The Partner

Also By A. A. Chaudhuri

CARVER AND KRAMER SERIES
Book 1: The Lawyer
Book 2: The Partner

THE PARTNER

A.A. CHAUDHURI

LUME BOOKS
A JOFFE BOOKS COMPANY

Revised edition 2025
Lume Books, London
A Joffe Books Company
www.lumebooks.co.uk

First published in Great Britain in 2019 by Lume Books
Please note this book was previously published as *The Abduction*

This paperback edition was first published in Great Britain in 2025

Cover design by Nick Castle

ISBN: 978-1-83901-596-0

For my dad

Chapter One

Boredom dripped off her.

Off her and her watching audience. Watching but not listening. Their constipated expressions voicing a desperate, yet vain attempt to mask their urge to yawn. Their minds focussed on anything but the dreary speaker and her tedious talk on insurance law. *Dinner, sex, last night's TV, that dress in the sale, I'm still so hungover from last night, I could so do with the loo, when the hell can we frigging get out of here?!*

A miserable uncomfortableness hung in the air. Suffocating, draining. Like high humidity in forty-degree heat. Making existence almost unbearable. Looking around the room, rising star fourth-year associate Madeline Kramer suspected these, amongst other thoughts, raided the minds of most of her colleagues. She could practically see the speech bubbles trailing from their heads, like cartoon characters from some satirical magazine.

At least the trainees – sycophantic brown-nosers, never off duty, desperate to impress, who'd wipe a partner's backside if it meant

1

guaranteeing a job at the end of the day – were staring in the right direction. In contrast to the associates, who simply stared into space, fighting the impulse to check their iPhones, or glance at their watches. But the partners had no such scruples. They were the worst. They did what the hell they wanted because no one was going to stop them or berate them for it. They were in charge. The *untouchables*. Their arrogance was as blatant as fresh blood on snow. And yet they were so full of themselves, they were completely oblivious to it.

Maddy glanced right at Richard Barker, the soon-to-be-retired Head of Litigation. Maddy's department. Just nine months to go, and then he'd be a free man. Leaving the shackles of City law behind him. *See ya, so long, I'm off to get a life. I'll be thinking of you… not! Suckers!*

He was a bird-like, pale-faced man. Almost bald, with a smattering of white hair thinly covering the back of his head, he was looking much frailer of late, and much older than his fifty-four years. Although that didn't seem to incapacitate his relentless work ethic. At his desk by 7.30 a.m., never leaving the building before 8 p.m. A personable character, albeit as sharp as nails, and a Rottweiler in court. Always there for his clients, come hell or high water, in sickness and in health. Much like a marriage, only politer and without the added complication of sex.

The gathering of ten associates, three trainees, and four partners (the rest of the team – three senior associates and two trainees – were caught up in all-day hearings and client meetings, the lucky bastards!) was seated around a large, shiny oak conference table in the firm's impressive ground-floor conference suite. A space usually reserved for lavish client events, boozy firm socials and external training courses. But today it was the site of the litigation department's obligatory weekly lunchtime talk. A burden that fell upon associates and trainees on a rota basis. A burden that no one got out of, and most – aside from the mega-geeky, work-obsessed arse-lickers – dreaded like the plague. A burden that sagged upon one's shoulders like a dead weight. A burden that detracted precious time from racking up billable hours on *real* work but required almost as much effort if one wanted to put on a convincing show in front of one's team. And, of course, impress the partners with one's solid legal prowess. Lack of preparation showed, and only made the exercise more painful. More humiliating. The only plus side was the free sandwiches, Kettle crisps and fruit basket, although on a day like today – a deliciously warm, sunny day in late July – it would have been nice to get out, loosen the joints, enjoy some natural warmth and light for once.

The room smelt of bread and coffee, with a touch of stomach-curdling body odour thrown in for good measure. The usually immaculate table was littered with evidence of lunch, as well as a selection of firm-embossed notepads on which some of the assembled pretended to take notes with equally impressive firm-branded pens, though most were in fact doodling aimlessly. Although the room was kept at a fresh fifteen degrees, the sheer number of bodies made it feel oppressive, and most had removed their suit jackets, loosened their ties, kicked off their heels underneath the table.

Maddy continued to watch Richard from the corner of her eye. He'd pulled back his chair, his wiry legs stretched out in front of him, head down, incessantly checking his iPhone as if a second's absence might cause him to go into anaphylactic shock. He eyed his Rolex impatiently between the furious tapping of his screen, every now and again fidgeting in his seat as if he was high on espresso and sitting on a nest of ants. And the other partners – James Canton, Colin O'Shea, Gavin Turner – were much the same. Part of Maddy wanted to give them an earful for being so bloody rude. After all, they were the ones who inflicted this weekly torture on the team. But the other part wanted to laugh out loud because their flagrant arrogance was kind of comical. And besides, she liked Richard. By far the nicest of the four. Who might actually have red blood running through his veins. He was a decent, fair man. She had him to thank for hiring her when many might have questioned whether she was up to the task after a six-month absence from law for personal reasons.

He was much more human than the likes of Turner. A short, rotund man with a flushed complexion and toothbrush moustache, Turner swaggered around the firm's corridors like Napoleon, ogling cleavages, barking at his poor secretary and putting the fear of God into his trainees. Classic short-man syndrome, that's what he suffered from. Big time.

In contrast, Canton was tall and athletic, the pin-up partner of the firm. Only just made up, he'd not quite left associate mode. At thirty-five, he was an attractive new piece of furniture amongst a building full of fading antiques, and keen to remain 'cool' amongst those he'd left behind. But he was also too spineless to dare disagree with anything his senior partners said, a trait which made him untrustworthy as far as the associates were concerned. He'd gone over to 'the dark side', and there was no turning back.

As for O'Shea, speculation abounded that he might be an alien sent from outer space. Bookish, spindly, with sallow grey skin and hair that never moved, he'd been deprived of the personality gene at birth, but made up for his lack of social skills by being technically brilliant. He was also exceptionally mean with money when it came to entertaining clients, but they let him off because he won cases. Insurance litigation was his speciality, a painfully dull but intellectually demanding area of law. Of all four partners sitting around the table, he would be most disgusted by the speaker's feeble performance.

Poor Charlotte Dempsey. Twenty-four-years-old, rake-thin, with mousy brown shoulder-length hair, a pale freckled complexion, and sporting a perpetually worried look on her face, she didn't instil a lot of confidence in those around her. Maddy noticed the piece of paper she was holding quiver in her hand as she read her notes out parrot fashion with no trace of inflection or enthusiasm for her subject. Head down, her cheeks every now and again turning rose pink, she looked like she wished she was anywhere but there.

Trainees at Sullivan, Blake, Monroe worked in four different departments over their two-year training period, before qualifying into their department of choice. If, that is, they impressed the powers that be enough to be kept on.

But Charlotte hadn't. Far from it. She still had eight months left before qualifying next year, but her fate had already been decided. Although she didn't know it yet. She was way out of her league at a firm like Sullivans. A drain on resources. A no-hoper. A huge mistake. Maddy hoped this wouldn't come as a shock to her. That way, the blow would be softened, and she'd have time to figure out an alternative career path.

It wasn't just her monotone delivery, nervous disposition and ability to send an audience to sleep when giving a talk. She was slow, made mistakes, got the simplest of tasks wrong, failed to speak up or take the initiative. All big 'no-nos' as far as the bigwigs at Sullivan, Blake, Monroe were concerned.

Although Sullivans wasn't a 'magic circle' firm in terms of size, its profits per partner matched all the big boys. Established over one hundred and fifty years ago, its building was situated in the thriving financial heart of London, a few minutes' walk from Shoreditch High Street station. It prided itself on a reputation for excellence, a partner-led approach and the ability to present clients with teams of uniformly excellent lawyers. Realistic in terms of the work a firm of its size could take on (it didn't pretend to take on matters it couldn't handle efficiently), it fought legal battles on behalf of its clients like a battalion of Roman gladiators. A fight to the death. Maximum effort, no stone left unturned, no obstacle too great.

Clients were like their children. They always came first, and they would go to the ends of the world for them. As a result, the firm attracted a loyal client base.

Its building was neither huge nor small, but it was slick, modern and eye-catching. With pristine marble floors, minimalist glossy furniture, state-of-the-art technology, it oozed money. All employees were provided with their own laptops and iPhones and went about the six-storey building in sharp dark suits. Not a ladder, scuffed shoe, mismatched tie or stray hair in sight.

Charlotte was like a fish out of water, and it made Maddy wonder why Nigel Davenport, the firm's senior partner, had hired her in the first place. His firm, renowned for its ruthless work ethic, only retained winners, and had no time to babysit associates who didn't come up to scratch.

In the City, you either had it, or you didn't. And Maddy had it, in bucketloads. It was there in her voice, in her demeanour, in the way she got a handle on problems in their infancy. It was there in the hungry glint in her ebony eyes, the excitement she felt when a problem presented itself and the ensuing heady rush of adrenaline that motored through her when trying to solve it. She guessed it was something she'd been born with, although losing her parents in a car crash when she was nine had probably contributed to her resilience, her hunger to succeed. Having said that, she could so easily have gone off the rails, descended into a bottomless well of self-pity and depression, but her beloved grandmother, Rose, had seen to it that she hadn't. She'd made sure she was loved and cherished, encouraged and supported, right through her childhood into womanhood.

Maddy may have been tough and ambitious, but Rose had also nurtured a soft, loving side to her granddaughter. A side that was now looking at Charlotte with genuine sympathy.

But also, a sense of realism. In truth, deep down she knew the reason why Charlotte was there. Connections. Charlotte's father – media tycoon, Charles Dempsey – had been Davenport's client for twenty-five years before he'd sold his company and retired. And as with so many walks of life, it wasn't *what* you knew, but *who* you knew, and no doubt a quick word from Dempsey in Davenport's ear went a long way.

The one thing that puzzled Maddy, and which she planned on asking Charlotte during her end-of-seat appraisal, was what had happened to the girl who gained a high 2:1 at Bristol, aced her law exams and impressed the hell out of the partners during her two-week induction? All that can't have been a fluke, surely? Perhaps it was simply the nature of the job that intimidated her, threw her into a state of flux? Maybe she'd be better off in a less cut-throat environment, where she wouldn't have to talk much, and the pressure was less intense?

As she watched Charlotte stumble through her lecture, her cheeks now turning cherry red, her delivery more rushed, Maddy felt increasingly sorry for her trainee. Again, she hoped she wouldn't be too distraught by the news that there'd be no job for her on qualification. She hoped she found her true vocation—

It was like a car backfiring. A sudden clap of thunder. The door flung open with such force, it rebounded hard against the wall behind it. Maddy's heart kicked violently at the unexpected noise. She and the rest of the room – a tapestry of shocked, terrified faces – instinctively jolted in their seats, then looked in alarm towards the door. Seventeen previously lifeless faces, suddenly very much awake, their attention caught in the blink of an eye.

iPhones nowhere in sight.

There were two men. Dressed in black turtlenecks, black combat trousers, black balaclavas, black rucksacks slung across their backs. 'Get down on the floor, all of you!' shouted the taller, slimmer one of the two. They both carried SWAT guns in their leather-gloved hands. 'Now!' the same man repeated when several bodies in the room failed to do as instructed. He slammed the door shut. Maddy wondered how they'd got past security, then shuddered as the disturbing range of possibilities raced through her mind.

Everyone did as they were told. Including the partners, all of whom looked like they might wet their pants any second. Or worse. Suddenly, they were just like everyone else. Vulnerable, scared, fallible. Turner looked the most frightened. Mute, for once, his eyes filled with fear. All too aware of his own mortality.

Then the shorter, stockier man spoke. He had a deeper, gruffer voice. 'Except for you. Get up.'

He was staring at Charlotte, whose previously nervous bearing had switched to one of abject terror. 'Me?' Her voice was unsteady, barely audible. Struggling to get up, she glanced nervously at Maddy – her supervisor – as if for reassurance, direction.

8

'It's OK, Charlotte,' Maddy said with a faint smile, trying to keep her own voice steady. She looked up at the thickset man. 'What do you want with her?' Her heart hammered in her chest as she asked the question, conscious of the gun in his hand.

'None of your fucking business. Now get your pretty little head down like the rest of them. And you, come here.' He made direct eye contact with Charlotte once more.

Maddy wavered, caught Richard's eye. He was crouching down on his skinny pins like a dog on its hind legs. 'Do as he says, Maddy. This isn't the time to be a hero.'

'He's right,' snarled the shorter man. 'Now get your head down, and you, come here.'

This time, Maddy did as she was told as the man roughly beckoned for Charlotte to join him at the door. As Maddy lowered her head, she slyly watched her trainee gingerly walk over to the man. To her credit, she didn't wail or cry, but she looked terrified. Maddy caught the gaze of a couple of associates hunkered down on her side of the table. She could practically hear the beating of their hearts, feel the fear, terror, generating off them. Janine Grant, a one-year-qualified associate, had tears in her eyes and looked like she was about to vomit. 'It's OK, keep calm,' Maddy mouthed. She inhaled slowly and deeply, gesturing for Janine to do the same. Janine, a petite, pretty brunette, nodded gratefully, and followed Maddy's lead, gulping in air like a pregnant woman in labour.

'Under the table, all of you!'

Everyone clambered under the table. Huddled together on all fours, like caged animals in some humiliating circus act. All except Richard, who bravely stood up, and asked, 'What is it you want? Maybe we can come to some agreement?' Maddy was stunned, particularly as he'd just asked her not to be a hero. She hadn't pegged him as the courageous type. And looking at the other three partners, quivering like frightened rabbits, neither had they.

'This isn't a fucking negotiation for one of your money-making deals.' The taller man's tone was harsh, uncompromising. He grabbed Charlotte's wrist, then pulled her aggressively towards him before putting his gun to her left temple. Everyone under the table winced as Charlotte shrieked with fear. 'You're coming with us.' Another yank of her wrist.

'What do you want with me?' she stammered. 'Please, I've done nothing wrong. I'm just a trainee. Please don't take me.'

'Shut your mouth!' came the brutal response. Then, 'And on second thoughts, you've pissed me off so much, you come too. I've heard you're a popular man around here.'

The man stared at Richard, whose face turned paler than ever. 'Move! Or I'll blow your fucking brains out!' A sudden trudge of feet, and then Maddy heard the man digging his gun into Richard's ribcage. He cried out in pain.

'OK, please, calm down, I'm coming,' he wheezed, trying to catch his breath. Then came the sound of his footsteps shuffling around the table. He asked hesitantly, 'What is it you want with us?'

'No questions. You'll know soon enough.' He paused, then lowered his head under the table, singled in on Canton. 'When we're gone, you get up and lock the door, got it?' Canton nodded vigorously. 'Good. Once you've locked it, get back under the table, and all of you stay put for ten minutes. If you don't, we'll blow this building to kingdom come. And we're not fucking joking.' He scanned the band of faces. Maddy saw two dark eyes. Cold and resolute. They lasered through her and her scared stiff colleagues. No one said a word.

Just then, Janine, still crouched under the table like the rest of them, vomited on the deluxe cream carpet. Clearly, the deep breaths had had their day.

The man sniggered, 'Priceless,' before raising himself up. Everyone winced at the vile smell but dared not speak.

And then, just like that, they were gone. The room remained as quiet as a gathering of Cistercian monks. Canton scrambled out from under the table, locked the door, then rejoined his petrified colleagues. He pointed to his watch and indicated to everyone that he would keep track of the time until ten minutes was up. Turner, red-faced and sweaty, nodded in agreement. He glared at Janine, back to his usual portentous self now that the men had gone. It sickened Maddy, and she could only imagine the grief he'd give the poor girl once the time was up.

With fifteen bodies trapped together under the table, it was clammy and airless, the pungent blend of perspiration, body odour and vomit making Maddy want to hurl herself. It felt like an eternity waiting for the time to pass. As she kept her head down, in a bid to stop light-headedness setting in, she wondered why trouble always seemed to follow her round.

Towards the end of October 2014, she had become embroiled in the hunt for a serial killer, coined the Scribe by the press, very nearly losing her life. Seven women, each of whom had slept with one of her former law tutors, Professor James Stirling, were violently murdered in the space of three months, seven different legal subjects inscribed across their chests. The first victim had been a trainee at Maddy's then firm, Channing & Barton, but after victim two turned out to be one of her best friends from law school, Maddy became obsessed with helping the police hunt down the murderer. But the truth had lain closer to home than she could ever have imagined. Her mentally unhinged flatmate had played an instrumental role in the murders by helping the killer. Finding out the truth about Paul, whom she'd loved like a brother, had very nearly broken Maddy. Feeling unable to show her face again at Channings, despite none of it being her fault, she'd quit, and taken six months out to get her head together, before landing the job at Sullivans in late July 2015. A fresh start. Given to her by Richard, when others might not have been so generous.

But she'd never given him, nor his fellow partners, cause to doubt his judgement. Two years on, she was considered one of the most diligent, popular, talented associates at Sullivans, and provided she kept up the good work, she was well on track for partnership.

But this afternoon's abduction was a bolt from the blue, certain to turn her ordered life upside down once again in the days ahead.

Who were those men, why had they taken Charlotte and Richard, and what would it take to get them back?

Chapter Two

The detective chief inspector watched the men drag Richard and Charlotte across reception, brandishing their guns at the terrified receptionists before exiting the building through the swish revolving doors. As well as the firm's CCTV capturing the moment, several eyewitnesses had spotted all four scrambling into the rear of a blue Ford Transit van parked outside the firm's reception, before it sped off. There was clearly another player in the game, but no one had seen the driver's face, or been quick or astute enough to note down the number plate. The DCI made a mental note to have his team check the street CCTV, including any available imaging detailing the van's route in and out of the City.

That was how they left…

But how had they entered? No one had seen them come in, and neither had the camera. It was as if they were ghosts, appearing from nowhere.

'Play it back again,' DCI Jake Carver said. It was 2.45 p.m. and his stomach felt as raw as a fresh graze. The call had come through as he was contemplating lunch. He'd worked out for an hour at 5 a.m. and hadn't had time for anything more than a protein bar and his usual black coffee en route to Hackney Central police station where he and his senior command team were based. The immediate area where the abduction had occurred wasn't usually in his remit, but the previous day the local area DCI had been taken seriously ill, and so Carver, being the nearest and most experienced officer to hand, had been called to the scene. He'd previously spent eighteen months heading up a team in north London, having fancied a change of area, but in truth he was an East End lad at heart and felt out of sorts up there. So, when offered the move to Hackney a little under three months ago, Carver hadn't hesitated. Better still, he'd managed to take his DS, Benjamin Drake, with him.

Since solving the Scribe murders together, a serial killer investigation that had pushed them both to the limit, Drake had become Carver's right-hand man. Lewis to his Morse. Hastings to his Poirot. And for Drake, it had been a no-brainer. He worshipped Carver, despite his prickly temperament. His mentor, his friend. And so the opportunity to work a different area with a man he trusted and admired almost as much as his own father, was one he'd grabbed with both hands.

Famed for his brusque manner, Carver, now approaching forty-five, had mellowed somewhat under Drake's influence. Unlike his younger charge, who'd joined his team a fresh-faced, optimistic, easy-going detective constable, albeit exceptionally bright and ambitious, Carver was like a well-ridden warhorse. He'd seen and been through a lot – shaped by the stresses of life, the vagaries of time, and only a year out of a bitter divorce. And, trying his best to remain a good father to his son, while competing with his ex's new man for his affections.

But break all that down – the hard veneer, the impatience, the irritation – he was a good, fair man. A brilliant officer and an astute judge of character, it didn't take him long to sort the wheat from the chaff. He'd been impressed by Drake's enthusiasm, intuitiveness and devotion to the case. Loyalty was important to Carver. And he never doubted he could count on Drake.

Carver's terseness continued to get on the wrong side of people, but it was also part of his charm. He was charmingly curt, charmingly offhand, and always one to give praise where it was due. Besides, he was now on civil terms with Rachel, his fiery ex, and had finally accepted her new husband, Carl. Seeing his eight-and-a-half-year-old son, Daniel, every other weekend, kept him in touch with his softer, human side. He loved his boy like crazy. So much so, it sometimes scared him. Daniel made bearable the shit life threw at him, the ugliness of his job, the monsters he frequently put behind bars. He had no time or inclination for cheap dates or booze. Daniel, work, boxing. His three loves in life, in that order. That was enough for him.

He stood looking over the shoulder of the salt-and-pepper-haired security guard, along with Drake, and Nigel Davenport, Sullivans' senior partner, hoping he might have missed something. But he hadn't. Forensics were on their way, but Carver wasn't confident they'd find much. The men had been wearing gloves, and aside from Charlotte and Richard, hadn't laid a hand on anyone. Fingerprint or DNA evidence was therefore highly unlikely. Even so, every inch of the building would be combed.

'Is there a back entrance?' he asked the guard.

'Yes, it's mainly used for deliveries.'

'I assume it has CCTV?' A nod. 'Can we see it? Try midday onwards for starters.'

The guard switched screens and rewound the tape monitoring the back entrance as Carver had directed.

'That's odd.' The guard frowned. He began to fast forward the tape.

Still hovering over the guard's shoulder, Carver immediately understood his confusion. The tape was blank between midday and 1.15 p.m.

'Some clever bugger's been busy,' Carver muttered.

He glanced at Davenport, who all at once twigged, his eyes wide with alarm. 'Technology's a wonderful thing, Mr Davenport, but it's also spawned a new kind of criminal. Hacking into your firm's CCTV wouldn't exactly be rocket science in this day and age.'

The surprised look didn't wane. 'Why so shocked?' Carver's tone was deliberately patronising. 'As a City law partner in the twenty-first century, I assume you're only too familiar with cybercrime?'

'Do I need to tell everyone to go home?' Davenport ignored the comment. He was fifty-four, about six-three, broad-chested, with hazel eyes and close-cut grey hair. Carver imagined he'd once been very handsome, but years of indulgent City life had clearly taken their toll. He had large bags under his eyes, a slight double chin which spilled over his top collar, and red spider veins crawling up both cheeks. Signs of a drinker, of someone who didn't get an awful lot of sleep. Although he was dressed in an obscenely expensive suit, cut to fit its wearer to a T, it couldn't disguise his paunch, his jacket buttons stretched to the limit. He also wore a permanent scowl on his face. Carver, who had little patience for rich City suits, especially when they let their mercenary objectives hamper his investigations, took an instant dislike to him.

'Yes, my men need the space to work freely. We can't risk cross-contamination.' He paused, then said with a wry smile, 'Everyone hates Mondays. I'm sure your staff will be delighted to have the afternoon off.' As he said this, he imagined Davenport was on the verge of having a coronary. He fought the urge to grin at his discomfort.

'They can work remotely.' The senior partner's voice was calm, but his face was an atlas of irritation.

16

'I'll be issuing a statement to the press later,' Carver said.

'Really? Don't you keep this sort of thing under wraps, for the hostages' safety, I mean?' Carver studied Davenport, wondering whether he was more concerned about protecting his firm's reputation, rather than the hostages' well-being. He'd made a good point, though.

'That's true, under normal circumstances, where we're dealing with an individual kidnapping. But this is a different situation, and in a firm of this size, with hundreds of employees, there's no hope of keeping this quiet. But don't worry, I'll keep it brief.' He paused, then said, 'But for now I need to speak to everyone who was in that conference room.'

'They're still in there. Pretty shaken up.'

'Lead the way.'

'That went smoother than expected,' the driver said, glancing at his accomplices as he finally came to a stop at the hideout. Seven miles out of the City. Their third stop after making their getaway.

'They're lawyers, what do you expect?' the slimmer one grunted. 'None of them have got the balls to be heroes. All big talk, and no fucking action.'

'True,' his stockier counterpart sneered. 'Except for Madeline Kramer. Should have known she'd speak up.' He filled the driver in on what had happened in the conference room.

'I've seen her photo on the web,' the driver said. 'She's pretty hot. That takes some guts to put away your own flatmate.'

'He did help some psycho-bitch kill seven women, including her best friend. You can hardly blame her.' The leaner man paused, then turned to look at the other three. 'You still want to hold off on sending our demands?'

'Yes. We wait until tonight,' their leader said. 'That'll give us time to beat up Charlotte and make Davenport sweat. He's a callous bastard, but hopefully even his heart will thaw when he sees his poor trainee's face beaten black and blue.'

'How should we play it with the others?'

'We do nothing for now. Charlotte is his friend's daughter. Smacking her around should be way more effective.'

The driver suddenly looked uneasy, his eyes flitting nervously between each of his co-conspirators. 'I've told you before, I can't do it. I don't have it in me, it's too hard.'

He received a sympathetic hand on his shoulder. 'It's OK, we've discussed this before, and we're all agreed. I'll do it.'

It was her, although Carver blinked three times just to make sure his eyes weren't deceiving him. He'd spotted her almost as soon as he'd followed Davenport into the room. Like a bright star in the night sky. Unmistakeable. Her right arm cradled the shoulders of a pretty, slightly built girl, whose face was ashen. The air smelt of stale vomit. Looking at the girl, he suspected she was the culprit.

Maddy instantly looked up. Almost as if she'd sensed his gaze fall upon her. Time had enhanced her loveliness, as it so often did with naturally beautiful women. She gave him a half-smile and he felt his cheeks colour. He smiled back. Resisted the urge to wink.

They hadn't seen each other since the day Paul King had been sentenced. That was nearly two years ago.

There'd been no denying the chemistry between them, right from the start of the case, even though neither had admitted it out loud. It had been implicit in every look, every soft intonation of voice, in the sexual tension stalking the air around them. Carver had been enchanted by Maddy's spirit and intellect, as well as her beauty. And for Maddy, she'd been attracted to a genuine decency behind Carver's tough-guy veneer, as well as a handsome face that seemed to tell a tale of its own. Maddy's biggest flaw was not being able to commit. She shied away from relationships because men were complicated, and she didn't like complicated. Having lost her parents as a child, she was perhaps afraid of getting too close.

Carver was different to the men she worked with, the boys she'd studied with and dated casually. It wasn't just his looks. He was interesting, had a cracking dry humour that made her smile. And she liked the fact that he wasn't perfect. Divorced, with a kid he adored but didn't see enough of, there was a vulnerability about him she found attractive. Like her, he was slightly chipped at the edges. But despite their similarities, they'd still been creatures of two very different worlds, separated not only by the material world they operated in, but by a seventeen-year age gap, and the fact that Carver had a child. Neither was the one-night-stand type, so there hadn't seemed any point in starting something that surely had no hope of a future. On top of that, the case had very nearly destroyed Maddy. By the time Paul was behind bars, the last thing she needed was a constant reminder of his cruel deception. She'd wasted no time in shifting from Bow to Southfields, the other side of London, moving into a flat with Cara, an old university friend, also keen to make the move from east to west. Feeling the need to extricate herself from everyone and everything associated with the case just to pull through, to survive, to start to live again.

And that included Carver, as well as Channing & Barton.

But seeing him now stirred all sorts of feelings inside her. He hadn't changed much. Maybe a little greyer around the temples, a few more lines circling that strong square jaw of his. But he was still handsome, still had that honest, decent look about him.

'Everyone, this is DCI Carver.' Davenport brought Maddy back to reality by introducing Carver to the roomful of zombies. Still in shock, unable to comprehend what had happened to them barely ninety minutes ago. It remained a surreal dream for most of them. Or rather, a nightmare.

They'd given it fifteen minutes, just to be on the safe side, before finally crawling out from under the table, despite hearing Davenport's fist thumping on the door, his booming voice ordering someone to 'Let him in, for Christ's sake!' barely five minutes after the men's departure.

Ann Stevens, the firm's longest-serving receptionist, had alerted Davenport the minute the men drove off with Charlotte and Richard. Davenport had been on a conference call in his office when she'd burst into his room. Seeing the distraught look on her face, he'd immediately cut the call short, much to his client's irritation. A quaking bundle of nerves, almost hyperventilating as she'd tried miserably to get the words out, it was only after he'd sat her down on a chair, made her take deep, dragged-out breaths, along with a large dose of the Hennessy XO brandy he stored in a crystal decanter in his office, that he was able to get anything logical out of her.

What had happened was unprecedented in the history of City law firms, and it had immediately set alarm bells ringing in Davenport's head.

Why the hell had they picked on his firm? On his staff? There were bigger, richer firms than his. It had made him wonder what else these men had on Sullivans – on the people who ran it. Including him. The only thing he could think of was that they knew who Charlotte's father was. But if extracting money from Charles was their objective, why not

20

just take his daughter from her home and blackmail Charles directly?

He needed to schedule a partners' meeting. But first he'd see what DCI Carver had to say. He had a familiar look about him, but he couldn't think why. He could tell from the first that their bread was buttered on very different sides. *Bloody working-class socialist.* Getting along with the man wasn't going to be easy, but he knew he needed to set his disdain aside if he wanted to get his firm back on track.

He went around the table, introducing everyone. Then Carver went and stood at the head. 'None of you are hurt?'

Drake stood back and took notes.

James Canton was the first to speak. 'The men had guns but didn't use them, except to poke and prod Charlotte and Richard. None of us were physically harmed, although I don't think they would have hesitated to use force had any of us failed to comply.' He eyed Maddy with irritation, a look that didn't bypass Carver.

'Something you need to tell me?' Carver looked from Canton to Maddy.

Maddy wasn't about to let Canton get away with his dig. She looked directly at Carver, chin up, her voice level as she explained, 'I just asked them what they wanted with Charlotte, that's all. She's my trainee and I felt responsible.'

Carver suppressed a grin. There she was. The same plucky Ms Kramer. Unchanged by time or circumstance. He had no doubt that she had bigger balls than all the men seated round the table put together.

'That was very brave of you.'

'Stupid, more like,' Turner sniped. 'Could have got us all killed.' He gave Maddy a look of contempt, and suddenly everyone was staring at her. Some of them sympathetic, even admiring. Including Janine, who smiled gratefully. But others, like Turner, were shooting daggers. Maddy felt her face flush. She focussed on Carver, hoping he'd read her mind and rescue her from her awkwardness. Thankfully, he did.

'This is not the time to point the finger.' Carver glowered at Turner. 'You've all been through a deeply distressing situation, and some, if not all of you, will still be in shock, even if you don't realise it yet. We have people who can help with that. But for now, I need to have a chat with each of you.'

'Today?' asked Colin O'Shea, who'd been silent up to this point. Carver's back stiffened. *What does he expect? That he can just go back to his office and act like none of this has happened?*

'Yes, today. We don't know where Ms Dempsey or Mr Barker are being held, or what their abductors plan on doing with them, but I'm guessing they'll be in touch soon with their demands.'

'Surely we can't be expected to comply with their demands?' Davenport said, glancing at his partners. Making sure they were on his side and in sync with his way of thinking. City law was all about being a team player. Except, of course, when there was just cause to stab your teammates in the back.

'That depends,' Carver said.

'On what?'

'Your conscience. I'm sure both abductees' families would think differently. As will the press.'

'Why do you suppose they took Charlotte and Richard?' Canton asked.

'Perhaps because of who Charlotte's father is?' O'Shea suggested, looking at Davenport for verification. Seeing Carver's perplexed look, Davenport explained.

'That doesn't explain taking Richard, though,' Canton observed.

22

'Other than the fact that he seriously pissed them off,' O'Shea said. 'They knew he was a partner. Which isn't exactly surprising. You can look any of us up on the firm's website. Christ, the way the net is these days, you'd probably be able to find out what our first words were.'

In your case, some obscure Latin legal term no doubt, thought Maddy.

'It could still have been random,' Carver said. 'But I agree the internet's a wonderful, yet highly dangerous, vehicle of information. Did any of you recognise the men's voices?'

'No,' O'Shea replied. 'The shorter man's voice was thicker, huskier, that's all I can tell you.' Everyone around the table shook their heads: *No, they weren't familiar.*

'I don't know about Richard, but it seems clear to me that Charlotte was their target from the outset,' Maddy said.

'Why do you say that?'

'They picked her out almost immediately. No hesitation.' She paused, then said, 'Wouldn't that mean they had help on the inside? I mean, how would they have known Charlotte was going to be giving a talk in here over lunchtime?'

'Good point. Of course, it's also possible they hacked into her calendar.' Carver scanned the room. 'I'm assuming you all have electronic calendars?' Sixteen nods. Including Davenport.

His question brought back memories for Maddy. Paul had been a computer whizz. Hacking was one of the ways he'd helped a fanatical killer frame Stirling for the murders. Carver read her mind. They held each other's gaze, and all at once Davenport twigged, his face lighting up with recognition. 'Ah, yes, that's right, you were the officer who solved the Scribe murders.' He wagged his finger at Carver. 'I knew I remembered you from the television.' He shook his head. 'A ghastly affair. It seems trouble follows you round, Ms Kramer.'

He gave a little chuckle, amused by his own wit, but his attempt to lighten the mood didn't help Maddy's unease. In fact, she'd never felt so bloody awkward. 'Yes, it seems like it,' she spluttered.

Carver wanted to punch Davenport on the nose. Instead, he kept his cool and cleared his throat. 'Is there another room I can use for interviews? Forensics will be here soon, and we'll need to cordon this room off.'

'Of course,' Davenport said, thankfully letting the subject rest. He looked at his staff gravely. 'I expect you all to cooperate with DCI Carver. We can't let these loathsome men get the better of us.'

'To be honest, they could have chosen a better pair to take. Charlotte's useless and Richard's on his way out.'

The man's insufferable, Carver thought. He and Drake were sitting across from Gavin Turner. Excruciatingly smug. With beady black eyes and a permanent smirk on his face. Carver didn't think he could trust anything that came out of the weasel's mouth. He was no doubt a brilliant lawyer.

'Ms Dempsey isn't being kept on?'

'No.' Turner shook his head emphatically, then tittered. 'She's probably the most incompetent trainee we've ever had.' He let out a self-satisfied chuckle. As if he'd just made a statement of global importance. Carver glanced at Drake, wondering what venom the arrogant snake was going to spout now. 'In fact, the intrusion was a blessed relief from the drivel coming out of her mouth.'

Little shit. 'I understand she was speaking at the time?'

'Yes, she was supposed to be giving a talk on insurance law. Not the most riveting of topics under normal circumstances, but Charlotte's no doubt put everyone around that table off it for life.'

24

Enough's enough. 'You clearly have it in for the girl.' Carver glared at Turner, who immediately shrank back in his chair. Gave a less confident chuckle.

'Steady on. If you're insinuating that I had anything to do with her being taken, you're very much mistaken.'

'Am I?' Carver shot back. In truth, he didn't think Turner did have anything to do with the abduction, but it was fun making the arrogant prick think otherwise.

'Yes, you are.' As Turner shuffled in his seat, his shirt slightly gaping between buttons, revealing his unsightly black-haired belly, he started to backtrack. 'Charlotte's a nice enough girl, and I wish her well once she finishes with us. Her abduction benefits me in no way whatsoever. Maybe Colin, my partner, was onto something when he mentioned the father, Charles Dempsey. He's a very rich man, who's given us a lot of business over the years through his friendship with Nigel.'

Carver kept up the pressure. 'And Richard Barker? How does his abduction benefit you?'

'It doesn't. Richard's been a fantastic head of department, and a tremendous asset to our firm since long before I can remember. He's like a piece of the furniture and will be sorely missed when he retires next April.'

'And who will replace him as head of department. *You?*'

Turner's ruddy face turned redder, his forehead glistening. 'Look here, I don't like the tone of your questioning. Yes, as it happens, I will be replacing Richard as head of department next year. But that's exactly the point. It's all been decided, so I have no reason to want shot of him, particularly for the sake of another nine months.'

Carver was bursting inside. He deliberately avoided Drake's gaze.

Finally, he eased up. 'Very well, Mr Turner. We may need to question you again, but for now, you can go.'

Turner got up and left the room without saying another word.

'Conceited little twerp,' Carver muttered under his breath once the door had closed. Men like Turner reminded him why he loathed the City. Although he'd grown up in a loving family, he'd also witnessed his parents struggle daily. It had pained him to see his mother, a bright, kind-natured woman, constantly having to cut corners, never being able to afford a new dress, or go out for a meal, while bankers and lawyers like Turner dined like kings every day and brought home obscene bonuses they didn't know what to do with, on top of their overinflated salaries. They had no grasp on reality. On the hardships ordinary people endured. 'Who's next, Drake?'

Drake looked down at his notepad. 'Maddy Kramer.'

A rush of excitement hurtled through Carver. He suddenly felt warm, and immediately took a sip of water from the glass in front of him. Had Drake sensed the chemistry between them? He was smart and intuitive – he must have done. But he was also discreet. He'd never say anything unless his boss broached the subject first.

Carver cleared his throat, trying to compose himself. 'Right, go call her in then, Drake.'

'I can't believe we're here again. Is it me, or you? One of us must be jinxed.'

Carver smiled at Maddy, sitting across the table from him. Drake had popped out to use the gents'. *Thank God.* 'Well, as this is my job, I'm guessing it's you,' he replied. She smiled back, her face colouring slightly, her eyes twinkling.

'So, you like your new firm?'

'Yes. I took a six-month break, you know, just to get my head together. But I also kept my eye out for anything interesting. And this came up. It's a great firm to work for.' She stopped short, appeared to hesitate.

Carver raised his eyebrows. Read her mind. 'But they work you like dogs?'

'Yes. Usual City mentality. Rest is for wimps. On the plus side, my salary and bonus more than make up for it.'

'Do they?' The question hung in the air as Carver's gaze lingered on Maddy. He wanted to ask, *And what about relationships? Does it bother you not having a personal life?* But he didn't, of course. He pretty much knew the answer. It pleased, and yet, saddened him.

Maddy didn't know where to look. She knew what he was thinking, and his ability to penetrate her mind thrilled her, yet also made her feel vulnerable. Seeing him up so close, he was more attractive than she remembered. Just then, Drake returned, saving her from her awkwardness.

'Sorry about that,' he apologised, glancing at both in turn. It was a strange situation. Almost like a reunion of friends, if only the circumstances had been different.

'So, you're Charlotte's supervisor?' Carver asked.

'Yes, she sits with me in my office. Litigation's her penultimate seat. She's got two more months with me, then moves to Banking for her last six months.'

'I hear from Turner she's not being kept on.'

'I haven't been told that categorically, but the partners have certainly inferred it. Poor thing obviously doesn't know. They're not really supposed to decide until her last seat.'

'Why are they letting her go, do you think?'

Maddy sighed. 'Basically, she's just not up to it.' She hesitated again.

'What?'

'It's strange. Her academic record is faultless, and she must have interviewed well. I'm certain Nigel wouldn't have hired someone he didn't think was up to the job even if she was the daughter of a major client. But since starting, you wouldn't have guessed she'd done so well in her exams or impressed at interview. She lacks confidence, she's disorganised, fails to take the initiative.'

'Maybe she's one of those intellectual nerds?' Carver suggested. 'Good at burying her nose in books, completely out of her depth in the practical world.'

Maddy shook her head wearily, as if struggling to reconcile this. 'Maybe.' She paused, then said, 'It makes me sound hard-hearted, but she's simply not tough enough. The City's full of sharks, who won't hesitate to gobble up girls like Charlotte. She's a sweet girl, and although she'll no doubt be devastated at not being kept on, I'm sure it'll be a blessing in disguise for her in the long run.'

'If she's that bad, she must suspect?'

'Maybe. I hope so.'

'Tell me about her father.'

'Nigel's the one you should really be asking. My knowledge is limited, save that he was one of the firm's biggest clients until he sold his company and retired last December. Apparently, he and Nigel go way back.'

'Hmm. As they say, it's not what you know, it's who you know.'

'I'm sure it happens in every line of work.' Maddy gave Carver a hard stare. 'Even yours.'

28

There was silence as their eyes remained locked on each other. Drake didn't know where to look. He stared down at his pad and began to doodle.

'What's Richard Barker like?' Carver finally broke the excruciating tension.

Maddy sat back in her chair and thought for a moment. 'He gave me the job. Didn't view me as some sort of pariah, despite what happened at Channings.' She paused, then said gloomily, 'He may think differently now.'

She quickly gathered herself. 'He's a good team leader. Very fair and approachable. Traits that are often lacking in partners, especially in someone of Richard's seniority. He gets on with the other partners as far as I can tell, plus he's one of the more popular senior figures amongst associates and trainees. You can actually have a laugh over a pint with him without feeling like you're being analysed.' Carver smiled inside. He was finding it hard to imagine Maddy with a pint in her hand.

'But I understand he's due to retire?'

'Yes, he turns fifty-five next year. Although it's quite early, it's not unheard of for City partners to retire in their mid-fifties. Some of them keep their foot in the door by staying on a consultancy basis.'

'Is Richard?'

'I don't know.'

'Is he married?'

'Yes. Very happily as far as I know. He has a grown-up son and daughter.'

'And wealthy?'

Maddy looked at Carver as if he'd just asked her whether Earth was round. 'He's a partner at a leading City law firm. Yes, he's very well off. Probably takes home over a million a year.'

Carver was about to respond, when she beat him to it. 'But so do the other senior partners. It doesn't explain why they picked on him especially, other than the fact that he pissed them off by speaking up. Or why they took Charlotte. Aside from who her father is, as we've discussed.'

'A trainee to pull on the public's heartstrings, and an esteemed partner with a large equity stake to rattle his partners?' Carver suggested.

Maddy frowned. 'Hmm, maybe.'

'You've not noticed anything unusual recently? Anyone acting suspiciously, in or outside the firm? Even clients?'

Maddy shook her head. 'No, not at all. That's what makes all this such a shock. It was so out of the blue.' She paused, then asked, 'Have you got many more to interview?'

Carver glanced at Drake, who flipped his notepad back several pages. 'Two trainees to go, sir. Then we're done.'

Maddy looked at her watch. Just gone 7 p.m. 'If that's all, I'd like to make a run for it. I'm shattered, and it takes me pretty much an hour to get home.'

'Of course. Thank you for your help.' Carver stood up, irritated with himself for feeling disappointed that their discussion had come to an end.

'I'm not sure I've been that helpful. I just pray Charlotte and Richard haven't been harmed and that we hear from their kidnappers soon.'

Carver was grave-faced. 'I can't guarantee the first. But I'm pretty confident about the second.'

Chapter Three

An hour earlier, at just gone 6 p.m., the men responsible for kidnapping Charlotte Dempsey and Richard Barker sat around a table reviewing a DVD in the company of their leader, their driver and a woman.

'Perfect,' said the woman. She took a protracted sip of Scotch, then said, 'They can't say no to that. One look at poor Charlotte's face and they'll be putty in our hands.'

'Maybe,' said their leader. Older, wiser, than the rest. 'But we can't be certain. We all know what these suits can be like. They're ruthless. Davenport would sooner sell his soul to the Devil than part with money. Especially for the sake of dead wood.'

'Even when it comes to his friend's daughter?'

'Even then. Christ, his own children can't stand him.'

'If that's the case, we'll have to use other leverage. You can be damn sure he won't want his secret out in the open. And neither will his partners, or his so-called friend.'

'Very true.' Their leader grinned. 'In fact, I'm rather hoping Davenport won't cave just yet. Personally, I'd forgo the money just to see the look on his face when he realises what we're threatening to tell the world.'

The bulkier man, yet to speak, piped up. 'Don't take this the wrong way, but you're in quite a different position from me. I'm in it for the cash. Plain and simple. That's always been my objective. I've not risked everything to come away empty-handed.'

The woman smiled. 'Don't worry, you'll get your money.' She turned to their leader. 'But you know I feel the same way as you. His shame will be the icing on the cake.'

'Well, that's that,' Carver said. 8 p.m. He and Drake had just finished interviewing David Lynsey, a second-seat trainee. Like everyone else who'd been in the room when the men had stormed in, the intrusion had come as a complete shock. He hadn't seen anyone or anything suspicious before or since, and he was just grateful to be alive.

Forensics had so far found nothing of substance to go on. There'd been no blood or sexual assault involved, and the men had been gloved. Charlotte's and Richard's computers had been removed for analysis, and Carver was still waiting to hear back on that front. The hostages' families would shortly join Carver at the station for a press conference. It was late, and the media had yet to be informed. But they couldn't wait any longer. Someone was bound to leak it. A statement had to be made even though they didn't yet know what the kidnappers wanted. Carver was certain, however, that they'd make contact soon.

He was spot on. The phone rang. It was Davenport. His voice was shaky.

'Has something happened, Mr Davenport?'

Carver heard him swallow hard. 'Yes. About fifteen minutes ago, I received a DVD by courier.'

'The hostages?'

'Yes,' came the faint response. 'But it wasn't just Charlotte and Richard on the recording. There were two others.'

Carver's interest quickened. 'Others?'

'Yes. Stephen Baines and Matthew Gerard. Both second-year trainees. Same intake as Charlotte. This is like a bad dream, DCI Carver, you need to do something for pity's sake!'

'Christ.' Carver glanced at Drake, then said to Davenport, 'Stay put in your office. I need to see it.'

From the little they could decipher of the footage, the room was sparsely furnished and dimly lit. The four hostages were seated on chairs next to each other, their hands tied behind their backs, blindfolded, gagged. Apart from Charlotte, whose lips remained unmuzzled.

Aside from the fact that Richard looked like skin and bones, the men appeared unharmed. Their shirts were unbuttoned down to the navel, their shoes removed. But Charlotte had not been so lucky. When the camera zoomed in on her, Carver saw bruises on her left cheek, and cuts to her lips which were red and swollen. Her white work blouse had been ripped apart, and as the camera zoomed in closer, he thought he saw a burn mark on her chest. Possibly from a cigarette stub.

Her uncontrollable sobbing was interspersed with hysterical screaming as she writhed around on the chair like a wild animal. The men were calmer, but Carver was certain that inside they were as frightened as Charlotte. After a few minutes, a man's lower half appeared behind her trembling shoulders. The same black combat trousers. He undid her blindfold, and she instinctively tried to open her eyes, but struggled. Like a newborn baby seeing light for the first time. Her eyelids were a deep purple and inflamed. She was clearly in a lot of pain.

Carver watched Davenport recoil in horror as Charlotte's engorged left eye came into full view, her lids fighting to open. A single sheet of paper was suddenly thrust in front of her. Realising this was a clear direction, she managed, with some difficulty, to open both eyes, then started to read out loud, her voice faint and wavering.

'The bruises on my face, the burn mark on my chest, are just the tip of the iceberg. If you do not comply with their demands, they will do much worse, not only to me, but to the other hostages.' The others flinched. Charlotte looked up for a second, terror-stricken. Her fear no doubt intensified by the horror of not knowing when her ordeal would come to an end. She looked down at the words again. 'So here are our captors' demands, all of which must be complied with by 4 p.m. on Friday.'

It was Monday evening. *I have less than four days*, thought Carver.

'Firstly, they require the resignation of Nigel Davenport as senior partner of Sullivan, Blake, Monroe, to be publicly announced to *The Lawyer* magazine at 3 p.m. on Friday afternoon.'

A quick glance at Davenport and Carver thought he was about to pass out. His face was pale, his brow shiny with sweat.

'Secondly, six million pounds to be transferred from the firm's office account to an account they will make known to you in due course. Thirdly, they require that Mr Davenport personally donate one million pounds to the national charity Rape Crisis.'

Carver frowned in surprise, while Davenport avoided his gaze.

'If you do not comply with their demands, they will make Davenport's shameful secret known to the world, and we will never see our families again. My captors hope they've made themselves clear, and that you know they're not fucking around. They're also not bothered about their demands being made public. The more damage done to Davenport's reputation the better as far as they're concerned.' Carver noticed Davenport tug at his collar, as if struggling for air. 'They'll be in touch again. Around this time tomorrow.'

Charlotte looked up, her expression a fusion of unbridled fear and blind hope. Then, after a few seconds, the screen went blank. For a while, no one spoke. Davenport poured himself a large brandy. His hand shook like he was suffering from the worst case of Parkinson's as he lifted it up to his lips and necked the golden-brown liquid like apple juice. He immediately poured another.

Sensing Carver's gaze, he met it, then said, 'I suppose you want to know what shameful secret they're referring to?'

'It's the obvious question,' Carver said. Inside, he was surprised at the kidnappers having no beef with the world being informed of their demands. Covert action was usually a given in hostage situations. But this case was different from the norm. It seemed ultimate exposure and humiliation for Davenport was high on the kidnappers' agenda.

Davenport took another sip, this time more prolonged, then walked over to the window. 'There's only one thing I can think of. I was falsely accused of rape at Cambridge.' His tone was matter of fact. Neither apologetic nor defiant. His back still to Carver.

'Falsely accused,' Carver repeated. 'By the victim, I assume?'

'By the troublemaker who made the whole thing up,' Davenport retorted sharply. He turned around to face Carver. 'There was no victim.'

Carver didn't much care for the man, but it was too soon to make assumptions as to whether he was telling the truth. He'd fight to the death to get justice for a genuine rape victim. But there were always those who lied. Who ruined innocent men's lives by falsely accusing them. For now, he needed to give Davenport the benefit of the doubt. 'Who was she?'

'Another student at Cambridge. Same year as me.'

'What happened?'

'She reported me to the master of my college, Trinity.'

'And who was that?'

'Stewart Larson.' Carver signalled for Drake to make a note. 'And the girl?'

Davenport took a deep breath, as if stalling to answer.

'I need the name, Mr Davenport.'

'OK. Mary. Mary Jacobs.'

'Thank you. Please, carry on.'

'But when he called us both to his room,' Davenport continued, 'I pointed out that she'd slept with half the year, and she realised she didn't have a leg to stand on. She was the college party girl. Although, to be honest, there were a lot of those at my college. Why she decided to accuse me, rather than any of the other men she slept with, I'll never know. Perhaps because I was house captain and pretty popular.'

Carver studied Davenport's face. There was no doubt he was a highly intelligent, articulate man. Whether he was also a brilliant liar, Carver couldn't yet tell. 'Did you sleep with her only the once?'

'Yes.'

'So the whole thing was hushed over?'

'Yes. She never reported me to the authorities, and it was never mentioned further. In fact, she was so ashamed of what she did, she left the following week, and I never saw her again. I have no idea how these men found out about it. As far as I know, only she, the master and I knew.'

Davenport paused, looked earnestly at Carver. 'I am not a rapist, DCI Carver. I had my wild days at university.' He let out a grunt. 'Didn't we all? But it was just a phase that I, like so many youngsters, went through. I'm a fifty-four-year-old man, married for nearly thirty years. I love my wife and I love my children. I have nothing to confess, and I refuse to give in to these kidnappers' obscene demands. Good

36

God, I don't have a million pounds to throw around, and the firm certainly can't afford to lose six million.'

That's debatable. Carver leant back in his chair. 'Is there anyone else you can think of who might bear a grudge against you? Against the firm?'

Davenport was silent for a moment. 'No, not that I can think of. I have a very good relationship with my clients, and I cannot think why anyone would want to target my firm specifically. Other than because of what we've just heard, of course. But as I said, I refuse to relent. If we cave, what kind of message will that send? We'd be opening a can of worms. Other loons out there will undoubtedly jump on the bandwagon and start making similar demands of other firms. And that's not going to make us popular.'

What he said was true. But when there were lives at stake, it was never that simple. 'I understand, Mr Davenport. It's not the police's policy to give in to ransom demands either. But the injuries to Ms Dempsey's face illustrate that these men mean business, and won't hesitate to go a step further if we refuse to comply. What do you think Ms Dempsey's family would have to say about that? I understand her father is a good friend of yours, as well as an ex-client. Or the public for that matter? Think about how the firm will be perceived by clients, by the world, by the press.'

Davenport tossed back the rest of his brandy, then gave Carver a hard look. 'I am not giving in, DCI Carver. You need to find them. That's all there is to it. Find them and end this nightmare.'

'You heard him,' the woman said, thankful for the listening device installed in Davenport's office. 'The bastard's not giving in. So much for his friendship with Charlie-boy. We go to stage two.'

'So soon?' one of her peers asked.

'She's right,' their leader said. 'We only have four days. The supercilious son of a bitch needs to realise we're not dicking around.'

'OK.' The taller man nodded. 'I'll see to it.'

Back at the police station, Carver sank down into his chair, having just briefed his team. As a senior officer, he had a sizeable room to himself, which looked out onto the open-plan station floor. He kept his desk reasonably tidy. Just his computer, various bits of stationery, the odd file and a photo of his son. But the shelves around him were full to the brim with files and books, the neutral cream walls dotted with whiteboards on which Carver liked to scribble his thoughts. It was 10 p.m., and everyone looked spent. Pasty, jaded faces, twitching with too much caffeine, hankering after a shower and a good night's sleep.

They'd only recently wrapped up a fraud case and hadn't expected to be thrown into another investigation so quickly. No time to breathe, rest, recharge their batteries.

Carver had charged Drake with the grim task of breaking the news of Stephen Baines' and Matthew Gerard's abductions to their respective families, while he had stayed a while longer with Davenport. Davenport had told him that Stephen was currently working in Corporate on the fifth floor, Matthew in Property on the fourth. Both were popular, hard-working members of the firm, and as far as Davenport knew, no one had a bad word to say about them. Carver would verify this with other members of staff tomorrow, although his sceptical side wondered whether anyone would dare utter anything derogatory about two kidnap victims. Aside from jerks like Turner, of course.

Everyone had long gone home, but having got their contact details off Davenport, Carver had since spoken to both Matthew's and Stephen's secretaries about the two trainees' movements that day.

Around 12.30 p.m., Matthew had told his secretary that he was popping out with Stephen for a sandwich – they were good mates and often grabbed a bite together – in need of some fresh air and the chance to stretch his legs. Matthew was a creature of habit and nearly always took his lunch around this time unless something urgent had cropped up. The question put to her, she realised she didn't remember him returning. And the same went for Stephen. At the time, with everyone in a panic about Charlotte and Richard, and then Davenport telling his staff to go home, no one had registered their absence.

Logically, given the timing, it seemed unlikely that the same two who took Charlotte and Richard could have taken Matthew and Stephen. Unless, of course, they'd seized the men first, before quickly handing them over to their accomplices, enabling them to move on to Charlotte and Richard. Either way, Carver was certain the masked men were part of a larger group. Strangely, the main reception CCTV hadn't captured Matthew and Stephen leaving the building around that time. Did this mean that, like Charlotte and Richard, they were abducted from inside the building? Matthew's secretary had said that it was possible they'd taken the stairs and gone out the back entrance. But of course, the CCTV covering the back exit for the time period in question was blank. Perhaps this explained why? Carver also had members of his team checking CCTV footage of the entire Square Mile, with specific attention paid to the getaway vehicle's route to the firm, and its path out of the City with the hostages.

As well as Drake, Carver had enlisted two more bodies on his team. He liked to keep his teams small and tight. For now, there was no need for any more players in the squad, and he hoped that ordinary investigative reactive techniques would suffice, omitting the need for a specialist surveillance response under the remit of the

Human Trafficking and Kidnap Unit based at New Scotland Yard. Even so, the HTKU DCI had insisted on Carver keeping him aware of developments with a view to intervening if necessary.

'Do we know who the courier was? Where he picked up the DVD from?' DC Carly Rivers was a tough-talking, pint-sized girl of twenty-four, with frizzy strawberry-blonde hair which she scraped back into a bun. She was ambitious to the point of scary, a confirmed lesbian and proud of it. At times, she scared the shit out of her peers. There was no messing with Carly.

'CitySprint,' Drake answered. 'They collected the package from some derelict office building in Stratford. The courier was slightly freaked out as it was handed to him by some weirdo wearing a Batman costume. He was standing in front of the building when the courier got there.'

DC Tom Coombs let out a snigger. Gangly, ginger-haired, and only just turned twenty-two, he was a smart, promising officer, who'd sailed through his probationary period. But he was also cocky and frequently childish. Carver glared at him. *I'll soon beat the wise guy out of him*, he thought.

'Something funny, Coombs?' His eyes continued to blaze through the rookie.

Coombs's face fell. 'Er, no, sir.'

Carver sighed with irritation. 'Carry on, Drake.'

'Yes, sir. I checked out the address, but it appeared to be an abandoned building, as I said. No sign of anyone using it. No CCTV.'

'No eyewitnesses?'

'Afraid not, sir. We asked around the area, but the building was on a tiny side street, and the courier confirmed there was no one about at the time.'

Carver stood up, walked over to a clean whiteboard, and began to scribble his thoughts.

'So, we have a respected partner due to retire plus three trainees, one of whom isn't being kept on, taken most probably between the hours of 12.30 and 2 p.m. this afternoon – 2 p.m. being roughly the time Gerard's and Baines' secretaries realised they hadn't seen them return from lunch. We know the partner and the girl were snatched by two armed masked men, who escaped in a blue Ford Transit van, driven by another individual, also donning a balaclava. But we don't know if they, or further unidentified members of their gang, took Baines and Gerard. The latter seems likely given the timing. The girl's been badly beaten, but we don't know where she and the others are being held. The captors haven't appeared on screen, except for the lower half of one of them, but it's clear they have it in for Davenport, demanding his resignation and that he donate a substantial sum of his own money to Rape Crisis. They have somehow discovered some very personal information about him, information which he claims was kept under wraps between him, the girl he allegedly raped – Mary Jacobs – and the then master of Trinity College, Cambridge, Stewart Larson. They have also demanded six million of the firm's money, presumably a bonus gift to themselves, although we don't know this for sure. We have until Friday 4 p.m. to figure out who they are and where they are holding the hostages before God only knows what they'll do to them if their demands aren't met.' Carver looked at his team expectantly. 'Any thoughts?'

'Talk to Larson?' Rivers suggested. 'Get him to verify that no one else knew about the rape allegation. There's every chance he let it slip. And the same goes for the girl. I suggest we track her down, question her. Find out who else she told. Boyfriends, husbands, girlfriends, there're any number of possibilities.'

'Good, Rivers. You and Coombs, track them down ASAP, then pay both a visit. Larson first. We need to see if his story fits with Davenport's before we go questioning some poor woman about an extremely delicate issue. We also need to question the hostages' friends, families, neighbours. Also, other trainees. See if they remember any of the hostages mentioning seeing or speaking to anyone suspicious.'

'Yes, sir.' Coombs nodded, his expression now deadpan. *Perhaps he's learnt his lesson*, thought Carver.

'In the meantime, I need to let the world know we've got a hostage situation on our hands.'

The lights were blinding. The noise incessant. Flash photographers clicked away as Carver made a formal statement to the press and nationwide TV audience. It had just gone 11 p.m. Later than anticipated. He was flanked on either side by the hostages' families. All of them distraught. In the case of the trainees, their choked-up fathers: Frank Gerard, Charles Dempsey and Mike Baines. All three trainees had lost their mothers. Coincidence or not?

Stephen's parents had split when he was only five. Mike had remarried shortly after, and had a daughter, Sophie, but she wasn't there with her father. Matthew was an only child, while Charlotte had a younger brother, apparently too cut up to attend. Also present was Stephen's Venezuelan girlfriend, Celeste. She was stunning. Carver noticed she barely made eye contact with Mike, and it made him wonder whether father and son shared a frosty relationship. Finally, there to beg for Richard's safe return, were his wife and two grown-up children, Justin and Stella. Mrs Barker was an elegant, eye-catching woman. It was clear she took care of herself. Her nails were French-manicured, her hair dyed to perfection with subtle highlights woven in to soften her

42

advancing years. And she had the figure of someone who ate like a bird and worked out like a long-distance runner. Outwardly, she was the calmest of the lot, but Carver suspected it was a different story inside.

He'd begun by summarising the situation, omitting, for the time being at least, the kidnappers' personal demands of Davenport. There was no point humiliating the man until all hope was lost. Despite the kidnappers' obvious desire to do so. All they needed to know was that a large sum of money had been demanded. The fathers and Mrs Barker had then made separate impassioned pleas for the public to come forward with any information they might have, however trivial, and to the kidnappers not to hurt their loved ones. Celeste, along with Richard's children, wept, while the fathers fought back tears and Mrs Barker remained stoical, yet glassy-eyed.

'Do you have any idea where the hostages are being held, DCI Carver?' asked a female reporter sitting in the front row.

'No, we do not. The recording gave no indication as to the hostages' whereabouts. As I explained, all we're sure of for now is that there are at least three hostage-takers who made their getaway with Ms Dempsey and Mr Barker, and that one of them was the driver of a blue Ford Transit van, last seen parked outside Sullivans' offices. At this moment, we do not know who took Stephen Baines and Matthew Gerard, but based on the last time both men were seen, we believe it was sometime between 12.30 p.m. and 2 p.m. today.'

'What about CCTV?'

'We're checking that.'

She didn't stop. Aimed her next question at Charlotte's father. 'Mr Dempsey, do you think your friendship with Nigel Davenport, and the fact that you were, up until last December, a pre-eminent client of Sullivans, has something to do with your daughter's kidnapping?'

43

'You don't have to answer that,' Carver whispered in Dempsey's ear.

Dempsey gave him a resigned look. 'It's OK, I don't mind.' He was a man of average height, sturdily built, with unnaturally white teeth and a full head of dark brown hair despite being in his mid-fifties. It was patently dyed. But like Davenport, he had the look of someone who'd enjoyed an extravagant lifestyle. The bloodshot tinge to his eyes, the puffy bags underlying them, the ruddiness of his skin. Carver wondered if he and Davenport were still close. It was a question he chalked up to ask both men later.

'I suppose it's possible,' Dempsey replied. 'But if that's the case, I don't understand why these men have demanded money from Mr Davenport's firm, rather than from me? And why did they take the other three, as well as Charlotte?' He gave those around him sympathetic smiles, then looked back at the reporter.

For once, she appeared lost for words. She changed tack. Fixed her gaze back on Carver. 'And what is the firm's position on the kidnappers' financial demands? Will Mr Davenport fulfil them?'

Carver leant into the microphone. 'We are reviewing all options at this point in time, and we will update the press and public accordingly. For now, that's all I have to say.' Before the reporter could get another word in, he stood up and ushered the families out of the room. Leaving behind a disappointed press to gossip amongst themselves.

'Dempsey actually looked upset.'

The woman rolled her eyes and tutted. 'Don't be fooled. It's all a fucking act. I bet he's been on the phone to Davenport, and now he's scared for his own skin. He's just playing the role of dutiful father for the public's benefit. But he doesn't fool me. Not for one second.'

Chapter Four

Maddy muted the TV, then tossed the remote on the coffee table with a heavy sigh. She and Cara had just watched Carver's press conference. It was hot and humid, and the clammy air seemed to cling to her. She was tired, but it was hard sleeping in the sweltering heat, and she needed more time to unwind. The second she'd got home, she'd changed out of her heavy suit into a light cotton nightie, stripped her face bare of make-up and flopped down on the sofa with a tall glass of lemonade, mentally and physically exhausted from earlier. Now, feeling a little more relaxed, having moved on to something stronger – ice-cold Sauvignon Blanc – she still felt hot. They had a fan blowing cool air at them at full blast from one corner of the small, yet smartly furnished living room. But the minute they switched it off, it was as if it had never been on.

Maddy had first met Cara at King's College London, where they'd both read English Literature as their first degrees, remaining firm friends ever since. Cara was like the Duracell bunny. A bouncy blonde, with ice-blue eyes and a gymnast's body, she had limitless energy. Previously a features reporter for a national newspaper, she'd since ventured into magazine writing, and now wrote the health and beauty column for a women's magazine. She'd been a rock of strength for Maddy after Paul's conviction, and had secretly talked at length with Rose about how best to get her granddaughter through one of the darkest moments of her life. They'd agreed that being alone was the last thing she'd needed. More than anything, she'd needed companionship and support. So, Cara had insisted that they move in together, and to her and Rose's relief, Maddy hadn't needed much convincing. The week after Paul was sent away, she said good riddance to the two-bed Victorian flat they'd shared in Bow, moving to a smart modern duplex in Southfields with Cara. And not too far from Rose, in Barnes.

'Those poor families,' Cara said. 'I can't imagine what they must be going through.'

'Hell,' Maddy said bluntly. Her mind flashed back to lunchtime, and the heart-stopping terror she'd felt. Her pulse accelerating, she reached for her wine, took a large gulp, then swallowed hard as if to swallow away the memory. Although she knew she should count herself lucky, coming away free and unscathed, she was still shaken up. Plus, she was annoyed with herself for speaking up to the men. He might have been a jumped-up twat, but Turner was right. She'd put her life and the lives of her colleagues in jeopardy. It was both her strength and her weakness. Never afraid to stand up to bullies, to speak her mind. But one day, if she didn't watch out, she'd go too far, and someone would end up getting hurt. Badly.

'You OK?' Cara asked with concern. 'You've been through hell yourself today. It's late. Why don't you hit the sack? I'll load the dishwasher.'

Maddy smiled gratefully. 'That's a nice idea. Thanks.'

Ten minutes later, as she stood in front of the bathroom mirror brushing her teeth, all sorts of questions buzzed around in her mind.

How did the men get inside the building unseen? What made them target Charlotte, Matthew, Stephen and Richard? And why pick Sullivans out of all the law firms in the City? Something didn't add up, and she had a feeling Carver hadn't told the world the whole story.

It bugged the hell out of her. So much so, tomorrow she planned on doing a little detective work of her own.

Tuesday, 8 a.m., Nigel Davenport was seated at the head of another equally impressive oak conference table in meeting room three on the sixth floor. The largest meeting room in the building, where *important* decisions were made at *important* fortnightly partners' meetings. Not all the partners, just the senior and managing partners, plus heads of department. But this meeting would be different. For one, they were missing one notable head: Richard Barker. And two, also invited were James Canton and Gavin Turner. Right now, they were one short of a full house, still waiting on Canton.

Davenport looked down at his agenda. Until yesterday afternoon, next month's annual client summer party had been top of his list. Followed by projected billings for the third quarter. But these had been brusquely knocked off the top spot. There would only be one topic of conversation at today's meeting, and he wasn't looking forward to it. Not one bit.

For most of yesterday, he'd managed to avoid Charles's phone calls. 'What the hell is going on, Nigel?' 'Is there something you're not telling me?' 'I hope you're fucking going to pay the money with my daughter's life at stake?'

Finally, wide awake, and seeing Charles's number appear again at 1 a.m., he'd answered his mobile lying on his bedside table, and taken it down to his study, not wanting his wife to overhear his conversation.

He'd known Charles for over thirty years. His closest friend. A man he trusted. A man who knew his murkiest secrets. A man who had murky secrets of his own. So, he'd bitten the bullet, and told him the truth. Every scrap of it. And for a while, neither had spoken. Shock, fear and regret stalking the line.

Then, finally, Charles had asked the inevitable. 'Do they know about me? Have they mentioned me? How the fuck did they find out, for Christ's sake?'

Now, Charles wasn't just worried for his daughter, he was worried for himself, but he'd made one thing clear before hanging up. For both their sakes, it wasn't worth standing up to these bastards. If they did, it could backfire catastrophically and cost them dearly.

And now, as he sat facing his fellow partners, Davenport knew he had a more pressing decision to make. Did he, or did he not, tell them about the personal demands being made of him? It was a question he'd wrestled with for much of the night. Unbeknown to his snoring wife, Pamela, oblivious to the secret her husband had kept from her all their married life. Just as she was oblivious to his favourite pastimes.

As far as Pamela was concerned, they'd simply picked on her husband's firm because it was rich and successful. She'd sympathised with him and his difficult decision, but surely saving lives was more important than saving money?

What did she know?

Just then, Canton appeared, looking unusually gaunt and harassed. 'Sorry I'm late,' he apologised, sliding his fingers through his perfect hair. His apology was met by a roomful of sympathetic smiles.

'It's quite all right, James,' Davenport said. 'No one would dare give you grief after what you've been through.'

Davenport surveyed the sea of faces and caught Turner's eye. Noting his put-out expression at not being included in this show of sympathy, he quickly added, 'And you of course, Gavin.' This did the trick, Turner's grimace swiftly transmuting into an oily grin.

Canton took a seat next to Turner. 'It's nothing compared with what Charlotte, Stephen, Matthew and Richard must be going through.' He looked directly at Davenport. 'Tell me, Nigel, was the DVD truly ghastly? Can we see it?'

All eyes focussed on Davenport, and his throat suddenly felt constricted. Blocked by panic, shame, fear. He reached for his glass of water and took a large swig. 'It's not pleasant,' he replied. 'I'm not sure there's any need to subject the rest of you to something so unspeakably horrid. They want money, plain and simple.'

There it was. In one fell swoop, he'd made his choice. He'd withheld crucial information from his partners. But for how long could he get away with his deception?

'I know we discussed this briefly yesterday, Nigel,' Mark Simmons, the managing partner, said, 'but why do you suppose they picked on us? The City is chock full of rich firms. Bigger and richer. What's so special about us?'

Simmons was an earnest sort of a fellow. Straight up, hard-working, boring some might say. Medium-build, late forties, receding brown hair, Clark Kent glasses, it was no surprise he'd chosen to specialise in tax. He was also one of the firm's few teetotallers.

He'd made a good point. One his senior partner couldn't answer. Or, at least, not without revealing the truth. 'I really don't know, Mark.' Davenport shook his head sombrely. 'It's something of a mystery.'

'And it's nothing to do with Charles being a wealthy ex-client and Charlotte's father?'

Oh, how he longed to say, *Yes, it's all because of him*. That would be so simple. Take the pressure off him, off his firm. But he couldn't, of course.

'They've not mentioned him.'

'You heard what Charles said at the press conference last night.' Turner stuck his oar in. 'He made a damn good point. If it's his money they're after, why haven't they contacted him directly? And why take the others? It makes no sense, particularly as he's no longer a client.' He looked at Davenport, who looked around the room. A grave unanimous nodding of heads. They were all highly intelligent men, and that scared him senseless.

'So, what's the plan, Nigel?' Frederick Houseman, Head of Property, asked. Originally from Texas, he'd retained his broad Texan twang, and towered over his fellow partners at a strapping six-six. 'We've got the families to consider, and Richard's like a part of the furniture. He's put years into this firm. Think of Marianne. Plus, how do you think we'll be perceived if we allow innocent trainees to be harmed, possibly killed, by refusing to pay out? No one will ever apply to us again. As it is, I'm certain applications will be down next year. I've not talked to HR yet, but I wouldn't be surprised if we've got incoming trainees rescinding their training contracts already.'

Davenport felt sick. Claustrophobic. Every word of what Houseman said was true. But it wasn't as simple as that. 'You expect me to just hand over six million of the firm's money' – he looked around the table as if the idea was preposterous – '*our* money, our *hard-earned* money, *clients'* money – to these nut-jobs?' Known for his unflappable disposition, the partners were stunned to see him looking so rattled.

'Calm down, Nigel,' Simmons urged.

'I can't calm down! This is a bloody nightmare. OK, say we give them the money, what assurances do we have that they'll return the hostages, that they're even still alive? And what kind of precedent would we be setting? We could be opening a Pandora's Box. And no one will thank us for it.'

'But we can't just sit by and do nothing,' Canton said. 'If we let them die, our reputation will be in the gutter, and we'll lose clients as well as staff. It's that simple.'

Either way, they were screwed. For a while, no one spoke. It felt like there was no air in the room. Davenport was about to speak when his iPhone, sitting on the table in front of him, pinged. It was a text. He rarely got texts, so he was intrigued to see who it was from. He picked it up, clicked on the message from a number he didn't recognise, then immediately wished he hadn't. Or at least, he wished he'd waited until he was alone in the privacy of his office.

As he stared at the screen, he felt the bile rise in his throat, his brow suddenly moist, his armpits sweaty, his head spinning.

'Nigel' – he just made out Simmons's concerned voice – 'you don't look well. Are you all right?'

Davenport looked up, but his vision was fuzzy. 'Er, no, actually, I'm not feeling too good. I'm afraid I'm going to have to cut the meeting short.'

'But we've not discussed our game plan,' Turner said.

Davenport saw the irritation on his partners' faces. He didn't blame them, but it couldn't be helped. He had to get out of there.

He hastily gathered his belongings, and walked quickly to the door, pausing briefly to look back over his shoulder. 'I'm sorry, I really do have to go. I'll get my PA to rearrange the meeting for this afternoon sometime.'

'But…' He vaguely heard Turner protest. Then he was out the door, deaf to the volley of abuse now being fired his way by Turner.

Davenport put his head over the toilet bowl and threw up. He'd checked that he was alone in the basement toilets, which were rarely used, then opted for the last cubicle. He slumped back against the locked door, tore off some toilet paper and wiped the dregs of vomit from around his mouth.

He felt dizzy and his heart was racing. Had he not recently undergone his annual BUPA check, which had confirmed his ticker to be in tip-top condition (surprising really, considering his lifestyle), he might have concluded that he was on the verge of having a heart attack, rather than a panic attack. Panting heavily, inhaling the acrid air, his chest felt tight as he viewed the text again – and stared down at the image of him lying flat on his stomach, butt naked, a blonde hooker bent over him, dressed in PVC bondage gear with holes in all the right places, and brandishing a whip across his naked bottom. He remembered her well. For more reasons than one. It had only been a couple of months ago. She'd looked like a *Playboy* model: all breasts, lips, hips, a shapely bottom and peroxide hair. His ultimate fantasy, his escape from his dull, fat wife and her constant nagging. A girl who'd ordered him to whip her, beat her, fuck her from behind. Not like those upstart Cambridge girls. With their come-to-bed eyes and false promises. Liars, all of them! They'd sent mixed messages. They'd been too full of themselves. They'd asked for it. Wanted it. Fucking little prima donnas. What did they expect would happen to them if they behaved that way?

Particularly *her*. She'd been the worst of them. Had known how beautiful she was, in that innocent, butter-wouldn't-melt kind of a way. And she had flaunted it in his face for an entire year. He'd been a Cambridge star. A golden boy. He'd had a right to her, and she had given him that right, by the way she'd behaved around him.

But then she'd had the nerve to complain about him. At least none of the others had. They had succumbed without protest. Considered themselves lucky. Enjoyed the experience. Thankfully, the master had dealt with it. He'd known how to silence her. He did silence her.

But somehow, the kidnappers knew. They knew about an incident that had happened over thirty years ago. And they knew about his fetish for sadomasochistic sex with buxom blonde call girls.

Who had they got this information from, and how was he going to stop them from telling the world?

'Are you OK, Nigel?'

Still in turmoil, Davenport had barely noticed Maddy board the lift on level one. Her question brought him back to reality with a start. He flashed her a nervous smile, and quickly wiped his damp brow with a handkerchief, hoping she wouldn't notice how much he was perspiring, or that his breath smelt rank.

She did. But didn't let on. 'Yes, thank you, Madeline. It's all this nasty hostage business. So unexpected, so upsetting, it's rather got to me. How are you coping?'

Maddy gave him a sympathetic smile. He had to have had the weight of the world on his shoulders, with such a huge choice to make. 'I'm fine, thank you. I just count myself lucky. Have the kidnappers been in contact again?'

Richard had been spot on when he'd hired Maddy Kramer. She was sharp, exceptionally bright, and exceptionally nosy. Perfect traits in a litigator. But right now, he wished she'd mind her own bloody business. Why did it feel like she was cross-examining him? Making him feel like a liar even though he'd said nothing. Why couldn't she just shut her mouth, and stop asking questions?

'No,' he said quickly. With a little too much conviction.

Maddy held his gaze, then asked, 'What are you going to do?'

'We're still working on that. The partners and me. But it's not that simple.'

Maddy was about to respond when the lift stopped on Davenport's floor. 'Have a good day,' he said abruptly, before dashing out.

That was weird, thought Maddy. Davenport had always struck her as an OK sort, albeit a little shifty, and he'd always treated her with courtesy. But just then, he'd lied. She was sure of it. The kidnappers *had* been in contact again. She'd seen it in his eyes, heard it in his voice.

She wondered if Carver knew. *Maybe not.*

She felt certain there was more to the kidnappers' demands than money. Davenport just seemed too personally affected. She'd give Carver a call, fill him in on her boss's strange behaviour.

Four lives were at stake, and he had no right to hold anything back for the sake of his own reputation.

Chapter Five

For a man of eighty-five, Stewart Larson was faring well. Tall, lean, upright, he had retained a thin dusting of snow-white hair, walked with a spring in his step, and spoke with authority.

All in all, he seemed mentally as sharp as he was physically able. There was no tremor in his voice, no confusion in his misty blue eyes, no timidity in his demeanour. DC Carly Rivers had no doubt she was looking at a man who would have no problem recollecting the events of over thirty years ago.

Maybe it was his third wife, Julia, thirty-five years his junior, who kept him so lithe and spritely on his feet. She looked like she spent a lot of time at both the gym, and with her plastic surgeon. Everything was tight and pointed north, her stretched face plastered with several layers of make-up, her smile pearly white, her cream pencil skirt pulled a little too tightly around her pert derrière.

Larson also appeared to have done very well for himself on the financial front. He lived in a six-bedroom detached house situated in large landscaped gardens on a peaceful no-through road in one of the best and most highly regarded residential areas of Cambridge. The gardens were a mix of mature and rare trees, shrubs and flowers, and the front of the house was screened by a maturing yew hedge and a pretty Japanese-style garden, along with a gravelled drive with ample parking.

'You have a very nice house,' Rivers commented as Larson led her and Coombs through to one of the property's four reception rooms while Julia went out to make coffee.

'Thank you, yes, I'm very fortunate. The land on which the house is built was originally in the ownership of a Cambridge College. During the time I was master of Trinity, plots of land were handed out to Fellows, giving us the chance to design and build the house of our choice.'

It's all right for some, thought Coombs, who'd attended the local comprehensive and grew up on a council estate in Hackney. *Posh bastard.*

'So, what can I do for you?' Larson gestured for them to take a seat on one of two black leather sofas. The décor was surprising. Way more modern than one would have guessed from the outside. The floor was glossy laminate wood, the coffee and side tables solid glass, the walls adorned with various pieces of modern art Rivers couldn't quite decipher.

Probably the wife's influence again, she thought.

Just then, Julia appeared with coffee and a plate of biscuits. As she served up the coffee, Rivers responded to Larson's question. 'As I explained over the phone, DC Coombs and I are part of a team investigating the recent abduction of a partner and three trainees at the London law firm of Sullivan, Blake, Monroe.'

Larson pressed his fingertips together. 'Yes, I caught the press conference on television last night. A terrible situation.' He shook his head gravely.

'The senior partner is a man named Nigel Davenport.' Rivers paused and waited for a reaction but got none. 'He was one of your students, from 1981 to 1984. Do you remember him?'

Larson sipped his coffee slowly, as if sampling the taste for the first time. A drawn-out sip, his eyes peeping over the rim like a well-trained spy. Eventually, he said, 'Yes, of course I do. He was a brilliant student. I'm not surprised he went on to become so successful.'

'And well liked?' A deliberate scepticism underlined Rivers' question.

Larson raised his eyebrows in surprise. 'Yes, very. He was house captain, and team rowing captain, as I recall.'

'Popular amongst the female students?'

Larson furrowed his brow. 'What's all this about? What's that got to do with your investigation? Why so much interest in Nigel?'

Rivers glanced at Coombs, then lowered her voice. 'Was Mr Davenport ever accused of raping a female student, Mr Larson?'

Larson jolted in his seat. He glanced nervously at his wife who'd been munching away happily on a custard cream, but had stopped mid-chew, her cheeks bulging like a chipmunk, her eyes awash with surprise and alarm. Her ears no doubt burning with intrigue.

'Really, this is quite out of order,' Larson finally said. His voice had gone from caramel calm to rocky road edgy. 'As far as I can tell, your question has no bearing on your current investigation.'

Rivers leant forward. 'Mr Larson, that's not for you to decide. Now please answer the question.'

'OK, yes,' he finally conceded. 'But it was all a misunderstanding. The girl dropped her claim, and it was never spoken of again.'

'Who was the girl?'

'I really don't remember.'

'Mr Larson.' Rivers gave him an icy stare.

'Really, I don't. Genuinely. It may have been Mary something or other.'

'Mary Jacobs?' Another steely look.

'Er, yes, that rings a bell. I seem to recall she had dalliances with a number of male students.'

'So, there was no truth to it as far as you knew?'

'No, none whatsoever.'

'Did you tell anyone about the girl's allegation?'

'No.'

'What about the girl? Did she tell anyone?'

'How would I know that?'

'Please answer the question.'

'No, not that I'm aware of. She swore she wouldn't, but I can only go by her word.'

'Do you know what happened to her?'

Larson cocked his head to one side, tapping the side of his face with his forefinger. 'Come to think of it, she dropped out soon after. Too ashamed of what she'd done, I suppose. Almost ruining the reputation of a perfectly innocent young man. Her leaving only proved her guilt for what she'd done.'

Or the fact that she'd been humiliated, and couldn't bear the sight of Davenport or you, thought Rivers.

'And you don't know what happened to her after she dropped out?'

'No idea. She didn't strike me as the ambitious type. Probably went on to marry some wealthy banker or some such like.'

How cliché of you to assume so, Rivers thought irritably.

'Why are you asking all these questions about something that happened over thirty years ago? How can it possibly have any relevance to your investigation?' He looked from Rivers to Coombs. Their failure to respond spoke volumes. 'Ah, I see.' Larson smiled, his eyes lighting up with triumph. As if he'd just solved the Enigma Code. 'Because it *does* have something to do with the investigation. The kidnappers know about the rape allegation. Are they blackmailing Nigel?'

He stared at the helpless young officers, who were sadly too inexperienced to know how to deal with the situation. The more mature man had the upper hand. And, once again, he had the answer he needed. Finally, a slightly pink Rivers said, 'Mr Larson, we would really appreciate your discretion at this point in time.' She turned to Julia. 'And yours, Mrs Larson. If word gets out to the press, you could be jeopardising the safe return of the hostages, and ruining a man's life, not to mention his poor wife's.'

Julia nodded, but Rivers saw the glint of excitement in her eyes. Some juicy gossip for the tennis club coffee mornings.

'Of course.' Larson nodded soberly. He turned to Julia. 'We won't say a word, will we, my sweet?'

Julia shook her head vehemently, before tucking into her third custard cream. *She'll probably vomit them up after we leave*, Rivers mused.

A thought sprang to Coombs's mind. 'I assume college photos were taken at the time? Do you have any?'

Larson sighed with irritation. As if the same notion had crossed his mind, but he was hoping it might have bypassed the officers' callow brains. 'Yes,' he said grudgingly. 'I keep them upstairs, in the loft.'

'May we see them?' Rivers asked. She held his gaze. There was only one correct answer to her question, and Larson knew that.

'Yes, of course,' he replied tersely.

'Darling, you shouldn't be taxing yourself, going up those narrow stairs,' Julia said. She gave Coombs and Rivers a vicious glare, but it didn't faze either officer. Her husband looked fitter than a lot of men half his age. They didn't expect a few extra stairs were going to prove too taxing for him.

They followed him up the bare wooden stairs to the loft. More a study than a loft. Clean, light and airy, the room smelt of fresh paint, with shelving on either side, a chunky mahogany desk set against the window, the off-white walls decorated with various academic and sports certificates dedicated to Larson. There was also a filing cabinet in the far corner of the room. Larson went over to it, bent down and pulled out the second drawer from the bottom. Rivers edged closer and watched him flick through the numbered dividers. It wasn't long before he pulled something out from a clear plastic wallet. An unframed colour photograph, probably around ten by eight inches. Larson considered it for a while before holding it up for Rivers and Coombs to see.

'This is Davenport's year?' Rivers asked.

'Yes. There he is.' Larson pointed to an athletic-looking young man, standing in the back row, arms crossed. He was good-looking, but there was also an arrogance about him. Almost a smirk on his face, an overconfident glimmer in his eyes. The type who felt they had the right to take whatever they wanted, behave however they wanted, whenever they wanted. Rivers took an immediate dislike to the younger Davenport. She couldn't imagine the older one was much different. Leopards never changed their spots.

'And Mary?' Coombs asked.

Larson's eyes flitted across the photo, squinting every now and again, as if he was having trouble recognising her. But then his gaze rested on a girl sitting on a bench in the front row. 'There.' He pointed. A second's pause, then, 'Come to think of it, I don't believe this was taken too long after the incident. Maybe the same week. She left soon after.'

The girl was beautiful. She had long, sleek dark hair, full lips and intense mocha-brown eyes. The kind of eyes that seduced you, swallowed you up whole. Both Rivers and Coombs could see the attraction. Both imagined themselves taking a fancy to her. She wasn't smiling. She looked sad. Like she didn't want to be there.

'Is Charlotte Dempsey's father in this photo?' Coombs asked. 'We understand he was also at Trinity, and is a good friend of Davenport's. And one of his best clients up until his retirement last year.'

'Hmm,' Larson pondered, scanning his eyes across the photo once more. 'Ah, yes, Charles, there he is.' Larson's finger paused on a boy standing in front of Davenport in the second row. They couldn't have been more different. Dempsey was several inches shorter and stout all over, with a stubby nose and horn-rimmed glasses. His smile revealed a crooked set of teeth. It was no surprise they needed Larson to point him out. He appeared very different to how he looked now: at least twenty pounds lighter, no sign of the glasses, and perfect teeth.

It's true what they say, thought Rivers, *men really do improve with age. Bastards. Although, pots of cash to preen, fix and tighten every nut and bolt no doubt helps.*

'He was a quiet boy,' Larson explained. 'Kept himself to himself. Shy around the girls, didn't have much luck on that front, I'm afraid. But clearly, he found his soulmate, else there wouldn't have been a Charlotte. I must say, I hardly recognised him on TV last night.'

'Yes, he's changed remarkably.' Rivers nodded, wondering why Dempsey's 'soulmate' had killed herself. That's what Carver had told her late last night.

She continued to study the photo. Then something caught her eye. A face that for some reason looked familiar. As if she'd only seen him recently. 'Who's that?' She pointed to a young man standing on

61

the far left of the back row. He had a strong physique, classic features. But he wasn't smiling. In fact, he looked troubled, anxious about something. Almost haunted.

'That,' Larson said, 'is Richard Barker.'

Rivers and Coombs looked at each other in amazement. 'As in one of the hostages?' Rivers turned back to Larson. Barker looked so different to recent photos they'd seen. Now, it was as if he'd shrunk a few inches and was suffering from a wasting disease.

'Yes,' Larson confirmed. 'You mean you didn't know that he, Charles and Nigel were at Cambridge together? I'd assumed you did. I'd assumed that was why you were here?'

'Why didn't Davenport mention he and Barker were at Cambridge together?' Rivers mumbled to herself.

'Maybe he just assumed you knew?' Larson offered.

'So they were friends back then?'

'Yes, good friends. Both sporty, ambitious types. They shared a friendly rivalry, always trying to outdo the other.' Larson noted the look on Rivers' face and immediately knew what she was thinking. 'And before you say it, DC Rivers, although they were both popular with the ladies, their rivalry was limited to the academic and sports fields. Not as far as girls were concerned.'

Rivers didn't buy it. Two good-looking guys at Cambridge, who enjoyed competing at sport and academically, had even more reason to try and outdo the other with the girls. If anything, it was a mark of status, another string to their bow. A sign of their virility. She was so grateful to be gay. 'OK, well thanks for your time, Mr Larson. You've been most helpful.'

'Not at all. I only hope you find the poor souls before it's too late. Especially dear Richard. I was fond of him.'

62

'Ms Kramer, what can I do for you?'

It was midday on Tuesday. Carver was in his office, wolfing down a sandwich, feet up on the table, shirtsleeves rolled up, when the phone rang. The air con wasn't working, and the room felt like a sauna – oppressive and airless. How he wished the weather would break. He'd just got off the phone with Rivers. She and Coombs were on their way back to London, but she'd wanted to brief him on their meeting with Larson straight away.

They'd yet to track down Mary Jacobs, and so Larson was the only witness to Davenport's version of events they had at present. Carver wasn't surprised to hear a clever man like him had worked out that Davenport was being blackmailed. It couldn't be helped; they had needed to speak to him. He just prayed his wife kept her mouth shut.

He also wondered why Davenport had never mentioned Barker being at Cambridge with him. If Davenport and Barker had been good friends back then, as Larson had claimed, perhaps Barker was also aware of the rape allegation, and had stuck up for his chum at the time.

In which case, is that why the kidnappers took him? As punishment? Was the brains behind the operation a friend of Mary's? Had one or more of the kidnappers been at Cambridge with Davenport, Dempsey and Barker? Did Dempsey also know about the allegation? Was the intention to make all three suffer?

Perhaps Davenport had assumed it was common knowledge that he and Barker had been at Cambridge together? Or maybe he didn't want the police digging deeper into his past? Whatever his reasons, it felt more than coincidental. He needed to go back and grill Davenport on that.

CCTV had confirmed that the getaway vehicle entered the City from the west around 12.15 p.m., making its way east and eventually disappearing onto a side street which ran off the back of Sullivans. Unfortunately, it had no CCTV. It seemed plausible that this was the moment Gerard and Baines were snatched. Later, the van reappeared on CCTV, pulling up in front of the firm's main reception, where it waited for Charlotte, Richard and their kidnappers to appear, at which point they all bundled in via the back doors before the van sped off and headed east out of the City. Carver's analysts had traced the van as far as Bow Road but after taking a series of turns onto minor residential streets, the trail ended. Carver had analysts checking all available CCTV on major roads in and around the area, but it was a massive job, and one he feared would prove hopeless. While some motorways and A roads had cameras designed to monitor traffic flow (even these were few and far between and rarely recorded in the same way as CCTV), most, in fact, weren't monitored by CCTV, and the same went for areas less populated than central London. To make matters worse, it appeared that the number plate caught on the street CCTV had been cloned, a common tactic used by criminals, and which in this case had led Carver's team to the house of a married couple in Southampton. The husband was a roofer and drove a blue Ford Transit van similar to the one in which the abductors fled the scene.

'I think the kidnappers may have contacted Davenport again,' Maddy explained, giving her reason for calling. With Charlotte gone, she had her office to herself. Even so, she'd made a point of closing the door and told her PA she wasn't to be disturbed.

Carver swung his feet off the table. 'What makes you think that?'

'I bumped into him this morning. He looked incredibly flustered.'

64

'That's not exactly surprising. Four of his staff have been abducted, and he has less than four days to decide between them and six million of his firm's money.'

'Is that *all* they've demanded?'

She was too smart. Thank God it was just a phone call. If she'd seen the look on his face, she'd have had her answer. But his silence also gave him away, and he knew there was no fooling her. He wondered whether she'd ever consider switching professions. He could do with someone like her on his team.

'What makes you say that?'

'It's not, is it?' she persisted.

Carver sighed. 'No. But keep it to yourself, Ms Kramer. There's a very good reason why we've not made it public knowledge.'

'I understand.' She paused, and Carver knew what was coming. 'But you can tell me, right? I won't breathe a word.'

He smiled, admiring her nerve. Even so, he didn't yield. 'No, Ms Kramer, I can't.'

'OK, worth a try.'

Carver grinned again. He couldn't see that she was also grinning. 'So, indulge me,' he said more seriously. 'What makes you think Davenport's received another message? Aside from him looking flustered.'

'I asked him, and he point blank denied it. But his response was too quick, and way too defensive. I could see it in his eyes, in his behaviour. He was perspiring, looked ill. They've been in touch, I know it. Plus...'

'Plus?'

'When I got back to my floor, I ran into James Canton, who I'm pretty friendly with.'

'Really?' Carver's tone was mischievous. Why did he always try and play the rogue around her? He wasn't like that normally. He was a sulky bastard around everyone else.

'Not like that.' Maddy let out an exaggerated sigh. 'He'd pushed back a client meeting we'd had scheduled for 8.30 a.m. because of an urgent partners' meeting Davenport had called for 8, regarding the kidnapping. So, I was a little surprised to see James back at his desk at just gone 8.20. He said Davenport had dashed out of the meeting after reading something on his iPhone. Said he turned quite green as soon as he read it.'

'He told you that?'

'James is a bit of a gossip. Newly made up, not quite made the transition from associate to partner.'

'Right, I see. Well, thanks, Ms Kramer. I'll have a chat with Davenport.'

There was a pause. 'He's in trouble, isn't he?' Maddy finally broke the hush. 'They've got something on him.'

'Yes,' Carver said softly.

'Should I feel sorry for him?'

'That depends.'

'On what?'

'On whether he's telling the truth.'

'Do you think he's telling the truth?'

'There are those who say he is. But you never know with people. You never know what secrets they harbour, or the personal agendas that drive them.'

66

Chapter Six

'Yes, Richard was at Cambridge with me. What of it?' Davenport looked at Carver crossly. More bad-tempered than yesterday.

'I thought you might have mentioned it. You both go back a long way. You must be good friends, as well as partners? His disappearance must therefore be exceptionally distressing for you?'

Davenport sighed heavily. 'Of course it's distressing. And yes, we were very good friends back then.'

'Not now?'

'It's different now. Back then, we were lads. Got up to all sorts of mischief, like lads do. But we grew up and moved on. Got married, had children, focussed on our careers.'

'Have you always worked together at this firm?'

'Yes. We both trained at what was then Sullivan Grant. When it merged with the firm Blake Monroe, and Peter Grant took early retirement, it became a very different outfit.'

'What happened to Mr Sullivan?'

'He died.'

'And you managed to climb to the very top of the ladder. Taking his place.'

'Bit of luck, really.' Davenport shrugged. 'To be honest, sometimes I wish I'd never let my ambition take hold of me. It's a lot of stress, being senior partner. Take times like this, for example. It falls heaviest on me. Always does.'

'Richard never wanted to be senior partner?'

Davenport eyed Carver guardedly. 'No. Head of department was enough for him. He's much more of a family man than me. To his credit.'

'Tell me, did Richard make any enemies at Cambridge that you can remember?'

Davenport thought for a while. 'No, not that I can recall. He was very popular. Always has been.'

'Did he know about the rape allegation?'

A slight trepidation in Davenport's eyes, then, 'No.'

'And what of Charles Dempsey?'

'Charles?'

'Yes. Mr Larson showed my officers a photo taken at Cambridge. You, Barker and Dempsey were in it. Dempsey looked very different to how he does now. A bit of a loner, so Larson said. Didn't have much luck with the girls.'

Davenport laughed quietly. 'Ah yes, that's true, poor Charles. But he did all right for himself in the end. Probably the most successful of the three of us. Damn shame about his wife, though.'

'Did he know about the allegation?'

More apprehension. As if he was deciding how best to answer. 'Charles was my best friend. Still is, in fact. So yes, he knew. I should have told you last night, I realise that now. I simply thought he had enough on his plate. Poor chap's in bits over Charlotte. But I can tell you now he was on my side. He never doubted me.' A brief pause, then, 'Which means he's not likely to be behind his own flesh and blood's kidnapping to teach me a lesson, is he? I know the thought's crossed your mind.'

'I accept that. But if the kidnappers think he covered for you, that could explain why they took his daughter.'

'I told you,' Davenport hissed, 'there was nothing to cover.'

Carver leant forward, rested his elbows on his knees, his eyes hard and uncompromising. Davenport froze, wondering what the hell was coming next. 'Mr Davenport, have the abductors been in contact again?' Carver held his gaze, unblinking.

'Yes,' Davenport admitted, looking down. Carver could tell he'd been desperate to lie.

'When?'

'This morning, at the partners' meeting.'

Damn, that girl's good. 'You should have told me straight away,' Carver almost shouted. 'Four lives are on the line, and time is running out. It's imperative that you don't withhold anything, particularly information as important as that.'

Davenport sprang up from his chair and loosened his tie. 'This is a fucking nightmare.' His face was pale and twisted with anxiety as he paced the room.

'What did they want?'

'It's an extremely delicate situation.' He kept pacing.

'Tell me,' Carver demanded.

Davenport came to a standstill, reached inside his trouser pocket for his iPhone, then brought up the text. He pressed play, then turned the screen around so that Carver could see it.

Carver's initial bewilderment swiftly turned to anger and repulsion. 'Jesus, you've got to be joking me!'

Davenport said nothing.

'When did this happen?'

'Around two months ago,' came the sheepish, barely audible, response.

'Where?'

'An establishment in Soho. A place I've used for some time.'

'How long exactly have you been using these *establishments*?'

Davenport swallowed hard. 'About twenty-five years.'

That's it! Carver had lost all sympathy for the man. The man who'd said only yesterday that he loved his wife and kids and had put his wild days as a youth behind him. Who'd claimed only a few minutes ago to have grown up and moved on. He was a morally reprehensible, cheating bastard, who deserved all that was coming to him.

'And your wife and family have no idea?'

'No, I don't believe so.' He shook his head feebly.

'This is a warning, Mr Davenport. A warning that if you don't give in to *all* of their demands, this video will go viral.'

Davenport slumped down in his chair as if all the energy had gone out of him. 'Yes, I realise that. But you haven't heard the worst of it yet.'

Carver gave a tilt of his head. 'Go on. Hit me.'

'The girl in the video. She's Richard Barker's niece.'

His revelation took the wind out of Carver. 'You knowingly slept with your partner's niece? Are you crazy? Completely sick?'

'No, of course I didn't knowingly sleep with her. I had no idea he even had a niece. It was only when I was paying her that she let it slip. Although, come to think of it, I think it was more deliberate than a slip of the tongue.'

'What did she say exactly?'

'Something along the lines of her uncle being wrong about me. That I wasn't the dinosaur he made me out to be.'

'And what did you say?'

'I asked her who her uncle was, and when she told me I nearly had a coronary.'

Poor you, thought Carver. 'How would she have known who you were? I assume you don't disclose your real name at these places. You definitely never met her through Richard?'

'Of course I don't disclose my real identity, and no, I never met her! Do you think I would have done what I did with her if I had? Clearly, she must have seen a photo of me or something, I don't know. What I do know is that I didn't want to engage her further on the subject. I simply told her never to speak a word of what we'd done to anyone, including her uncle, and she said it went without saying in her line of business.'

'Any idea how she managed to end up in that *industry*?'

'No idea. Part of me was desperate to know. But the other part thought it best to let the matter rest, and not draw further attention to myself. I didn't want her talking about me to her colleagues.'

'But that doesn't seem to have worked out, does it, Mr Davenport? Either she filmed you, and is part of this whole thing, or you were followed and filmed by someone else that night. Either way, this whole situation appears to be some sort of personal vendetta against you. Forward the text to me, and the name of the *establishment*.'

Carver made for the door.

'Where are you going?'

'Soho.'

'He's scared.' The woman grinned.

'Yep, the sick shit's not such a tough guy now,' the slimmer of her male accomplices said. 'That was a brilliant move to accelerate the plan. There's no way he's going to allow that video to go viral. Can you imagine? His life won't be worth living.'

She grinned again. 'It almost makes me want to waive the money and let it happen. Let the bastard get what he deserves.'

'No,' her sturdier partner-in-crime said. 'That was never the plan. This is *your* personal crusade against Davenport.' He gave the woman a hard stare. 'You, him and him.' He acknowledged one of two other men in the room with a tilt of his head. Their leader. 'It doesn't affect me. It's never affected me. But I've been deceived, taken advantage of, and I want the cash. I *need* the cash.'

'Calm down, will you?' the woman said. 'Do you think we'd have gone to all this trouble if we didn't want cash out of him? We could just have easily released the tape, settled for his resignation, and stopped there.'

'She's right,' the driver said. 'You need to stop worrying. You'll get your money. And Davenport will still be suitably punished.'

It was only Tuesday, late afternoon, but the streets of Soho were already buzzing. The air was close and oven-like, but it didn't deter London's revellers from making the most of a rare heatwave. Perfect weather for a cool crisp Chardonnay or a refreshing beer. Perfect weather to start drinking early, finish late, and worry about the midweek hangover tomorrow.

Carver wandered up Dean Street until he spotted the address he was looking for. Number 29, Madame Giselle's. The name was written in scrawly italics, and before long, as night fell, it would be lit up in shocking pink neon lights. He walked up to the door and pressed the buzzer, half expecting no one to answer. If that was the case, he'd just have to come back later. But to his surprise, the door

72

was quickly opened by a pale-faced brunette, dressed in torn jeans and a green vest top. She was thin all over, except for her chest, which was huge. He tried to steer his vision away from the obvious, but it still felt like he was talking to her breasts. She eyed him distrustfully, a lit cigarette perched between her fingers.

'Yeah? Can I help you?' she asked curtly.

Carver produced his ID. She immediately drew back. 'Look, we don't want no coppers in 'ere, push off, mate.'

'I'm not here about your establishment as such.'

'Good,' she said a little less defensively. 'This is a licensed business, and we've done nuffin wrong, all right?' She took a drag and blew smoke rings in Carver's direction.

Carver cleared his throat as he put his ID away, then pulled out his phone. It was debatable whether this girl read the papers or watched the news, but it was worth a shot. 'I'm investigating the recent abduction of four employees at a City law firm.'

'Yeah, saw that on the news last night. Come to think of it, you look familiar.'

Wonders will never cease. *I really should stop being so judgemental.* 'Perhaps you watched the press conference I gave with the victims' families?'

She looked him up and down, inhaled, then blew another plume of smoke directly into his face. He coughed. 'Yeah, that's right. It was you I saw.' She paused, gave him another distrustful glance. 'So, what you doing 'ere, then?' Her suspicion was replaced by a suggestive grin. 'Looking for a good time?'

'No,' Carver replied firmly. He clicked on the video and paused on a close-up image of the girl's face, making sure Davenport was out of the picture. Then he showed it to her. 'Do you know this girl?'

She squinted at the image, then cocked her head at him. 'What if I do?'

'Please, it's vital you tell me the truth, or if you don't feel able to, maybe I can speak to your boss? Neither you nor your boss are in trouble. I just really need to find this girl.'

She seemed to consider this for a while, then opened the door further, gesturing for Carver to come through. *Progress.*

As he expected, it was dark and seamy inside, while the air stank of booze, nicotine and sex.

He followed the girl downstairs where she knocked on a door marked, 'The Madame'.

'Come in,' came the low, raspy response.

The Madame was seated behind a decrepit wooden desk, strewn with loose papers and stationery, and an ashtray full of cigarette butts. The entire room reeked of smoke. The walls were a shocking fuchsia pink, while a garish black chandelier hung from the ceiling. As he took in her appearance, Carver soon realised that the Madame was no madame at all. She, or he, looked like an extra from *Priscilla, Queen of the Desert*, minus the headpiece, with full-on make-up and pencilled-on black eyebrows that gave rise to a permanently surprised look. He/she also appeared to be dressed in some kind of Abba tribute costume – a pale blue polyester jumpsuit with flared arms, the image rounded off with a long ash blonde wig. Carver was having a hard time keeping a straight face. He thought about his ex-wife's marriage to Carl, and that did the trick.

'I was hoping you could tell me whether this young lady still works for you?' He attempted to pass her his phone, still stuck on the image of Barker's niece. At first, she ignored it, looked up at him with her severely made-up panda eyes.

'I must protect my girls' identities.'

'I understand that, but I am investigating the disappearance of four employees from a City law firm, and this girl may be able to help us with our investigation.'

'Ah yes, I read about that in this morning's paper. How could one of my girls possibly know anything about that?'

Carver had no choice but to explain. But he didn't want the skinny brunette listening in. He glanced her way and the Madame took the hint. She gave her a stern look. 'Leave.' The girl bowed her head and was gone.

Even so, Carver kept his voice low. 'Because in this footage, she's having sex with one of the firm's partners. A partner who's being blackmailed by the kidnappers into handing over six million pounds. We also have reason to believe the girl is related to one of the hostages.'

Silence.

'Please, we have a very short window to find the hostages,' Carver persisted. 'Three of them are young, in their early twenties, and the partner is one year away from retirement. They have families.'

'Lucky for them,' came the unfeeling response. 'Some of us are alone, and we manage fine. Shit happens. That's life.'

Carver felt his pulse quicken, his blood pressure rise, but despite being fit to explode, he somehow kept his voice level. 'If I'm forced to get a warrant to search this place, I will. Who knows what my officers might turn up?'

This earned him a sickly sweet smile in return. 'OK, tough guy, there's no need to make threats.' She took the phone and considered the image. 'She was very popular that one, but she took off without so much as a word. Can't abide disloyalty like that. Silly little bitch.'

'When?'

'Not long after this was taken, I think. When was it? About two months ago?'

'Yes.' Carver nodded. 'What was her name?'

'Who knows, honey? She said it was Katrina, but my girls never use their real names. And I don't ask for second names. I don't need surnames, and neither do my clients.'

'How long was she with you?'

'Not that long at all. About six months, tops. She was good, I'll give her that. Built up quite a clientele of regulars in that short time, then disappeared.' She clicked her fingers, adorned with lethal-looking flamingo-pink stick-on nails, then cracked her large knuckles. Carver tried not to cringe.

'Where did she come from?'

'I don't know. She didn't give me her family history. She was young, hot and willing, and that was more than enough for me.'

Carver thought for a moment. Pondered whether he could trust the Madame to keep her mouth shut. Time was short. He had no choice. 'I want to show you the man she entertained in this video,' he began. The Madame smiled at his polite turn of phrase. 'But I need you to give me your word that you won't speak to anyone about this. It's imperative we keep his identity a secret.'

'Look, darling, my outfit relies on repeat business and survives on discretion. If word gets out I leak the names of my clients, I'll be out of business.' Exactly what Carver had been banking on.

Satisfied that she'd keep quiet, Carver said, 'OK, then. Please go ahead and press play.'

He studied her face as she watched the footage. Despite the sound of grunting, groaning and whipping, it remained impassive. As if she was watching an advert for life insurance.

'You recognise him?'

'Yes, he's one of my regulars.'

'But he only slept with this girl once?'

She paused to observe her nails. 'Yes, yes, I think that must be right. He likes them blonde and buxom. I seem to remember the girl he usually requests being struck down with a bug, and Katrina kindly offered up her services.'

'Is that normal? To be that keen?'

'Listen, honey, in this industry, nothing's normal. These girls aren't in it for the love of the job. They're in it for the money, pure and simple. She probably heard he was a stinking rich lawyer and she smelt a big tip. That's what my girls rely on. A big fat tip at the end of the night, thrust down their G-strings.'

'OK, thanks. If you should see or hear from the girl again, please get in touch.' Carver slid his card across the table.

'No problem, sugar.'

As he made his way upstairs, Carver felt a tap on his shoulder. It was the same brunette who'd let him in. She spoke in hushed tones. 'I saw her, two days ago.'

'The girl in the video?' Carver asked keenly. Finally, a break.

'Yes.'

'Where?'

'Spearmint Rhino on Tottenham Court Road. She was one of the lap dancers.'

'That's great, thanks for your help.'

The girl smoothed her finger along Carver's jawline. 'No sweat, babe. Maybe see you again sometime?'

Hopefully not, thought Carver, then left.

Chapter Seven

'Hello, Nigel. I thought you should know that I had two police officers come to the house asking questions earlier today.'

Davenport was seated at his desk. He rolled back his chair, phone pressed to his ear, a glass of brandy in his free hand. It was 6.30 p.m. Not long to go until he'd hear from them again. He needed something strong to steady his nerves. Who knew what they were about to throw at him this time?

'Hello, Stewart, yes, thank you. I warned you they would, didn't I? It went smoothly? You were convincing?'

'Yes, they seemed to believe everything I told them. Were very persistent, mind you. Made me dig out old college photos.'

'I can't believe this is coming back to haunt me, all this time later. Do you think it's her? Do you think the bitch is trying to take revenge?'

'It seems unlikely. So much time has passed. Why wait till now?'

'That's what stumps me.'

'Perhaps it's someone who found out by chance and saw a way to make a quick buck out of your firm?'

'But they've demanded my resignation and a substantial donation to Rape Crisis. It doesn't feel like we're dealing with a group purely in it for the money. It cuts deeper than that. It feels personal.'

'Yes, I see what you're saying. I'm sorry I can't be of any more help, Nigel.'

'No matter, Stewart. You've done everything you can. It's a grave only I can dig myself out of.'

It was just on 7 p.m. Maddy was in her office, packing up for the evening, when she looked up and spotted Richard's wife walk past. She'd met Marianne Barker several times. Except for O'Shea (as tight as a duck's backside), the litigation partners were a sociable, generous lot. They liked to eat and drink well, and were in the habit of hosting lavish Christmas parties and summer BBQs at their impressive homes, no expense spared – champagne, Chablis and Pimm's on tap. Marianne had always been extremely polite and welcoming, and Maddy had been struck by how much in love she and Richard appeared to be, even after twenty-seven years of marriage.

So, despite Marianne having been a model of poise and discretion at last night's press conference, Maddy wasn't surprised to see her now looking somewhat fraught, dabbing her eyes with a tissue as she walked by. Clearly, her husband was everything to her, and his unexpected abduction had to have been heart-wrenching.

Maddy dashed out, called her name from behind. 'Mrs Barker.'

Marianne stopped short, swivelled round. In her early fifties, she was a perfectly groomed, stately woman. But today, she didn't look quite so spruce, quite so composed.

She walked up to Maddy. 'Hello, Madeline. Please, call me Marianne. How are you? I do hope you've fully recovered from yesterday?'

Maddy smiled. It was kind of Marianne to ask after her well-being considering her husband's current predicament. Looking at her sad, bloodshot eyes, Maddy could tell she'd been crying for some time. They were almost dead with despair and fading hope.

'I'm fine, thank you,' she replied guiltily. Guilt for standing there free and unharmed, while her boss remained captive, God only knows where, and subject to who knows what abominable treatment. 'It's so dreadful, and I am so sorry about Richard. I am – we all are – praying for his safe return. And for the others, of course.'

Marianne sniffed, dabbed her eyes once more. 'Thank you, that's very kind. DCI Carver seems very able. I understand you know him from a case he investigated a few years back. One that you were heavily involved in. You've never mentioned it before.'

Maddy was surprised Richard hadn't discussed her past with his wife. It made her respect him even more. Not a gossip like Turner. 'I… I don't really like to talk about it. It concerned my ex-flatmate, who I thought was my friend but turned out to be a far cry from the person I believed him to be.'

Even thinking about it now, all this time later, it wrenched at her soul, and she had to blink back tears. 'But, on the plus side, I can certainly vouch for Carver's ability. He's a brilliant police officer. If anyone can find your husband, it's him.'

'Thank you, Madeline. That's most reassuring.' She paused, then appearing to read Maddy's mind, explained, 'I just dropped by to see Gavin. I had something delicate to discuss with him. Something I only found out about last night. Quite by chance, in fact. And it made me wonder if Gavin knew.'

Should she ask, or shouldn't she? Maddy was in two minds. Her nosiness had got her into trouble in the past, but it was partly what made her so good at her job. She liked asking questions, and she wasn't afraid to ask them, even if it meant getting on the wrong side of people.

But lucky for her, this time Marianne solved her dilemma for her.

'I found a letter from my husband's doctor last night. Tucked away in a shoebox at the top of Richard's wardrobe. I shouldn't have been prying, but when I got home from the press conference, I couldn't sleep. I was on edge, felt like I had to do something, search the house for any information, any clue, as to why those men took Richard.' She paused momentarily. Maddy could tell that whatever was coming wasn't good news. Her heart raced at the thought of what it might be.

'My husband has advanced prostate cancer. He only has six months, at best.'

Maddy was paralysed with shock. 'Oh my God, I'm so sorry.' She just about got the words out. She placed a hand on Marianne's shoulder.

'Thank you. It came as a complete shock, as you can imagine.'

'Of course. How long has he known?'

'Well, the letter was roughly three months old, but I'm guessing he's been living with it for some time. Perhaps even a couple of years. You know, I'd suspected something was up. He's lost a lot of weight over the last year. Gets tired easily. Complains about pain in his joints, barely eats. But I brushed it off as too much work, him simply getting older.' She sighed heavily, then said, 'I've been so stupid, and I'm so cross with the bloody man for not telling me. For suffering alone when I could have been at his side, helping him through the pain, the treatment. Now I don't know whether I'm ever going to see him again. Get to say goodbye. And I have no idea what medication he's on. He won't have it on him, and he'll no doubt be in terrible pain.'

The tears were there again. Forming like puddles of water in a blocked drain. Maddy glanced around. Thankfully, the secretaries had long gone home, and any lawyers left were tucked away in their offices. She put her arm around Marianne's shoulder. Could feel her body trembling.

'Did Gavin know?'

'No.' Marianne shook her head, then blew her nose into a fresh tissue. 'He was as shocked as I was. I thought the cancer might have been the reason for his early retirement, and he therefore might have told his partners in confidence. But he never mentioned it to anyone here.' She raised her eyebrows, gave another slight shake of her head. 'That doesn't mean it's not the reason, of course. He simply told Gavin what he told me. That he wanted to spend more time with me, do other things. We're not exactly short of money, I'm rather ashamed to say.' She paused, then continued, 'I'll have to tell DCI Carver, of course. But please don't tell anyone here, will you? My husband's a very private man.' She grunted bitterly. 'Christ, the fact that he didn't feel able to tell me is proof of that.'

'I'm guessing he didn't want to upset you. Wanted his last few months with you to be happy ones.' Maddy smiled weakly. She knew this was probably little consolation for Marianne.

'Perhaps. But it's not worked, has it? Now he's been taken, and I don't know if I'm even going to get to say goodbye to him.'

'Sir, Mary Jacobs is dead.'

Carver sat behind the wheel of his car in thick traffic on Charing Cross Road. Painfully chugging along in first gear. He had the air con on at full throttle, suit jacket off as he drove one-handed with his elbow resting on the door. When his phone rang, he'd half expected it to be Davenport, not Drake. It had gone 7 p.m. and the kidnappers were due to make contact. He had men in place to trace the call, of course, but he was certain the kidnappers were prepared for that.

'Christ. So far, this case is non-stop dead ends. How?'

'Suicide. That's the conclusion the police came to, at least. Her family reported her missing on New Year's Day 2016, after she'd failed to return home, having popped out to buy a few groceries. Two weeks later, they found the scarf she'd been wearing wedged into some stones on Southsea beach. Her hometown.'

'So trying to find out if she told anyone about the rape allegation is going to be nigh on impossible.'

'I could ask the husband, but I'm not sure how receptive he'd be right now.'

'Why's that?'

'Because his son is Matthew Gerard.'

'What?' Flabbergasted, Carver nearly hit the car in front of him which had stopped rather abruptly at a temporary red light. He brought his foot down hard on the pedal. 'This is all getting stranger by the minute. Surely that can't be a coincidence?' He already knew that Frank Gerard's wife, Mary, had died, but there were a lot of Marys in the world, and there'd never been any indication she was the same Mary Jacobs who'd been at Cambridge with Davenport, Dempsey and Barker. The same girl who'd accused Davenport of rape. Then again, why should there have been? Frank Gerard didn't know Davenport was being blackmailed, or that the police had been looking for his dead wife because of what happened between her and Davenport over three decades ago.

But he needed to be told now. 'Question the husband. We need to know if she told anyone else, aside from Larson. Including him.'

'Who is this?'

Davenport knew very well who it was – the timing of the call, coupled with the hostile voice, was a sure giveaway – but he asked the question all the same.

'That's none of your concern. Are you going to meet our demands?'

Davenport sucked in the artificially controlled air in his magnificent office. He'd reached the very top of his game. Rich, successful, respected. And yet, at that moment, he felt as vulnerable as a child abandoned by its mother. 'Why are you doing this? Why have you taken four members of my staff? Those four especially. I demand to know.'

'You are in no place to demand anything, Davenport.' His name was spoken with exaggerated scorn. 'Have you learnt nothing over the last two days? Your reputation will be in ruins, and your life won't be worth living if you fail to comply with our requests. But even now, I can tell that overinflated ego of yours is finding it hard to let go of your greed and thirst for power. No matter, we'll just have to take things a step further.'

'What do you—'

Davenport didn't get the chance to finish his sentence. The line went dead.

'Sorry, sir, we couldn't get a trace. Must have used a burner phone, as with the text.'

'Damn,' Carver cursed, despite not being in the least bit surprised. Like so many criminals these days, these kidnappers were sophisticated, smart, and technologically savvy. Unlikely to make such a basic mistake as dialling from a registered number when they knew he'd be monitoring Davenport's phone.

It was 8 p.m. He'd still been knee-deep in traffic when Davenport had called around 7.30, hysterical, demanding to know if he had any leads on the hostages' whereabouts, despite his rational side knowing it was like trying to find a needle in a haystack. Carver had pulled over into a space, tried his best to calm him down, made him recount every word of his conversation with the kidnappers. Not that it helped much. Davenport's stubbornness had only served to make things worse for himself.

They had less than seventy-two hours left. It wasn't looking good, and Davenport was facing a tough choice. His reputation versus the lives of four innocent members of staff. Either way, his name would be mud. It seemed his days as Sullivans' senior partner were numbered.

After hanging up, Carver got out of his car and made his way to Spearmint Rhino on Tottenham Court Road. He walked in, received a moderately suspicious glance from the burly bouncer on the door, paid the door charge, and headed for the bar. He glanced at the stage en route but didn't spot Katrina. It was piercingly loud, the entire place heaving with excitable men desperate to be titillated by young, ravishing, scantily dressed women. Most were in suits, knocking back booze until their livers could take no more, their chatter resembling a drone of flies alongside the thumping music.

'What can I get you?' the barman asked. Carver ignored the question. Thrust his phone in the man's face. 'Does this girl work here?'

The barman, young and tanned with olive-black eyes and reeking of cologne, immediately stepped back, having realised he wasn't dealing with a regular punter. 'Look, man, we don't like your sort in here.' He glanced around, afraid that his boss might be watching.

'Don't worry, no one here's in trouble. I just need to find this girl. Other people's lives depend on it.'

The barman gave the room another quick scan, then looked at the photo. 'Yeah, that's Cherry.' *Cherry now, is it?* thought Carver.

'She works here. I think she might be entertaining someone at this minute.'

'Will she be out soon?'

'Yeah, she'll be back on stage when she's done. I can't say when exactly, but it shouldn't be too long.'

'It's OK, I'll wait. I'll have a tonic and lime please.'

The barman nodded, visibly relieved the questioning had stopped. He set about making Carver's drink. Carver checked his phone for messages as he waited. He was surprised to see a text from Maddy.

Found out that Richard Barker has advanced prostate cancer. Six months max left. His wife told me. I'm sure she'll be in touch soon. She found out by accident. No one else knows, aside from Turner, and she wants to keep it that way. Don't know if it's helpful in any way, it probably isn't, but thought you should know. MK.

Carver read the message a couple of times. He wondered if the kidnappers knew about Barker's cancer, and why Barker hadn't told anyone? Would this be their next line of attack against Davenport? Not only would he be exposed as a rapist and an adulterer, but selfish and mean enough to allow a cancer victim – his friend of thirty-six years, his partner – to remain in enemy hands, no doubt weak and in terrible agony. And, just to incite the public's wrath further, denied the chance to spend precious time with his devoted wife.

He texted *Thanks* back, felt a pat on his shoulder as he pressed send.

'That's her,' the barman said. 'There, on the left.'

Carver glanced up to see a gorgeous blonde cavorting on stage in nothing but a gold tasselled G-string, her bronzed Amazonian legs wrapped around a pole, her large breasts on full display. She'd already attracted a table of suits sitting that side. Carver expected it wouldn't be long before she was giving one of them a private dance. He needed to act now.

He went up to the stage and caught the girl's eye. Sensing a few notes to add to her G-string, she gave him a suggestive smile, then bent over, receiving several leery cheers from the sloshed suits. One of them – a *Wolf of Wall Street* wannabe – gave Carver the evil eye. Clearly, he'd hoped to get in there first.

'Can we talk?' Carver shouted above the din of music, chatter and jeering. He slyly showed her his ID.

The girl flinched, glanced around nervously. 'I don't talk, especially to coppers.'

'Please, it's important I speak with you.'

'I'm not going anywhere with you.' She glared at him.

'If you don't come with me quietly, I'll be forced to arrest you here in front of everyone. Is that what you want?'

'You can't arrest me if I've done nothing wrong,' she said. Her eyes darted nervously around the room again.

'Stop the talking, old man, and get on with it!' the Wolf shouted.

Carver ignored him. Noticed a man standing the other side of the stage eyeing him warily. He looked back up at Cherry. 'Are you going to talk to me civilly, or will I be forced to make a scene in front of your customers and your boss?'

'OK,' she spat, before elegantly rolling onto her bottom then stepping off the stage. She took Carver's hand. 'Follow me, sugar,' she said loudly with a wink, aware of her boss's gaze.

She led him across the bar, then through a door into a box of a room. There was only one chair in it. 'Sit down,' Carver said.

'You sure you don't want…'

'No.' He introduced himself and explained why he was there.

Cherry gave a slow nod. Guilt was written all over her face. Carver pulled out his phone and played the video of her with Davenport.

'This is you with Nigel Davenport, the senior partner of law firm, Sullivan, Blake, Monroe, a couple of months or so ago. He claims you told him you were Richard Barker's niece. Is that true?'

She bit her lip nervously.

'Tell me,' Carver demanded.

'No. I don't even know who Richard Barker is.'

'You're lying. He's one of four lawyers who've been kidnapped from Sullivans. And you know it.'

'Fuck. Really, I didn't know that.'

'Did you know you were being videoed?'

She nodded. 'I put the camera in the room.'

'Why?'

'Because he told me to. The man. Paid me a shitload of cash.'

'What man?'

'I dunno, he didn't give me his name. Just showed me a photo of the lawyer, this Davenport you mention. Told me to make sure I fucked him and filmed us in the act.'

'And also to say you were Richard Barker's niece?'

'Yes.'

'What did he look like?'

'He must have been in his early twenties, tall, dark brown hair, dark eyes. Posh voice, quite good-looking, or he could have been if he lost twenty pounds.'

'You'd call him chubby?'

'Yeah, I'd say so. Slight double chin, soft around the waist. And then there was…'

'Then there was what?'

'He had this scar. Running across his chin.'

Carver made a note. 'Do you know where to find him, or how to contact him?'

'Not a clue, sorry. He didn't give me his number. Just came and took the tape off me later that night.'

'Why did you agree to this?'

'Told you, he paid me a grand. I was skint at the time. Couldn't turn down an offer like that, now could I?'

'Why did you leave Madame Giselle's?'

'The same bloke told me to find a job elsewhere. Said the police might come knocking, so I should clear out of Soho.' She sighed, ran her hands through her hair. 'But here you are. You still found me.'

'If the man tries to contact you again, you call me straight away. Is that clear?' Carver handed her his card and a twenty-pound note. 'Sorry, that's all I've got.'

'No matter.' She slid the note down her G-string. 'Sure you don't want a dance while you're here?' She kept her hand down her crotch and pressed up against him. She smelt of booze and aftershave. He wasn't the least bit turned on.

'You seem like a bright girl.' Carver looked her straight in the eye. 'Go get a decent job.'

Chapter Eight

'What is it, Nigel? Have they been in contact again? You've gone so pale.'

Nine p.m. Davenport sat at the dining table with his wife, Pamela. As usual, their lack of conversation enhanced all extraneous noise. The clunking of cutlery on plates, the ticking of the carriage clock, the outside traffic. They rarely ate together. Two or three nights a week he usually dined out with clients or attended firm marketing dos. And then there were his extra-curricular activities, disguised as *work*, which took up the rest of his time.

But recent events had quashed Davenport's normally rampant sex drive. All he felt like doing was going home and barricading himself inside with a bottle of brandy. Blunting his senses. Sending him into an alcohol-induced coma. Fooling himself into imagining he'd wake up to find it had all been a hideous dream.

He was tormented by the past that had come back to haunt him, and the tough decision he was facing. All the money, power and influence he wielded suddenly meant nothing. But even at home, there was no escape. He looked down at the text. Another video. Sent a couple of minutes ago. From a different number to the last. He lowered the volume, pressed play. Watched in horror at the footage of Matthew Gerard being repeatedly punched in the face and stomach by a man dressed in black with a balaclava over his head, his back to the camera. He winced at the sound of knuckle on skin, and at Gerard's cries of pain. After about a dozen brutal punches, the man stopped. Gerard was a good-looking boy, but now it was hard to tell – his face nothing but a bloody puffed-up mess. The man walked away. Noiseless. Merciless.

The promising young trainee sat there limply. Then he slowly looked up, dazed and confused. Tried his hardest to focus on the camera, although it was clear that simple movements like blinking and opening his mouth took every ounce of effort. Finally, he spoke, his voice weak, flat and despairing. Every word uttered causing him immeasurable pain. 'Please help us,' he begged. 'Please give them what they want. I'm too young to die. Please, I'm begging you. Have mercy on us before it's too late.'

The screen went blank.

'Nigel, talk to me. What is it you're looking at?'

Davenport realised his hand was shaking. He laid down his phone, picked up his crystal wine glass, threw the twelve-year-old Burgundy down his throat as if it was nothing more than cheap plonk, then looked directly at his wife. Plump, plain and dowdy, but someone whose loyalty he'd never questioned. He knew how much she adored him. That she'd stick by him, come hell or high water. This was largely the reason he'd married her so soon after they'd graduated from Cambridge. She'd worshipped him from the moment she'd set eyes on him at a college party. She'd been a safe bet, a smokescreen to hide behind while he dabbled in his tawdry pursuits to his heart's content.

But the way things were going, with so little time left, he'd have to come clean with her, before he came clean with the world.

* * *

'I hope that did the trick.' The kidnappers' leader spoke quietly into the receiver, awaiting reassurance from his mole.

Thinking back, he was pretty confident no one had seen them arrive at the hideout. His driver had parked the blue Ford Transit van (whose cloned number plate they had quickly exchanged for another replica bought off a back street vendor after taking a detour off Bow Road) inside a steel-clad industrial unit they'd sublet in the six-acre Leyton Industrial Village. They swapped it for the white Volkswagen Transporter waiting behind the unit's roller shutter doors, which he'd then driven to Riverside Industrial Estate in Barking. Both premises were monitored by CCTV, but only his driver had got out to unlock the units, and in any case, his face had been hidden from view by a balaclava. They'd also been careful to remove the licence plate from the VW, so that the police would have no means whatsoever of tracking the vehicle should they be spotted leaving the premises on CCTV. It had been risky driving without a plate, but unlike the first leg of the journey, the drive to the hideout was relatively short, and it had been considered a chance worth taking. Better than using yet another duplicate or stolen plate, where there was always the chance of the forgery being traced back to them. What's more, the hope was that the CCTV tail had been lost long before, following their first detour off Bow Road.

Even so, he was starting to feel a little on edge. As were the others. They still didn't know whether Davenport would cave. Had received no firm assurances that their demands would be complied with. But if their terms weren't met by Friday afternoon, what then? It wasn't a question he enjoyed contemplating, but he knew it was something he must consider. Davenport was a despicable human being. It wasn't out of the question that he'd opt to save his own skin over that of four innocent victims. But his spirits were buoyed by the response he got now.

'I'm confident it did. Very soon we'll have our answer. The answer we want.'

'Great.' He exhaled with relief. 'This place is starting to get to me, starting to get to the others. I need to get home. I miss Annie.'

'I know. It won't be long. Three more days, and you'll be free again, and we'll have our revenge.'

'I'm going to tell the partners this morning.'

Wednesday. 7 a.m. Davenport stood in front of his wardrobe mirror, fixing his tie. Pamela was seated at her dressing table, pinning a brooch on the lapel of her jacket. On Wednesdays and Thursdays, she worked in a charity shop, a short walk from Sloane Square Tube station, and not too far from their three-million-pound two-bedroom apartment in Cadogan Square, to where they'd downsized after the children had moved out of the five-bedroom house in Hampstead in which they'd grown up.

Almost the entirety of Pamela's adult life had been devoted to her husband and their two children. But when Jennifer and Simon flew the nest, she was left with a big hole in her life. She had to occupy her spare time with something, for fear of going insane. Especially as the menopause had hit her hard, making her feel almost suicidal at times. She was a kind, generous woman who liked helping people. Charity work suited her to a T, and she enjoyed the busy, sociable nature of shop work. Also, the feeling that she was contributing something, doing something good in a world that often seemed very unfair.

She'd met her husband at the beginning of her third year at Cambridge, where she'd read Classics at Clare College. He'd caught her eye during a college party one night, and she'd been putty in his hands. He was popular, handsome, charming, and confident. So unlike her: plain, shy, introspective, *square*, as Lucinda Barrington – one of the most popular girls in her year – tall, blonde, leggy, and a genius to boot – used to sneer about her to the other pretty girls behind her back. She'd been fully aware of his reputation for being a cad but had been too smitten to see sense. She'd delighted in the attention, in Lucinda's shock and disdain when they'd started dating. Being Nigel's girlfriend did wonders for her confidence and popularity, and when he proposed at the end of her third year, she couldn't believe her luck. Although there'd been times during their engagement when she'd found herself pausing to ask why he'd chosen her for his wife, having had his pick of beauties, she'd quickly brushed her misgivings aside, chiding herself for questioning her good fortune. She'd married Nigel at twenty-four, had their first child a year later, their second eighteen months after that, while her husband forged a successful legal career. A career that went from strength to strength, brought in pot-loads of cash, but ensured he never had much time for his wife or children. She hadn't been hugely bothered for the first eighteen or so years of it. She knew his job was demanding, and she didn't feel she had the right to complain. She adored her children, with whom she'd forged close, loving relationships. But the last few years had been lonely ones, creating a vacuum that was hard to fill.

Davenport studied his face in the mirror. He felt like he'd aged about ten years in three days. Both mentally and physically. Last night, he'd told Pamela everything. She'd sat there in silence the entire time. Leaden-faced, too shocked to speak. But then the tears had come.

Thick and fast. He'd tried to put his arms around her, but she'd sat there rigid and unresponsive. Unable to look her depraved, cheating husband in the eye.

He wondered if she'd ever suspected. She wasn't a stupid woman. Surely, she had? He tried to convince himself of this to appease what little conscience he possessed. But perhaps she'd preferred to brush the truth under the carpet, because the truth hurt when said out loud. It was easy to turn a blind eye, pretend all was fine and dandy while the subject remained a suspicion rather than a fact.

But now she knew for sure, and before long, her husband's good reputation would be in shreds. And that would surely have consequences for her too?

After telling her about the video featuring him and the hooker, he'd told her about the rape allegation, his version of it, at least. He couldn't tell if she was more shocked by this – something he'd kept from her for over thirty years – or his extra-curricular activities.

'You'll tell them everything?'

'No, not everything. Just that they're demanding my resignation, in addition to the money, in exchange for the release of the hostages. They can draw their own conclusions.'

'The whole world will do that once they hear about your donation to Rape Crisis. The press will smell blood; they'll be all over it. They'll start looking into your past, and then it won't be long before it's front-page news.'

'Maybe.' Davenport turned around. He couldn't be angry with his wife for digging her nails in. She had every right. He was a selfish man. Always had been. 'Let them. I'm certainly not going to volunteer up the information. And if the bloodhounds do come sniffing, I'll tell them exactly what happened. That nothing came of it, because it never happened. No matter what these kidnappers say or choose to believe.' He paused. 'Plus, the woman's missing, presumed dead. Carver told me last night. So she can't hurt me. They have no evidence.'

Davenport thought back to his conversation with Carver. He'd breathed a sigh of relief at the news. But finding out that Matthew Gerard was Mary's son had come as a shock. What point were the kidnappers trying to make? That although he'd hurt the mother, surely he wasn't such a bastard that he'd hurt the son as well? Albeit, indirectly.

Pamela said nothing. Analysed her husband like an ugly, yet absorbing piece of art. She knew he was lying. Knew what kind of a man he was underneath that smooth, distinguished, respectable facade. She'd long stopped believing anything that came out of his mouth, and he deserved everything that was coming to him.

But *she* didn't deserve to suffer. She'd cleaned, cooked, reared his children, pandered to his every need for almost three decades, and now it was time to look after herself. To save herself from the scandal he'd created. The scandal she didn't deserve to be a part of.

D-Day was coming. A day that could be life-changing for them both.

Chapter Nine

'Do you have an answer for us?'

Davenport put the familiar voice on speakerphone. For the benefit of his partners, Carver and his team. Ten a.m. Wednesday. This was it. The moment of truth. There would be no going back after he'd given his response. There was only one possible answer, but it was torture saying it all the same. He felt sick, dizzy. All those years of hard graft, blood, sweat and tears. *Scheming*. Striving to be the best and taking down others to get there. All down the plughole. He was starting to believe in karma.

He gave the rest of the room a slow nod, as if to confirm what they were already prepped for. 'Yes. I will abide by all of your demands.'

It was done. His life as he knew it was over. There was silence at the other end of the line. Carver wondered whether the kidnappers were high-fiving each other, doing a celebration dance round the room. Finally, the man spoke. 'Good. This is what you're going to do. And by the way, I know you're there, DCI Carver.'

All eyes focussed on Carver. He tensed. 'What did you expect?' he asked.

'Don't get me wrong. Naturally I expected you to be listening in. I expect you've been working non-stop since Monday trying to find us. But even a clever detective like you won't succeed. We've covered our tracks, thought of everything. Don't be too hard on yourself. This is one battle you're going to have to concede defeat on.'

Carver reined in his anger. The bastard's cockiness made him want to nail him and his scumbag accomplices more than ever. Once he got the hostages back, he wasn't going to stop there and let it rest. He'd pursue the investigation, make it his mission to hunt them down, even if it took him the rest of his career. Besides, he still had two days.

He leant in closer, his mouth hovering over the phone. 'Why are you doing this? What's your motive, aside from money? Why pick on those four especially? What have you got against Mr Davenport? If you tell us, maybe we can try and negotiate something?'

Davenport looked aghast. He'd specifically told Carver he'd withheld the rape allegation from his partners and intended to keep it from both them and the world. Carver ignored him. He didn't expect an explanation, just wanted the man to talk some more.

The caller gave a snigger. 'There was no magic to the chosen four, Chief Inspector. It was random.'

'Bullshit,' Carver said.

'Tut tut, language, DCI Carver. As for Davenport, he's our concern, not yours.'

Painful silence ensued as the man's response seemed to reverberate in the air. All the partners wondering what the hell their senior partner had done to tick him off so violently. Then he spoke again. 'So, once again, these are our terms, Davenport. One, you announce your resignation to *The Lawyer* magazine at 3 p.m. on Friday afternoon.

Two, at 3.30 p.m. you transfer one million pounds of your own money to Rape Crisis.' Davenport's partners immediately looked at him in alarm. He gulped in air, avoided eye contact and focussed on his notepad. 'Three, at 4 p.m. you transfer six million pounds from your firm's office account to this account. Take it down. Now.'

Everyone picked up their pens.

'Account number: 59670321, sort code: 91-37-22.'

'Is that an offshore account?' Carver tried his luck.

'If you think I'm going to tell you that, you're either stupid or desperate. I think I know which.'

'And the abductees? When will they be released?'

'As soon as I have confirmation the money's gone through, they will be released.'

'But that could take two or three days.'

'Not if you use the priority option. As I said, as soon as I get confirmation the money's been received, the four will be released the same day.'

'Where?'

'You'll find that out later. We'll give you a time and place where they can be picked up.'

Carver didn't feel good about this. Obviously, his main concern was the hostages' safe return, and to avoid taking any action that might jeopardise that. But he'd be stupid to comply with all of their demands before seeing the hostages with his own eyes. What guarantee did he have that they'd be returned once the terms had been met? And even if he was given a time and location where they could be picked up, who was to say his officers wouldn't be walking into a trap? He needed to make the kidnappers come to him. He needed a bargaining chip.

'If you think I'm going to give you all that you want without proof the hostages are alive, without seeing them with my own eyes, you can think again.' A second's pause, then, 'Mr Davenport will not be making the donation to Rape Crisis until we have the hostages in our grasp. You drive them to a prominent location where we'll be waiting at a specified time, and you release them to me in the open air. I'll not have my officers walking into some remote building which, for all I know, could be a trap.'

All eyes were on Davenport again. The same questions running through his partners' minds. Carver held Davenport's fretful gaze, making it clear he wasn't negotiating on this point.

Silence, then, 'No deal. The donation needs to happen before we release them.'

Now Carver was the point of focus. *Will he cave, or won't he?* He knew that's what they were thinking. *What if neither relents, and the hostages are never released, or worse, found dead?* It might spell the end of the firm, their illustrious careers, their big fat pay slips and juicy bonuses.

'Fine,' Carver said. 'It's your choice, but I don't believe you want their blood on your hands. I don't believe this is just about money.'

More unbearable silence. Although he appeared calm on the outside, Carver's chest was burning. He prayed he hadn't misjudged the kidnappers' motives. If he had, and they didn't relent, he was stuck. He glanced at Drake, who read his mind.

Then the same voice said, 'Hold the line.'

Carver cast his gaze around the room. Fear, panic, a feeling of total helplessness etched across Davenport's and his partners' faces. He realised the kidnapper had gone to consult with his fellow conspirators. Did this mean he wasn't the chief amongst them? That he took orders from another?

100

Finally, after a few agonising minutes, he came back on the line.

'OK. You have a deal. But the minute you have the hostages in your grasp, Davenport makes the donation. If we learn that he has not, and believe me we will – we even know when he takes a shit – his worst nightmare will come true. No tricks, understood?'

Davenport was under the spotlight again. *What worst nightmare?* He knew the answer to that, of course, and so did Carver. The video. It would go viral. Carver was even more convinced the kidnappers had a mole at the firm feeding them information. But who? There were infinite possibilities, but no one they'd questioned thus far had aroused his suspicions.

He caught Davenport's eye and received a subtle nod. 'OK, it's a deal. Where and when will you release them? Remember, somewhere prominent, in the open.'

'We'll let you know the details later. But you remember this: once everyone's happy, you let us drive away, no funny business. Try any stunts and Davenport will wish he'd never been born.' Carver glanced at Davenport again, and realised the same question was running through his mind. *Were they also threatening to tell the world about Mary? Did they have evidence to prove it?* 'Just make sure Madeline Kramer doesn't leave the office on Friday before we make contact.'

Carver straightened. 'What? Why her?'

'Ms Dempsey appears to have developed something of a soft spot for her. And the men seem to like her too. They say she's one of the more human types at the firm.' Carver glanced around the table. A montage of put-out, crimson faces. 'Dempsey wants her at the drop-off. Carver, you bring her. But you'll stay nothing short of two hundred feet clear while she picks them up. Got it?'

'Yes.' Carver nodded down the phone. 'Got it.'

Twelve hours earlier

The young woman was mesmerised by her reflection. She stared intently at her bruised face. Admiring it, rather than resenting it. Fascinated by it, rather than repulsed by it. Proud of it, rather than ashamed of it.

She lightly touched her left cheek, still raw and swollen, then gently traced her skin like a blind person reading braille. Like a lover discovering the object of his desire's curves for the first time.

And like her own lover, pain didn't faze her. Not like it had at first. Not now they were so close. She'd wanted to feel the stinging, throbbing ache. She'd wanted it to be convincing. She'd wanted them to see that she was genuinely suffering at that moment in time. Wanted to force even a heart as hard as his to melt.

It hadn't even been thirty-six hours, but already her wounds were starting to heal. Her cheeks and lips were a little less inflamed, and the deep purple colouration encircling her eyes was slowly dispersing. And with time, the burn mark would fade. Even so, there would still be enough damage left for the world to see when they emerged on Friday. The poor, innocent, defenceless abductees. Ruthlessly seized by brutal, mercenary thugs who bore a grudge against Nigel Davenport, the esteemed senior partner of top City law firm Sullivan, Blake, Monroe, and whose whiter-than-white reputation was suddenly called into question with his quick resignation and substantial donation to Rape Crisis. A donation that was sure to ignite cries of: *Why?*

Why had they chosen this particular charity, and what was Davenport's connection to it? Had he been harbouring a disturbing

102

secret all this time? Fooling his partners, his clients, his friends, his family, all these years? The possibilities were tantalising.

Charlotte Dempsey smiled to herself, forgetting the pain that accompanied this simplest of actions, as she thought about Davenport's fall from grace.

'You OK?' She heard his silky-smooth voice before his face appeared in the mirror. Black and blue like hers. Worse, in fact – his wounds inflicted only that evening.

He came up behind her, wrapped his arms around her tiny waist, and nuzzled the side of her neck.

'I just want to have an answer, for Friday to come and all of this to be over,' she replied, enjoying the sensation of his tongue on her skin, the heat of his breath. She shivered with desire.

'I know, but we're so close now. Davenport will make the announcement soon, I'm sure of it. The money will be wired, and we'll be free and avenged.'

Charlotte turned around. 'We have so much to thank Richard for.'

'Yes, we do. Recruiting us like that was a work of genius.' He grinned, looked at her adoringly. 'If only they knew what a smart cookie you really are. It must have been hell playing the class idiot for so long.'

'Actually, it was kind of fun,' she laughed, stroking his chest. 'And Maddy Kramer's not so bad. I think she genuinely feels sorry for me, rather than angry. Not like that bastard, Turner.' Her eyes narrowed as she pulled Matthew Gerard in close, then brushed her bruised lips against his.

'God, I hope these heal quickly.' He grinned naughtily.

'Me too.'

There was a knock on the door to the small office belonging to the warehouse where they had concealed themselves.

'Come in,' Matthew said.

It was Barker. The boss and genius behind their brilliantly crafted plan. 'Sorry to interrupt you lovebirds, but I've just been on the phone with our mole. She had some good news.'

Charlotte looked at Richard expectantly. At the same time saddened by his rapidly declining health, evident with each passing day. The sunken cheeks, the hollow eyes, the way his clothes seemed to hang off him. Only last night, as they'd tucked into pizza, he'd nibbled at his, his appetite for food not even close to his appetite for revenge. He'd assured them he'd never bail; that he'd see this through to the end and ensure that every last detail was tied up before he passed away. And for that, they were grateful.

He needed to get back to his wife, spend what little time he had left with Annie, his nickname for Marianne. But his hatred of Davenport was just as potent as Charlotte's and her brother Isaac's. And Matthew's, of course. Only Stephen was in it for the money. But that was fine. Richard was certain he could be trusted. That no one was ever going to find out.

'And?' Matthew asked, his eyes as bright as a shooting star.

'Friday's a go. Isaac will make the call tomorrow at 10 a.m. We'll need to be ready to put plan A into action as soon as we hear all the terms have been met.'

Charlotte beamed at Richard, wrapped her arms around his frail frame. 'That's fantastic news, well done.'

'Couldn't have done it without you both.' He looked at his protégés with genuine affection.

'Soon our mothers can rest in peace,' Matthew said to Charlotte. 'Come on, let's go tell the other two. After all, Isaac's the one who's going to be doing the talking, again.'

Chapter Ten

Matthew Gerard
Late January 2016

Matthew felt an arm around his shoulder. He glanced up, locked eyes with his father, an inch or so taller. Grieving, like him.

'You OK, son?' Frank Gerard gazed down at his handsome son with sad, earnest eyes. When he looked at Matthew, he saw her. It was both a curse and a blessing. A constant reminder of the beautiful, loving, wonderful woman he no longer woke up with.

A retired police officer of fifty-seven, fairer-haired than Matthew, Frank was a gentle, easy-going man, who'd happily dedicated his life to his wife and son.

'I can't believe she's gone. I won't believe she's gone. Not until I see her body.'

'I know. I can't either, son. I know how hard it is to believe. But she is. She made that clear in her note.'

Matthew bit his lip. Fought back tears. He felt hollow, sick, numb. Incomplete without her. Unable to believe he'd never hear her voice or feel her touch again.

His father continued. 'But we'll get through this together. We're a team, you and me. And you're a strong lad, always have been.'

Matthew laid his head on his father's shoulder as the tears trickled down his face, nearly anaesthetised with the biting cold. It was a bleak January day. Fitting as far as Matthew was concerned. Symbolic of the despair he felt at the loss of his mother, Mary. Devoted mother and wife. Wonderful, kind, generous. Beautiful on the inside, as well as on the outside. But hiding a deep depression that would lead her to take her own life.

The trees stood bare and emaciated, the sun concealed under a thick film of grey. Father and son had gone for a walk in Queen's Park, near the Gerards' family home in north-west London. A pretty park, popular with mums and childminders, where Matthew and Mary would stroll on crisp winter mornings, stopping at the café for hot chocolate, or play tennis in the summer, rewarding themselves with an ice cream afterwards. Where she'd first brought him as a baby, watching the joy on his chubby round face as he'd ridden the swings for the first time. Giggling at his adoring mother, the one person in the world whom he trusted completely, who made him feel safe. How could she leave him and his father like that? He wanted to be angry with her, but he couldn't. He loved her too much.

Matthew fought back more tears when he thought about her last words to him as they'd toasted the New Year. She'd turned to him, whispered in his ear, 'Live life to the full, Matthew. And never let anyone walk all over you. Fight for justice, and never be silenced if a truth needs to be said out loud.'

He'd thought her words strange at the time. But he'd quickly brushed them aside, put it down to the fact that they'd both had too much champagne.

The following day, she'd taken the car, left a note on the kitchen table saying she was popping out for some milk and bread from the local Tesco Express. But she never came home. The next day, Frank found a letter in her dressing table drawer. Addressed to him and Matthew. Telling them how much she loved them, but that she had too many demons. Demons that haunted her and were making life impossible for her to live. Two weeks later, police found the scarf she'd been wearing that day jammed under some pebbles on Southsea beach. Her home town. Where she'd returned to die. The coastguards had searched the area tirelessly, but her body was never found. The family car had been abandoned just off Southsea Common. Apparently, it was common for suicide victims who chose drowning to end things, to fill their clothes with heavy objects. And it was presumed that she'd abandoned her scarf as a sign that she was gone, a parting farewell of sorts. Although Matthew didn't want to believe it, his mother's body no doubt lay somewhere at the bottom of the English Channel.

And now, standing there, he realised she'd chosen those words deliberately. Her parting shot. And it made him wonder whether they'd held a deeper, personal resonance. Almost as if she was telling her son to face life in a way she hadn't.

'Come on, son, we should go now,' Frank urged. 'You'll catch your death out here.'

'Do we really have to do this?' Matthew asked his father. He felt seven years old again. Doubtful, scared, unsure. Needing his father's reassurance. The only difference was, now that he was older, he knew how cruel life could be. That his father didn't have all the answers. That life was fragile. And that neither he, nor his parents, were infallible. It scared him, and he wished he was seven again. In some ways, he'd been stronger then than he was now. Because knowing how hard life was – how utterly shit it could be at times – could weaken a person, rather than spur them on to face life head-on, all guns blazing. The ignorance of youth was a strength, rather than a weakness. He realised that now.

He knew what Frank's answer would be, but he felt driven to ask it all the same. Mary had made it clear in her will that she wanted all her clothes and shoes to be given to charity. Two charities, in fact. Refuge and Rape Crisis. Matthew hadn't been surprised by the former. She'd been a social worker for many years. But the second had baffled him slightly. It had just seemed so specific.

'She was a staunch champion of women's causes, always had been,' his father had explained. 'Many of the women she worked with were sexually abused. I'm not surprised at all.'

Matthew had accepted his father's explanation, and no more was said on the subject. As Frank had pointed out, Mary had been a social worker for twenty-nine years. Caring for abused children and female victims of domestic violence. He'd asked his mother once, when he was only twelve and getting increasingly curious about the world with every passing day, what had prompted her to enter her field of work.

'Because I want to make a difference,' she'd replied with a smile. Not a full-blown grin. It had been a wistful, almost sad, smile. 'Not everyone's as lucky as we are. Not everyone has someone to stick up for them.'

Matthew remembered feeling mildly jealous of those who took up so much of his mother's time. He was still so young, and being an only child, the apple of his parents' adoring eyes. Especially his mother whom he'd loved fiercely. More than his father, in fact; although he'd never told him so to his face. There was just something about the mother–son bond. A bond as unbreakable as reinforced steel. He'd felt guilty for loving one parent more than the other. Felt almost disgusted with himself. But he couldn't help it. He wasn't used to sharing, and he had wanted her all to himself.

Now, looking back, he was ashamed of his envy, but he let himself off; after all, he'd only been a boy. And now, he craved another blood tie to share his pain and grief. Even though he had his father, he felt alone in the world because he knew his father wouldn't be around forever. When he died, what then?

Matthew clutched the empty bin liner, awaiting his father's response. 'It's what she wanted, son. We must respect her wishes.'

They spent the next few hours carefully sorting through Mary's drawers and wardrobes. Every now and again, Matthew would catch his father pressing an item of clothing to his cheek, inhaling his wife's scent as if he was trying to bring her back to life. Clinging on to every bit of her.

His parents had been married for twenty-eight years. They'd met when Frank was just a young green constable. He'd been called to the scene of a reported domestic abuse incident. Mary had been the social worker assigned to the case, and it had been a simple case of love at first sight. For Frank, that is. He'd pursued Mary relentlessly until she'd finally agreed to go on a date with him. From their first kiss, they both realised they'd found the person they wanted to spend the rest of their lives with. As he considered this, Matthew thought how lucky they were to have found each other. He prayed that one day, he'd find his soulmate, the glove that fitted his hand, who understood him completely, unconditionally. Who would always stick by him, no matter what he did.

They'd worked all morning, and Matthew's insides were crying out for food. His stomach let out a mournful growl. 'Heard that.'

His father grinned. 'Not much left to do, by the looks of things. Just those couple of top drawers. Why don't you make a start on them while I whip us up some sarnies?'

'Thanks, Dad, will do.' Matthew watched his father walk away, then headed over to a tall chest of drawers they'd yet to inspect. It was chock full of underwear. As he began to fish the contents out, feeling slightly weird rifling through his mother's underwear and wondering whether he should, in fact, leave it to his father, he felt something hard and rigid. He pulled it out. To his surprise, it was a leather journal, wrapped within one of his mother's petticoats. Her diary for last year, 2015. The last year of her life.

His heart pounded as he ran his hand over the cover, then inhaled the combination of leather and his mother's familiar perfume. In the distance, he heard the radio playing and crockery being shifted as his father prepared their lunch. He knew he should respect her privacy, but he was far too inquisitive by nature. Probably one of the reasons he'd been attracted to law. In less than two months' time, he'd start his training contract. His mother had been so proud of him when he'd gained a first in law from UCL, then a distinction on the Legal Practice Course. And then, when he'd told her he'd bagged a job with a top City firm, she'd been overjoyed. But then, quite suddenly, her enthusiasm had plummeted. Like a jumbo jet that had been soaring high, only to have sudden engine failure. He might have been imagining it, but her change of heart had seemed to coincide with the moment he'd told her the firm's name.

'Were they the only firm to offer you a place?' she'd asked. 'You don't have any other options?' He remembered her words as if they were yesterday. The curtness of them. The shock, almost the sound of fear in her voice.

He'd been cross at the time. Cross with her questions. Cross with her for dampening his elation at being offered a training contract with one of the most highly regarded firms in London. It was like a dream come true. A dream that she was souring. She'd sensed that. And later that night, she'd swiftly apologised. Scooped him up in her arms and congratulated him on his success.

They never spoke of it again.

Matthew couldn't wait to start work. To get stuck in. Immerse himself in law in a bid to numb his pain. Bury the loss that terrorised his heart.

He backed away from the chest of drawers and sat on the edge of the bed. The door was open, and he had a bird's eye view of the stairs from where he was sitting, so he'd know the minute his father was on his way up. The last thing he wanted was to be caught by his father snooping in his mother's diary.

To Matthew, it had always felt like his mother had been hiding something from him. Perhaps her diary would reveal what that something was?

Running his fingers over the cover again, he tentatively opened it, and began to skim-read its contents. Dating back to exactly a year ago. She wrote of daily humdrum events. Her work, her clients, painful cases, her friends, funny things that had happened, her love for Matthew and Frank.

Matthew blinked back tears, flicking the pages until he reached the last few entries, being sure to catch every tear that escaped, so as not to smear his mother's neat scrawl. But then, an entry she'd written two weeks before her death, on 16 December, nearly made Matthew's heart stop.

I pray more than anything for God to take away the shame I feel. As I near the last chapter of my life, my soul is tormented by that night at

Cambridge. For so long, I've managed to push it far to the back of my mind, almost pretend it was a terrible figment of my imagination. Frank and Matthew helped me to do that. My work, ironically, helped me to do that. But lately, the memory is so vivid, it's as if it happened yesterday. And with Matthew starting at that firm – his firm – I feel torn between my love for my son and my hatred of the man who very nearly ruined me. In fact, I still wonder if he succeeded. I can still feel his hands around my neck, pinning me down as he took away my dignity while the others watched. Leering at me like a piece of meat. I should never have let them silence me. I should have gone to the police. Too much time has passed now, but I still pray that ND will somehow get his just deserts, although I fear my prayers are in vain.

Matthew was in shock. His stomach felt knotted, his head spinning with confusion and disbelief. He sat motionless on the bed, his eyes scanning the words again and again, scarcely able to believe what he was reading. It couldn't be true. It was too shocking, too horrific, to contemplate. But his mother's words were clear.

ND had to be Nigel Davenport, and he – the senior partner of Sullivan, Blake, Monroe, the firm Matthew was going to work for – had raped his mother.

There was no other meaning to grasp from her words. He'd forced himself on her in front of a complicit audience. The fucking bastard. Anger bubbled up in Matthew, and he was too late to stop a tear from splashing onto the page. It left an unsightly blue smudge. 'Shit,' he cursed out loud, while fishing out a tissue from his jeans pocket and gently dabbing the page.

So many thoughts and questions raced through his head. Fast and furious, like an express train. This was the real reason his mother had quit Cambridge. She'd told him she'd missed home and wanted to be closer to her parents. But now he knew that was just a story she'd made up to fob him off.

This was why she'd chosen social work – to help others like her. And it also explained her donation to Rape Crisis, and why she hadn't reacted well to his job offer. Of all the firms to offer him a place, why did it have to be that one?

Who had been watching? Why had she allowed herself to be silenced? Did the college master know? Why had Davenport picked on his poor, darling mother?

Just then, Matthew heard his father's footsteps. Glassware and crockery rattling against the tray he was carrying.

He quickly hid the diary under the bed. His father was upset enough. If he saw what she'd written, who knows what it might do to him. Destroy him, send him mad, cause him to confront Davenport and then do goodness knows what.

No, Matthew couldn't let his father – the only blood relation he had left – bear that burden. He'd bear that burden. He'd suck it up and channel his pain for a greater good.

To right an unforgiveable wrong.

To bring Davenport to heel and get justice for his beloved mother once and for all.

He'd make him suffer in the most humiliating way conceivable. Just as his mother had suffered. The only question was, *how*?

Chapter Eleven

Charlotte Dempsey
December 2015

'What's wrong, Mum, why are you crying?'

It was 7 p.m. on a glacial mid-December evening. Charlotte cuddled up to her sobbing mother on the sofa. Although she no longer lived with her parents, Diana and Charles Dempsey, she was only a twenty-minute walk away in West Hampstead, and still had a key to their splendid house, just off Hampstead Heath. The home she and her younger brother, Isaac, grew up in.

In just over three months, Charlotte would be starting her training contract at Sullivan, Blake, Monroe. But before then – next month, in fact – she was heading off to Thailand for a month with Becky, her best friend. Another aspiring lawyer, who'd been offered a place at a smaller West End firm, just off the Strand. They saw their trip as a last hurrah before real life kicked in.

Her mother's face was buried in her cupped hands, further obscured by her shoulder-length brown hair, streaked with strands of grey, hanging loose on either side. Charlotte was always urging her to dye it, but Diana said she over-fussed. That a few grey hairs were part and parcel of growing old, and that it didn't bother her. She was unpretentious like that. Not like her husband, who not only dyed his hair so that it covered every speck of grey, but whitened his teeth, Botoxed his face, and regularly detoxed his self-abused system. Everything about him was artificial as far as Charlotte was concerned. Including his love for his family.

But Charlotte adored her mother. Unlike her father, who'd always been too busy for her and Isaac, married to his work, Diana had practically brought their children up single-handedly. Although they could easily have afforded a nanny, she'd refused. Just as she'd refused to go on faddy diets, spend hours in the gym, stick needles in her face, as other women with rich husbands did. She'd showered her children with love and affection for as long as they could remember. Making up for their father's cool indifference and long absences.

Charlotte remembered reading with her mother as a little girl, the endless trips to the park, baking cakes, throwing snowballs, snuggling up together on bitter nights with crumpets and hot chocolate topped with marshmallows. She'd felt guilty for moving out, but Diana had insisted. 'You need to learn to survive without me,' she'd said. 'As much as it kills me to see you go – as much as I'd like to cling to my little girl forever – I want you to be able to take care of yourself.'

Diana had cried a lot when Charlotte and Isaac were children. Usually in the privacy of her bedroom because she was too selfless to inflict her misery on them. But they weren't stupid. They knew how unhappy she was. And they knew about the pills she took to combat her depression. Clutching hands, they'd stand outside her door, and listen to her sobbing, wondering if their father knew how sad she was, but too afraid to ask him. Wondering why he didn't seem to care. Why he was hardly ever home. Too young and unworldly to consider the dark answers to these questions, to know how to help Diana themselves, and yet desperately wanting to.

But once they were grown up, they understood why Diana cried. She cried because their father was as cold towards their mother as he was towards his children. When he wasn't working, he was out on work jollies, or socialising with his obnoxious City friends. One of them was Nigel Davenport, soon to be Charlotte's boss. Her father and Davenport were old friends from Cambridge. Back then, Charles had been the fat, geeky, timid one. Too uncool for the cool boys, too ugly for the pretty girls.

But for some reason, Davenport – clever, handsome, popular – had taken Charles under his wing and moulded him into a lesser version of himself. By the time they'd left university and headed for the big City, Charles was barely recognisable. Twenty pounds lighter, he'd binned the glasses, acquired a sense of style and a whole repertoire of cheesy chat-up lines. He was also Davenport's first major client, and still a firm friend.

Finally, Diana looked up, her red blotchy face smeared with streaks of black mascara, tattooing her nude foundation. 'It's our wedding anniversary today.'

Shit, Charlotte cursed inside, guilt consuming her. She'd been so preoccupied with her forthcoming trip, she'd completely forgotten. 'Oh, Mum, I'm so sorry for not remembering. For not getting you a card. Isn't Dad coming home? Is that why you're crying? Has he forgotten as well?'

Diana sniffed and lightly wiped her eyes with the cuffs of her jumper. 'Pathetic, aren't I?' She smiled. It was a sad, desperate smile that brought tears to Charlotte's eyes.

'No, Mum, of course you're not pathetic. Dad's an absolute arsehole.'

'Charlotte!'

'What? It's true. How could he possibly forget your anniversary? I'm gonna call him now.' Charlotte made to get up, but her mother pulled her back down.

'No, I don't want you braving my battles for me. Besides, it'll only make him resent me more. Make me seem more pathetic in his eyes.' Now the tears flowed fast and furiously. 'I had a pair of cufflinks made especially for him. White gold, engraved with his initials. I planned on giving them to him before he left this morning, but he was already gone when I got up. Almost as if he was avoiding the chance of me catching him. Like some disease.'

Charlotte felt sick hearing her mother talk like that. She was worth so much more. Why did her father not see that? He must have done when he married her. The way her mother told it, they'd been so happy the first five years, having met through a friend at a Christmas party. Maybe it was her and her brother's fault. Maybe she and Isaac destroyed the passion between them. Drove him away. She wished her mother had left him long ago. In all honesty, it had always felt like it was just the three of them. They would have coped, and Diana might have got a second chance at happiness. 'And he's not been home since?'

'No.' Diana shook her head. 'I haven't heard a peep out of him.'

'Do you think something's happened to him?' Charlotte almost hoped that something had. At least then there would be a genuinely good reason for his silence, his absence. At least then her mother wouldn't feel her husband was deliberately avoiding her.

'No. I would have heard by now. No, I suspect he's got some work function or other to attend. Either that, or Nigel's taken him out.'

Fucking Nigel. Charlotte's blood boiled. She didn't know how best to phrase her next question. Finally, she just came out with it. 'Taken him out where?'

Diana looked into her daughter's eyes. 'There are some questions you're better off never asking. Just because…' She sighed. 'Just because the answer might hurt too much. Might even kill you.'

Charlotte hadn't really needed to ask. Her father, like Davenport, had a roving eye. But it was Davenport who encouraged it. Davenport who, as far as Charlotte could tell, led her father astray. She'd witnessed this for herself last summer, when he and his poor long-suffering wife, Pamela, had come over for dinner one balmy August evening. The men had gone out into the garden, overlooked by the kitchen, for a cigar. At the time, Charlotte had been washing up at the sink, the windows open to let in what air there was. And that's when she'd overheard them discuss a particularly attractive female lawyer at Sullivans. Charlotte had nearly vomited when her father had made some crude comment about how he'd enjoy looking at her *briefs*. Davenport had professed his comment to be hilarious, and even offered to arrange an introduction. Charlotte wasn't naïve. She suspected Davenport's client dinners were often followed by trips to so-called respectable men's clubs, and she shuddered at the thought of what her father did behind her mother's back. If only she'd had the courage to leave him. Realised her children were much stronger than she'd given them credit for. That they would have preferred her to be single and happy, as opposed to being trapped in a loveless marriage, a sham of a happy family.

And now Charlotte was struggling with the idea of working at Davenport's firm. She'd tried others but faced rejection after rejection. It was a tough industry to crack, and you took what you could get. She was as good as anyone else – her grades demonstrated that – but training contracts were few and far between, and it was often a quick whisper in a contact's ear that made all the difference.

'Mum, do you think I got the job at Sullivans because of Dad's friendship with Nigel?'

Charlotte knew the answer. Of course, it had helped. No question. But she was too proud to admit it, and she knew her mother would give her the answer she needed to hear.

Diana brushed a loose strand of hair away from her daughter's face and smiled at her with adoring eyes. 'No, my sweetheart. You got that job on merit. And don't let anyone else tell you otherwise.'

'Thanks, Mum.' Charlotte smiled. She hesitated, then said, 'But I'm not sure I want to train there anymore. I mean, I can't wait to be a proper lawyer, but I resent Nigel for the way he takes Dad away from you. It's like Dad's under his spell. Nigel clicks his fingers and Dad comes running like an obedient puppy. It makes me sick. He's a bad influence.'

'Your father feels he owes everything to Nigel. He befriended him when many of his peers at Cambridge shunned and made fun of him. I guess, in his view, if it wasn't for Nigel he wouldn't be the successful man he is today.'

'That may be so,' Charlotte said, 'but on the other hand, he might have been a whole lot nicer, as opposed to a complete fuckwit.'

'Language, Charlotte,' her mother remonstrated.

Charlotte didn't apologise. She meant every word of what she said. She gave her mother a playful nudge in the side. 'Come on, Mum, if Dad's not going to take you out, I am. Go clean your face up and put on something nice. We're going out for a slap-up dinner.'

Although Diana didn't feel like it, she saw the determined look on her daughter's face. There was no arguing with Charlotte when she put her mind to it. She was a stubborn, determined young woman, and Diana had every confidence she'd go far. So, she did as she was told, and they ended up having a wonderful evening getting tipsy on Mojitos at Gaucho Grill. Diana couldn't remember the last time she'd enjoyed herself so much. And when she'd said goodbye to her daughter at Heathrow airport a month later, she did so with fond memories of their evening together.

It was a memory Charlotte would also treasure. More than she could ever have imagined at the time. Midway through her trip of a lifetime, she was woken by a phone call in the dead of night. It was her hysterical brother, who'd found their mother's lifeless body less than an hour before. Slumped up against the side of the bath, an empty paracetamol bottle lying beside her cold, rigid form, along with a handwritten suicide note saying she was sorry, but that she was too tired with life to carry on living it. Charlotte had returned home immediately, although how she'd made it through the plane journey she'd never know.

She and Isaac knew the truth. They knew what had driven Diana to an early grave. It was their father. Along with his vile friend, Nigel Davenport. The night her mother had killed herself, the poisonous pair had been out together. Locked in the basement of some seedy club in Soho, where no signal could be found. Her father had been too caught up in ogling scantily dressed women to bother checking his phone until emerging four hours later at 2 a.m.

Charlotte had been tempted to give up her training contract. Cut all ties with Davenport. The last thing she wanted was to help line his pockets further.

But then she'd had an idea. What if she could use her position to make him pay? Devise a plan to ruin the bastard. Her instinct

120

had told her to start her training contract, and see what options materialised.

Her instincts had been right. Because four months into her first seat, she found herself having a conversation with two like-minded men. Two men who bore equally fierce grudges against Nigel Davenport. Two men equally united in their desire to bring about his downfall.

One was Matthew Gerard. The other was Richard Barker.

Chapter Twelve

Richard Barker
May 2016

'I'm afraid it's not good news, Richard.'

A sickness Richard had buried deep in the pit of his stomach rose to the surface. 'Tell me,' he said to Dr Lewis, a consultant clinical oncologist at the Royal Marsden. In truth, he knew what the answer would be. It was implicit from his face, from the tone of his voice, despite his professionalism. It helped prepare Richard for hearing the truth out loud, even though he already knew it in his heart of hearts, based on his recent symptoms.

Dr Lewis replied gravely, 'It's spread to your pelvis, ribs and lungs.' He held Richard's gaze, a genuine look of sympathy and concern in his. Then his face lightened a little. 'There's some good news, though.'

'What's that?'

'It's not got to your spine yet.'

'Fabulous,' came the sarcastic response. 'What are my treatment options?'

'I'd recommend a combination of hormone therapy and surgery to drive down your testosterone levels, which the cancer thrives on, as you know. That, plus chemo, will give you the best chance of surviving for longer.'

Until now, Richard had been insistent on keeping a watchful eye on his PSA levels which a routine blood test had proved to be alarmingly high. When he was first diagnosed, the cancer was found to be confined to the prostate, and as he hadn't had any other symptoms, Dr Lewis had been content to delay treatment and the unpleasant side effects that often accompanied it. More recent check-ups, however, had shown Richard's levels to be rising, but despite Dr Lewis's insistence that Richard start hormone treatment, he'd maintained he was feeling OK and could bring down the levels by diet alone. But, having lost a lot of weight in the last month or so, along with feeling rather breathless, Richard had reluctantly agreed to an all over body scan to see if the cancer had spread, the results of which now confirmed that the watchful waiting was well and truly over.

'I don't want chemo,' Richard said bluntly. 'Just do the hormone treatment, cut my balls off if you must, and radiate me if that's an option. That'll do.'

Dr Lewis looked aghast. 'You're not thinking straight, Richard. I think you need more time to think this through. Radiation's too dangerous. We typically only use radiation when the cancer hasn't spread. The bones can often be managed with hormone therapy alone, but I'm afraid the lungs are another story.'

'I'm perfectly lucid, and I've made up my mind.'

Dr Lewis leant forward, tilted his head, and stared into his patient's eyes. 'Look, I know chemo's a nasty business, and the side effects can be unpleasant, but we need to be vigorous with your treatment. Don't you want as much time as possible?'

Richard was angry. Of course he wanted more time. He wanted not to have fucking cancer! But he did, and the way he saw it, eventually it was going to get him. He didn't want to spend what little time he had left tied up in hospital, puking up every five seconds, and feeling like he was already dead. He wanted to work, spend time with his wife, make amends for his cowardice in failing to stand up to Davenport what felt like a lifetime ago. Maybe he'd finally got his comeuppance. Karma at its most ruthless.

He flexed his jaw, felt his face go red. 'Of course I do. But I don't want to spend it in here, throwing up, with my arse hanging out of a hospital gown. I want to work, I want to socialise, spend time with my wife. I want to *live* the rest of my life.'

Dr Lewis sat back and sighed. There was no use arguing. He didn't agree, but he'd given his patient his best advice, and in the end, it was his patient's choice. Just like it had been his patient's choice not to tell his wife he had cancer. But now things were different. Surely, he'd tell her now? He leant forward, clasped his hands together. 'OK, Richard. Would you like to come in with Marianne? Let me help you break it to her? Patients often find it hard to tell their loved ones alone, for fear of their reaction.'

Richard filled his diseased lungs with as deep a breath as he could muster, his face impassive. 'I still don't want her knowing. Another reason I don't want chemo.'

Dr Lewis sat back with a start, not expecting this second bombshell. 'Richard, I understand your urge to protect her, but you must tell her. She's your wife, and she'd want to be there at your side. You can't do this alone, Richard, you need her. Especially when you come in for surgery. How will you hide that from her?'

'Can't you use silicone or something?'

'We can insert artificial silicone sacs into your scrotum, yes, but I'm not sure you've got to grips with the other physical side effects, or, indeed, the psychological ones. You'll have a lower sex drive, possible hot flushes, breast tenderness, anaemia, depression, to name but a few.'

'I'm tough, I'll be fine.'

'But you can fight this thing better with Marianne at your side. Hiding it from her will exhaust you.'

Richard wouldn't be turned. He'd made up his mind and his steely look said as much. 'I told you, I don't want her knowing. At least, not for now. It'll kill her, and I can't do that to her. As for the surgery, it's an outpatient procedure, right?' Dr Lewis nodded. 'Good. So just reconstruct me, load me up on pain medication when I get out, and she won't know the difference.'

'But if the worst happens, Richard, what do you think that will do to her? The shock will be even greater. She'll be hurt that you kept something so huge from her. Plus, although external beam radiotherapy might be an option, this has its own side effects. Tiredness, nausea, hair loss.'

'I've already got that going for me.' Richard attempted a joke, gave a half-smile as he rubbed his shiny temples.

'Seriously, Richard.' Dr Lewis wasn't seeing the funny side. 'She's a smart woman and she'll cotton on.'

'Maybe, but I just can't handle her knowing I'm that sick. Not for now, anyway. I'll put the tiredness down to work, the hair loss to age, and the sickness to a bug. The lack of sex drive can be blamed on all three. Plus, you can give me meds for any nausea I might suffer, right?'

Dr Lewis remained silent.

'Right?' Richard widened his eyes, immoveable.

Once again, his doctor gave a heavy sigh. 'Right.'

'Good. I appreciate your concern and your discretion. Now, tell me, how exactly does the treatment work, how much will I need, and when do I start?'

Later, as he lay in bed, his wife sleeping peacefully at his side, oblivious to the cruel invasion of her husband's increasingly fragile body, Richard began to devise a plan. A plan he'd vaguely considered for some years now, but which he'd thought about more seriously since first learning of his cancer, and after finding out who his new trainees would be.

A plan which had now taken on a greater urgency and needed to be fleshed out.

A plan that could not be put in motion effectively with him chained to a hospital bed, although, of course, poor well-meaning Dr Lewis could never know that.

With his health in the balance, he needed to move quickly. He'd make contact again, and hope she agreed the time was right to hasten the plan.

July 2016

Richard was nervous.

He was sitting at a table in a snug corner of the Berners Tavern. Across from him were Matthew Gerard and Charlotte Dempsey. His trainee mentees. At the start of their training contracts with Sullivans, it was routine practice for trainees to be assigned a specific partner mentor, who would help steer them through their two years of training. Basically, they were to look out for them. But it wasn't a coincidence that they'd been assigned Richard. That was an arrangement of his own subtle engineering.

Richard had chosen this table deliberately. Unobtrusive and out of the way. It was a popular, cavernous, bustling restaurant situated in the glamorous London Edition hotel, a restored Edwardian building, located just off Oxford Street in the heart of Fitzrovia. The walls were covered with magnificent paintings, the high ceilings adorned with ornate plasterwork and chandeliers, the lighting low and atmospheric. Being a weekday lunchtime, it was mostly filled with suits who were too wrapped up in their own concerns to be bothered by yet another City partner and a couple of insignificant trainees. But you never knew who might be listening… speculating… gossiping, even though, as their mentor, he had every right to take them out for a mid-seat treat. One had to be careful. It wouldn't be a dignified end to his career, his life, if someone overheard and spilled the beans. But then again, what right had he to dignity after his cowardice?

Be that as it may, Richard was tense, because today was make or break, and it could all go horribly wrong. He was about to lay his cards on the table with two young fresh trainees who, should he totally have misjudged them, might go running to Davenport and unveil their mentor's deception of him. But he saw no other way. *She* had seen no other way. He had to be the one to make the first move. His plan was never going to work without them. Plus, he consoled himself with the fact that even though the surgery and hormone therapy seemed to be stemming the aggressive nature of his disease, the cancer would kill him in the end. So why should he care about being exposed?

He selected a bottle of Saint-Emilion for himself and his companions, they ordered starters and mains, and then he kicked off with some pleasantries.

127

'So, how are you two finding your feet? Settled in OK?'

Charlotte and Matthew exchanged furtive glances, shy grins, then Matthew said, 'Yes, thank you, Richard. I think I could find myself steering towards securitisation on qualification. Craig's a good guy to sit with, and the hours haven't been as bad as people make out.'

Richard chuckled as he took a slug of wine. 'Don't be fooled. You've lucked out there, Matthew. As you know, they closed a big deal just before you started, and now they're taking a breather. But only a temporary one. I understand there's a massive new deal in the pipeline, so be prepared. You might not see the light of day for the rest of your seat.'

Matthew smiled, sipped his wine, then said, 'Thanks for the heads-up, Richard. I'll make the most of lunches like these, then.'

Richard turned his attention to Charlotte. 'And how's Property, Charlotte?'

'Pretty slow actually. I mean, I'm steadily busy, but Robin takes off around six every evening, and sometimes I'm twiddling my thumbs come five thirty.'

'Again, enjoy it. That's fairly typical of Property. A good one to ease yourself in. I understand you're going to Corporate next, so be ready to go up a gear. It might come as a shock to the system.'

Charlotte smiled, sipped her wine, her eyes creeping over the rim of her glass as she fixed her gaze on Richard. 'Don't worry, I'm fully prepared.'

'Litigation's where you want to be,' Richard said. 'The true *legal* department, the brains of the firm. The team that sorts out the other departments' messes.' He paused, gave a sly grin. 'I'm biased, of course.'

Charlotte grinned back. 'Naturally.'

They chatted about this and that over their food, along with a second bottle of red.

Then, as they waited for their desserts, Richard asked, looking at both in turn, 'So your parents must be delighted with your success so far?'

'Er, you mean my dad?' Charlotte said. 'You must know that my mother died in January? With my father being who he is, I mean.'

Matthew turned to Charlotte in surprise. Although they'd chatted a bit during induction week, they'd barely crossed paths since, aside from passing glances at client dos, and trainee drinks down the pub. 'Your mother died in January? So did mine.' He looked away, reflective. 'Well, we think she did. She went out to buy milk and bread on New Year's Day but never came back. They found her scarf on Southsea beach, along with a note in her dresser drawer.'

Charlotte looked momentarily shocked, then said, matter-of-factly, 'Sorry to hear that. But I can equal you there. Mine killed herself too.'

It was Matthew's turn to look surprised.

The red wine had loosened Charlotte's tongue. But she was still lucid enough to recognise this and told herself to be careful.

'I'm so sorry,' Matthew said.

'Yes, me too,' Richard echoed. 'I rather feel like I've stuck my foot in it.'

'Don't be silly, you weren't to know,' Matthew said. Then, quickly glancing at Charlotte, he said, 'At least, not about my mother.'

'Their deaths must have hit you both very hard,' Richard said softly. He noticed his protégés squirm in their seats. Could tell they were irritated by his failure to quit the painful topic, but at the same time, didn't want to appear rude to their partner mentor.

'Yes, I was devastated by her death, we were extremely close,' Charlotte said. Matthew just nodded.

'And are you close to your father, Charlotte?' Richard persisted. 'I know him from way back, you see.' He slyly glanced at Matthew. 'We were in the same year at Cambridge. Me, Charles and Nigel.'

He saw it. The tensing of shoulders, the apprehension, the hatred in their eyes. The relaxed, congenial atmosphere had quickly evaporated, and he realised he'd struck a chord. Matthew knew the truth. Richard already knew that from his mole. And even though he didn't have absolute proof, he was almost sure Charlotte bore a similar resentment.

'Really?' Matthew said. 'Were you all good friends back then?' He'd tried to phrase the question casually. But he wasn't fooling Richard.

'The best of friends.' Richard smiled. 'As thick as thieves.'

Matthew fiddled with his tie, stretching his neck this way and that as if he was struggling for air. He then gulped his wine and was about to say something when Charlotte beat him to it. 'The way I understand things, Nigel was very popular back then – like he is now, I suppose?' She leant in, a glint in her eye. 'Obviously, please don't tell him I asked this, but was he like, the ringleader? I mean, there's always a wild one at uni. I don't know about you, Matthew' – she glanced slyly at Matthew, who was still looking uncomfortable – 'but we had one at Bristol. The popular Lothario who the girls worshipped, and the boys envied. Although, of course, there were some who followed him around like the Pied Piper.'

She gave a little laugh, the same glint in her eye. But there was more to her query than a cheeky nosiness. The girl was fishing for something.

Richard sat back. Looked from one to the other. 'He was certainly that.'

Matthew cleared his throat. *Is that a line of perspiration developing across his forehead,* Richard wondered.

'I gather my dad was a bit of a geek back then?' Charlotte continued to fish. 'Chubby and not a hit with the ladies, unlike Nigel. I guess we have Nigel to thank for making my dad the dashing, successful man he is today.' She gave a false smile, while her eyes, though not unfriendly, seemed to drill through Richard.

'I guess that's true.' Richard continued to keep his comments brief. Goading them to spout more questions. He needed to arouse their interest. Be certain of the difference between innocent curiosity and veiled interrogation.

'And what about you?' Matthew finally spoke. 'Should we thank him for making you the man you are today?'

'In part, I suppose.' Richard nodded. 'But I'd like to think I've learnt a lot of lessons since university. That I'm my own man, and not a product of someone else's making.'

Matthew couldn't resist. The temptation was too great. Particularly after four glasses of wine. He now realised Richard had barely touched his since his first glass. 'My mother was at Cambridge the same time as Nigel.' A pause, then, 'So you must have known her too?'

'Mary Jacobs.' Richard didn't hesitate, stop to think for one second, or even frame his response as a vague query.

His decisiveness patently unsettled Matthew. As had been the plan. 'Yes, yes, that's right,' he stammered.

'She was a lovely woman, and I am so sorry to hear of her passing. A terrible way to die for anyone, but especially one so intelligent as well as beautiful.'

'Thank you,' Matthew stammered again, his eyes suddenly watery. Richard knew what was running through his mind. He was wondering if his mentor had lusted after his mother, the way

Nigel had. Whether he'd stood by and watched, delighting in her suffering and humiliation. 'So, you must have some stories to tell from back then?'

'Yes, I have a lot of stories. Good ones, bad ones.' Richard paused. 'But there are some memories I would rather forget.' He stopped. Looked straight into Matthew's eyes, as if trying to prise a truth out of him. He noticed the quizzical look on Charlotte's face. She clearly knew nothing about that night. It was up to him to seal the common bond between them. He knew about her father's extra-curricular pursuits with his best friend, and he was sure she had as much cause to despise Nigel Davenport as Matthew did. But the two were still clueless of their mutual hatred.

'Correct me if I'm wrong, Matthew – Christ, tell me to shut the fuck up, but is there something specific relating to your mother's time at Cambridge that you'd like to know about?'

Just then, a waitress appeared with their desserts. A few seconds of uneasy silence passed as she set them down, before leaving them alone once more.

Matthew glanced nervously around the crowded restaurant. The noise level was such, there was no way anyone could have heard Richard's question. But he couldn't help himself. He may have been overthinking things, but it was almost as if his mentor had invaded his mind and was challenging him to voice the one painful truth that plagued it night and day.

'Like what?'

Richard silently prayed that his instincts were right about Matthew knowing what happened to his mother at Cambridge, then went for it. He spoke slowly, quietly. Like a spy divulging some coveted secret. 'Like your mother's relationship with Nigel?'

He kept his gaze on Matthew, willing him to be brave and ask the one burning question he was dying to ask.

'You know?' Matthew looked stunned, his voice catching.

'Know what?' Charlotte couldn't resist asking. Right now, she felt like she was eavesdropping on their conversation, but as it involved Davenport, and something told her not in a good way, she was intrigued and wanted in.

'I know that something bad happened to your mother while we were at Cambridge, and I'm guessing that if you know what that something is, you're at my firm for one reason only, and it isn't to prove to us that you're the best lawyer that ever walked the planet.'

Grim-faced, Matthew tossed back the rest of his wine even though it was the last thing he needed. His head and heart were suddenly pounding, his stomach churning. He stared long and hard at Richard, as if trying to suss him out. They were like opponents in a deadly game of chess.

'She was raped.'

Charlotte gasped, while the men were silent. The air simmered with tension, until finally, Richard nodded. 'Yes, that's right.'

'Please tell me you weren't there,' Matthew said, trying to keep his cool.

He was so like her, thought Richard. He had her eyes – large and chocolatey – the same Mediterranean skin colouring, the rich dark hair.

He lowered his gaze, felt the guilt that had been eating away at him for what seemed like an eternity, swell. While the cancer steadily ravaged his body, the guilt grating at his soul was somehow more potent, more painful, to bear. He looked up. 'I'm sorry, but I was.'

Matthew gritted his teeth, anger consuming him. He wanted to punch the motherfucker in the face there and then. But he told himself to stay calm, that punching him wouldn't do his mother's memory any good or help him get his revenge.

But what now? He'd been exposed. How *was* he going to get his revenge on Davenport now that his reason for being at Sullivans was out in the open? He still hadn't a clue how he was going to make Davenport pay; it had only been a few months and he'd wanted to settle in, see what developed.

But that was going to be impossible now.

Or was it?

Based on the tone of Richard's voice, the guilt in his eyes, the incognito feel to their lunch meeting, something told him his mentor wasn't about to rat him in. Matthew glanced at Charlotte, wondering what her part in all this was. Why Richard had deliberately chosen to disclose something so hateful, so personal to them both, in front of her. Surely there was a good reason?

Charlotte was still in shock. But then, as the magnitude of what she'd heard sank in, she suddenly felt a profound connection with Matthew. Just like her own mother, his had suffered at the hands of that despicable man. Was this why Richard had brought them both here today? Because he knew about Diana, as well as Mary? Because he knew they both wanted revenge for their mothers' suicides?

Richard looked at Charlotte and read her thoughts. It was her turn now. He held her gaze and said, 'I know Nigel led your father astray. He did it at Cambridge and he's continued to do so for the last thirty-odd years. I know what he and your father got up to behind your poor mother's back, and I'm guessing you blame him for her suicide.'

Now Charlotte's eyes were wet, while Matthew looked astonished.

They looked at each other, realising that their fates were somehow entwined, and that they'd both been exposed before they'd even begun.

'It's OK,' Richard said. He noted the confusion on their faces. 'I'm not going to tell Davenport, or anyone for that matter. Your secret agendas are safe with me.'

'Why?' Matthew asked, somewhat relieved but still puzzled. What the hell was he playing at?

'Because I have an agenda of my own.' He gave a dramatic pause, then said, 'Because I also want revenge.'

This was startling news. So unexpected. Could he be trusted?

'Why?' Charlotte asked.

Richard reached for the bottle of mineral water lying in the centre of the table and poured himself a tall glass. He drained half of it, pushed his untouched dessert to one side, clasped his hands, rested them on the table, then explained.

'I was in love with your mother, Matthew. From the moment I set eyes on her. She was bright, beautiful, like a breath of fresh air. Genuine and unspoiled, unlike many of the girls at Cambridge. But – and I don't blame her for this – she didn't give me a second look. Don't get me wrong, she wasn't cruel or unpleasant, I simply wasn't her cup of tea.' He paused, gave a half-smile, but Matthew remained stony-faced, waiting for Richard to continue. 'She was chased by all the men, and yes, she flirted, as pretty women do, as they have every right to do when they're in the prime of their youth, barely out of their teens, all sorts of hormones racing around inside them. She slept around a bit, who didn't…'

Matthew's face turned scarlet. The anger was there again. He glanced around the room, said through clenched teeth, 'Are you calling my mother a whore? Because if you are, I'll punch your lights out.'

'Calm down. That's not what I'm saying. All I'm saying is that it's normal, it's university. I dare say the same sort of thing went on at your universities. Am I wrong?' He stared at them and got two slow shakes of the head in return. 'Right' – he nodded back – 'so, as I was saying, she was popular with the boys, and disappointed a fair few. Including Davenport.' Another pause.

At the mere mention of Davenport's name in the same context as his mother, Matthew felt his back stiffen. 'Go on,' he said.

'Nigel was very popular amongst staff and students alike. He was handsome, clever, witty, sporty, and a charmer. So, when your mother turned him down, he didn't take kindly to it. It was a massive blow to his ego. And to his reputation as a ladies' man.'

Matthew felt the sixty-pounds-a-head lunch he'd just eaten rise to his throat. He knew he wasn't going to like what was coming next, but he had no choice but to hear Richard out.

'Like most students, Nigel liked a drink. And drugs. Of any variety. One night – the same night your mother turned him down at a house party – he was completely out of it on vodka and cocaine. He had the Devil inside him, I guess. He rounded up three of his hangers-on, your father included.' Richard looked at Charlotte and she felt her cheeks burn with shame. 'And they grabbed Mary on her way back from the party to her halls. The same halls Nigel and I lived in.'

Another pause. Matthew felt his eyes moisten. He bit his lip to stop himself from making a scene. So hard, it drew blood. He tried desperately to control his breathing, which was becoming increasingly shallow. 'And where were you?' he asked with a shaky voice.

'I was still at the party. I'd seen them go, knew something was up. I left about twenty minutes later. I lived on the same floor as Nigel. Mary was the floor below. Going up the stairs, I heard several voices, a faint squeal, the shuffling of feet coming from Nigel's room.' He stopped talking, a single tear falling from his right eye as he looked up to the ceiling, then slowly back down again. 'When I walked in, I saw your mother on all fours on the floor, her head pressed up against the bed, Nigel behind her, doing – well, I don't think you need me to spell it out for you.'

There was silence. Matthew looked away, his heart thumping, his mind spinning, his stomach heaving. 'What about her father?' He shot daggers at Charlotte.

'He simply watched, as did the others.'

Charlotte bowed her head, disgusted.

'And you?' Matthew asked bitterly.

'I told him to get off her – said I'd report him, but he said that if I did, he'd see to it that your mother ended up dead in a ditch somewhere.'

'You believed him?' Matthew looked incredulous. 'It was all just talk, surely?'

'I couldn't be sure. I wouldn't have put it past him.'

Matthew took a deep breath, but it didn't help. The pain was there, tearing through his body, his mind, his soul, making him sick to the stomach. 'Excuse me,' he said, quickly standing up, then bolting across the restaurant.

Richard and Charlotte sat in silence for a few seconds, realising he'd gone to the gents' to throw up his expensive lunch.

Finally, Charlotte looked Richard in the eye and asked, 'Why are we here? I mean, I get why Matthew's here. You feel guilty for being a coward, and keeping your mouth shut…'

'I've explained my reasons for that.'

'Yes, I know, but something tells me – and I'm sure Matthew's thinking the same thing – you could have tried a little harder.'

Richard sighed, sucked his stomach in tight, as if trying to compress his guilt. 'Maybe,' he said faintly.

Charlotte continued. 'So why have you told me about this? Surely not to ridicule me for having a scumbag of a father?'

'No, I don't want to ridicule you, I want to help you. Help Matthew.'

'Help us how?' Matthew was back. He didn't look well. He sat down and poured himself a large glass of water before guzzling half of it.

Richard leant forward, his elbows resting on the table. 'By exposing Davenport in the most dramatic, humiliating way possible.' He paused for effect, could see he'd caught their interest.

'How?' Matthew asked.

'By obtaining his resignation, plus a couple of added bonuses.'

After Richard explained what he had in mind, and how his master plan would work, the two trainees sat there, speechless. It was a brilliant idea, but one question rang out, loud and obvious.

'Why?' Charlotte asked. 'Why would you do that? Risk your life, your reputation, your career?'

'Because I hate him for what he did to Mary, and because he cheated his way to senior partnership by bribing certain of my fellow partners to vote for him, rather than beating me fair and square. And, because I have terminal cancer, with at best five, but most probably far fewer, years left on this screwed-up planet.'

Matthew's and Charlotte's faces dropped. More silence as they tried to digest this last piece of news. It was the last thing they'd expected.

Finally, Charlotte said quietly, 'I'm sorry.'

'Thanks.'

'Do the partners know?' Matthew asked.

Richard shook his head. 'Not even my wife knows, and I'd like to keep it that way. Understood?'

They both nodded.

'So,' Richard continued, 'I have nothing to lose with this plan. You, on the other hand, do, if it all goes terribly wrong. Which is, of course, a possibility.' He let his words hang in the air as Matthew and Charlotte looked at one another, trying to gauge what the other was thinking. 'So, what do you say?'

'If we do this,' Matthew said to Charlotte, 'we'll be risking everything. Our futures, our freedom. But I, for one, am prepared to do that. I found out what Davenport did to my mother only by accidentally finding and reading her diary after she died. It was a total shock. And it's been hell imagining the burden she carried all those years, the pain she went through. I've not slept through the night since. It torments me every second of every day, and until he pays for what he did, I'll not be able to rest. If I don't do this, my life will be wasted anyway.' He paused, then continued. 'But you – you're in a different position. Your father may have watched, stood by like a spineless coward, but he's not Davenport, he's just weak and easily manipulated. Plus, Davenport didn't hurt your mother like he hurt mine.'

Charlotte shook her head, her eyes angry. 'No, that's not true, my father's just as bad. And Davenport may not have physically hurt my mother, but he was the instigator who sent her to her grave. He led Dad astray for years, to strip clubs, brothels and God knows where, with God knows who. Until finally, poor Mum couldn't take the hurt and humiliation anymore. She killed herself while I was travelling. I didn't even get to say goodbye. I blame my father – of course I do – but he's a weak man like you said, and it's Davenport who brainwashed him, who turned him into the selfish fucker he is. Davenport's a cold, calculating bastard. He's the one who should pay, and I want in on any plan that can make that happen.'

Richard saw the determination in Charlotte's eyes, saw what he'd seen at her interview, knew she had what it took to see his brilliant, yet highly dangerous, plan through to the end. He felt imbued with a new lease of life. He'd played by the rules all these years, and it was exhilarating just contemplating something so dangerous, so unethical, so daring, after a lifetime of living on the straight and narrow.

He looked at them both, then said in a low voice, 'It will take a lot of planning, and we'll have to be careful, do our research. As I said, the main aim is to engineer his resignation, but I also want his integrity called into question.' He paused, then said, 'So I'm thinking we should get him to make a personal donation to Rape Crisis, which I know is a charity your mother held dear to her heart.' He fixed his gaze on Matthew.

'How would you know that?' Matthew shot back.

Richard tensed, then said, 'Just conjecture, in view of what happened to her, that's all.'

Satisfied, Matthew nodded, and Richard continued. 'But Nigel's a selfish man, like you said. Likely to sacrifice his staff rather than concede his position or his money.'

'So what do you propose?' Matthew asked.

'Blackmail.'

'Explain.'

'The request for a donation to Rape Crisis should make it obvious to him the kidnappers know about the rape allegation. But the kidnappers also need to make it clear that they're aware of his frequent use of prostitutes. I propose that we pay one of his regulars to film him in the act, and send him a clip, threatening to make it viral if he doesn't do as we ask.'

'I like it,' Charlotte said, her eyes lighting up. 'But can we take the chance that an outsider won't blow our cover? If she can be bribed by us, who's to say she won't talk to the police and ID us?'

'That's why we need a couple more bodies on the team. At least one other person whose face won't end up on the news or in the papers like ours. For one, we need a driver, plus someone who's good with computers, that sort of thing; and another would be useful for sheer manpower.'

'I have an idea,' Charlotte said.

'Yes?'

'My brother, Isaac. He hates Davenport and our dad as much as I do. We're very close. Always have been. I can trust him. He's also a complete IT nerd. I suspect hacking's one of his specialities.'

Matthew shook his head. 'I don't know, it's risky.'

'I know my brother. We can trust him.'

'I'd like to meet him,' Richard said.

'You mean assess him?' Charlotte simpered.

'Yes, I suppose. Like I assessed you. It's the only way.'

'Agreed.'

'OK.' Matthew nodded.

'We still need another body.'

'Maybe a professional?' Charlotte suggested.

'Perhaps. It's got to be someone who can be bought,' Richard said. 'Perhaps we also demand money from the firm, which we pledge to our other recruit. I, for one, know we can afford to spare a few million. I also know it'll kill Nigel to have to do this.' He paused for reflection, then said, 'It has to be someone who's desperate to make a lot of money, and who's willing to stake their freedom for the sake of it.'

'I have someone in mind,' Matthew said. 'Give me a week, just to check some stuff out, then I'll get back to you.'

'OK.' Richard nodded. He hesitated, then said, 'I also have another pair of eyes and ears to be our contact on the ground while we're hiding out. Someone who can report back on Davenport's state of mind, and the likelihood he'll cave.'

'You can trust this person?'

'Without question.'

'Who is it?'

'Someone who hates him as much as we do.'

'And who would that be?'

'His wife.'

They agreed to strike in a year's time. Midway through Charlotte's and Matthew's third seats. Although they were desperate for revenge, and Richard's time on Earth was limited, they had to be patient. It would be important for Charlotte and Matthew to establish themselves at the firm, build up trust, so that no one would suspect them.

Matthew would continue to be himself. A grade A student, impressing in all his seats, a star pupil whom the partners would want to retain as an associate. Charlotte, on the other hand, would fail to live up to her grades. So timid, so inept, so inefficient, no one would think her capable of pulling off her own abduction. And Richard, well Richard would continue to be Richard. A much-loved, diligent, respected partner – quite simply, indispensable. It remained to be seen which two would join their operation, but as far as Matthew, Charlotte and Richard were concerned, the only thing that needed to be running through people's minds when they were taken was: *Poor them – the most blameless, innocent, harmless souls to have been picked.*

Chapter Thirteen

Stephen Baines
January 2017

One unusually mild evening in late January, ten months into their training contracts, Matthew Gerard met his best mate, Stephen Baines, for a pint. They sat perched on stools in the Castle on Commercial Road. The pub was jam-packed. Mainly with stressed-out, burnt-out City bods. Over-excited monkeys, delighted to have escaped their cages, and devouring booze like it was their only lifeline. Christ, they'd have it via a drip if they could. It was noisy, and Matthew had to speak up to make himself heard.

'So, how's it going in Litigation, mate? Like it?'

Stephen slugged his beer, then grimaced. 'Worst one yet. Bloody hate it. Too much niggly procedure. Too much bloody law. Can't wait to move to Corporate next month.' He grinned. 'Give me a meaty transaction any day.'

Matthew laughed. 'You never did have much patience, Stevo.'

They had known each other since primary school. Stephen was around five-ten, three inches shorter than Matthew, broad all over, with blue-green eyes, a steadily receding dark blond hairline and an eternally sunny temperament. Being a jovial sort, he was popular, made friends easily, and was fun to be around. It was funny to think that they'd not only chosen the same career path, but had ended up in the same firm, despite attending universities at opposite ends of the country – while Matthew had stayed in London, Stephen had gone up north to Leeds. But their solid friendship had ensured they remained close, meeting up during the long university breaks, and keeping in regular email contact during term time. They had applied to the same firms as a bit of a joke, never for a minute believing they'd both be offered a place at Sullivans.

Celebrating their training contracts over tequila slammers, they'd vowed not to let their healthy competitiveness at work affect their friendship. But Stephen wasn't to know that things had changed radically for Matthew. That he no longer cared two hoots about shining at work. That all he wanted was revenge against the tyrant who ran the place.

Mary had treated Stephen like a second son. Shortly after his parents split when he was only five, his father remarried, a child following soon after. Stephen had remained with his mother, whom he'd adored, but thirteen years later, she died of breast cancer. Her death hit him hard, in the same way Mary's, eight years later, devastated Matthew. To Matthew, it now felt like they had more in common than ever. He'd been desperate to tell Stephen about the diary, and his desire to make Davenport pay. But with no plan on the horizon, he'd been too afraid.

But things were different now. Now, a firm strategy was in place. A strategy being steered by one of the most influential men at the firm. Matthew had convinced Richard that Stephen was the one to help them, but only now was it the right time to bring him in.

'How are you getting on in Corporate?' Stephen asked.

'Good. George is a decent guy, and the hours, although at times shocking, haven't been consistently bad.'

'I know for sure that Corporate's where I want to qualify. I plan on making that clear to George from the start.'

Matthew's face suddenly darkened.

'What is it?' Stephen asked. They knew each other's looks, oddities, foibles, inside out. He could tell that Matthew was keeping something from him. Something he wasn't going to like.

'Listen, mate, I've heard something.'

Stephen gave a nervous laugh. 'Heard what?'

Matthew necked the rest of his pint, his heart hammering. This was it. Make or break. He realised how Richard must have felt when he recruited him and Charlotte. He was about to tell his best friend a big fat lie, and he felt terrible for it.

'You're not being kept on.'

At first, Stephen thought he was joking, playing a friendly trick – the kind of thing they did to one another. But Matthew remained poker-faced.

Stephen shifted uneasily in his seat, his eyes darting around the room. He didn't suffer from claustrophobia, but the room was closing in on him. 'Stop bullshitting me, mate.' He laughed nervously. 'You can't know that, only halfway through our training contracts!'

'I'm not bullshitting you.'

The room was smaller still, and Stephen felt overheated. He was banking on a permanent job in a year's time. For more reasons than a love of law. Matthew knew why, but for now, he didn't let on.

'Spit it out, man, you're really starting to piss me off. This healthy competition thing is getting out of hand.'

Matthew's heart was still thumping, but somehow, he kept his voice steady. 'I'm not dicking around, mate. This has nothing to do with any playful rivalry between friends. I only wish it was.'

Stephen realised his friend was telling the truth. He breathed in deeply, trying to settle the queasy sensation roiling through him. 'How the hell do you know? Are you sleeping with Betsy Carter?' Another nervous laugh.

Betsy Carter was the Head of Securitisation, where Stephen, like Matthew, had done his first seat. He'd messed up big time on a piece of work for her, and despite trying to make up for it by working his socks off for the rest of his time there, she never let him forget it.

'No, course not.'

'So what, then? How can you possibly know that? Tell me, for God's sake!'

'Before I do, I need you to confirm something.'

This was getting weirder and weirder. 'You've just told me I'm out of a job, with no explanation, and you want *me* to confirm something?' Stephen heard his voice getting louder, but he didn't care. This was his life he was talking about. His ticket out of the shit he'd landed himself in.

'Please, Stevo.'

Stephen inhaled sharply, then said, 'OK, yes, what is it you want me to confirm?' He felt like a spy being interrogated by the enemy.

'Are you shit-deep in debt?'

One bombshell after another. Stephen felt woozy, even though he'd only had one pint. It was stuffy in the pub, and he'd started to develop damp patches under his armpits. 'What?' he said faintly.

'You can tell me, mate. Are you struggling?'

146

Stephen fiddled with his collar, undid the top button. 'What makes you say that?'

'The gambling.'

An uneasy chuckle. 'What gambling? I may have a flutter now and again, but nothing more.'

Matthew looked at his friend with genuine sympathy. 'It's more than that, Stevo. I've seen how you get when we're out. Not so much now, but before we started at Sullivans. It's where we always ended up after a few beers. I saw you lose at least a grand on more than one occasion.'

'So? That automatically means I'm in debt, does it?'

'No, but it might explain why you're so reluctant to buy a place with Celeste, the love of your life. Why you sold your car last month, your other love. Why you still live in that shit flat in a scummy part of town ten months into your training contract.'

A few seconds of silence elapsed, during which time Stephen's face grew redder, and Matthew said a silent prayer that his friend would let him in.

Finally, he did. He ran his fingers down the back of his head, and Matthew saw tears in his eyes, the stress on his face blatant. *I'm such a bastard*, he thought. But it was a necessary means to an end.

'OK, yes, I'm in deep shit. I owe two hundred grand.'

He hadn't expected that. 'Fuck, mate. How the hell did you rack up that much?'

'Credit cards, loans, overdraft. All to get my fix. I know I have a problem, and I've been getting help. Attending meetings every Thursday night when Celeste's at her Zumba class.'

'Why didn't you tell me, for God's sake? We're best mates.'

Best mates wouldn't con each other though, like I'm conning you.

147

Stephen looked away briefly. Then faced Matthew square on. 'Precisely because we're best mates, I guess. I felt ashamed, like I'd let you down. And when things got really bad, you'd only just lost your mother. I didn't want to burden you with something that was my own doing.'

'Mate, don't be silly. What are friends for? You're like the brother I never had.'

Yeah, like Cane and Abel.

Stephen choked back tears. 'So that's why I need to be kept on. Because I'm in a steady, well-paid job, my creditors have agreed to a payment plan.'

'An IVA?'

'Yes. That's why HR didn't rescind my training contract after they found out through the background check. They threatened to, but when I pleaded with them, pointing out my straight A grades, my character references, and got my creditors to write a letter detailing the IVA, they agreed to give me a chance. That's why I've been working my backside off. To prove to the powers that be that I'm reliable, that I'm partner material. But also, so I can guarantee a well-paid associate's position at the end of it. A trainee salary over two years isn't going to cover my debts, for obvious reasons. When you factor in council tax, rent, bills, day-to-day existence. I need something permanent.' A pause, then, 'So now I've answered your question, and been made to feel like the biggest loser ever, you need to answer mine. How the hell do you know I'm not being kept on only a year into our training contracts?'

'Because Richard Barker told me.'

Another lie. But another necessary one. *We need to make it personal for Stephen, like it is for us*, Richard had said. *It's not enough that he's in debt. What we're proposing is highly dangerous. He needs another motive to join us. He needs to feel wronged, like we do.*

'Barker?' Stephen repeated in amazement.

'Yes. He's my mentor, as you know. Can't keep a secret for shit. Took me out for drinks last week, we got talking about this and that, and after five pints he told me the partners don't think you're the right fit. And yes, I think Betsy Carter had a strong hand in that, being the HR liaison partner. And from what Richard said, she's not one to forgive people's mistakes, particularly ones made by lowly trainees with massive debts.'

'What does "not the right fit" mean exactly?' Stephen's pulse was racing.

'What can I say? They're snobby bastards, shallow as fuck, with a stick up their arses.'

The penny dropped. Stephen understood what he meant. He didn't fit the firm's 'image'. 'You mean because I don't look like Bradley Cooper? Or *you*, for that matter.'

'I'm sorry, mate.'

'Sorry! What the fuck am I going to do now?'

This was it. He was nearly there. Matthew willed himself to hold it together. 'I think I have a way to solve your financial difficulties, but it's risky. Are you in?'

'Hang on,' Stephen said, 'you can't expect me to say yes before I even know what the hell it is you want me to do.' In his mind, he'd all but agreed to whatever it was Matthew was proposing. He was so mad, felt so wronged by the firm who had pretended to give him a second chance, that reason no longer came into play. He wanted revenge, pure and simple.

Matthew made Stephen swear on his mother's grave not to breathe a word of what he was about to tell him to anyone.

Then he told him about Cambridge, about the diary, about Richard's plan. A plan that would ensure Stephen earned more money than any Sullivans associate could ever dream of making and end his financial woes for good.

Thursday, 27 July 2017

Stephen unzipped the now familiar green two-season sleeping bag, which was lying on the worn carpeted floor, and got in. He lay down flat on his back and stared up at the ceiling. This time tomorrow, if all went well, he'd be back in Celeste's bed, a rich man. He prayed she'd missed him as crazily as he'd missed her. Judging by the press conference he'd watched on TV, she had.

He'd watched her sob, her characteristically bright coffee-coloured eyes lifeless, her lively, melodious voice, dull and flat. He'd felt so guilty for making her suffer like that. But he'd told himself it was worth it. He was doing all this for them both. For their future together. Hopefully as husband and wife.

He craved her touch, her smell. He longed to trace the small of her back, the curve of her hips, taste her luscious lips. He never tired of her. Every time they made love, it was like the first time. Full of wanton desire and a sweet fascination. He knew he was batting way out of his league. She was Latin American, as hot as hell. But for some reason, she wanted him. He lived in constant fear that she'd leave him for someone as good-looking as she was.

They'd met in a bar in Leeds, where she'd been waiting tables. Until then, he hadn't believed in the lightning bolt, but he was proved wrong the moment he set eyes on Celeste. After bravely ordering two obnoxious upstarts to back off when they'd repeatedly tried to grope her shapely behind, she'd insisted on buying him a drink. No one had ever done anything like that for her before, she'd told him. Usually intimidated by beautiful women, Stephen had been imbued with a formidable courage hitherto alien to him. He'd asked her out, and she'd miraculously agreed.

That was three years ago. After he finished university, she'd agreed to move to London with him, and they were still together. Somehow, he'd managed to hide his gambling addiction from her. An addiction which had started at university, and which he knew, in his heart of hearts, stemmed from his mother's death, and which had mushroomed out of control.

Even though he hadn't gambled since starting at Sullivans, and was attending weekly meetings, he wasn't sure how much longer he could keep his debts from her. He longed to take her away from the grim apartment they shared, a good twenty-five-minute walk from London Bridge station. Was sure that if he didn't do so soon, she'd leave him. It was dirt cheap, and Celeste deserved so much more. She'd asked him recently why they couldn't get a mortgage, considering he was training at a top City law firm, and he'd made up some baloney that his student debts made him a risky bet for a lender. He'd told her that as soon as he qualified, and had a steady job, things would change, and she, being the trusting soul that she was, had believed him. But the bastard partners had put paid to that, and Matthew's proposal, although highly risky, had been too tempting to turn down. Not if he wanted to clear his debts and hold on to Celeste.

It had been torture continuing to work his butt off for the firm, but Richard had made it plain it was essential he keep in character. *He* knew they had no intention of retaining him as an associate, but the point was, *he* wasn't supposed to. Slacking off completely, coupled with an attitude problem, would only draw undue attention to himself.

Stephen wasn't particularly good in stressful situations, or at lying. Unlike Matthew, whom he trusted implicitly, who had nerves of steel, and a silver tongue when needed. The night before their ruse, he'd thrown up, blaming it on something dodgy he'd eaten, when inside, he knew it was the thought of being caught that had made his stomach flip. On Monday, he'd secretly swigged some vodka, and taken a line of coke in the basement toilets before he and Matthew had burst into the conference room. Substances that gave him the courage to see it through, and act like someone he was not. Substances that gave him the resolve to put on the gravelly voice he'd rehearsed repeatedly at the cottage, and when he was alone.

The worst part over, he had relaxed a little, but Carver had since put a spanner in the works. He thought back to yesterday morning, when Richard, who had been at Isaac's side during his call with Carver, had dropped the bombshell that their original plan was no longer viable. 'We'll need to be ready to put plan B into action as soon as we get confirmation that two of our terms have been met,' he'd said.

All three trainees' faces had dropped. 'Plan B? Two of our terms?' Charlotte had repeated, hoping Richard had made a mistake, but knowing this was highly unlikely.

'What happened to plan A?' Matthew had asked.

They'd listened with glum faces as Richard had explained what happened on the call with Carver.

'It's not ideal,' he'd acknowledged, 'but we always knew it was a possibility. That's why we planned for it, why we're prepared for it.'

'It's risky,' Matthew had said, shaking his head. 'How can we be sure Davenport will keep his word? It makes us look weak. Carver might get suspicious.' Stephen had agreed. Plan A had been so simple, so airtight. Isaac would inform Carver that the hostages could be found at a specified time in Unit H at Riverside Industrial Estate, apparently abandoned there by their kidnappers who, it would seem, having got what they wanted, had vanished off the face of the earth. He would make the call after disposing of both vans, thereby leaving no trail for Carver to pursue. Perfect. Although they knew it was prudent to have a reserve plan in place, they genuinely hadn't believed Carver would be prepared to bargain with the hostages' lives and force them to implement it. A much more flawed, dangerous alternative.

'We don't exactly have a choice,' Richard had said. 'Not if we want Davenport to make the donation to Rape Crisis.' He'd held their gaze long and hard. 'And I think we're in agreement that we do?' Three nods. As he'd expected. It was the most important term of all. It implied Davenport's guilt. 'That's what Carver's banking on. He knows this isn't just about money for us; that we want Davenport's integrity called into question, and for him to account for what he did to Mary. We don't look weak. We made sure of that by threatening to release the video. There's no way Davenport's going to risk that happening. Point is, Carver doesn't know we faked it. He's fully justified in thinking his officers might be walking into a trap. That's why he's insisting on a prominent open-air location.'

'Don't worry, Richard's right,' Charlotte had said, squeezing Matthew's shoulder. 'We just need to stay calm and it'll all be fine.'

'And Zac's OK with this?' Matthew had questioned, still unconvinced. At the time, Isaac had been updating Pamela on the change of plan.

'Yes.' Richard had nodded. 'He's fine. He's prepared and he knows what's got to be done. The main thing is we've got everything we wanted. Davenport's fate is sealed.'

This had calmed the three trainees somewhat, and now, despite still feeling a little anxious, Stephen reminded himself how close they were to pulling it off, and that he and Celeste could look forward to spending the rest of their lives together in blissful happiness. If she asked how he'd found the money for a deposit, he'd say it was an unexpected inheritance from a dead relative, or some such. She wasn't to know, plus, stranger things happened every day. He'd tell the same to the police if it ever came to that. Although, God willing, it wouldn't.

Stephen turned over on his right side, nervous and excited about the day that lay ahead. He closed his eyes, and dreamt of Celeste, and the new life awaiting them.

Chapter Fourteen

Friday, 9 p.m. Maddy sat in the back of Carver's car, nerves prickling through her like little electric shocks. Carver drove while Drake rode shotgun. Two more police cars and an ambulance tailed them on their way to the meeting point, Leyton Industrial Village. A well-configured industrial estate of 135,000 square feet comprising a wide selection of industrial units and located seven and a half miles north-east of central London. Half an hour's drive on a good day, considerably longer in heavy traffic. One side of it backed onto a vast playing field and woodland, another onto a railway line.

They'd received the call less than an hour ago. A smart move, as was the decision to release the hostages at night. No chance for Carver to monitor the estate until the last minute. They'd also made a further request – that the estate's CCTV be switched off from 9.10 p.m. for an hour – accompanied by a stern warning that the repercussions would be nasty if their instructions weren't followed to the letter.

Maddy had slept badly, despite telling herself there was no reason for the kidnappers to backtrack on their word, provided all their demands were met. Which, according to Carver, two of them had been, that afternoon. Six million pounds had been wired to Pellington

Corporation's account with Ansbacher (Bahamas) Limited, the oldest private bank in the Bahamas. Pellingtons was no doubt a shell company set up by the kidnappers to act as a front for the money and conceal their identities. Maddy knew of local Bahamian law firms that would readily, for a hefty fee, set up secret bank accounts for international clients through the mechanism of a shell Bahamian international business company. All the client had to do was submit the paperwork by email – usually a one-page form attaching a photocopied passport photo and driver's licence – and the lawyers would take care of the rest. Within forty-eight hours, the lawyers would then be able to open a bank account in the name of the newly formed company. There was no requirement to file a public notice of who the company's officers and directors were, and it was perfectly acceptable for the law firm's address to serve as its local office. Carver had told her he wasn't about to dig any deeper until the hostages were home and dry. Besides, he suspected he'd have to get a court order to get anything out of the bank, or the law firm used. He'd seen what the kidnappers were capable of, and they'd made it clear on the phone he wasn't to snoop around. It wasn't worth risking their lives for the sake of another day or two.

Even so, a lingering doubt tugged at Maddy's insides. What if they changed their minds? Had something else up their sleeves? What if it was all a trick? She told herself to get a grip, and stop being so pessimistic, particularly as Carver had assured her the kidnappers weren't likely to do anything stupid if they wanted their last term met. She was dying to know what it was, at the same time surprised that Carver had been able to negotiate like this. It seemed a highly unusual scenario, but she had refrained from probing any further on the basis that she might be endangering the hostages' lives in doing so. Charlotte, Matthew, Stephen and Richard were counting on her.

She pictured Charlotte's battered face, and it gave her the strength to see it through.

Carver caught Maddy's eye in the mirror, noted the pensive look on her face, indicative of the way he felt inside. He wished it wasn't her they wanted. Anyone but her. 'Are you sure you're OK with this?' he asked.

'Certain,' she said with a half-smile. 'Besides, what choice do I have?'

'There's always a choice.'

'Tell that to Mrs Barker and those poor fathers. Imagine if it were Daniel.'

Carver couldn't. The thought of any harm coming to his boy terrified him. Every day he lived in fear of something bad happening to him. Because he, more than most, knew what a dangerous world it was out there. And he was the one who helped put away the scum who made it so.

'Point taken.'

'Besides, I'm wearing this vest' – she patted her chest – 'and you'll be two hundred feet away. They've got nothing to gain from hurting me.'

All logical points. But emotion was stronger than reason. And right now, Carver's emotions were getting the better of his usual common-sense approach, notwithstanding the deal he'd struck with the kidnappers.

Just five minutes away. Maddy reached inside her handbag and pulled out her phone. She'd already read the article once, but she couldn't help taking another look at the breaking news headline on *The Lawyer*'s website. '*City shocked by sudden resignation of Nigel Davenport following hostage crisis.*'

The article quoted Davenport's resignation for 'personal reasons' but not what those 'personal reasons' entailed. Even so, it was rife with speculation. Had the pressure of the last few days simply got to him? Perhaps he'd had a nervous breakdown. Perhaps he was ill? Perhaps he and the firm were hiding something? Something so big, so ugly, he'd been forced to resign?

Maddy was certain there was more to it than money. She'd seen the look on Davenport's face, while Carver's silence on the matter had been telling. There was something terrible in Davenport's past; something the kidnappers knew; something that had enabled them to use the hostages as bait to get what they wanted.

She cranked her neck and looked out through the back window. Marianne Barker, Charles Dempsey, Frank Gerard, Mike Baines and Celeste, all following in the other cars. She'd spoken to them briefly, before they'd set off. They'd been so grateful, and she'd found their appreciation touching.

Almost there. Maddy's pulse accelerated, memories of two and a half years ago, when she'd been held hostage, flooding back to her. She would have died, had it not been for Carver, who'd found her in the nick of time. He'd had her back then, and as she caught his glance in the mirror, she felt certain he'd have her back today.

She'd convinced herself that her feelings for Carver had been a fleeting by-product of *that* case. But seeing him again these past few days, in her heart she knew otherwise. No one since had made her feel that way. The attraction was still there, as strong as ever. And she didn't know if she had the strength to fight it.

Focus, focus, she told herself. She tried to play out the next half hour in her mind. The plan sounded simple enough. They'd stop two hundred feet clear of Unit 25, turn off their headlights, then wait for the van to arrive. Once the van had parked up, she'd get out of the car and, after five minutes, walk up to it, alone. The hostages would be released through the rear doors, and they'd then walk round to the front, where Maddy would be waiting. There would be no talking, no hugs, no contact whatsoever until all five had walked the two hundred feet back to Carver. At which point the van would take off.

But what then? Surely, the kidnappers expected to be followed? Surely, they had some fail-safe plan? Granted, they'd given themselves the best chance of escape by making the drop at night, and requesting that the CCTV be switched off, but how could they be certain the police wouldn't be waiting for them at the exit gates once the hostages were handed over? Maddy couldn't help shuddering at the thought of what the kidnappers might have planned. Dynamite strapped to one of the hostages being one of the nasty images running through her mind.

Finally, Carver turned onto Argall Avenue, and after checking in with security and the site manager, both of whom had been forewarned, they entered the dark, deserted industrial estate. All tenants, who usually had twenty-four-hour access, had been ordered to clear out.

Having asked Drake to pull up a map of the estate en route to their destination, Carver already knew it backed onto an expansive playing field. He had men currently looking into the identity of the unit's tenant, although he suspected the kidnappers had anticipated this move, and weren't about to hand him the information on a plate.

Carver made sure he parked no less than two hundred feet away from Unit 25, then turned off his ignition and lights. The other two cars and the ambulance, having parked up beside him, did the same. Carver looked back at Maddy. He knew she was scared, but as usual, she was trying not to show it. He gave her one of his reassuring smiles, then checked his watch. Any minute now. 'Ready?' he asked.

Maddy's mouth was as dry as sand. She took a sip from the bottle of Evian clutched in her left hand, then nodded. 'As ready as I'll ever be.'

'There it is, sir,' Drake said. A white VW Transporter suddenly appeared. It parked directly in front of Unit 25 so that its bonnet faced Carver's head-on, its rear backed up against the unit's roller shutters which Carver had previously noticed were closed. There was no sign of a number plate, and it was impossible to make out the driver in the dark. A few seconds passed, then Carver thought he detected movement. Perhaps the driver moving to the back of the van. He wondered what they'd done with the blue Ford Transit van in which they'd made their getaway. *Perhaps torched it somewhere?*

Carver set a timer on his watch so that he'd know when five minutes was up, then quickly got out and opened Maddy's door. She'd changed out of her work clothes and heels into joggers, a light baggy jumper (concealing the bullet proof vest) and trainers before leaving the office. She wanted to be able to run if she needed to.

Just then, Charles Dempsey came up to her and extended his hand. She shook it. 'Thank you, once again,' he said.

'It's nothing,' she said. 'Nothing compared to what poor Charlotte's been through.'

She'd met Dempsey several times before, when he'd still been a client. She didn't like him much. He always seemed to stare at her a little too intensely. There was something oily about him, and she never felt entirely at ease in his company.

'Still, it's a brave thing to do.'

'Charlotte's a lovely girl. I hope you realise how lucky you are?'

'Yes, it's taken these past few days to make me realise that.' Dempsey sighed. 'I've not been there for Charlotte over the years as much as I could have been. It was her mother, you see. She was Charlotte's and Isaac's rock. She held us together.'

Maddy saw the guilt in his eyes. His wife's suicide had to have been hard on him. But she wondered what had driven Diana Dempsey to it. Had he been an inattentive husband as well as a neglectful father? Had her death brought him and Charlotte closer together, or driven them further apart? Charlotte certainly never talked about him.

'It's time.' Carver stirred Maddy from her thoughts.

She turned to him, held his gaze and took a deep breath. 'OK, let's do this.'

The weather had broken that morning. After a prolonged spell of baking hot conditions, the sky had been overcast all day, the temperature ten degrees cooler. And now that night had fallen, it felt cooler still. A faint spit of rain permeated the air as Maddy walked past Marianne, Mike, Celeste and Frank.

They all gave Maddy grateful nods of appreciation, faint smiles of encouragement. It willed her to keep walking. But she couldn't help looking back as she did so, catching Carver's steady gaze, his eyes not leaving her for a second. Then she faced forward again, kept going, slow and steady, until she was there. She stopped in front of the bonnet. The driver's seat was empty, no indication of movement. All that could be heard was the faint sound of traffic, the odd rumble of a distant plane. The situation was disquieting enough, but it was that much more alarming in the dark of night. The onlookers stood like statues, hardly able to breathe, waiting, praying, for the hostages to emerge.

Two, three minutes passed, and still nothing. Maddy jigged from side to side, her hands plunged deep in her pockets, as she recalled her grandmother's words on the phone that morning.

'Be careful, my darling girl,' she'd said. 'Don't do anything stupid. Do exactly as you're told and come home safe.'

More time passed. Carver was looking fidgety, and Maddy was starting to wonder whether there was, in fact, anyone in the van. But then suddenly, she heard movement, a door being unlocked. This was it. Her heart raced, adrenaline pinballing through her. She was tempted to go round the back. But her instructions had been clear. On no account was she to move from that spot. She caught Carver's eye and gave him a subtle nod. He immediately stood to attention, Drake at his side. Maddy strained her ear, trying to make out voices, but heard none. Just movement. Footsteps shuffling closer, until their owners appeared. One by one. First Stephen, then Matthew, then Charlotte, and finally Richard.

They were like zombies. Still wearing Monday's clothes. Fear and bewilderment haunted their eyes, like small lost children. Maddy tried not to react as she took in Charlotte's and Matthew's bruised faces. But worst off was Barker. Despite the darkness, she could tell he'd lost more weight, hardly surprising given his condition, and the fact that he wouldn't have had any medication on him. He managed a half-smile for Maddy as he dragged his feet feebly towards her. She made eye contact with all four and pressed her finger to her lips as if to confirm that no one should speak. There was no obvious sign that any of them was strapped up with explosives, but that didn't mean it wasn't concealed somewhere more obscure. Maddy cocked her head in the direction of Carver and the anxiously awaiting crowd, indicating to the hostages that they should start heading that way. They all nodded, walking alongside Maddy, every second feeling like hours, always the worry that it was a trap, that something nasty was about to happen.

But it didn't. They made it, at which point Carver signalled to Drake to alert Davenport to the fact. He didn't doubt the kidnappers would follow through with their threat to upload the video if

Davenport failed to make the donation immediately. Frank Gerard was the first to reach out and embrace his son, tears of joy and relief hurtling down his cheeks as Matthew allowed himself to be scooped up like a child who'd lost, then found, his parent. Stephen and Celeste did the same, after he and his father shared a much stiffer embrace, while Marianne clung to her brittle husband like she'd never let him out of her sight again. 'You stupid man,' she sobbed into his chest. 'Why didn't you tell me, stupid, stupid man?' Now he was crying, not questioning how she knew, but burying his bald head in her bosom, weeping uncontrollably.

But like Stephen and Mike, it was a different kind of reunion for Charlotte and Charles Dempsey. Although Maddy saw tears in Charles's eyes as he went up to his daughter and attempted to hug her, Charlotte remained dry-eyed, as rigid, and as unresponsive, as stone. It saddened Maddy, and it made her more certain that Charlotte blamed her father for her mother's suicide.

She continued to watch them as Charlotte leant in closer and whispered something into her father's ear. Was she imagining it, or did he flinch? He slowly broke away from his daughter, looking at her with a puzzled expression. What had she said to make him look so—

Maddy didn't have time to finish her thought, her ears ringing from the massive blast that had interrupted them, her lungs suddenly clogged with smoke and dust. She had instinctively ducked down behind Carver's car, Carver quickly at her side, her heart beating double time, shouts, screams, chaos all around her. Then, after a moment or two, they both slowly got up, straining their eyes to see what had caused it.

The van was a ball of fire. The kidnappers had only gone and blown themselves up.

Chapter Fifteen

After the explosion, things turned crazy. Drake wasted no time in calling the fire brigade, who were quick to fan the flames, a team of paramedics on their tail, and not long after, the press, who'd been banned from the drop, but had quickly got wind of the unexpected turn of events. There'd been a further surprise, however. Another vehicle concealed behind the steel shutters of Unit 25 – it turned out, the shutters hadn't been completely closed at the time of the explosion, a gap of around three feet separating them from the ground – had been blown to pieces; most probably, the blue Ford Transit van the kidnappers had made off in on Monday. It remained to be seen whether anyone had been inside the unit when the vehicle exploded, but it did indicate to Carver that at least one of the kidnappers had got out of the white van and opened the shutters at some point. But why? To detonate the van inside, to run, or both? If so, did he alone escape, having betrayed his accomplices, or did they all make it out? Alternatively, had the driver been flying solo? It was mere conjecture at this stage. For now, he kept his theories to himself.

The hostages were taken to nearby Whipps Cross Hospital, their loved ones following on. Carver told Maddy he'd question the hostages tomorrow. First and foremost, they needed medical attention and a good night's rest. For now, having been quick to get forensics on the scene, his priority was to stay behind and assess the damage. Although it was dark, they could work through the night under artificial light, and make a preliminary assessment. It was a misconception that fire proved lethal when it came to identifying bodies and retrieving DNA, especially if the blaze was put out quickly, as it had been in this case. Unless a body was reduced to ash, DNA identification could still be made from bones and teeth. Although it was clear that some form of high explosive was used to detonate the van, assuming some or all of the kidnappers had been inside it when it blew, there was every chance of making identification through bits of anatomy which would have been sent flying. Working through the debris would, of course, take time, but on the plus side, being a fairly contained area, dotted with high rise buildings, the search parameters would hopefully be less extensive than they would have been had the explosion occurred in a large flat open space. Even so, Carver had men combing the wider area, the railway, roads and playing fields encircling the estate, for anything of interest.

It was now 11 p.m. Maddy sat sipping coffee in the hospital waiting room. She was physically fine, mentally a little shaken, but didn't feel able to go home until she'd spoken to Charlotte. She was her trainee, and she owed her that.

Charlotte was currently being treated for her injuries, but a nurse had informed Maddy that she'd be able to see her soon. After being checked over, a police car had shuttled Richard and Marianne to the Royal Marsden, where his doctor was waiting. He'd looked so weak, Maddy was doubtful he'd last another month, let alone six. She hoped he'd see sense and bring his retirement forward. See out his final days at home with Marianne and their children.

Just then, Charles Dempsey appeared, a Styrofoam cup of tea in his hand. He sat next to Maddy. 'How are you holding up?' he asked. He looked deadbeat.

'OK. A little in shock. I think it was the last thing any of us expected.'

'That's for sure.' Dempsey gave a heavy sigh. Inside, he felt an overwhelming relief that the kidnappers were dead. Hopefully, his shameful secret had died with them.

'How's Charlotte? I thought I'd hang around to make sure she's OK once the doctors are done examining her.'

'That's very kind of you. I'm sure she'd appreciate that. You're the only one at Sullivans she seems to like.'

Maddy hesitated for a second, then couldn't resist saying what was on her mind. She phrased her question carefully, tried to keep her tone light. 'It must have felt wonderful to hug your daughter again. If you don't mind me asking, what did Charlotte say to you? I couldn't help notice her whisper something in your ear.'

For a moment, Dempsey said nothing, and Maddy feared she might have irritated him. But then he answered, 'She said that I am to blame for all of this.'

'Why would she say something like that?'

Dempsey stalled again. Finally, he said, 'I'm as flummoxed as you, Ms Kramer. I really don't have the foggiest what she was on about. I think she was just a bit disorientated.'

He avoided Maddy's gaze as he said this, and she was sure he was lying. Just as Davenport had lied to her in the lift. They were both hiding something, but what?

'Hey there, how are you feeling?'

166

Maddy popped her head around the door of the examination room. Charlotte had changed into the top and jeans her father had brought for her and was stuffing her soiled work clothes into a rucksack. She looked up with a start.

'Sorry, I didn't mean to make you jump,' Maddy apologised. 'I just wanted to check you're OK?'

Charlotte smiled. 'I'm fine, thanks. Feeling better now the doctors have given me something for the pain.' She touched the side of her face. 'When I lie down, it hurts.'

'I'm sure,' Maddy said soothingly as she came closer. She put her hand on her trainee's shoulder. 'I can't even begin to imagine what you've been through. Tell me, did they beat you solely to make a point? Or did you try and escape?'

'They beat me because they're evil, and they could. But more to make a point, as you said.'

'To anyone in particular?'

'Yes. Nigel Davenport.'

'Charlotte, do you know why they wanted Nigel to resign?'

'No, but the leader said he needed to be punished for something terrible he'd done in the past, at Cambridge. When Richard demanded to know what it was, he wouldn't say.'

'The leader? How many of them were there?'

'Five in total. The two who took me and Richard, and another two who took Stephen and Matthew. There was also a driver, but he wore a mask and we never saw him again after he dumped us at the hideout.'

'Do you have any idea where you were held?'

'Not really.' Charlotte shook her head. 'It was some warehouse, I'm guessing in the back of beyond. It must have been at least ten miles away, because it felt like we were driving for some time. Although

I suppose we could have been driving in circles. We made a quick stop five or ten minutes into the journey, then stopped again roughly halfway through, when they made us get out, before bundling us into another vehicle. Then we took off again. They blindfolded us all the way there, and before we left this evening.'

'Richard was at Cambridge with Nigel. You know that, right?'

Charlotte's eyes widened. 'You're kidding me? No, honestly, I didn't. Richard kept that quiet.'

'It's true. Are you sure he had no idea what Nigel might have done to tick these men off?'

'He claimed not to.' She paused, then said, 'I have my doubts about that, though.'

'Why?'

'Because on the first night, one of the men came and took Richard away. He must have been gone about twenty minutes or so. Clearly, it was important enough for them to want to speak to him in private.'

'Did you ask Richard what they wanted when he came back?'

'Yes. But he said he couldn't tell us. Not if we wanted to stay alive.' She was silent for a while, as if reflecting on her suffering, then added, 'Whatever Nigel did, it was obviously bad enough to have led us to this.'

'Whoever this leader was, he should have sorted it out face to face with Nigel.'

'Perhaps he already tried that, and Nigel wouldn't listen? Or perhaps he wanted to make Nigel suffer?'

'Perhaps.' Maddy paused, then said, 'So I'm guessing you never got a glimpse of their faces?'

'No, they wore balaclavas at all times. Matthew went crazy on day two. Told the bastards to show their faces.'

'And that's when they beat him?'

168

'Yes.' She started sobbing. 'I was so frightened, Maddy, I really didn't think I was going to make it out alive.'

'There, there,' Maddy said. 'You did, and you're here, thank God.'

Charlotte hesitated, then said, 'Do you think they were religious fanatics, or maybe part of a cult? I mean, why blow themselves up after getting what they wanted?'

'It's possible, Charlotte, but we may never find out now. Of course, it's also possible the van was sabotaged. Tell me, how did Richard manage?'

'How do you mean?'

'He's sick. You must have realised that? Being together, twenty-four seven.'

Charlotte's face grew sad. 'Yes, he told us on the first night. Although we guessed something was up when the leader came in and gave him pain medication.'

'He did?'

'Yes. It was strange. They beat me and Matthew but gave Richard pain relief.' She sighed, then said, 'His illness came as such a shock. We just presumed his appearance was down to a combination of working too hard and getting older.'

'We all did,' Maddy sighed. 'Even his poor wife.'

'She didn't know?' Charlotte gasped.

'No, he kept it from her all this time.'

'Unbelievable.'

'Listen, Charlotte, you don't have to answer this, but I spoke to your father earlier and he mentioned that you blame him for what happened. Can I ask why?'

Charlotte's shoulders tensed. Then she sighed. 'Well, I just reckon they picked on me because of who my father is: a very rich ex-client of the firm's, who also happened to go to Cambridge with Nigel.'

'That makes sense, I guess. Still, you mustn't be too harsh on him. I'm sure he's been through hell these last few days.'

'Maybe,' Charlotte said. 'But my dad's not the sentimental type. He doesn't do tactile. That was my mum's job, and she did it brilliantly.' A tear appeared, and she wiped it away.

'You must miss her terribly?'

'I do, every second of every day.' Charlotte grabbed a tissue from a box resting on a table by the bed. 'But that's life, isn't it? It stinks sometimes. Some people get all the luck, while others get one bad break after another.'

'At least you have good times to look back on and treasure. I only wish I'd had the chance to spend more time with my mother and father.'

Charlotte suddenly looked embarrassed. 'Oh, gosh, I'm sorry, Maddy, that was incredibly insensitive of me.'

'Don't be silly. It was nearly twenty years ago. I miss them every day, but time numbs the pain.'

'Does it? My pain still feels so raw. That's why I feel I can relate to you, Maddy. You get me. You know what it's like to lose someone you love.'

Maddy gave a faint smile, then said, 'You need to take as much time as you feel you need before coming back to work. Understood?'

Charlotte slumped down on the bed. 'I don't know if I can face going back there. As it is, I'm going to suffer nightmares about this for some time. But being in that building all day, every day, will only make things worse.'

'I get where you're coming from.' Maddy sat down next to Charlotte. 'That's how I felt after Paul's arrest. It took me some time to get my head together. But I was already qualified. I could afford to take time off, look elsewhere, but you need to finish your training.'

'Do I?' came the quick response, coupled with a hard look. Maddy was taken aback. She saw a resilience in Charlotte's eyes she'd never seen before.

'Yes, I mean – don't you want to qualify?'

'I know I'm not being kept on, Maddy. I'm not cut out for law, and it's obvious all the partners think I'm a waste of space.'

'That's not true,' Maddy said half-heartedly.

Charlotte gave a sardonic smile. 'You're a good person, Maddy, one of the better ones. You don't have to soften the blow for me. I'm tougher than you think.'

Maddy didn't doubt it for a second. As the saying went, what doesn't kill you makes you stronger. It made her think. Had the last few days made Charlotte stronger? 'Yes, I can see that,' she said, smiling. Just then, there was a light rap on the door. It was Matthew and his father.

'Hello. Thought I'd drop by to see how you're doing? I've just been discharged.'

'Better thanks.' Charlotte smiled. 'How about you?'

'Not too bad. The doctor I saw thinks these wounds will heal in no time.'

Matthew was still handsome, despite his injuries. Maddy wasn't surprised the female staff at Sullivans lusted after him. Probably the best-looking guy at the firm. Tall, thick dark hair, dreamy rich brown eyes, a sexy smile, a lean physique. What wasn't there to like? But he was somehow too perfect for her. 'Matthew, I'm so sorry for all you've been through.' She turned to Frank. 'And you, of course, Mr Gerard. You must have been through hell as well.' Frank seemed like a nice man. Genuine to the core, who loved his son unreservedly.

He patted his son's shoulder. 'He's all I have left. I can't imagine life without him, and I'm grateful to the man upstairs for bringing him

171

home safe.' Father and son shared an affectionate look, so different to Charlotte and Charles, then Matthew turned to Maddy. 'Thanks for coming today. After you got blasted for sticking your neck out in that conference room, I wouldn't have blamed you for steering clear.'

Maddy creased her brow. 'How did you know I got blasted?' She glanced at Charlotte, who appeared frozen to the spot, her eyes locked on Matthew. He coughed lightly, then explained, 'Charlotte and Richard told us what went on in there. When we were alone.'

That makes sense, Maddy told herself. 'I see. So, you weren't gagged the whole time?'

'No,' Charlotte said. 'That was all for the camera. We were untied most of the time. They locked us in a room with no windows, let us out just to use the loo, and fed us bread and water three times a day.'

'We're all very grateful to you,' Matthew repeated.

'That we are,' Frank echoed.

Maddy was dying to ask Matthew how he and Stephen got taken, but she decided against it. He and his father were on their way home, and in any case, Carver would find out tomorrow.

'Well, I'd better get going. You guys get a good night's sleep, and I'll see you both soon, I hope.' Her eyes lingered on Charlotte.

'Thanks, Maddy, I'll think over what you said.'

In reception, Maddy spotted Stephen and Celeste heading for the exit. She guessed his father had already left. 'Stephen,' she called out. They turned around in surprise as she came rushing up.

'How are you? I've just been with Charlotte.'

'I'm fine. I'm the fortunate one.' Stephen had his arm around Celeste's waist. He pulled her closer as he said this. 'Poor Richard really suffered. I can't help feeling guilty, coming away physically unscathed. Unlike him and the others.'

'Thank God you're unhurt,' Celeste sighed. 'You can't blame yourself for that.'

'Celeste's right.' Maddy smiled. She hesitated, then asked, 'Was there any particular reason they left you alone?'

Stephen shook his head. 'No, I just got lucky, I guess. I mean, who knows, if Davenport hadn't agreed to the terms, they might have moved on to me? I'm sure that's why they beat Matthew up. To put more pressure on Davenport.'

Charlotte had said they beat Matthew after he demanded to see their faces. Why hadn't Stephen mentioned that? It was rather a big point to overlook, but it was late and she didn't want to press the issue further.

Maddy took in Stephen's appearance. He looked well. Better than she'd expected. He'd always been on the chubby side, but he didn't look like he'd lost half a pound surviving on bread and water for four days. His cheeks had a healthy glow to them, and his eyes were bright and animated. Maybe he wasn't the worrying sort? Maybe he'd taken it in his stride, like some people are able to do in tough situations. Then again, this was contrary to what she'd heard. That Stephen was prone to stress.

'Shall we go, baby?' Celeste asked. 'You need your rest for tomorrow.'

'Sure, hon. I expect the police will want to ask a lot of questions, although now those psychos have blown themselves to kingdom come, I'm not sure there's much point.'

'I disagree,' Maddy said. 'There's always a point. Criminals out there need a deterrent; they need to know they can't get away with committing unforgiveable crimes.'

Stephen lowered his eyes. 'True.'

'Besides, DCI Carver said there's a very good chance identification can be made from the wreckage.'

Stephen looked up. 'He did?'

'Yes. In any case, aren't you curious? Surely you're burning to know who held you hostage for four days? Who beat your friends and let a terminally ill man suffer?'

Stephen lowered his eyes to the floor again, then glanced up sheepishly. 'Course I do, I didn't mean to sound flippant.'

Celeste gave Maddy an angry glare. 'He's tired. He just needs a good night's sleep. Come on.' She grabbed Stephen's hand and frogmarched him out through the revolving doors.

As she watched them disappear, Maddy was left in no doubt as to who wore the trousers in that relationship.

'So that's it? Thirty years of marriage and you're throwing me out like yesterday's news?'

Davenport stared at the two suitcases standing upright in the hallway. Packed by Pamela, and filled with some of his clothes, shoes and toiletries.

'I'll send the rest on once you give me an address,' she said dispassionately.

He couldn't believe what was happening to him. In the space of five days, his career and his marriage were in ruins, his bank balance had taken a serious hit (he'd been forced to sell his holiday home in Majorca), and his reputation had been permanently tarnished. Mary Jacobs was dead, so she couldn't be behind it. And now it seemed they may never know the truth, the cocksuckers having blown themselves to smithereens.

It didn't make sense. They'd got everything they'd asked for. Why, then, had they opted not to hang around and enjoy the fruits of their victory? Including his own fall from grace. It was as if it had all been for nothing.

'Don't you dare play the hard-done-by card with me, Nigel,' Pamela went on. 'I've devoted the best years of my life to you. Cooking, cleaning, bringing up our children, while you cheated on me left, right and centre with fucking whores.' Davenport winced. His wife was not a swearer. The worst he'd ever heard her say was 'bloody'. He was seeing a whole new side to her. A side he'd brought out. 'Even a long-term mistress would have been better. But to think that you've been visiting brothels, sleeping with women young enough to be your own granddaughter, disgusts me to my very core. You deserve everything that's come to you. But most of all, you deserve to rot in hell for raping that young woman.'

Davenport's chest felt tight. If his wife didn't believe him, what chance did he have with the police? Still, surely it was unlikely they'd start investigating something that allegedly happened over thirty years ago? It was ancient history. Mary was dead, Stewart had his back, as did Charles, and there was no proof.

He knew what he'd do. He'd lie low for a while, and once the dust had settled, maybe try for a partner position elsewhere, or offer his services on a consultancy basis. The kidnappers were dead, so his secret had safely died with them. It was just a matter of biding his time, and letting the scandal blow over.

'Well, if that's how you feel, Pam, then so be it.' He picked up his cases and left, not seeing the broad grin that had spread across his wife's face.

She picked up the phone and dialled a long-distance number. 'Hi, just to let you know, I'm finally rid of him. You can go ahead and move the money.'

Chapter Sixteen

Carver entered his flat off Hoxton Square, tossed his keys on the hall table and, without turning on any lights, headed straight for his bedroom and collapsed on the bed. He'd lived there since buying the place with his then new wife, Rachel. That was nearly thirteen years ago. Since then, they'd had a child, divorced, and Rachel had married Carl. Although at first the split had been acrimonious, and Carver had feared being 'replaced' by Carl, both he and Rachel had softened, and they were now on civil terms.

Things could have been worse. Carl could have been a gambler, a druggie, an alcoholic, a child abuser. But he was none of these. Carl was a decent guy, a little boring maybe – after all, he was an accountant – but boring was better than unhinged and unreliable. Unreliable was what Rachel had called Carver when the rows had grown more heated and she was on the verge of leaving. His job ensured he could never guarantee being there for that school play, that Saturday morning footie practice, that all-important parents' evening. Some women could live like that. But Rachel couldn't. She needed stability, and she wasn't strong enough to bring up a child virtually alone. But alone is what she'd felt most of the time being married to Carver. He'd been angry at first, but he'd since come to understand and respect her reasons. And besides, he saw Daniel, who worshipped his biological father, regularly. The eight-and-a-half-year-old had a wise head on his young shoulders and he had assured his dad umpteen times that, although he liked Carl very much, he'd only ever have one dad, and that was him. Carver went to sleep every night comforted by this, but also by the fact that his only child lived in a safe, loving environment.

After spending some time at the crime scene, Carver and Drake had headed back to the station for a team briefing. The smoke had eventually cleared, enabling forensics to work more productively. Although it had yet to be confirmed, it was suspected that some form of high explosive was used, which, once detonated, blew the petrol tank, thereby causing the fire. As the van exploded upwards and outwards, various bits of debris had been flung in all directions, hitting the ground, surrounding buildings, and such like. Although it would take time to trawl through the wreckage, Carver's Crime Scene Manager, Jonas Mead, had already made an interesting observation: one that stuck in Carver's mind as he'd sat down to brief his team, and which continued to do so as he lay on his bed staring into the darkness. In an explosion such as this, with four, possibly five bodies thought to have been in the blast – either a suicide mission or sabotage was Carver's immediate thought when it first happened – one would have expected to see some evidence of human life, given the relatively small size of the vehicle and the contained area in which it exploded. A body part – for example, a large bone, the femur being a prime example, and one that was often found intact in cases like these. But so far, they'd found nothing, and the position hadn't changed twenty minutes ago when he'd called Mead on his way home. That being so, was there something to his theory that the kidnappers had made their escape through the unit and out onto the playing field during the ensuing chaos? Or maybe only the driver had been at the drop? Much easier for one man to escape unseen, than five.

In truth, Carver knew it was far too early to make assumptions, and still possible that proof of life would be found. All he could do was speculate at this stage. Hopefully, he'd know more tomorrow.

For now, too tired to bother getting undressed or brush his teeth, Carver shut his eyes and prayed for sleep to come quickly. Acutely aware of his stress levels, and not wanting a case like this to cause him to lean on booze as a crutch as it had done in the past, he planned on hitting the gym first thing tomorrow in order to clear his mind and set himself up for what he was certain, with four hostages to question, would be a taxing day ahead.

The gym was muggy, the air soiled by sweat and pungent body odour, generated by men boasting impressively toned physiques. Groaning like women in childbirth as they pumped iron, jumped rope, crunched their six-packs until their stomachs were tight and knotted, and the sweat dripped off them in puddles. Maddy let her eyes wander around the room until she spotted him. At the far end, throwing punches. At first, she didn't venture too close. Just stood there for a few seconds, watching him. Until now, she'd only ever seen him in a suit. He didn't appear to have an ounce of fat on him. His Nike top clung to his chest and abdomen with perspiration, the muscles in his strong, lean calves flexing as he danced around the bag.

Maddy hadn't slept well again. Although she'd felt physically shattered, she'd been too wired to switch off. Unable to lie in bed a second longer, she'd slipped out of her flat a little after 5.30 a.m. – Cara still dead to the world – bringing forward her usual Saturday morning swim at Putney leisure centre by an hour.

Swimming was Maddy's meditation. Her way of ridding her mind of the stress and clutter (which was normally work-related) that built up in it every week. But work had taken a back seat this week. A crazy week that hadn't, as far as she was concerned, resolved itself satisfactorily. Yes, it was fantastic that they'd got the hostages back safe and sound, but it bugged the hell out of her that their abductors' identities remained a mystery. Unless, as Charlotte had speculated, they were members of a fanatical cult on some kind of suicide mission, it didn't make sense for them to blow themselves up. And what the hell was going to happen to the six million they'd effectively stolen from Sullivans? Was it just going to sit in an offshore account forever?

It made her wonder whether one of the kidnappers was still out there. And, if so, had that someone betrayed his team, and taken the money for himself?

Maddy knew Carver was a creature of habit. Working together on the Scribe murders, he'd told her that boxing was his meditation. She took a chance he hadn't changed gyms and was relieved to discover her hunch was right. She could scarcely believe she'd trekked fifty minutes across town to Old Street. But the impulse had been too great. She watched him pause, take a swig from his water bottle, then glance her way. They instantly locked eyes. Looking surprised, he walked over to her, and she immediately felt self-conscious, her heart thumping hard inside her chest.

'Hello, what brings you here?' His eyes twinkled as he asked the question. It was more than just a superficial look. It felt like he was taking in every detail of her, and it sent goosebumps crawling all over her. He was standing so close, she could smell him: a combination of his natural scent and aftershave. She edged back a little, tried to compose herself.

'Have you questioned any of the hostages yet?'

Stupid question, given the hour.

Carver raised an eyebrow and glanced at his watch. 'No, it's not even 8 a.m. Doing that at twelve. Why? Have you?' His eyes drilled through her, amused rather than hostile. Maddy felt her face flush.

'No, I mean, not really,' she replied. She recounted her conversations with Charlotte, Matthew and Stephen at the hospital. And her exchange with Charles Dempsey. Including what Charlotte had whispered to him.

'There's clearly no love lost between her and her father,' Carver said.

'No. Like Stephen and his father, theirs didn't appear to be an overly emotional reunion.'

'The mother died by suicide, right?'

'Yes, not long before Charlotte started at the firm. They were very close, and I can tell she misses her terribly.' She paused, then said, 'It's strange, don't you think, that both Charlotte and Matthew lost their mothers around that time, and both were taken hostage? I mean, do you think the kidnappers knew both mums had killed themselves?'

'What difference would it have made if they did? What purpose would it serve?' Carver kept his questions general, but he was tempted to tell Maddy about Matthew's mother and the rape allegation. In his mind, he knew she was onto something. They must have known that Mary was Matthew's mother. It was too coincidental. But if all this had been about getting revenge for Mary, why punish her son? That made no sense at all. And he was sure Davenport hadn't known Matthew was Mary's boy until he told him.

'I don't know.' Maddy shrugged. 'Maybe to pull on the heartstrings a bit more? Or maybe it goes deeper than that?'

'Dempsey's a stinking rich ex-client, and a good friend of Davenport's. Maybe they thought taking Charlotte would give them more leverage. As for Matthew, money doesn't come into play as far as his family's concerned. I understand his father's a retired police officer, and I can assure you, we're not loaded.' He dipped his eyes, and they shared a smile.

Carver looked around. Thought, *What the hell?* 'But listen, you're right, there is more to it than that. Have you had breakfast?'

Maddy shook her head.

'I make a mean eggs Benedict if you can overlook the state of my living room.'

It was an invitation she hadn't expected, and one that sent all sorts of questions running through her mind. She told herself not to be dramatic. It was only breakfast. They'd discuss the case, and then she'd leave. Perfectly innocent.

'Sure, I'm starving.'

'Sorry again about the mess,' Carver apologised as he opened his front door.

He ushered Maddy through the small hallway, and into the living room. It was a bit of a tip as he'd forewarned. Several editions of *Men's Health* were strewn across the glass-topped coffee table, also stained with coffee cup marks, a 'Best Dad' mug half-filled with cold black coffee, as well as a ceramic bowl containing the remnants of dinner from who knows when. There was one black leather three-seater sofa, as well as a tired-looking armchair, Carver's pullover draped across the back of it. In one corner of the room she saw a bookshelf stacked with various historical fiction novels and West Ham United annuals, and in the other, a small dining table with four chairs squeezed around it. The place also felt like it could do with a dust, and Maddy fought to suppress a giggle as she watched Carver make a vain attempt to tidy up, flinging the magazines under the table and darting to the kitchen with the mug and bowl.

'You like historical novels?'

'I do,' Carver replied, casting his eyes over the bookshelf. 'The past, particularly ancient Rome, fascinates me. I loved history at school, and I would have liked to have studied it, but my parents were working class and I couldn't afford to go to university. So I'm catching up now. Not that I get a lot of time to read mind you, between work, boxing and seeing my son.'

'How is Daniel?'

Maddy noticed Carver's eyes light up at the mere mention of his son's name.

'He's good. He'll be nine in October. Bright lad. Brighter than me. He'll be moving up to senior school before long. It's hard to believe. It seems like only the other day I was picking up this tiny thing, worried that I might drop or break him.' He smiled. A proud smile, full of love for his son. 'Time goes so fast.'

He was an attractive man, with his sharp features, soulful grey eyes, crew-cut hair. But there was also a kind, gentle side to Carver underneath the surly exterior he presented to the world. Maddy wished others saw what she saw, but she also guessed his tough persona was what made him such a good police officer. Someone who commanded the respect and loyalty of his team, who was never taken advantage of, and got results.

'Right.' Carver broke her thoughts. 'Breakfast first, then we talk.'

Twenty minutes later, they sat at the compact dining table, eating eggs Benedict, toast and real coffee. Carver's one vice was coffee; she'd witnessed his craving before, and she wondered how he ever managed to sleep with the amount of caffeine he got through in a day.

'Have forensics come back with anything?' she asked, before taking a bite of toast.

Mead had, in fact, sent an update overnight. 'Still waiting on the white van,' Carver said. He omitted to recount Mead's observation about there being no sign of human life at this stage; there was little point until he knew more. 'Obviously, the search radius is more extensive than inside the unit. But it looks like the other van was empty on detonation, as was the unit itself.'

Maddy took a moment to digest this, then, leaning forward, asked, 'So, what is it you're keeping from me?'

Carver sat back, wiped his mouth with a paper napkin. He knew she was referring to Davenport. He also knew she'd never let up until he told her the truth. He sighed, in his mind telling himself he could trust Maddy to keep the information to herself. 'I'm only telling you this because I know you'll never rest until I do and because I feel I can trust you.' He paused, then said, 'Plus, I already know what a good amateur detective you are.' He grinned, and she grinned back.

'You plan on using me?' she said in mock horror.

'Yes,' he replied, unashamedly. 'Don't tell me this case isn't going to carry on bugging you until you know who's behind it all?'

Maddy pushed her chair back, sipped her coffee, trying not to grimace at the strength of it. 'You're right, it is going to bug me. Something doesn't make sense. So tell me, or I'll hound you forever.'

Why doesn't that feel like a bad thing to me? Carver mused.

He leant in, rested his elbows on the table and clasped his hands together. 'I'm pretty certain Nigel Davenport raped Matthew Gerard's mother while they were at Cambridge together.'

183

Maddy's jaw dropped. She hadn't seen that coming. 'Jesus.'

'Quite.'

'Have you questioned Davenport about it?'

'Of course. He flatly denies it. We've also spoken to his old college master, a man named Stewart Larson, who claims the girl, Mary Jacobs as her name was then, was a bit of a flirt and made it all up. Just to spice things up further, Charles Dempsey and Richard Barker were at the same college at the same time. Dempsey was something of a misfit and Davenport, the college hero, took him under his wing and apparently helped make him the man he is today.'

'And Barker? Was he friends with them at the time?'

'That's a little unclear. Like Davenport, he was popular, which makes me wonder if a bit of friendly rivalry went on there.'

'So this was all about getting revenge for the fact that Davenport raped Matthew's mother over thirty years ago?'

'It has to be. The resignation of Davenport, the donation to Rape Crisis, the video, it all adds up.'

Maddy frowned. 'What donation? What video?'

Carver filled Maddy in, including details of his conversation with Cherry at Spearmint Rhino and the man who'd approached her to film Davenport.

'But why punish Mary's son?'

'That, I don't get. It would only make sense if Davenport had known Mary was Matthew's mother before he and the others got taken. But I don't believe he did until I told him. Alternatively, it's possible the kidnappers believed Matthew knew Davenport had raped Mary, and therefore wanted to punish him for taking a job at his firm.'

'Have you questioned Frank Gerard?'

184

Rivers had questioned Frank on Thursday. On learning that Mary had been at Cambridge with Davenport, and that he might have raped her, his face had apparently fallen in disbelief.

Yes, his wife had told him she was raped – long ago, on the night he had proposed, in fact. She hadn't wanted it hanging over them. But she had never revealed the identity of her attacker, or where it had happened, and he had agreed never to raise the subject again.

'It must have come as such a shock,' Maddy said, after Carver finished explaining.

'Yes. But like the rest of us, he couldn't understand what the point was in taking Matthew hostage, when Davenport apparently had no idea he was Mary's son. Plus, he said there was no way Matthew could have known his mother was raped.'

Maddy considered this for a moment, then moved on. 'So, we're looking for a man with a scar on his chin, according to this Cherry you questioned?'

'Yes, but it appears he might be dead. Assuming he was caught in the explosion.'

'What about the estate's CCTV?'

'Good question. It picked up the blue van, with a different number plate, cloned like the first, entering the estate the day the hostages got snatched, and parking up in front of Unit 25. A man got out, but he had a balaclava on, and kept his head down. It's impossible to make an ID from that. He unlocked and raised the unit's roller shutter doors, got back in the van, drove inside, then shut them again. Not long after, the doors rolled up again and a white van emerged. Someone, probably the same guy, got out of the driver's seat, pulled down the shutters, locked the unit, got back in the van, then drove off, having removed the number plate completely.'

'Smart.'

'Indeed. CCTV from yesterday showed the white van arriving at the estate around 9.08 p.m., but then, as you know, the imaging was switched off for an hour, so we have no means of ascertaining whether one or more of the kidnappers got out of the van. They must have done, though, because we now know that the roller shutters weren't completely closed when both vans blew. At some point, someone opened them.'

'Christ. Do you think whoever it was escaped through the unit and blew the vans, intending to bump off his accomplices and take the six million for himself?'

Carver smiled at Maddy's ingenuity. 'It's possible. Of course, it's also possible that the driver was on his own and blew both vehicles to buy himself time to escape while also destroying any evidence. We won't know the answer to that until I have the forensic report. Either way, it's another reason for making the drop at night, and requesting that the CCTV be switched off for an hour.'

'And what about the unit itself? Did your men find out who it's leased to?'

'Yes. Turns out it's leased to a bogus company the National Crime Agency's only recently been alerted to. Stanislav Textiles was created online through Companies House six months ago. Its directors are two Romanian brothers, Alexandru and Andrei Constantin, and they are suspected of preparing false invoices, amongst other things, as a means of laundering money. They also employed an English accountant, a man named Gareth Bright, who we understand was made redundant from his firm around eight months ago and was clearly desperate to provide an air of legitimacy to the company by opening up bank and trading accounts, and adapting the company's business model so as to ensure it appeared to meet the minimum standards required under the money-laundering regulations. The company therefore passed the usual comprehensive tenant checks used by reputable commercial property agents. But all three appear to have vanished off the face of the planet. My guess is that they knew the NCA was onto them, and when the opportunity arose to make a quick buck by subletting the unit to the kidnappers, they took off as soon as the deal was done.'

'Bloody hell. These kidnappers aren't stupid. Who the hell can they be?'

'Well, first things first, I need to talk to the four hostages. See if they can shed light on any of this, although if they never saw their faces, I'm not holding out much hope.'

'And the six million? Are you monitoring it to see if it's been moved or accessed at all?'

'Don't worry, Ms Kramer, I've got that covered.' Carver nodded as he reached over and took her plate, and his, to the kitchen. Maddy got up and followed him, watched him dump the dishes in the sink. She had a broad grin on her face.

'What are you smiling about?' he asked.

She tilted her head. 'The fact that you still call me Ms Kramer. It's rather sweet.'

Carver felt himself colour. He cleared his throat. 'You were a civilian who helped me with a case. That's how we met. It just stuck, I guess. Plus, it's been more than two years since we last saw each other.'

Boy, didn't she know it. Maddy held his gaze. There was an extraordinary electricity in the air. She suddenly felt warm, dizzy with it. She'd fended it off too many times before, but here, the two of them alone in his flat, she couldn't help herself.

'What the hell,' she said, throwing herself at him and kissing him square on the mouth. Carver stood there rigid, as her lips attacked his with such force it startled him. She withdrew, looked at him with apologetic eyes. 'I'm sorry,' she said. It was her turn to redden. What if he didn't feel the same way, and she'd just gone and made a complete idiot of herself? She'd never live it down. She'd never be able to look him in the eye again.

'Don't be,' he said. And then it was his turn. He grabbed her waist and pulled her towards him. Kissed her with equal hunger.

Desire overwhelmed them, superseded all sense of reason. She could smell his sweat from earlier as she pulled off his top, tracing his back, his stomach. And then he was lifting off her T-shirt, pulling down the strap of her bra, diving into her neck, driven by a need, a craving that had longed to be satisfied.

He lifted her up, still kissing her, her legs wrapped around his waist. 'You sure about this?' he asked, almost breathless.

'Yes,' she whispered, breaking away and cradling his head in her hands. 'I've never been surer.'

It was everything they could have hoped for, and more. Connecting – no longer two separate entities concerned solely with their own needs and desires, but one, driven by a deep longing to please the other, to get truly lost in the other. All of life's stresses and strains, trials and tribulations, hopes and fears, buried for a while, nothing more important than luxuriating in the smell, touch, desire of each other. Everything else was immaterial for that blissful period.

But now reality beckoned. It had gone 11 a.m., and Carver was meant to be picking Drake up from his flat at 11.30. From there, they'd head to Richard Barker's home, and begin a long afternoon of questioning. And this evening, once he was through with questioning, there would be a press conference.

Carver had just taken a shower. Maddy watched him put on a clean shirt, still on a high. Still unable to believe that what had always felt inevitable had finally happened. Had it been a mistake? It hadn't felt like it at the time. But what about later, tomorrow, the next day? Was there any future with Carver? He was seventeen years older than her, divorced with a child. He led an unpredictable life.

Plus being together would cause a scandal. Not just the scandal of a seventeen-year age difference, but the chance of Carver's unblemished reputation as a brilliant, respected police officer being blackened by him getting involved with a civilian caught up in two of his investigations.

'What are you thinking?' Carver asked, gazing down at her.

Maddy lowered her eyes. 'Oh, it's nothing. Just feeling a little dazed, I guess.'

He leant over and kissed her softly. Then, his face still only an inch or so away from hers, he said, 'I know, I'm that good. I have that effect on women.' He grinned, and she pushed him away playfully.

'Ha ha, you can stop that cheek, DCI Carver!'

She swung her legs off the bed, covering her modesty with the duvet. He sat down beside her, and tilted her face towards him, cupping her chin like a delicate piece of china.

'It was amazing, you are amazing, and I have never felt more wonderful.'

It was the most wonderful thing anyone had ever said to her, and she couldn't help but smile. She kissed him on the mouth. 'I think you can call me Maddy now.'

'Yes, I think I can,' he said tenderly. 'Look, I have to go. Take a shower, stay as long as you need, and just pull the door to when you leave.'

'Thanks, will do.'

Another warm kiss, then Carver got up and walked to the door, before pausing to look back over his shoulder. 'I'll call you later, OK?'

'Great.' She smiled. 'I hope you find some answers.'

'Me too.'

And then he was gone, and she was alone. In DCI Jake Carver's flat. She lay back down on his bed and stared up at the ceiling. She felt radiant, on top of the world, and she wondered how she was ever going to come back down to earth.

Chapter Seventeen

The exact same thought sailed through Carver's mind as he drove to Drake's flat. She did something to him that sent him crazy with desire, the likes of which he'd never felt before. Not even with Rachel. For sure, it had been nice with her – good, in fact. It had produced Daniel. But it had never been as fierce, hot, all-consuming, downright breathtaking as it had been with Maddy. He was a disciplined, guarded man by nature, but somehow, she brought out a whole other side to him. Wild and licentious. It was exhilarating, but also terrifying.

Although she'd fobbed him off, pretended it was nothing, he knew what she'd been thinking when he'd asked her what was up.

The exact same thing he'd been thinking as he'd looked down at her. The moment over, reason conquering emotion.

What now? How was this going to work? What would people say? The scandal, the age difference. A senior police officer mixing business with pleasure. Distracted from the job at hand.

He reached his destination. Drake was already waiting outside. Carver prayed his smart sidekick wouldn't catch on. 'Pull yourself together,' he muttered as he pulled up to the kerb.

'Sir.' Drake got into the car, strapped himself in. 'Good workout this morning?'

Carver turned to him, said with a smile, 'The best.' Then drove off.

'Hello, DCI Carver, DS Drake, please come through.'

Marianne Barker was a striking woman. A fact that had immediately struck Carver when they'd been introduced just before the press conference on Monday evening. But today she appeared more fragile than she had five days ago. Worry was stamped all over her face. Worry and fear. Fear that she'd soon lose her husband to the merciless disease ravaging his body, having had barely enough time to come to terms with it.

The Barkers lived in a four-bedroomed 1950s terraced house in Pimlico, not far from the river. Spread over four floors, it was modern, spacious and tastefully decorated. White walls, light oak wood flooring, minimalist furnishings, and filled with family photographs and quirky pieces of modern art that might sit well in Tate Modern.

Marianne steered them upstairs to the main reception room, where her husband was resting on a pale blue fabric sofa. Carver had yet to meet any of the hostages, yesterday's explosion causing a speedy exodus from the scene.

'Mr Barker, please don't get up,' he said as he went over and shook Richard's hand. It felt so cold. He looked ill, frail. Every inch of him wasting away like kindling in a fire. *Poor man,* thought Carver as he and Drake sat down on the sofa opposite. Marianne sat by her husband.

'Excuse my state,' Richard apologised with a faint smile. 'I'm just feeling rather spent. The last few days have taken their toll. Would you like some tea, coffee?'

'We're fine.' Carver glanced quickly at Drake. 'I'm sorry for what you've been through. It must have been especially hard, given your illness.'

'It wasn't easy, I'll grant you that.' Richard glanced at his wife. Her eyes were moist. 'You must think me terrible for keeping such a thing from my wife, but I didn't want to burden her, you see. I saw no point in two of us suffering.'

Marianne clutched her husband's hand. 'Oh, Richard, you daft fool,' she sobbed.

Carver knew genuine love when he saw it, and the Barkers' was as genuine as it got. He gave them a moment, then said, 'I understand the kidnappers were aware of your condition?'

'Yes,' Richard replied.

'How? Only your doctor knew, isn't that right?'

'Yes, that's right. I really have no idea. Who knows how criminals find these things out? They could have hacked my records, anything like that, I suppose.'

'That's certainly possible. And indicates to me that their picking you wasn't random. Perhaps they saw it as a bargaining chip to get Nigel Davenport to agree to their demands?'

'Yes, perhaps.'

'Charlotte told Maddy Kramer the kidnappers gave you painkillers.'

'Yes, that's right. It was most astonishing.'

'And yet they beat Charlotte and Matthew?'

Richard sighed, ran his hand over the back of his scalp. 'Yes, and it's something I feel very guilty about. Those poor kids.'

'So, you think they were softer on you because of your illness?'

Richard nodded. 'It seems that way. They said it was never their intention to let anyone die. They knew how ill I am and they didn't want to chance that happening. But the leader said he needed to make a point. Somehow, they knew Nigel was wavering, and I guess beating up Charlotte and Matthew was the only way to get him to agree to their demands. Although I don't think Matthew helped himself when he demanded they show their faces.'

'Are you saying they had a mole at your firm, feeding back information?' It was, of course, something that had occurred to Carver.

'Possibly. How else would they have known Nigel was vacillating? Either that, or they planted a wire, tapped into his conversations, I just don't know. They never told us.'

Carver made a mental note to check Davenport's room for bugs.

'Aside from capitalising on your illness, do you think there may have been another reason why they picked you?'

The tone of Carver's question suggested he already knew the answer. Something that didn't bypass Richard. His expression became grave. 'Yes. And I think you know the answer to that already, Chief Inspector. It's because I was at Cambridge with Nigel. At the same time as Mary Jacobs. They took me into a separate room and told me as much. They also gave me strict instructions not to tell the others if I knew what was good for them, and for me.'

Now they were getting somewhere. Carver leant forward. 'Is it true, Mr Barker? Did Nigel Davenport rape Mary Jacobs? You know she's Matthew Gerard's mother, who went missing – is presumed dead – two months before Matthew joined your firm?'

Richard sighed again. Glanced almost apologetically at his wife, even though Carver was sure he'd already told her the full story.

'Yes, I know, but as far as I can tell, Matthew doesn't know we were all at Cambridge with Mary. He was as confused as Charlotte and Stephen about the kidnappers' demands. I hope you won't tell him. It would devastate the poor boy. He's suffered enough.'

He was right, but Carver had no choice. 'I have to, I'm sorry, Mr Barker. All the facts need to be out in the open if we're ever going to get to the bottom of this.'

'But they blew themselves up. What's the point?'

'You've not answered my question, Mr Barker. Did Davenport rape Mary Jacobs?'

Richard lowered his head, seemingly ashamed. He kept it down as he said, 'Yes, he did. I walked in on him doing it, jeered on by the others.'

'Including Charles Dempsey?'

'Yes. But again, Charlotte doesn't know.' Richard looked up, tears in his eyes.

'How do you know she doesn't?'

'How could she? Her father's not likely to have mentioned it, is he? And as I said, like the others, she was baffled by their request for a donation to Rape Crisis. Although, I suppose it must have set alarm bells ringing.' A pause, then, 'But why should she or Matthew have any reason to think it might have a connection to them?'

'I'm afraid Charlotte will know soon enough about her father.' A pause, then Carver asked, 'When they took you aside, did they say anything else?'

'They said they wanted me to suffer. Not physically, but mentally. They wanted to remind me that I was weak back then. That I failed to do the right thing, which was to turn Nigel in and make him account for his actions.'

'Do you regret keeping quiet, Mr Barker?'

Carver didn't really need to ask the question. He saw from Richard's pained expression that he did. 'It's my biggest regret in life, DCI Carver.'

'And yet you've worked with Davenport all this time?'

Richard coughed. A deep chesty cough that seemed to wear him out. He sighed, gave his wife another guilty look. 'I was young, and I was weak. And I guess, because Mary left Cambridge soon after the incident, and never took things further, I let things carry on as normal. Pushed it far to the back of my mind, almost like it never happened, as if I'd imagined it. After all, we'd been at a house party, and we were all very drunk. A couple of years later, Nigel and I happened to land articles at the same firm, we worked our way up to partner, and got stuck with each other, I guess. I had to live and let live, for the good of the firm.'

The man genuinely regretted his actions, Carver saw that. But it only served to fortify his own loathing for the City, and all the greed and selfishness that went with it. He'd lost any shred of compassion he might otherwise have had left for Nigel Davenport. The bastard deserved to be punished for what he'd done. The fact that over three decades had elapsed was irrelevant. A crime didn't become less evil because of the passage of time.

Although he didn't in any way condone the way the kidnappers had gone about it, he understood their motivation. Their goal. Which was to get justice for Mary.

But so many unanswered questions remained. Questions that baffled and niggled him. What was the kidnappers' connection to the horrific events of that night in Cambridge? And why go to all that trouble only to blow themselves up? If, in fact, it turned out they had been inside the van when it blew, although Carver had serious doubts on that front.

Before he and Drake left, Richard confirmed what Charlotte had already told Maddy. That he never saw the kidnappers' faces, and that they'd all been blindfolded to and from the hideout. He also couldn't say how many of the kidnappers had accompanied them the previous night. They had ridden in silence to the drop and only one voice, low and gruff, had given them their instructions. Probably the same individual who'd snatched him and Charlotte from the conference room.

Outside on the street, Carver tossed Drake his keys. 'OK, Drake, let's head to Gerard's place.'

'You want me to drive?'

'No, I just wanted to play catch,' Carver mocked. Drake's face turned crimson, the way it had so many times in the early days of their relationship. 'No need to blush, Drake, you should be used to my outstanding wit by now. Truth is, I need to check in with forensics as we go. See if they've found anything.'

As Drake drove, Carver held the line for Mead. Mead was a skinny, meticulous sort, with a slight stoop, who peered at everything and everyone suspiciously over the top of his half-moon spectacles. He also drank copious amounts of tea, giving his skin a yellowish tinge, while his social skills left a lot to be desired. He was second to none at his job, though, and that was all that mattered as far as Carver was concerned.

He didn't answer immediately, and Carver began to lose patience as he continued to hold the line, Drake negotiating the Saturday afternoon traffic in the direction of Queen's Park, where Matthew Gerard still lived with his father. Finally, Mead picked up.

'Mead, what have you got?' Carver asked impatiently, hopeful of a breakthrough.

'That's exactly the problem, sir,' Mead replied in his customary nasal tone. Almost as if he suffered from chronic sinusitis.

'What do you mean?'

'We don't have anything, sir. No trace of a single body. No sign of human life whatsoever.'

Chapter Eighteen

Carver silently wrestled with Mead's revelation all the way to the Gerards' four-bedroomed Edwardian flat in north-west London. Drake sensed this. He knew his boss's moods, and although he was dying to discuss the implications with him, he knew now wasn't the time. Carver needed time alone to think and mull it over, before bringing it to the floor for discussion.

Drake turned off Kilburn High Road, lined on either side with a somewhat seedy mix of cheap bargain stores, Irish pubs and greasy spoons, onto the more civilised tree-lined Brondesbury Villas. A pleasant sloping road, flanked by graceful weeping willows, and attractive three-storey Edwardian period houses converted into airy, high-ceilinged flats.

He drove slowly, pulling up in front of number eighty-nine, a handsome white building, approached via an intricate black wrought-iron gate.

Drake switched off the engine, then turned to Carver. 'You ready, sir?'

Carver gave him a steadfast look. 'This changes things, you realise that? It's a whole new ball game. Of course, it's still possible someone was in the van when it blew, and I've told Mead to keep sifting through the wreckage; every last fragment needs analysis before we can conclude otherwise. Even so, my gut tells me only one of the kidnappers drove the hostages to the drop. That same individual let them out the back, and while we were busy watching them coming towards us with Maddy, made his escape under the shutters, through the unit, across the playing field and into the woods. At this point, he blew both vans.' Carver paused, then said, 'They're still out there, Drake, who the hell knows where, but they're somewhere, I'm certain of it, and they need to be caught.'

'Yes, sir.'

'My son's just upstairs. He'll be down shortly.'

Carver and Drake stood watching Frank Gerard make instant coffee for four in his L-shaped kitchen. The flat had a lived-in, homely feel to it, and it didn't take a genius to work out that Matthew Gerard had been raised in a secure, loving environment. There were family photos everywhere. Some of Matthew with both his parents, but mostly of Matthew and his mother, Mary. There was no doubt how beautiful she'd been. Movie-star beautiful. Old school Hollywood, a la Rita Hayworth, only with chocolate-brown, rather than flame-red hair. Carver recognised the mutual adoration between mother and son, the special bond only they can share – he'd seen it between Daniel and Rachel – and he realised how hard her death must have hit Matthew. He hated having to tell him the truth.

They took their coffee into the sitting room. It had large windows letting in vast amounts of natural light, and a small dining table positioned against the wall opposite. Carver and Drake plonked themselves on a cream three-seater sofa. Across from them was an attractive artificial fireplace, bordered by a matching pair of china mantel dogs. Frank, who'd pulled out one of the dining chairs, caught Carver looking at them. 'My wife's choice,' he said with a fond smile. 'She loved dogs but couldn't have one due to her asthma. They were the closest thing she got.'

Carver knew the feeling. He was highly allergic to all sorts of things, especially cat hair, but unlike Mary, he'd never hankered after a pet.

Just then, they heard footsteps coming down the stairs. 'Sorry to keep you, gentlemen,' Matthew apologised, extending his hand to Carver, then Drake. 'I overslept and was late to take a shower.'

'No need to apologise.' Carver smiled at Matthew warmly. He had his mother's looks, despite his wounds, and in that first greeting displayed a maturity beyond his twenty-four years. He had partner-in-waiting written all over him. But not in an arrogant way. There was an unthreatening assertiveness about him. In his deep, steady voice, his earnest gaze. Carver liked him instantly.

Matthew sat by his father. Carver asked after his injuries, which were healing nicely, then got down to the nitty gritty.

Matthew confirmed much of what Richard had said, minus the hideous details concerning Mary only Richard knew. But he also shed light on something that Carver and his team had been itching to know since Monday evening. How were he and Stephen captured?

'I don't know if you've heard, Chief Inspector, but Steve and I are best mates from primary school.' Carver hadn't, in fact, realised the friendship dated back that far. 'We often grab a bite together at lunchtime, you know, just to catch up. Sometimes in the canteen, sometimes out if we fancy some fresh air. As was the case last Monday.'

'What time did you head out?'

'Around 12.30.'

'You say that with some conviction.'

Matthew smiled. 'Don't know if anyone's mentioned it, but I'm a bit OCD about these things, and unless something prevents me from doing so, I tend to take my lunch break around the same time every day.'

Carver glanced at Frank, who rolled his eyes. 'I can vouch for that. Not sure if it comes from Matt being an only child, but he's always been rather particular about things.' He smiled. 'Drives me mad.'

Carver smiled back, then returned his gaze to Matthew.

'None of the receptionists saw you leave?' He knew the front reception CCTV hadn't captured them leaving, but asked the question all the same.

Matthew smiled. 'We both took the stairs and snuck out the back way. We often do, when the courier guys aren't about.'

'Why?'

'Don't tell her this, but Ann Stevens is a terrible gossip. She's been at the firm almost as long as Nigel, and she tells him everything. It was a nice day, and we planned on having a leisurely lunch, despite it only being a Monday. We didn't want her timing us, possibly reporting back to Nigel or our supervising partners on how long we'd been.'

'I see,' Carver said. This struck him as a little odd, a bit childish, but nothing to get worked up about. It did make sense why the CCTV had been disabled, though. The kidnappers must have been monitoring Matthew's and Stephen's movements for some time, intending to grab them at the back of the firm, out of sight and on a tiny side street where no CCTV would catch them. 'Go on.'

'We often trek over to Smithfield. There's a great deli there which does the best meatball subs. But we never made it. No sooner had we stepped out of the building and turned right, we heard this vehicle speed up behind us, then screech to a halt. Both Steve and I turned around but the next thing we knew, we were being bundled into the back of a van.'

'And no one was around at the time?'

'No, not a soul. Not as far as I'm aware anyway.' He paused, then said, 'Vehicles aren't supposed to go down that street, except for deliveries. It was all so quick. All I saw were these angry eyes, hidden behind black balaclavas.'

'Jesus, son.' Frank rested his hand on Matthew's shoulder.

'What then?'

'They gagged and blindfolded us, tied our hands behind our backs and told us not to make a sound if we wanted to live. Then they drove off, and before we knew it, the van pulled up again.'

'Then what?'

'Maybe a few minutes max passed before we heard the back doors being opened and someone shouting, "Get the fuck in."'

'Charlotte and Richard?'

'Yes, I heard her crying, while Richard was trying to reason with them. But they told him to shut up, and the van took off. We made a brief stop around five, ten minutes after that, then must have been on the road for another thirty minutes before we came to another stop. I thought I could make out a garage door being opened. It sounded like roller shutters. Then we heard the van doors being opened, and they hauled us out and into another vehicle, although we never saw what kind it was until they released us last night.'

'Then what?'

'Then we drove for another half hour or so, to our final stop. All we could hear was Charlotte's muffled crying, and… fuck… I was so bloody scared, I… I…' Matthew got up. Carver watched him

202

pace the room, fiercely rubbing his eyes as if to erase the memory of his torment.

'It's OK, Matthew,' Carver said. 'I realise how hard this must be for you. Take your time.'

More composed, Matthew turned around. Explained how, like Charlotte and Richard, he never saw the men's faces, or had any idea where they were held. Only that it appeared to be some sort of industrial warehouse, with no windows, and sparse furnishings. He suspected they'd picked on Charlotte because she was a girl and the daughter of Charles Dempsey, and therefore more likely to shift Davenport's stance. And he explained how standing up to them had got his face kicked in.

He had no idea why they had it in for Davenport, or that they planned on blowing themselves up. Yes, Richard had told them he had advanced prostate cancer, and didn't expect to live much longer than six months. The men had known this, and they had given him pain relief. The four of them had feared for their lives, despite the men making it clear it wasn't their intention to kill them.

Every now and again, Frank gave his son an affectionate pat on the knee, his eyes watering on hearing what he'd been made to endure.

'DCI Carver, please explain to me why they wanted Nigel's resignation? And why the donation to Rape Crisis? I get the feeling Richard knows. The kidnappers took him out of the room once, but he wouldn't say what they discussed. Charlotte, Steve and I also have a right to know, don't you think? Considering what we've been through.'

Carver saw the strain on his face. Matthew had told him everything he knew, and now it was his turn to tell him a very difficult truth. He hated moments like this. He was good at interrogating criminals until they confessed to their crimes. He was comfortable with locking them up, going home satisfied that he'd done his job and got one more bad guy off the streets.

But there were shitty parts of the job. Like telling an innocent young man, who'd already suffered so much, that his mother had been raped by his boss thirty something years ago. Purely for selfish reasons, Carver felt relieved that Frank at least knew the truth. Just so he didn't have to bear the guilt of breaking two men's hearts at the same time.

'What?' Matthew barely got the word out after Carver broke it to him. His face full of disbelief. He gulped in air as he looked at his father helplessly. 'I… I don't understand, Dad. Is it true? Did Davenport really do that to Mum?'

Frank gave Carver a hard stare. He wiped away a tear with his sleeve, pulled his son towards him, and rested his head against his chest.

'I'm afraid so, son. But your mother made me promise never to tell you. She didn't want you feeling sorry for her or knowing that she'd suffered.'

'Hang on.' Carver shifted his weight, also noticing Matthew's shocked expression. 'You told DC Rivers that your wife kept her attacker's identity a secret from you. But you knew it was Davenport? Why lie? I would have expected more from an ex-policeman.'

'Because I felt ashamed, I guess. I didn't want the young officer to think ill of me. Wonder how I could have let my own son work for the monster who raped his mother.'

Matthew was still looking stunned by Frank's confession. He broke away. 'It's a bloody good question, though, don't you think? I had a right to know, Dad!'

'You say that, but what difference would it have made?'

'I wouldn't have taken the job at Sullivans for a start. Then perhaps none of this would have happened. That's why she sounded so upset

204

when I first told her where I'd be training. Why didn't she say something then, for God's sake? Why didn't you, Dad? I wasn't ten anymore, I was a grown man! Maybe she would still be here. It's my fault, I drove her to it! I brought back a memory she'd tried to forget!'

Matthew sobbed like a child as his father stroked his juddering head, anguish and regret swamping his face. Carver and Drake watched in uneasy silence. Father and son needed this moment, and it wasn't their place to interfere.

'It's not your fault, son. And what would you have done if you had known? Let the matter rest? Or would you have gone and done something stupid, like pay Davenport a visit and beat him to a pulp? It's what you'd like to do right now, isn't it? Tell me I'm wrong.'

For a moment, they just looked at each other, locked in a mutual pain they'd never be free from.

Finally, Matthew said softly, 'But, Dad, how could you have just stood by all these years without saying anything? Without reporting the matter? You were a police officer, for Christ's sake! You had a duty.'

'Yes, I had a duty' – Frank glanced guiltily at Carver – 'but your mother made me promise not to, and first and foremost my duty was to her. Believe me, I wanted to, but she was adamant I leave it alone. She said she wouldn't marry me if I didn't do as she asked. And believe me, not marrying your mother – that beautiful, wise, wonderful lady who was way out of my league – was not an option.'

Frank smiled lovingly at his son, the crow's feet around his tired eyes, eyes that had done a lot of crying, and endured many sleepless nights, creasing as he did so. And then they shared a warm embrace, Matthew's tears soaking Frank's shirt.

Finally, they broke apart. Matthew looked up at Carver with red puffy eyes. 'So now you've told me, Chief Inspector. Now I know why these men demanded Davenport's resignation. But are you any closer to finding out who they were, what connection they had to my mother, and why they blew themselves up?'

Carver leant forward. 'That's what I was coming to next.' Matthew and Frank looked at him eagerly. Both on tenterhooks. 'Forensics have so far found no sign of human life. They've not finished, of course. It's a painstaking process. But whoever took you, I'm almost sure they're still out there, and I'm determined to find them.'

He analysed their reactions. Both swallowed hard, no doubt sick at the thought of Matthew's kidnappers still being at large and possibly not done with him. Matthew got up and walked over to the window looking onto the street, his back to all three. 'That's why they let us out through the van's back doors.' He turned around. 'Why you were made to stay well away. Why Maddy was asked to stay at the front.'

'There was no one inside the other van, or the unit itself. The unit backs onto a playing field. My thinking is…'

'They escaped on foot through the back doors, through the unit, out onto the playing field and then they, or someone else, blew the vans remotely.'

Carver smiled at Frank. 'Your son has clearly inherited some of his father's investigative genes. It seems the only logical explanation.'

Frank turned to Matthew. 'Do you think it's possible that only the driver was with you at the drop?' He looked at Carver. 'Much easier for a single man to make a quick getaway, don't you think?'

'Yes, I'd agree with that.' Carver nodded. 'Do you remember hearing more than one voice in the van, Matthew?'

Matthew thought for a while, then said, 'Come to think of it, I don't. Just the one. Low and hoarse. He gave us our instructions at the drop. We were blindfolded, of course, but I don't think he was the leader. He untied our hands before opening the back doors, and made it clear we were to remove the blindfolds only after we got out.'

Carver glanced at Drake, taking notes, then fixed his gaze back on Matthew.

'We'll be talking to Ms Dempsey later, but there's something else you need to know. Something I'm pretty sure Ms Dempsey knows nothing about.' He paused, then said, 'Ms Dempsey's father was there the night Davenport attacked your mother.'

Another shock. Matthew sat back down next to his father. 'So that's why they took Charlotte? They wanted to teach her father a lesson too?'

'Possibly. It also explains why they took Mr Barker. You see, he was also there that night.'

Carver noticed the veins on Matthew's neck flex. Anger flooded his face. 'Lying bastard,' he said. 'And to think I felt sorry for him.'

'I don't believe Mr Barker played an active role in what went on that night or took any pleasure from it.'

'Is that so? He clearly played no active role in getting justice for my mother, working with that slime-ball all these years. And to think he lied to our faces, saying he had no idea what the kidnappers wanted.'

'He had no choice. They forced him to lie, and he did so to protect the three of you.'

There was no sign of Matthew's anger letting up.

'Please, son,' Frank urged, glancing at Carver as if willing him to do something.

'I genuinely believe Mr Barker regrets his silence,' Carver said. 'This has all come as a terrible shock to you. You're tired and emotional. Please don't do anything stupid.'

Matthew held his gaze, his eyes blazing anger. But to Carver's relief, he agreed. 'OK, I won't.'

'And don't take it out on Ms Dempsey. I'm certain she knew nothing about it.'

'Charlotte's a great girl,' Matthew said. 'I don't believe she has a malicious bone in her body.' He gave Carver a determined look. 'I hope you're going to arrest Davenport. He shouldn't be allowed to get away with this, just because it happened over thirty years ago.'

'After what Mr Barker's told us, yes, we'll certainly be bringing him in for questioning.'

'I want more than that,' Matthew said icily. 'I want a conviction. I want the bastard locked up for a very long time.'

Chapter Nineteen

'I'll call Rivers. She and Coombs need to bring Davenport in for questioning.'

Carver, sitting in the passenger seat, looked straight ahead as Drake negotiated the traffic. 'Matthew Gerard's right. The bastard needs to pay for what he did.'

'What about Larson? He helped cover it up.'

'Let's deal with Davenport first. He may try and shift some of the blame onto Larson, which will give us more leverage to bring him in. Right now, all we have is hearsay from Barker who, unfortunately, wasn't an eyewitness to whatever plan they hatched. Unlike the rape.'

'What about Dempsey? He watched the rape. Makes him an accomplice.'

'In that case, so was Barker. I'm not sure about you, but I think the man's been through enough. He deserves to live out his last months with his wife. If we bring in Dempsey, he'll mention Barker, guaranteed. Let's not go there for now. Are you with me, Drake?'

In his heart, Carver knew he was bending the rules to suit his conscience. But the fact was, his conscience couldn't handle the idea of a dying man, a man who regretted his actions, spending what little time he had left in a prison cell. Davenport was the ringleader, the real lowlife in all of this, and provided he was made to account for his actions, justice would be served in Carver's eyes.

'Yes, sir,' Drake said. Ever loyal, ever trusting of his boss's judgement. 'I'm with you.'

'What the hell happened to you? I was worried, especially as you took bloody long enough to respond to my texts. You decide to swim the Channel or something?'

Three p.m. Maddy walked into the living room and slung her gym bag on the floor. After leaving Carver's flat, she'd aimlessly wandered the streets. Walking from Hoxton all the way to Oxford Circus where, realising she was starving, she'd made a quick pit stop to satisfy her deprived stomach. She just couldn't come down from her high. Couldn't stop thinking about earlier that morning. It made her blush with embarrassment, just thinking about it. She longed for it to happen again and couldn't stop wondering what was going through Carver's mind. Whether he longed for the same?

Her grandmother was constantly on at her about getting a boyfriend. She knew why Maddy shied away from commitment. It stemmed from her parents' untimely deaths. If she didn't commit herself, she could never be hurt. A child of hers could never be hurt. That was Maddy's logic. Rose had told her numerous times that this was no way to live. And in her heart, Maddy knew she was right. If anything, her parents' deaths should have proved to her that life was too short to worry about getting hurt. But she couldn't help it. She was a naturally guarded person, and it took a lot to break down her shield.

But Carver had. And it made her think. Maybe it wasn't just her personality, or her childhood, that were to blame. Maybe she just hadn't met the right person. The person who made her feel giddy with excitement when she saw him, heard his voice, felt his touch. The person who made her eyes light up, made her laugh, made her cry, made her feel safe.

But she had. She'd first met him getting on for three years ago now, and fate had brought them together again. Her grandmother would be over the moon that she'd finally met the one person who sparked all these feelings in her.

If only he wasn't seventeen years her senior, divorced with a kid, who got out of bed every day knowing it might be his last.

'Sorry about not responding sooner,' Maddy replied guiltily. In truth, she hadn't known how to respond to Cara's messages, and in the end just said: *I'm fine, long story, will explain when I get home. x*

Cara was sitting on the sofa, flicking through a magazine, the TV showing reruns of *New Girl*. She gave Maddy a suspicious look. 'So, where did you get to? You'd gone when I got up. That was seven hours ago.'

'Oh, you know, I went for my swim, then for a walk, ended up having lunch on Oxford Street.'

'You ended up on Oxford Street? Come on, what's the real story? You always come home after a swim, without fail.'

Cara was a born journalist. Her speciality was prising truths out of people. Especially her best friend, whom she'd known the best part of a decade. Maddy adored Cara, but if she didn't know her, she'd be scared stiff of her. Physically, everything about Cara was dainty – from her teeny nose to her rosebud lips, her tiny feet, her delicate hands. But therein lay the danger. She was a deceptive little powerhouse, who never gave up on getting what she wanted, and always had the last say.

'What are you not telling me?' Her eyes, full of suspicion, lasered through Maddy, and all Maddy could think about was Carver gazing down at her as she lay in his bed. She was blushing inside, and she just hoped her face didn't show it.

'Well, something was bugging me about the case…'

'Shit, Mads.' Cara closed her magazine, sat up straight on the sofa. 'I hope you're not putting yourself in danger again? You did that once, and it nearly screwed you up for good. Nearly got you killed, for Christ's sake!'

'That was different,' Maddy protested. 'That was personal.'

Cara sat back again. Looked at her crossly. 'Don't try and fob me off. You're a lawyer, not bloody Jane Tennison.'

'Calm down, will you? I just went to see Carver at his gym to ask…'

'Carver? DCI Jake Carver. You went to see the man you had a thing for, at his gym, on a Saturday morning?'

Maddy's cheeks were suddenly hot. She could feel the heat radiating off them, and she couldn't look Cara in the eye.

Cara gasped out loud, her eyes wide. 'You slept with him, didn't you? That's where you were all this time!'

There was no point lying. She nodded. 'Not all this time. I left around midday.'

Cara grinned impishly. 'You little minx. I can't say I'm entirely surprised, what with the history you two have. And it's obvious you still have a thing for him. Every chance you've had this past week, you've dropped his name into the conversation. Carver this, Carver that.' Maddy was about to protest, when Cara beat her to it, her face suddenly serious. 'Do you know what you're doing, Mads?'

'No,' Maddy sighed, with a weary shake of her head. She slumped down on the sofa and laid her head on her concerned friend's lap. 'I haven't a frigging clue.'

* * *

A little after 4 p.m., and thoughts of Maddy resurfaced in Carver's head as they drove to Charlotte Dempsey's flat in St John's Wood. Just a short drive from the Gerards'. Her father had bought it for her after she graduated from university, but now she shared it with her brother, Isaac, who'd moved out of the family home in Hampstead following their mother's death.

Carver wasn't used to feeling so preoccupied. Not with matters of the heart, at any rate. For so long, his life had been simple. Although he'd missed a woman's touch, he'd reminded himself that romantic love had only brought him grief (aside from his son, of course, the one blessing) and since he and Rachel had split, his life, although a little dull, had been straightforward. But this morning had upset the order of things. Brought in a whole new, not to mention extremely complicated, equation. He'd let desire triumph over reason, his heart rule his head. Basically, he was in deep trouble.

But boy, had it been bloody fantastic. This was the conundrum he faced. She was so much younger, lived in a different world – a corporate world he resented and could never learn to embrace. Plus, he had a son.

But she was also wonderful – more mature than most girls her age, but also bright, beautiful, funny. They were good together. She made him feel alive, complete. And they'd connected physically, like two halves of the same coin.

'Something up, sir?' Carver turned to see Drake eyeing him with concern.

'No,' he replied quickly, 'nothing to bother you with, Drake, but thanks for asking.'

As he pulled up in front of an imposing mansion block on St John's Wood Park, he told himself to put Maddy out of his head. For now, at least. He had a job to do, and he couldn't let his romantic life distract him from the task at hand.

Besides, maybe his inner conflict was immaterial. Maybe she'd realised what a bad idea it had been, a mistake that should never have happened. Maybe she'd solved the problem for him already.

Chapter Twenty

'DCI Carver, DS Drake, it's good to finally meet you.' Charlotte Dempsey answered the door to her first-floor flat after buzzing her visitors up. She was dressed in faded skinny jeans and a pale blue tank top, her hair pulled back in a low ponytail, her feet bare, her toes decorated with chipped red nail polish. 'I caught a glimpse of you both yesterday, just before the explosion and things went mad. Thank you both, for all that you've done so far.'

'Not at all,' Carver said as she led them through the plush carpeted hallway into the spacious living room which overlooked the street. *A two-bedroom flat in St John's Wood must have cost Charles Dempsey a pretty packet*, thought Carver. But then again, he supposed that was small change for someone as rich as him.

He and Drake declined refreshments and sat down on one of two sofas opposite Charlotte. Her injuries were fading quicker than Matthew's, although she was perhaps wearing make-up to conceal them.

'Your brother not about?' Carver enquired.

'No, he plays football every Saturday afternoon.'

'I see.' *You'd have thought he'd have given it a miss today given his sister's recent trauma.* 'How are you feeling?'

'I think I'm still in shock, to be honest. Shock that I came out alive. I really thought I was going to die.'

'Did your abductors ever suggest that was a possibility?' Carver thought back to his earlier conversation with Richard. He'd said the kidnappers had made it plain they never intended to kill their hostages.

'No, in fact they said quite the opposite. But they beat me, as you can see.' She lightly touched the side of her face. 'It didn't exactly make me feel like I could trust them.' She fleetingly gazed out of the window, then turned back to Carver, her eyes watery. 'When you're trapped in a situation like that, you can never really be sure of a happy ending, despite what's told to your face.'

'I'm sorry for the terrible ordeal you've been through, Ms Dempsey, but I'm afraid I have some rather unpleasant truths to tell you; truths that must be told in light of new information we received earlier this afternoon.'

Charlotte cocked her head sharply, almost a look of alarm in her eyes. 'New information?' she repeated.

Drake updated her on the absence of bodies, the explosion inside the unit and the connection between Davenport, Barker, Dempsey and Matthew's mother.

'Oh my God.' Charlotte put her hand over her mouth, her eyes almost bulging from their sockets. 'I knew Richard was hiding something. But I honestly had no idea it was that. Matthew must hate me.'

'No, he doesn't,' Carver assured her. 'You were not to know and it's in no way your fault.'

'But still, I'm tainted by the same blood.' She clutched her midriff, shook her head forlornly. 'Sorry, but suddenly I feel quite sick. Please

216

excuse me, I need some water.' She dashed out of the room, quickly returning with a glass of water. 'Sorry again, it's just such a shock.' She paused, then said, 'So you think they're still out there?'

'It's highly likely, yes. How many voices did you hear in the van yesterday?'

Charlotte shook her head. 'I'm really not sure. The one who ordered us to get out had a deep, husky voice. Sounded like the same arsehole who stormed the conference room.' *Just as Richard said*, thought Carver. 'But that doesn't mean he was alone.'

'True.'

'Are you going to question my father about the rape?' Charlotte asked sternly. 'He needs to account for his actions, surely?'

Her gaze was unwavering. This was not the meek and mild girl Gavin Turner had ridiculed only last Monday. She seemed way more confident, way more on the ball, way more hard-nosed than he'd described her to be. And it was interesting that she didn't seem in the least bit bothered by the possibility of her father going to jail.

'You're not close, you and your father?'

'In one word, no,' she replied harshly. 'My mother practically brought us up single-handedly while my father made the money. As children, we only ever saw him at weekends. And even then, I'm certain he'd rather have been working.'

'Your mother's death must have been very difficult to come to terms with?'

'I was devastated, as was my brother. She was our rock, our best friend, and I think about her every day.'

Carver saw the despair in her eyes. He recalled how he'd felt after his own mother had passed away. Empty, vulnerable, alone, scared. A feeling that never disappeared completely. A feeling that stayed with a child until the day he or she died. His son would feel it, too, and it saddened him. Made him feel so helpless.

'I'm very sorry,' he said, then asked Charlotte the same questions he'd asked Richard and Matthew. In return, he got pretty much the same answers.

'Are you going to see Stephen now?' Charlotte asked.

'Yes, he's the last.'

'Do you have any idea how the kidnappers knew about Davenport's past?'

'No.' Carver shook his head. 'It's a complete mystery. But one that I'm determined to get to the bottom of.'

Charlotte stood at the window, watching Carver and Drake get into their car. It had taken all the will in the world not to smile broadly when Carver had answered her question with the words '*It's a complete mystery.*'

Having shown Carver what they were capable of with Charlotte and Matthew, they'd been confident he'd agree to all of their terms before they told him where the 'hostages' could be found. But Carver hadn't played ball. His persistence had been frustrating, but not a cause for panic. Although they'd known that Richard's back-up plan to blow up the white van and make it appear, initially at least, that the kidnappers had died in the explosion was in no way fail-safe – he himself had told them there was every chance of forensics eventually concluding that no one had been inside the van when it blew – they'd all agreed there was no better alternative. The main thing was, the explosion bought them time.

As soon as Isaac, dressed head-to-toe in black and wearing a back-pack, had let Charlotte, Matthew, Stephen and Richard out of the van, and they'd started making their way towards Maddy, he had opened and slipped under the unit's shutters, raced through the building and out onto the playing field, where he had detonated both bombs with the remote-control device he and Richard had previously fashioned. Crucially, the frenetic aftermath of the blasts had given him enough time to escape into the woodland, before changing into a fresh set of clothes stored in his backpack and taking off on the motorbike he'd concealed there. They knew that trawling through the wreckage was never going to be a quick process and it would therefore be some time, possibly weeks, before Carver established that the perpetrators were still out there.

The point was, in conceiving his fallback plan, Richard had felt it important to make an impact, create an element of uncertainty, drama, confusion, hysteria; yet another harrowing event the poor hostages had been forced to endure, as if being held captive for five days wasn't enough. None of them, however, had anticipated Carver's quickness to conclude that they were still out there, together with his resolve to hunt them down. Clearly, he was a man who acted as much on instinct as hard evidence. Of course, they could have just waived Nigel's donation and released the video before making it appear that they had been abandoned at Riverside Industrial Estate. But the donation was a vital element of Davenport's exposure as a rapist and the next best thing to Mary's diary which Matthew couldn't bear to make public. It was also infinitely preferable to the humiliation poor Pamela and her children would be forced to endure following the release of the video. None of them wanted her to suffer like that. And like Richard had said, the police would be hunting criminals who didn't exist. They would surely never consider what was right under their noses.

'You were good,' a familiar voice said from behind. Charlotte turned around to see her brother, who'd been hiding in his bedroom, standing there, full of admiration for his older, wiser sister.

She smiled. 'Thanks. I've got used to this acting thing. I think it quite suits me. Maybe after I quit Sullivans next week, I'll sign up for a drama course.'

Isaac grinned, then his expression became solemn. 'You still want to quit? Shouldn't you see it through? After all, you're only eight months away from qualification.'

'I may have pretended to be shit at my job, but that doesn't mean I didn't actually hate it. They're all the same, those partners. Fucking narcissistic upstarts like Gavin Turner, who look down on anyone who's not a partner like they're nothing. I'll be damned if I help make arseholes like him richer.'

'OK, sis, if you're sure.' Isaac knew better than to argue with his sister. She'd always been the same, even as a child. Stubborn, opinionated, decisive. The complete opposite to him: compliant, easy-going, hesitant. Now that their mother was gone, she was his tower of strength, the only one he felt able to trust, the only person he could count on.

'In light of what the police now know about our darling father's part in Mary's rape,' Charlotte continued, 'my decision to quit will be entirely understandable. In any case, as far as that issue's concerned, I'm not acting. I'm fucking ashamed of what he did, aren't you?'

'Course I am. What about Matthew? Is he quitting too?'

'He doesn't want to stay on, but I've persuaded him to. He wants to be a lawyer – he'll be a damn good one, and he can find a job elsewhere once he's qualified.'

'And what about the fact that you're together? How are you going to swing that one?'

'I told you before. We'll say that being held hostage brought us together, as did the fact that we both lost our mothers. That bit's largely true, anyway.' She shrugged. 'These things happen all the time. People growing close after sharing a distressing experience.'

'You've got it all figured out, haven't you?' Isaac kissed her cheek.

'I have.' She nodded. 'Including that war wound.' Charlotte traced her finger over the prominent scar running across Isaac's chin. Sustained after falling off his bike as a child. Apart from that, he was a decent-looking guy, with darker hair than hers, and intense brown eyes. 'When's the procedure scheduled for?'

'Monday.'

'Good. Stay out of sight till then. We can't take any chances the hooker won't come forward and identify you.'

Chapter Twenty-One

Richard closed the door to his study, went over to his desk, unlocked the bottom drawer with a key he never let out of his sight, and pulled out a brand new unregistered mobile phone. Marianne was busy preparing dinner, but he still couldn't chance her overhearing. For one, she'd endured enough over the last few days, and the shock of learning that her dying husband had engineered his own abduction might kill her. And two, he didn't want to put her in a difficult position. She was an honest, decent woman, and he knew she'd be torn between her loyalty to him and going to the police.

He dialled another mobile phone. Also unregistered. After four rings, Stephen picked up.

'It's me. Can you talk?'

'Yes. Celeste's popped out to the shops, but she'll be back soon.'

'Have they spoken to you yet?'

'No, but Charlotte called not long ago to say they'd left hers and were on their way here. Apparently, Carver's already decided we're still out there.'

'Yes, that's right. OK, so it's a bit sooner than we expected – this Carver guy seems like a bit of a maverick, by all accounts. But it's

222

not a problem. Just keep your head and keep to the story. Don't act like you know any of that, or about Davenport's past. You have to look and sound surprised.'

'I know, don't stress.'

Stress was exactly what worried Richard. Because he knew that Stephen was a *stresser*. He knew that from observing him at work. Unlike the other two, calm and unflappable, Stephen was a worrier. Good at his job, but a worrier all the same. He was a genuinely nice young man, but that was partly the problem. He worried too much about what people thought, about doing the wrong thing, about upsetting people, even strangers.

So, when Matthew had proposed bringing Stephen in, he'd had his doubts. Serious doubts. Concerned that Stephen would bail at the last minute, that he wouldn't be tough enough to see it through. That he'd crumble in the conference room and wreck all their best laid plans in an instant. But Matthew had assured him his friend would be fine. That he knew him better than anyone, and that the seriousness of his gambling debts meant he was desperate to get himself out of financial trouble.

And so far, Matthew had been on the money. Stephen hadn't yet buckled under pressure or shown any sign of weakness. Aside from the vodka and cocaine. Still, if that's what it took…

But today was crunch time. Today he wouldn't be wearing a mask. Today he needed to be sober in front of the police. Today he needed to act like the coolest customer in town.

'Just so you know,' Richard said, 'I've spoken to Pamela. One point eight million has been transferred to the Gibraltarian account, and 200 k will soon be with you. She'll let you know the pick-up point very soon.'

Stephen felt almost sick with elation. 'I still can't believe I'm going to have that much money. It feels so unreal.'

'It's very real, son. Just think of all those weeks of planning, the danger you've put yourself in. You deserve every penny.'

'You really never wanted any money out of this?'

Richard gave a droll smile. 'What's the point? I'm a dead man. And besides, I'm already a rich man. Annie won't have any financial worries.'

His comment saddened Stephen. He'd come to respect and care for the man. To have so much courage in the face of certain death, to have the guts to make up for a mistake he'd made over thirty years ago, when he could just as easily have let it wash over him and gone to his grave quietly, was quite something. He was a unique man, and Stephen wished he'd had a father like him. Loyal, brave, honourable. He'd be greatly missed.

They hung up, and Stephen went over to the window, wondering if the police would show before Celeste got home. They had a difficult drive across town, from St John's Wood to London Bridge, to the one-bedroom flat in a less-than-desirable council estate block, on a less-than-desirable road, that he and Celeste shared.

He constantly worried about her walking home late at night, especially in the dead of winter when darkness set in early. There were so many loons about, and he wasn't in the kind of job that allowed him to leave early and walk home with her.

But all of that was about to change. Soon they'd be able to buy their own place in a nice area of north London, and after he qualified, he'd get a job at another firm. Even if the bastards at Sullivans weren't keeping him on, he was sure he'd get a decent reference.

After all, he was a minor celebrity now who'd survived a terrible ordeal. Who in their right mind would have the heart to turn him down?

* * *

'Bit of a contrast to the other three homes, wouldn't you agree, sir?'

Drake stood with Carver, facing the block of flats Stephen and his girlfriend lived in. A grey, depressing concrete jungle in a dingy part of town.

He was right, thought Carver. Either Stephen wasn't into living the fancy City lifestyle, or he was still deep in debt from university. His money was on the latter. A salary of fifty thousand pounds would have been more than enough to rent somewhere nicer, in a better part of town.

They entered the estate, attracting unfriendly glares from a group of youths smoking something suspicious. A nauseating stench of greasy food, refuse waste, urine and marijuana hung in the air, and Carver found himself holding his breath as he followed Drake up two flights of stairs to flat 12. He was about to knock, when a voice called out from behind.

'Hello, DCI Carver, DS Drake. Good timing.'

Carver spun round. Celeste was standing there, holding a carrier bag which was bursting at the seams. They'd met before, of course, at Monday night's press conference, and briefly yesterday before heading to the drop. She was a striking girl. Legs that went on forever, long brown hair with natural golden highlights, cinnamon skin, Bambi brown eyes. But she acted like she wasn't aware of it, and clearly loved her very average-looking boyfriend to be living where they did.

'Can I carry that for you, Ms Ramirez?' Drake offered.

'No, thank you, I can manage.' She shuffled past, a set of keys in her right hand, and opened the door. 'Steve, darling,' she called out, 'I'm home, and the police are here.'

The place was tiny. Tiny entrance hall, tiny kitchen to the immediate right, tiny airing cupboard and bathroom to the left. Directly opposite the bathroom was the bedroom, just big enough to house a small double bed, and next to that, the living room, containing one sorry-looking two-seater sofa, a small TV, coffee table, and a couple of bean bags.

It struck Carver again that Stephen Baines wasn't exactly living the *LA Law* lifestyle. He was in the kitchen when all three entered.

'Hi, hon.' He kissed Celeste on the cheek as he took the shopping off her, throwing milk, butter and eggs straight into the fridge. He, Carver and Drake then exchanged pleasantries as Celeste made coffee, before they all sat down in the living room, Carver perched precariously on one beanbag, Drake on the other.

After enquiring after Stephen's health and general state of mind, Carver relayed forensics' findings, then told him about the rape allegation.

'My God.' Celeste squeezed Stephen's hand, looking horrified. 'So they might still be out there?' She looked at him directly. 'What if they're not done with you, my darling?'

Stephen put his arm around her shoulder. 'Don't worry, sweetie, it'll be fine. They have what they want, they have no reason to bother us anymore.'

Carver watched this exchange with interest. Stephen appeared amazingly composed and sure of himself for someone who, just over a day ago, was being held hostage by a group of thugs who beat up his colleagues.

'Isn't that right, Chief Inspector?' His eyes were bright and calm. Unnaturally so.

'Yes, I'm sure that's true,' Carver assured Celeste. She gave him a faint smile, looking marginally relieved.

'I just can't believe it about Nigel.' Stephen shook his head. 'Poor Matt, we're like brothers, as I'm sure he's told you. And Mary was always so kind to me.'

226

He was suddenly less poised, a look of genuine sadness veiling his face as tears filled his eyes. 'The thought of what he did to her.' He shuddered. 'It sickens me.' He paused, while Celeste stroked his shoulder sympathetically. Then he continued, 'And Charlotte must feel terrible, knowing that her father was there and did nothing to stop it. Will you press charges?'

'We've not got that far yet,' Carver said. 'We're bringing Davenport in for questioning.'

'I see.'

'Can you describe how you and Matthew got taken? What happened exactly?'

Stephen sipped his coffee, then said, 'Matt and I often get some fresh air over lunchtime. Usually around 12.30 because Matt's a bit weird like that; likes to go out the same time every day.'

'So I've heard.'

Stephen smiled. 'It's true. When we were in senior school, some of the meaner kids used to call him Rain Man, because he liked doing things a certain way.' He gave a wistful smile, and it was obvious to Carver how close the two men were. Stephen continued. 'We often walk over to Smithfield, where there's this great deli that sells the best meatball subs.'

'Which exit did you use?'

'We slipped out the back entrance, where deliveries come.'

'Why?'

'Ann Stevens on reception has an eagle eye, and a loose tongue. She reports everyone's comings and goings to Nigel. We regularly sneak out that way, when the courier guys are on a break. It's quite fun really, makes us feel like kids again. Anyway, the sun was shining, and we planned on being an hour or so, but we didn't want him to think we were slacking. It was only Monday after all.'

'So, you avoided the receptionists, but did you tell *anyone* you were heading out for lunch?'

The slightest hesitation, then, 'Er, yes, my secretary. And I think another secretary may have said "Enjoy the sunshine" as I got into the lift on my floor. Matt's one floor below me.'

Carver looked quizzically at Drake, then back at Stephen. 'Lift? Matthew said you both took the stairs.' He didn't take his eyes off Stephen, who suddenly seemed edgy. Clearly, something had unsettled him.

He gave a nervous laugh. 'God, yes, that's right, we did take the stairs. Silly me.' Another uneasy chuckle. 'Do you know, I'm so flustered by all that's gone on, I can't even remember what I did this morning, let alone last Monday. Guess my brain is more scrambled than I realised.'

Carver pondered his response. Why did he get the feeling there was more to it than that? Last Monday had to have been the most terrifying, yet the most memorable day, of his life. Surely, he would have recalled exactly how he'd left the building, especially if he and Matthew had been trying to avoid Ann Stevens by using the back exit? The young man was hiding something.

He mentally tagged it for later and moved on. 'What happened then?'

Stephen's strained expression relaxed a little. 'We never made it to the deli. No sooner had we turned right out of the back entrance, we heard a vehicle coming up behind us. Before we knew it, we were being bundled into the back of a van.'

'You never saw the men's faces?'

'No, not then, not ever. They wore balaclavas the entire time. I remember one of the men who grabbed us was noticeably shorter than the other, but that's about it.'

'And then you drove away?'

'Yes. They blindfolded us. The van took off, but maybe thirty seconds later, came to a stop.'

'What then?'

'A few minutes later, we heard the doors being opened and Charlotte and Richard being shoved inside by two more men. They were also blindfolded as we drove off.'

'So there were five men in total?'

'Yes.'

'How long were you driving?'

'Not long at first. We made a very brief stop, God knows where, then took off again.'

'How long for?'

Stephen shook his head, made a puffing sound. 'I don't know, about half an hour. Then we came to a stop. I think it must have been some garage or storage facility because we heard what sounded like a heavy door being raised, then the men hauled us out of the van, and into another vehicle.'

'You were still blindfolded?'

'Yes. Then we drove off again.'

'Again, for how long?'

'Maybe another thirty minutes. As I said, we were blindfolded, so I've no idea where we drove to. It was disorientating. They did the same before we left yesterday.' He paused, then said, 'Once we were inside the hideout, they removed our blindfolds, except when they videoed us. As far as I could tell, we were in a warehouse of sorts, but it had no windows. We could have been anywhere.'

Carver paused, then asked, 'Why do you suppose they beat Matthew and Charlotte, and not you?'

Stephen ran his hands through his hair, glanced at Celeste, then back at Carver. 'I thought it was because Charlotte's a girl, and the effects would be more shocking. As for Matt, he got mouthy with them, and I just figured he'd asked for it.'

'Thought? You've changed your mind? Why?'

'Isn't it obvious?' Stephen looked at Carver and Drake as if the answer should have been staring them in the face. 'You've already said as much. It's because of their connection to what happened all those years ago. Charlotte's Charles Dempsey's daughter, and Matthew is Mary's son.'

'So why take you?'

Stephen shrugged. 'Maybe they'd only intended to kidnap Matt and hadn't banked on me being around when the chance arose, but then had no choice but to take me too. Or, maybe they knew we were best mates.'

Something didn't add up in Carver's mind. Stephen's explanation was too simplistic. The back entrance CCTV had been disabled specifically around the time Matthew and Stephen nearly always took their lunch. A deliberate act which suggested the kidnappers had been monitoring their movements for some time and, quite possibly, had a mole inside the firm. Taking Stephen did not therefore appear to be random. 'Your kidnappers wanted Davenport to pay for what he did to Mary Jacobs. Why punish her son, who's done nothing wrong?'

'He took a job at Sullivans, didn't he? Davenport's firm. Maybe they presumed he knew what happened at Cambridge, and was therefore no better than Davenport for letting greed and ambition

230

overtake his conscience? Maybe they assumed he had no conscience at all?'

Carver had certainly considered this himself. After all, anything was possible. Even so, there was something unnatural about Stephen's answers that bugged him. Almost as if he'd been speaking from a script. It made him wonder whether the kidnappers had fed these answers to him under threat. He stored the idea in the back of his mind as he and Drake said their goodbyes and left the young couple in peace.

Chapter Twenty-Two

How are you?

Six thirty p.m. Maddy stared at Carver's text. She was supposed to be joining Cara for dinner and drinks with friends at a hip tapas restaurant in Notting Hill, at 8 p.m. But she hadn't even taken a shower, let alone thought about getting dressed. Since coming home, sitting still had proved impossible. She'd done a few mundane chores, started to watch a film, but she was too hyper to concentrate on anything for long.

She'd never been one to amble along in life, see where it took her. She was a planner, never did anything last minute, and she couldn't stand not knowing all the facts when it came to stuff that was important to her. And right now, that 'stuff' was Carver.

'OK,' she muttered to herself, 'so that's friendly, approachable, considerate.'

Good, thanks, how's your day been? She typed in a kiss, then deleted it, wrote it again, then deleted it once more. He didn't put one, and she didn't want him to get the wrong impression. Then again, wrong impression? What was she thinking? She'd slept with him, for God's sake! What other impression was there? OK, so she didn't want to appear needy before she knew how he felt. She left the kiss deleted, pressed send.

This was so unlike her. Strong, self-reliant, career-minded Maddy. Never one to get hung up on whether a guy she liked answered her texts within ten seconds, phoned her when he was *supposed to*, what that text/call, or lack of text/call meant? She usually didn't give a monkey's. She was too proud, too sure of herself, for all that crap.

But Carver was on the verge of turning her into one of those paranoid, needy women who monitored their phones twenty-four seven, jumping to attention whenever it buzzed or beeped.

'Get a grip,' she told herself, flinging the phone on the sofa. But just as she did, it buzzed, and she leapt to answer it. She was officially one of *those* women.

Had a long day. Could use a sounding board. Fancy grabbing dinner?

Maddy's heart raced. She shouldn't dis Cara, dis her friends. She was forever having a go at other friends who, once they became attached, seemed to disappear off the face of the planet. And now she was acting like one of them. But she couldn't help herself. For one, she wanted to see him, and two, she wanted to know what he'd found out from the hostages.

Sounds good, she responded. *When and where?*

Slowly, softly, sensually, he skimmed his finger along the back of her foot, her calf, her knee, where she shivered, her thigh, the curve of her bottom, the small of her back, between her shoulder blades, bringing it round to the side of her face, which he then tilted towards him, lowering his lips to hers, which he kissed with a tender passion. She shuddered again with a pleasure so exquisite, she felt like she could come again. Only five minutes after he'd made her groan like a wild animal.

She was living a dream, and sometimes she had to pinch herself just to make sure it was true. It wasn't that she was unattractive. She had her good points. Slim build, reasonably perky breasts, nice bone structure. But she wasn't a stunner. She wasn't the female version of him. So goddamn gorgeous. The guy every girl at the firm wanted to shag, and that probably went for the female partners too. She'd seen the way they sized him up from behind, flirted to his face, laughed at his jokes, funny or not. It sent her wild with jealousy, and at times she'd wanted to tell them to stay the fuck away, he was hers, and they needed to back off, bitches!

But she'd held it together by remembering their common cause – a cause they had all worked so hard for, and planned to perfection. If she blew their cover, none of them would forgive her, and most of all, she couldn't bear to let Matthew down.

Their love affair had developed fairly quickly. After their lunch with Richard, the three of them had met again in secret two weeks later, on a weekend. Richard had instructed them to travel separately to his cottage in the Cotswolds, where he'd be waiting. He'd been smack in the middle of a high court trial at the time, and Marianne hadn't given it a second's thought when he'd told her he had to work the weekend and prep a witness who was giving evidence the following week.

Charlotte had driven, while Matthew took the train, getting a cab from the station to the Barkers' charming cottage set in beautifully kept grounds in Lower Slaughter. There, Richard had welcomed them warmly, and before getting down to business, they'd chatted about this and that over sandwiches and tea in the quaint little kitchen, almost as if they were there purely for a social occasion.

But then, the idle chit-chat and frivolities over, they'd adjourned to the outside annexe – a mini cottage in itself – where Richard had

234

laid out a map of the firm on his desk, and gone over in detail his plan for the ultimate deception.

In a typically lawyerly fashion, he'd provided them with handouts, and they'd spent the next three or four hours fine-tuning how it was going to work. She remembered Richard's eyes. Animated, hungry to succeed. Their plan was the tonic that kept him going, gave him strength to fight the cancer. The thought of pulling off a crime – completely against his by-the-book lifestyle – had exhilarated him. It had exhilarated her, purely and simply because she'd been desperate to make Davenport pay, and her father sweat.

They'd agreed that Charlotte would continue to play the part of 'below-par trainee' (ever since their lunch her work had taken a sharp turn for the worse), the butt of jokes amongst the partners, while Matthew would continue to shine: the popular, handsome, meticulous, somewhat OCD partner-in-the-making who couldn't put a foot wrong. Either way, no one would suspect they planned on shaming their senior partner in the most humiliating way possible or screwing the firm out of six million pounds.

First and foremost, they had known that the threat of the past wouldn't be enough to scare Davenport, especially with no Mary to corroborate it. Yes, they had her diary, but Matthew didn't want that being made public if he could help it. It was his mother's private journal, and he'd wanted to keep it that way. They had therefore needed something current to sway him, and Richard, aware of his former classmate's regular trips to Soho, knew exactly what card to play. But they also knew it would be dangerous for one of them to hire the hooker. She'd likely see them on television and blow their cover to someone, if not the police. So, they'd needed another player. Someone outside the firm they could trust. Also, to organise the nuts

235

and bolts of their plan. Like purchasing their getaway vehicles and cloned plates, finding suitable premises to store the first van, and another property where they could hide. Not to mention ensuring the smooth facilitation of any back-up plan, should this option prove necessary. There was also the issue of getting the DVD laying out their demands to Davenport. In no uncertain terms could they risk it being traced back to them, so they'd needed another body to hand it over in person; it was too risky going to the post office with potential witnesses and CCTV.

Cue Charlotte's brother, Isaac. Frustratingly, despite force-feeding himself into gaining two stone before approaching the hooker, then crash dieting to lose it in the run-up to the abduction, they hadn't considered his scar. It was their one and only oversight – one that hadn't occurred to Richard until much later. But that would soon be taken care of. It was nothing to panic about.

It had been proposed that Richard would, at some stage, find the chance to tap Nigel's room. They were always in and out of each other's offices, and him walking in unannounced wouldn't be deemed unusual or suspicious. Later, listening in on his conversations from the hideout, they'd know how close he was to caving, and whether more pressure needed to be exerted.

On the day itself, Matthew, and another – probably Stephen, although this had yet to be confirmed – would go down to the basement toilets, which were hardly ever used, change into black combat trousers, black tops and black balaclavas, stuff their work clothes into rucksacks they were to wear on their backs, and, making sure no one was about, storm upstairs into the ground-floor conference suite, and take both Charlotte and Richard hostage. Isaac, having disabled the back entrance CCTV so there would be no way of verifying Matthew and Stephen's story about sneaking out that way, and using a laptop with a virtual private network – which he stored in the van and later destroyed – would be waiting in the vehicle purchased off Gumtree from a private seller up north (but now using a cloned plate), at a pre-agreed time on the road outside, and all five would make their getaway.

They would drive five or six miles to Leyton Industrial Village (having made a temporary detour off the main road to swap number plates) where a white VW Transporter, also purchased by Isaac from a private seller at the other end of the country, would be waiting inside a secure warehouse unit, serviced by steel roller shutters, sublet to Isaac for an extortionate fee by the director of a highly dodgy textile company operating in London's black market, who Richard had found through a trusted source. Richard would foot the bill. They'd park the blue van inside the unit and switch vehicles. They would then drive eight miles to Riverside Industrial Estate in Barking, having removed the second vehicle's number plate, where a single-storey industrial warehouse unit would be waiting for them, sublet to Isaac by the same dubious enterprise, but paid for by Richard. The hideout. They would buy several unregistered pay-as-you-go phones, and only use these when speaking with Davenport, the police and Pamela. And later, after the event, with each other. Isaac would also supply the warehouse with enough food and drink to last them the four nights they'd be hiding there, and would bring Richard's medication.

They would burn the 'kidnappers'' clothing and wait, hope, that things went smoothly. Of course, things hadn't panned out quite as they'd hoped, thanks to Carver.

But the hardest part of Richard's plan – the part that would be the real test of his protégés' nerve and desire to bring Davenport to justice – would be the injuries they must suffer.

They would have to be real. Make-up would not do. Richard knew they would all be checked over by medical staff as soon as they were free, and any attempt to fake their injuries would be obvious from the start. Charlotte's stomach had churned at the thought. She'd never suffered more than minor grazes from falling over, or from playful squabbles with her brother. The thought of suffering real pain had frightened her. But she also knew that Richard was right, and so both she and Matthew had agreed.

Now, lying in her lover's arms, Charlotte recalled the tears in his eyes when he'd taken a swing at her face. He'd uttered the words 'Sorry, my darling' repeatedly, and she'd known how much he'd hated himself for doing what he'd had no choice but to do.

Because it had to be him. Stephen had been too squeamish, Richard was physically incapable, and there was no way Isaac could bring himself to harm his beloved sister. Even if it was for a greater good. Afterwards, swigging whisky to numb the pain, she'd finished the job by stabbing her chest with a lit cigarette, a pain that had been strangely exhilarating.

It had been a different story with Matthew, though. Although they got on well enough, all Isaac had needed to do was imagine his father and Davenport in some seedy brothel drooling over a bunch of filthy whores, to ensure the police and medical staff never doubted the authenticity of Matthew's injuries.

That night, they'd got through a bottle of whisky to numb their pain and their guilt, hoping to God that it had all been worth it. Hoping and praying that their plan would succeed and that they'd make it out the other end.

That first rendezvous at the cottage, after Richard was done going over his plan, he'd given Matthew the go-ahead to make a move on

Stephen when the time was right. Matthew had hated the thought of lying to his best friend. Telling him he wasn't being kept on, even though, at that moment, his future at Sullivans had been far from decided. But as Richard had said, they had no choice; it was essential to make Stephen feel desperate.

Desperation was a powerful force – a force that often drove those afflicted to commit terrible crimes, achieve the unimaginable. Matthew was acutely aware of Stephen's gambling addiction which he'd thankfully appeared to have curbed, but which had left him with massive debts. The thought of no job at the end of his training contract would hopefully be enough to tip Stephen over the edge and convince him to join them.

Once Isaac and Stephen were both on board, the four would meet regularly at Richard's cottage until it was time to strike.

Getting Isaac to agree had not been too problematic. Although at first he'd told his sister that Richard was insane, that it was a crazy idea that would never work, that she was mad for putting her life and her future in jeopardy like that, once he'd calmed down, and she'd talked over the plan in detail with him, he'd realised this wasn't some ill-thought-through whim, and that she meant business. That, with or without him, she was doing this.

There was no way he was going to let her do this without him. She was the only surviving blood relative he gave a crap about. And besides, he didn't exactly have much of a future to lose. Isaac was a drifter, reluctant to commit himself to a steady relationship after witnessing his parents' unhappy marriage. A university dropout, he played local gigs in the same band he'd set up in the sixth form and worked at Starbucks during the day. The rest of his time was spent playing video games or surfing the internet. But there was one thing that motivated him. He'd wanted revenge on Davenport and his deadbeat father as much as Charlotte did.

Once their first meeting at the cottage was over, Richard drove home the same evening, but suggested that Charlotte and Matthew stay on and get to know each other better.

'After all,' he'd said with a sly grin, 'I've done my research on you two, and it seems to me you both have a lot in common but have yet to realise it.'

He'd obviously been confident that they'd agree. The fridge had been stocked with wine, pizza and dessert, and there'd been fresh towels and toothbrushes lined up in the bathroom. Neither had to be anywhere special, and as it was chilly, and already dark, they'd said, *what the hell?*

At first, things were awkward, but after a glass or two of wine, they'd relaxed. It was an unseasonably cold August, and so they'd made use of the real fire, munching pizza as they chatted about their childhoods, the good and bad times, realising how they'd both shared a special bond with their mothers. Mothers who had suffered at the hands of Nigel Davenport. And then, feeling increasingly drawn to one another because it had been the first time another person had really understood what they were going through, they'd moved on to lighter topics, talking about all sorts of things until they'd realised it was gone 1 a.m.

Now, one year later, Charlotte couldn't help but grin as she lay in Matthew's arms and thought back to their first kiss – when each had been reluctant to leave the other's company, despite the hour. Sitting on a rug by the fire, Matthew had looked into her eyes, said softly, 'You understand me so well.' She'd felt her face flush, and it wasn't because of the wine. He was so wonderful and handsome, but she also knew he was right. 'And you me,' she'd murmured. And then, he'd leant in and kissed her gently on the mouth, making her body tingle with desire, the way his kisses still did.

It hadn't been easy keeping their relationship a secret, although they'd confessed to Richard (who hadn't seemed surprised), after a month of secret trysts in unobtrusive hotel rooms. Never meeting at each other's homes, despite being desperate to act like a normal couple in public. It was crucial for the abduction to appear completely random. At first, at least.

But now they were almost home and dry. Now they could start their lives afresh. Together, and for all the world to see.

Chapter Twenty-Three

Maddy met Carver at a small Italian bistro nestled on the corner of an equally inconspicuous side street, a few minutes' walk from Old Street station. He was already seated at a table laid out for two set against the wall when she arrived. An inviting aroma invaded her nostrils as she handed the waiter her jacket, before joining him. His eyes lit up when he saw her. She was dressed in dark blue skinny jeans and an elegant black halter-neck top, and she'd accessorised with a pair of silver drop earrings and a matching chain. She looked incredible.

Butterflies gripped Maddy's insides as she sat down. Only that morning, they'd got naked together, and it was all she could think about as she smiled and said, 'Hello.'

There'd long been an awkwardness between them. The awkwardness of unfulfilled attraction. Now, despite this huge development in their relationship, there was the awkwardness of consummation. Neither knowing what the other was thinking having taken that giant step.

In need of some Dutch courage and noticing Carver's already half-empty glass of red wine, Maddy immediately ordered a large glass of the same.

Waiting for it to arrive, she took the chance to ask how things had gone with the hostages.

'OK. Tiring,' he replied.

'How was Charlotte?'

'Much better than I'd anticipated. Much more composed. After speaking to the likes of Gavin Turner, I'd expected her to be a mumbling bag of nerves. But she seemed quite together.' He paused, his eyes lingering on Maddy. Her stomach flipped, her pulse suddenly crazy, and she was relieved when the waiter arrived with her wine. No sooner had he put it down in front of her, than she took a large gulp. Then she spoke.

'Like I mentioned before, she was a model student, and obviously managed to impress the partners at interview. It's like Sullivans brought out this whole other side to her.'

'I get the feeling she won't see out her training contract.'

'She did hint at that at the hospital, but it seems a shame. A real waste. She could at least qualify. Maybe I'll pay her a visit. Try and convince her otherwise.'

It was so typical of her, thought Carver. Typical of her caring nature, but also her unwillingness to give in about anything.

'What about the others?' Maddy continued. 'How were they? Did Stephen and Matthew describe how they got taken?'

Carver explained what they had told him. Including the one difference in their stories.

'That is a bit strange. It was only last Monday, for goodness' sake. I'm not sure I would have forgotten a detail like that.'

'I agree.' Carver nodded. He hesitated.

'What is it?' Maddy probed.

'Something about Stephen's behaviour irks me. It struck me

as unnatural, his answers almost rehearsed, like he was keeping something from me.'

'Why on earth would he do that?'

'I don't know. Maybe the kidnappers gave him a script. Told him there'd be trouble if he didn't stick to it. He seems like the nervous type. And now we know they're all probably still out there, he'll be even more likely to keep in line.'

Maddy straightened. 'They are?'

Carver nodded, explained Mead's findings. Maddy was awash with intrigue, something she felt secretly ashamed of. She knew this meant the hostages could still be in danger, and that in many respects, it would have been better for all concerned had their abductors died in the explosion. But the challenge of tracking them down, of bringing them to account and finding out, once and for all, how they knew about Davenport's past, and their connection to Mary, appealed to her curious side. Her desire to solve a problem.

The waiter arrived, and they ordered.

'So how was your day?' Carver asked after he'd gone.

'Oh, you know, pretty uneventful.'

'Oh, I'm sorry to hear that.' Carver couldn't resist. 'Even this morning?' He smiled. She smiled back.

Her stomach flipped again. She had to say something; it was becoming unbearable. 'Carver,' she began, but he stopped her mid-flow.

'Jake, remember?'

She grinned, flicked a strand of hair away from her face. 'OK, Jake.' She smiled.

'Better.'

'Tell me what you're thinking, about us, I mean? Because I think we need to nip this in the bud before time runs away and we're both too chicken to say how we feel.'

She'd been shrewd in making her move. Smacking the ball straight in his court. Leaving him exposed and open to attack, while allowing her to form a response based on his. She was smart, she knew how to protect herself, and it only heightened her attractiveness.

Carver sighed, leant in. The background music had turned quieter. The last thing he wanted was to let the couple next to them in on their conversation.

'I think that this morning was amazing,' he replied, his eyes not leaving hers for a second. 'I always knew there was something between us two and a half years ago, and when I saw you in that conference room on Monday, I felt it again.' Maddy lowered her eyes briefly. He'd mirrored her thoughts. 'I don't regret it. Not one bit.'

Silence.

'But,' Maddy said. 'There's a "but", isn't there?'

Carver sighed again, this time more heavily as he took Maddy's hand in his. She felt both enlivened and comforted by his touch. 'But I worry about you, what people will say. Not about me, hell I couldn't give a shit. But you – you're seventeen years younger than me, with your whole life ahead of you, climbing your way to the top of the legal ladder as far as I can tell. You don't want to be tied down with a middle-aged divorcee, gossiped about behind your back. You and I know that what we have is pure, but people are shits, generally. They love to snipe and twist things to make a good story. Take that idiot Turner, for starters. He'd have kittens hearing one of his best associates was dating the senior police officer heading up two criminal investigations she was a part of.'

He was right, and Maddy knew it. But she'd done a lot of soul-searching since they'd parted that morning. Going over in her mind what the right step would be. She'd thought she'd reached a conclusion as she walked into the restaurant, but it wasn't until she'd spotted him, held his gaze, been in his presence once more, that she'd made up her mind.

She took a breath, took a chance. 'I know all that,' she said. 'But I guess, how shall I put this simply? I guess *I* couldn't give a shit.'

'You couldn't?' He looked knocked for six. It was not the answer he'd expected.

'I lost my parents when I was only nine. I was lucky. If it wasn't for my gran, I could have gone off the rails, turned into some delinquent screw-up. But she was there for me, every step of the way, and I turned out OK.' She paused.

Carver smiled. 'She did a fine job.'

'Thanks.' Maddy filled her lungs again, then said, 'But when it comes to relationships, I am a bit screwed up. I find it hard to commit, to truly let anyone in – a self-defence mechanism, I suppose. It's worked so far, but I know something's missing, and when I'm with you—' God, was she really saying this, really exposing herself like this? There was no turning back now, so she just pressed on. 'I know what that something is. Seeing Marianne has made me realise that life's too bloody short. When you find something good, you just need to hold on to it. So…' Another pause, then, 'So what do you think? Shall we have a go at making something of this? Of us, I mean?' She lowered her eyes, then looked up once more. 'I'm in, if you are?'

He didn't respond, and they continued to hold eye contact as if no one and nothing else existed. A powerful, tantalising moment. She had his answer. He didn't need to speak.

Later, after they'd made love, and Maddy slept peacefully in Carver's arms, it occurred to him how miserable he would have felt lying there without her – had she responded differently and decided to walk away. She was like a fine cognac. A tonic that warmed his insides, made him feel so damn good about himself. But she was also intoxicating. Dangerously addictive. In getting this close to her, he wondered how he'd ever free himself from her if things didn't work out.

He needed to live for the moment, enjoy what they had, while he could. But he couldn't lose himself in her completely. That was too dangerous.

Coombs and Rivers sat across from Nigel Davenport in an interview room at Hoxton East and Shoreditch police station. The décor was bland, harsh, uninviting. No windows or elaborate furnishings. Just a table, three chairs, and a door. It was a hostile, suffocating environment. Davenport found it hard to believe he was there.

If the abduction hadn't occurred, right now he'd have been sitting behind his magnificent mahogany desk, occasionally swivelling his shockingly expensive custom-made chair to admire the splendid view he had of the City. King of the Hill, the man everyone wanted to please, the man everyone looked up to. But now he was in hiding. Now he was nothing.

Having been kicked out by Pamela, he'd taken a room at a luxury hotel in South Kensington. Where Rivers and Coombs had found him, before bringing him in for questioning. At first, he'd been rude and aggressive. Said they must have been out of their minds to believe he'd attacked Matthew Gerard's mother all those years ago at Cambridge. The girl had been a liar, and her decision to quit had proved as much. But then they'd told him about Carver's conversation with Richard, and he'd nearly burst a blood vessel on hearing the bastard had ratted him in. Richard, who he'd thought was his friend, a man he could trust, a fellow alumni.

Now, having got over his initial shock, he claimed that his old friend had gone crazy; that clearly the cancer had tipped him over the edge, sent him doolally.

'Mr Barker was checked over by our psych team,' Rivers said. 'He's perfectly lucid. He remembers the night in question in some detail.'

'You can't possibly believe the word of a sick man, who's clearly been through a traumatic experience. It's pure hearsay; one seriously ill man's word against that of a healthy, perfectly sane one. You must have read about the sick having delusions. It happens all the time.'

The man knew how to argue, that was for sure. And he had a good point. They needed something more than Barker's testimony to make a charge like rape stick. But they wouldn't tell Davenport this just yet.

'So, you deny raping Mary Jacobs?' Rivers said.

'Of course I do! Like I told DCI Carver, we slept together, but only the once. Nothing more happened between us. You spoke to Stewart Larson, didn't you?'

Rivers didn't trust Larson as far as she could throw him. He was a slippery leech of a man, just like Davenport.

'You were Mr Larson's golden boy, or so I understand. The master always looks after his apprentice, isn't that what they say?'

Davenport's face reddened. He looked fit to burst. As if he'd never been so affronted in all his life. 'Stewart Larson is a respected academic, held in high regard by past and present Cambridge alumni. If you're insinuating anything untoward on his part, I would watch your back. Slander is a nasty business, DC Rivers.'

248

Rivers smacked the table hard with her fist, and it made Davenport recoil with fright. 'Don't you threaten me. Your fancy legal mumbo jumbo doesn't impress me. This isn't *Law and Order*, this is the real world. Got it?' She gave him a menacing look, and he nodded slowly.

'Mr Davenport, were you and Mr Barker close at university?' Coombs took it down a level, tried to play good cop.

Davenport sighed. 'Yes, for about the millionth time. We're still working together, for Christ's sake, or rather, we were. Doesn't that tell you something?' He paused, a look of recognition shrouding his face. As if a thought had just occurred to him, and the pieces of a challenging puzzle were suddenly fitting together.

'What is it, Mr Davenport?'

Davenport gave a knowing smile. Then said coolly, 'He's getting his revenge.'

'Revenge? For what?' Rivers and Coombs both looked perplexed.

'For me beating him to senior partnership. We both went for it at the same time, you see, but he lost out on the final prize. The one prize he'd had his eye on since we started our articles as lowly trainees.'

'But why would he be bitter about that? I assume you got the vote of the partners fair and square? To try and take revenge – what is it, nearly eight years since you were elected senior partner? – doesn't make sense.'

Davenport smoothed his fingers over his lips, as if prepping himself for a difficult truth. 'I might not have won the position fair and square.'

Rivers eyed him with disdain. *What's the tosser going to say now?* 'Meaning?'

'I may have made certain promises over the odd drink, the odd lunch, here and there, to various partners. Just to, you know...'

'You bribed them?' Rivers said bluntly.

'I wouldn't put it like that.' Davenport shifted uneasily in his chair. The room was starting to contract. He fiddled with his collar. He needed some air. He'd never been a religious man, but maybe there was a God after all, and now he was paying for his sins.

'I can't see there's any other way to put it.' Rivers leant in. 'And you think Mr Barker somehow found out about this?'

Davenport shook his head slowly. 'He's never said anything to my face, but I wouldn't be surprised. It'll only have taken one slip of the tongue on the golf course, or after one too many drinks at some dinner or other, and hey presto, the secret's out. And besides, partners talk, they love to gossip, they think they're above reproach.'

'You count yourself in that category, do you, Mr Davenport?' Rivers said.

'Yes.' Davenport gave a heavy sigh. 'Yes, I suppose I do.'

Rivers and Coombs excused themselves for a quick chat in the hallway. It was frustrating, but the fact was, they didn't have enough to charge him. It was one man's recollection of events versus the other's. Like Davenport said. Not only that, Davenport's latest revelation called into question Barker's motives.

Reluctant as she was to release him, Rivers knew she had no choice. But she didn't doubt the bastard was guilty. As was Larson. They just needed something tangible to prove it.

Chapter Twenty-Four

It was like it had never happened. The firm back to normal. Business as usual. An army of sharp suits patrolled the building, all with important calls to make, important meetings to attend, important documents to amend. Every employee on a mission. Not an idle bone in the building now that the hostages had been freed.

Every hour billed meant more money for the firm, and a potentially bigger bonus for staff. Lunch was for wimps, as was sleep and social time. Stepping into the spring-cleaned ground-floor conference suite, no one would ever have guessed that seventeen staff members had been held in there at gunpoint just seven days ago. Over the weekend, the room had been rearranged, redecorated and renumbered: a clever psychological tactic designed to disassociate staff and clients from any memory of last Monday.

The partners would be electing a new senior partner later in the week, but for now, Mark Simmons, the managing partner, was holding the fort. Of course, there was talk behind closed doors, and especially amongst the gossipy secretaries, as to why Davenport had resigned. Particularly as word of his donation to Rape Crisis had spread. But that was all it was. Talk. Idle speculation. They knew nothing material, could assume nothing. There was also no point. What was done was done. They had their staff safely returned, and it was time to move forward. Albeit with a few less clients who'd decided to play it safe and switch allegiance.

Charlotte hadn't yet resigned, and Maddy prayed she could convince her not to when she called by her flat later that evening. She just hoped she wasn't already too late.

At 8.30 a.m., Maddy sat down at her desk and logged in, glancing over at Charlotte's empty desk in the corner. Naturally, forensics had been all over it, including her computer, but found nothing helpful. Everything had been put back in the exact spot they'd found it, including an empty mug, its rim stained with lipstick. *I should wash that out*, thought Maddy. Needing a coffee herself, she went over and picked up the mug, her attention caught by a framed family photograph lying next to Charlotte's phone.

Maddy had noticed it before, but never seen it up close. She picked it up and took a moment to study the happy family. Charlotte must have been about sixteen. Hair in a ponytail, she still had braces, her figure still boyish. Her mother had a warm, kind, open face. Her arms were wrapped affectionately around her children's shoulders, while Charles Dempsey, although smiling broadly, stood a little apart. Almost as if he was a friend, rather than a family member. There was no doubting the special bond between his wife and their children, though.

Charlotte had mentioned Isaac several times. Maddy knew how close they were, even closer since their mother's death. He was a nice-looking boy, except for, she noticed, the visible scar running across his chin. A boyhood scuffle most likely, she thought. It made her think of Carver. He had a similar scar, not, as she'd romantically imagined, heroically acquired in the line of duty, but through tripping over his shoelaces as a kid, after his mother had reminded him several times to tie them up. Maddy couldn't help smiling as she thought back to Saturday night when, lying in bed, she'd finally plucked up the courage to ask him. Resting her head in her right hand, she'd traced the scar with her left index finger, then kissed it tenderly after he'd told her.

'Daydreaming, Madeline?'

Gavin Turner's strident voice nearly made Maddy jump and drop the photo. She recovered quickly and placed it down gently.

'Sorry, didn't mean to startle you.' *Like hell you didn't.* 'Still jumpy from last week, are we?' There was no concern in his voice. It was disparaging, rather than kind. And to think that the little shit had gone as white as a sheet and as quiet as a mouse when the men had burst in. Where had his smart comments been then? It was such a cliché, but so true. Turner had a complex about his height, or lack thereof. And he chose to make up for it by howling at everyone at the top of his lungs. And now he was set to replace Richard as Head of Litigation, things were sure to get worse. The man would be intolerable. Maddy wondered whether it was time to jump ship.

'You might want to get your PA to start packing up Charlotte's stuff,' Turner said.

'Why? She's not resigned as far as I know.'

'Yes, but she will,' Turner tittered. 'She couldn't hack it before all this happened, she'll be a complete headcase now.'

Maddy wanted to wallop him, but she restrained herself. 'Don't be so sure. She's stronger than you think.'

Turner looked at her as if she was mad, gave a little *hmm*, then strutted off imperiously.

He looked awful, and Rivers felt shitty for intruding, but she had no choice. His poor wife had answered the door, not looking too great herself, and after explaining their reason for calling, Marianne had reluctantly led Rivers and Coombs upstairs to the sitting room. Her husband's clothes seemed to hang off him, as did the skin on his face. Like melting plastic. But his sunken eyes still managed a smile as they shook hands.

They apologised again for the intrusion, then recounted their conversation with Davenport.

After they'd finished, Richard didn't respond immediately. Perhaps because he didn't know how to, or was working up the strength to do so, Rivers wasn't entirely sure. Finally, he said, his voice wheezy, 'It's true, I did discover Nigel bribed several of my colleagues to guarantee his appointment as senior partner. Their vote tipped the balance in his favour. It was my last shot at the post.'

Rivers glanced at Marianne. This was clearly news to her. What else hadn't he told her? 'Richard, you never mentioned this to me.'

'I didn't want to burden you, my dear. It was all so petty, really.'

Another betrayal. Tears glistened in his wife's eyes, like early morning dew. 'Another important thing you've kept from me.' She was trying hard to keep her voice steady, but it trembled nonetheless. Rivers sought a diversionary tactic.

'Mr Barker, Mr Davenport believes you fabricated a story about him raping Mary Jacobs to get your revenge against him.'

Richard laughed bitterly, shook his head as if he wasn't surprised. 'Oh, that's so typical of Nigel. Thinking others behave in the same underhanded way that he does.'

'So it's not true?'

'Of course not.' Richard swiped the air with the back of his frail hand. 'If I'd wanted to take revenge, I wouldn't have waited eight years to do so. It makes no sense. And I certainly wouldn't have made up a story as horrific as that. Why on earth would I want to drag a good woman's name through the mud? And besides, surely the fact that our abductors demanded Nigel make a donation to Rape Crisis suggests it's true?'

'That's a fair point. How did you find out about the bribes?'

'Over a drink with one of the partners. Someone whom I'd long considered my friend, and whose vote I had counted on. Nigel had promised him certain privileges in exchange for his vote.'

'I could kill him.' Marianne's face was contorted with rage.

'He's not worth it, my love,' Richard said soothingly. The man was near death, but he had such a peaceful air about him, thought Rivers. So calm, so content, despite the rough hand he'd been dealt. She admired him greatly.

'For what it's worth, I believe you, Mr Barker, but I'm afraid we don't have enough to charge Davenport with. It's your word against his, and unless and until we have something else, something tangible, to prove he raped Mary Jacobs, he's a free man.'

There was a flicker of apprehension in Richard's eyes, no doubt betraying the guilt he felt for having kept quiet for so long. Especially now that he knew Matthew Gerard was the poor woman's son. Rivers wondered if they'd spoken, whether Gerard had it in his heart to forgive a dying man and the poor choices he'd made.

She and Coombs said their goodbyes and left the Barkers alone. Hoping Mrs Barker wouldn't be too harsh on her husband for trying to protect her.

Richard stood by the window, watching his wife cross the street. She was on her way to meet a friend for coffee. She'd been reluctant to leave him, even for a second, but he'd insisted. He could see how stressed and tired she was, and he'd told her that the break would do her good.

He didn't want her to neglect her friends. She'd need them when he was gone. She needed to carry on living her life when his was over.

But he also had a selfish reason for persuading her to go out. He needed to make a call. In private. He left the room and made for his study. Once inside, he went over to his desk, unlocked the bottom drawer, and pulled out a phone different to the one he'd used to call Stephen two days ago, and which he'd since disposed of. Then he dialled a different unregistered number. 'They've released him,' he said when the other person picked up.

'Fuck, you've got to be kidding me?'

'No. The police have just left. They didn't have enough to charge him. It was my word against his. There's only one way now, and you know what that is. Question is, how much do you want him to suffer? He's resigned. That, and the personal donation he's made to Rape Crisis has sparked all sorts of gossip. Isn't that enough?'

At the other end of the call, Matthew thought for a moment. Was it enough? A man like Davenport – ruthless to a T – would probably bounce back before long. The City was fickle and forgiving of men who'd helped make it richer. Give it a few months and Davenport's resignation would be old news. Plus, he had contacts all over. A few words in the right ears here and there, and he'd be back on track. No, it wasn't enough. He'd reined in his anger for a year. Swallowed his hatred, his desire to pummel the bastard's face to a messy pulp every time he saw him. He'd sucked up to him, smiled at him, practically licked his backside, and he didn't want all that to have been for nothing.

No. He wanted the son of a bitch behind bars, with no chance of redemption or forgiveness. And there was only one way to achieve that, God rest her soul. His father might not like it, but then again, he was still angry with Frank for keeping it a secret all these years. Even if he didn't like the idea at first, he'd come round, eventually.

'No, it's not enough. And it shouldn't be enough for you. You loved her, didn't you?'

Richard felt his eyes water. Of course he had loved her. This was why the guilt ate away at him every day. She wasn't just some girl. She was special. She hadn't seen him as special, though, and perhaps that's what had stopped him from doing more that night. She hadn't been his to fight for.

'You know I did.'

'Well then, we're in agreement. I'll let the others know.'

Chapter Twenty-Five

Tuesday, 9 a.m. Carver hung up the phone, having just spoken to Mark Simmons, who'd told him that two hundred thousand of the six million wired to Ansbacher (Bahamas) Limited had been withdrawn on Saturday morning. The rest had been wired to a different account in Gibraltar, held in the name of a locally incorporated company called Jericho Ltd, no doubt set up in the same manner as Pellingtons, that is, using a local law firm, with falsified identification papers.

It was further proof that the kidnappers were still out there. But the question was, *who* had made the transactions? And who had set up Jericho Ltd, knowing that under local law there was no requirement to disclose the identity of the beneficial owner of a Gibraltar-based non-resident company, unless by order of the Supreme Court?

Bahamian secrecy laws also made it virtually impossible to determine who owned a Bahamian international company. And under local law, it was a crime to reveal account information without the owner's permission, unless by order of the court. Carver dialled Drake's extension and ordered him to get an order, pronto.

He'd also received confirmation that Davenport's office had been bugged. A tiny microphone had been concealed inside a framed photograph of his wife and children which sat on his desk. Giving credence to both his and Richard's theory that there'd been a mole on the inside. But who had placed it there? A secretary, another lawyer, a client, a security guard, even a cleaner perhaps, who knows? All had been questioned thoroughly, and none had given him reason to suspect their involvement.

Aside from a few texts, he'd had no contact with Maddy since she'd left his place mid-morning on Sunday. He'd spent the rest of the day with Daniel, kicking around a football in Victoria Park, followed by a movie and dinner at Pizza Express, Daniel's favourite. He smiled when he thought back to his son's comment about him seeming different. Had his new-found happiness, new-found life, been that obvious to an eight-and-a-half-year-old kid? Then again, children were often more perceptive than adults, who, so frazzled by everyday life, so consumed by their own problems, failed to notice what was right in front of them.

He'd nearly choked on a dough ball when his son had asked, matter-of-factly, 'Have you got a girlfriend, Dad?' He couldn't lie to his son. There was no point. Not if he and Maddy were trying to make a go of things. Daniel would have to meet her at some stage. And in any case, he was more fearful of Rachel's reaction than Daniel's.

'As a matter of fact, I am seeing a lady,' he'd replied.

His son had grinned, revealing a large piece of basil which had become wedged between his two front teeth. 'Can I meet her? Is she pretty?'

Carver had laughed. 'She's very pretty, yes. But it's early days, so don't get too excited just yet. If things go well, you'll get to meet her in time.'

'But she makes you happy, Dad?'

'Yes' – Carver had smiled, Maddy's face floating before him – 'she does.'

Daniel had given him another leafy grin and no more was said on the matter.

The phone rang, stirring Carver from his flashback. It was the duty sergeant. 'Got a girl down here waiting to see you. Says it concerns last week's hostage crisis.'

'Did she give a name?'

'Cherry, sir. She said that's all you'd need.'

Carver leapt up from his chair. Surely she had important news? Otherwise, why would she be here? Perhaps the scarred man had been in contact again?

'Take her to room three, Sergeant. And offer her a drink of something. I'll be right there.'

She looked very different to the first time they'd met. Dressed in a flowery summer dress, and cute powder-blue ballet pumps. Neutral make-up, her flaxen hair tied up in a high ponytail. Like Sandy from *Grease* before she became a Pink Lady.

She stood up as soon as Carver walked in. A barely touched cup of the station's finest in front of her on the table, an anxious look on her face.

'Hello, Cherry, you're looking…'

'Different?' The cheeky grin from Spearmint Rhino re-emerged. 'Yes.'

'You don't expect me to go around dressed in a bra and thong all day, do you? That's my job, Chief Inspector, where I like to think of myself as an actress, of sorts. *This* is the real me.'

'I like it better.' Carver smiled. She blushed, then sat down, as did Carver.

'So, what can I do for you?' he asked gently. He didn't want to come across as aggressive. Could tell she was already doubting her decision to come, and whatever it was she wanted to get off her chest, it needed gentle coaxing, not blanket interrogation.

She picked up her cup, took a nervous sip, then put it down and looked around as if someone might be watching.

'It's OK, you can tell me.'

'I saw him.'

'Who?'

'The guy who paid me off.'

'Are you sure? When? Where?'

'Positive. Yesterday. I walked straight past him on Sloane Street.'

'Sloane Street? What were you doing there?'

Cherry looked put out. 'Why shouldn't I have been there?' she asked crossly, her brow furrowing. 'It's a free country, isn't it?'

Carver squirmed in his seat. 'Look, Cherry, I'm not…'

'Save it,' she snapped. 'I was treating myself, OK? Had a bit of spare cash to spend, so I was having a nosy on the King's Road.'

'What time was that?'

'About 3.30 p.m. I'd just finished shopping and was walking back to Sloane Square Tube station when I saw him come out of some posh building on Sloane Street. Shoulders hunched, collar up, hands in his pockets, wearing a cap, like before. Like he didn't want to be recognised. He'd lost a load of weight. Not ultra-skinny, but lean, fit-looking. Even so, I knew it was him.'

'How?'

'From the eyes. Dark and very distinctive.'

'You made eye contact?'

She nodded. 'He glanced up, and we briefly caught each other's eye. But he walked right past. Even though he had a cap on, I noticed he had a giant plaster stuck to his chin.'

'Where the scar was?'

'Yep. I went and checked out the building he came out of. It was a private clinic, where they do plastic surgery and stuff like that. I'm guessing he had it removed or something.'

It was the biggest lead they had so far. One of the kidnappers was still in the country, but for how long?

'Cherry, I really appreciate you coming in. I'd like you to give a description of this man to one of our sketch artists. He may have had his scar seen to, but he's not had a face transplant. Will you do that for me?'

'Sure,' she said. 'But only if you get me a decent cup of coffee. This stuff tastes like shit.'

Forty-five minutes later, Carver gathered his team on the station floor, and held up two sketches of Target 1. The first sketch showed him to be around five-ten, approximately two hundred pounds, olive skin, brown eyes, Roman nose, probably short brown hair although he'd been wearing a cap. The second sketch had one big difference. He was now around thirty pounds lighter, sporting a strong, lean physique, his cheekbones more defined by his dramatic weight loss.

It wasn't much, but it was better than nothing.

Later, he and Drake would pay the clinic a visit, but Carver wasn't expecting much more than a polite steer towards the door. He knew as well as anyone that doctors were bound by the Hippocratic oath to keep details of their patients and their identities a secret. But this was a major police investigation, and if necessary, he'd obtain a disclosure order to get the information he needed.

Chapter Twenty-Six

That afternoon, Carver and Drake found themselves sitting across from David Middleton. A top consultant specialising in scar revision treatment. He oozed *public school boy*, dripped money and eyed his visitors with derision. With slick black hair, and a honed, bronzed physique, he looked like he spent half his day in the gym or on a tanning bed. His charcoal-grey, made-to-measure suit must have cost a thousand pounds minimum, and his teeth were unnaturally straight and white. Carver remained civil, explaining the purpose of their visit.

Middleton spent a few seconds studying the sketch, then handed it back with a shake of his head. 'I'm sorry, gentlemen, but you know as well as I do, I cannot divulge confidential information about my patients.'

His eyes were hard and unreceptive. Carver found him tricky to read. He forced a smile. 'I appreciate that. But I am conducting a police investigation. At least give me a name. At least confirm this is the same man you treated.'

'No.' Another scowl. 'I won't tell you anything without a court order. I'm sorry but your journey here has been wasted.'

Carver swallowed his disappointment. He'd expected as much but it had been worth a shot. After a brief thanks and quick handshake, he and Drake left empty-handed.

Walking down the road, a breathless voice called after them. 'Excuse me!'

They turned around in surprise to see Middleton's secretary standing there, catching her breath. She was fair-haired, attractive, with striking green eyes, and a gentle character. She'd been kind enough to bring them coffee as they'd sat waiting for her boss to become free.

'Yes, how can I help you?'

'You're investigating last week's hostage crisis, aren't you?' Her lovely eyes were filled with trepidation, and she glanced around fretfully as she spoke.

'Yes, do you know something?'

'I'm not sure, but my brother, Stephen Baines, was one of the hostages. I'd like to be of help, if I can?'

Carver studied her more closely but found it hard to believe they were brother and sister. Her features were so different, aside from the green eyes. She was a looker, while he, quite simply, was not. Then he recalled that they were half-siblings.

'We're half-brother and sister.' She'd read Carver's mind before he'd twigged, and had no doubt received the same quizzical look countless times before. 'My name is Sophie. Sophie Baines.'

'Yes, sorry, I realise that now.'

She lowered her gaze. Almost a look of guilt in it. 'I don't suppose Stephen's talked about me? You see, my father left Stephen and his mother for mine when he was only five. Despite Dad claiming he only got together with Mum after they'd split up. Stephen's not on speaking terms with Dad since his mum passed away from breast cancer.'

'When was that?'

'Steve had just finished his A Levels, poor guy. After she died, he moved as far away from us as he could. Went to Leeds University. Hasn't spoken to Dad or me since – aside from a few terse words with Dad last Friday, before the explosion. Before his mum's death, he'd see us on and off, and we all got on OK. Dad and I were both in bits last week. We were just so relieved when they got released.'

'What did Stephen say to your father at Leyton Industrial Village?'

'That he shouldn't have come.'

'I see.'

'We tried to make contact over the weekend, but he put the phone down on Dad, and when I tried, his girlfriend picked up and said he didn't want to speak to me. She was very nice, very apologetic. I don't blame her for a second.'

'I'm sorry, it must be tough on you.'

'He resents me.' A tear ran down her cheek, but she quickly wiped it away. Almost as if she felt she didn't deserve pity. 'I don't blame him. The fact is, our father chose my mother over his, and my mum's still alive, while his isn't. Of course, no one could have known she'd get cancer when Dad left her, but I guess that's small consolation for Stephen. It must have been incredibly tough for him.' She paused, then switched topic. 'I presume you came to see my boss because you believe he might be of some help to your investigation? Were you after details of a particular patient of Mr Middleton's?'

'Yes, I was.' Carver glanced at Drake. 'But you'll be getting yourself into a lot of trouble if you release confidential information to me behind Mr Middleton's back.'

Sophie gave a weak smile. 'I suppose you could call it a guilty conscience, but I want to feel like I've done something to help Stephen. Christ, he's been through enough in his twenty-four years.'

Carver was only too aware of the hot water Sophie might be landing herself in, but he wasn't one to play by the book; his urge to solve the case, the smell of a way in, however small, taking over. 'Show the young lady,' he directed Drake.

Drake was used to Carver bending the rules, but that didn't mean he was entirely comfortable with it. He didn't want the girl getting into trouble. Reluctantly, he pulled the sketch from his inside pocket.

Sophie studied it for a few seconds, then said, 'Yes, he was here yesterday.' Carver's heart raced at the news. 'Came in for scar revision treatment.'

'On his chin?'

'Yes. He was a morose sort. Not much of a talker, kept his head down, wore a cap. Twenty-three, or so I remember from the file.'

'And the name?'

Sophie looked over her shoulder, then back at Carver. 'That's not going to help you, I'm afraid.'

'Why's that?'

'He said his name was Al Capone.'

Carver thought he must have misheard. 'What?'

Sophie repeated the name. 'Private clinics like Cressingtons are prepared to overlook minor details like a patient's real name.' *In which case, how is a court order going to help*, thought Carver.

'What about an address?'

'I can check, but it's probably bogus, like his name.'

Carver sighed. *She's probably right.* 'No photo?'

Sophie shook her head.

'Is he scheduled for a routine check-up?'

'Yes, two weeks from now.'

'Call me as soon as he appears.' Carver handed her his card. Then smiled. 'Thank you, Ms Baines. You've been most helpful.'

A few minutes later, driving through heavy traffic in rush hour, Carver got a call from Rivers. The court order had come through, and now the Bahamian bank had no choice but to cooperate with his investigation. A couple of local officers were currently on their way to see the manager of Ansbacher. Hopefully they'd soon have an idea of who was handling the money.

Chapter Twenty-Seven

Six thirty p.m., Tuesday, and Maddy was running late. A last-minute visit from a partner in Corporate delaying her departure by a good forty minutes. Corporate were an arrogant bunch. Notorious for starting their day at least an hour after the rest of the firm had already accumulated several billable hours, blaming their erratic schedule on equally erratic clients who frequently dropped a ridiculous deadline on their desk one minute before close of business. They were also infamous for bothering the litigators with problems they themselves had created, and needed help extricating themselves from. Maddy didn't know how many times she'd helped some cocky corporate wise guy get out of a tricky scrape, receiving no more than a terse *thanks*, as if she didn't have work of her own to manage.

Thankfully, on this occasion, a thirty-minute discussion was all that was needed, and she took her chance to flee the scene, avoiding eye contact with everyone until she was out on the street. It was hot and sticky, the balmy weather of last week back after a brief lull over the weekend. It was only Tuesday, but summer nights in the City made every night feel like a Friday. City slickers sipping chilled, crisp white wine, cold bottled beer, al fresco, ties undone, jackets off, legs exposed, laughing and chatting in a favourite haunt, a trusty pub or a trendy bar. It didn't matter where you drank, only that you'd escaped the stress and tedium of the office for freedom, natural warmth and company. It made the long days shorter, the work more bearable. Maddy would have killed for a glass of Chablis herself, but right now she was sandwiched between two men with an apparent dislike of deodorant, riding the Jubilee line to St John's Wood, on her way to Charlotte's flat. She hadn't made it there last night, despite her good intentions. She'd been stuck on a conference call for two hours, then had some follow-up work to do, causing her to stay late at the office. There was still no resignation from Charlotte, so she lived in hope that she hadn't made her final decision yet.

The Tube train arrived at Swiss Cottage, made a brief stop, then pushed off swiftly. She was almost there, but she was glad she'd called ahead to make sure Charlotte was home. Apparently, she was going out at 8.30.

Ten minutes later, she stood in front of Charlotte's block, waiting to be buzzed up. She didn't have to wait long, and in less than thirty seconds, the two women were sharing a warm embrace.

Maddy was the first to break away. 'Let me look at you.'

Charlotte appeared much improved since Friday, her wounds fading rapidly. 'I've just been sitting around here on my butt most of the time,' she explained. 'My doctor instructed me to rest, so I have. But it means I've been raiding the biscuit tin, and my jeans are already feeling it.' She patted her hips.

'Nonsense,' Maddy said. 'Rest is what you need, and deserve, after the hell you've been through. And besides, you're a skinny mini, you can afford to put on a few pounds.'

Charlotte gave a half-smile. 'Thanks, I think.' She paused, then read Maddy's mind. 'Fancy some wine?'

'Love some.'

Five minutes later, they were sitting on the sofa with their wine. Maddy again asked how she was doing, while Charlotte enquired after things at the firm. It led Maddy to her main reason for being there.

'So, when can we expect you back?'

Charlotte's face dropped slightly. 'Like I mentioned at the hospital, I don't think I can face coming back.'

'But that's crazy. You're so near to qualifying. At least qualify, then you can tell us all to sod off.'

'I know I'm not being kept on, Maddy, it's obvious, even to a dumbo like me. Gavin Turner looks like he wants to spit in my face every time I walk past him.'

'Don't be silly, you're exaggerating.'

'Am I? I hate it there, Maddy. I was too embarrassed to leave before – too scared, if I'm being honest. But I guess it takes being in a situation like last week to give a person the strength to say *no, no more.*' She paused, then said, 'I won't stand for it a second longer.'

There was a grit in Charlotte's eyes that took Maddy by surprise. Was she referring purely to last week? Or was there something else on her mind? Something bigger?

Maddy made a last-ditch attempt to change her mind. 'They might be too afraid to drop you now. Afraid it'll make them look heartless.'

'I don't want their pity,' Charlotte said bitterly. 'I want to be there on merit.'

Maddy tried a different tack. 'How does your father feel about you quitting?'

'He has no say in the matter. I know what he did, or rather failed to do, all those years ago, and he's lost any scrap of respect I might otherwise have had left for him.'

270

Maddy tried to imagine how she'd feel. Knowing her father had witnessed a rape and done nothing to stop it. Not only that, had kept his mouth shut, and remained friends with the perpetrator ever since. How could you trust someone like that again? Look at him in the same way? Feel for a person so apparently callous? She couldn't help but sympathise.

'Have you spoken to the others since Friday?'

'Other hostages, you mean? It's OK, Maddy, you can say it, it's not a word I'm afraid to hear.'

Maddy smiled at her courage. 'Yes, the other hostages.'

'No. Well, only briefly to Richard. He's invited us to his place this evening.'

'Oh?'

'Yes. Marianne wanted to have us over for a meal. A celebration, I guess, that we're all still alive.' She paused, a heavy sadness cloaking her face. 'Poor woman. She's got her husband back, only too aware that he'll be taken from her again soon. This time, for good.'

Maddy saw how fond Charlotte had become of Richard. It was amazing how shared trauma drew people closer together, even in a short time. They'd probably had nothing in common before, and Richard had been dead against keeping Charlotte on at the firm. *Nice girl, but she's way out of her depth.* She remembered his words clearly, although she'd never tell Charlotte, of course. There was no point. It served no purpose.

Last week's events had ensured they'd always share a special connection. Their lives forever entwined. Bonded by a terrifying experience that others would never be able to truly understand.

As she contemplated this, Maddy didn't yet realise how right she was.

'Why are you calling me? I've told you before, I don't want to talk to you. I don't want anything to do with you.'

'Stephen, please, just hear me out,' Sophie Baines pleaded down the phone. 'I just want to help.'

'Help? Help with what? I don't need your help.'

'It concerns the men who took you.'

There was silence at the other end of the line. Finally, 'I'm listening.'

'I think one of the men who took you came into the clinic yesterday.'

'Clinic? What clinic?'

'Oh, that's right. You've been so busy wanting nothing to do with me, you've no idea what goes on in my life.'

More silence. They had barely said two words to each other in seven years. Stephen had no idea what his half-sister was up to because he'd had no urge to know. But now he did. Now he wanted to know everything. 'Go on.'

'I work at Cressingtons, a private clinic on Sloane Street. The consultants there conduct various surgical and non-surgical procedures, including scar revision treatment.'

Stephen's legs were suddenly wobbly, his throat dry and tight. This couldn't be happening. His half-sister had seen Isaac and knew about the scar on his chin he'd recently had treated. The scar that identified him as one of the kidnappers. The scar that would lead the police to the rest of them.

'So?' He tried to sound unmoved, forcing down the acid that had suddenly accumulated in his gullet. 'What's your point?'

'The police came knocking earlier. They seem to think this guy is one of the kidnappers. Showed me a police sketch, which certainly looked like him. Do you remember seeing a scar on one of them?

He'll be back for a routine check-up before long, and I'll make sure the police will be waiting for him. I told you, I want to help, make you see that I care for you and want the best for you. You can't blame me for Dad's mistakes. I played no part in them, and you know it.'

He couldn't be angry with her. It was a kind thing to do, and he realised she was risking her job for him. 'The men all wore balaclavas. I never saw any scar.'

'Oh, I see. Well, as I said, the police seem to have evidence proving this guy is one of them, so I just wanted you to know I plan on cooperating fully. Even if it costs me my job. I mean, I know you're free, but surely you won't be able to rest easy until they're caught? The papers say forensics are certain no bodies were in the van when it exploded, so they're obviously still out there, somewhere.'

That they are, thought Stephen. First, he'd made a blunder in his interview with Carver, and now his half-sister was meddling where she shouldn't. The others would start to wish they'd never brought him in. He was a curse. A chink in their armour. But surely, they couldn't blame him for this? How was he to know that the half-sister he never spoke to worked at the same clinic where Isaac chose to have his scar treated? He should have gone abroad to have it done. Why the hell hadn't he?

Stephen tried to stay calm. 'Thank you, Sophie,' he said. 'I appreciate your help. It is a worry, yes, knowing they're still out there, and we'll all feel safer once they're caught.'

It was the nicest thing he'd said to her in seven years, and it made Sophie smile. They said goodbye, one of them with a warm, fuzzy feeling in her stomach, the other feeling as sick as a dog. No sooner had Stephen put down the phone, he reached in his pocket for his pay-as-you-go phone and dialled a number. Waited, then said, 'We have a problem.'

Fortunately, Maddy Kramer had just left when Stephen called. Charlotte would, of course, have acted like nothing was up, but it was easier not having to. She was getting tired of acting, as much as it had been fun to begin with.

She couldn't believe such a coincidence could happen. She was angry with Stephen for not doing due diligence on his sister. When the five of them had gathered at Richard's cottage a few days after Matthew had recruited Stephen, Richard had made it clear that every angle needed to be covered. Family, friends, colleagues. No stone left unturned. No shortcuts, no secrets. And when Matthew had mentioned Sophie, Stephen had insisted she knew nothing about his life, and therefore could never cause a problem for them. But he'd been wrong, so wrong. And now they had not one, but two eyewitnesses to worry about. The hooker and Sophie. Not only had the hooker met Isaac when he approached her about filming Davenport, she'd walked straight past him on Sloane Street as he'd left the clinic on Monday, the two of them making eye contact. Based on what Sophie told Stephen, it was obvious she was the one who had gone to the police and provided a description of Isaac. He was still recognisable despite being twenty pounds lighter and missing his trademark scar.

Charlotte was also worried about Stephen holding his nerve. He was softer than the rest of them. Didn't cope as well under pressure. And on the phone, she'd heard the panic in his voice, sensed his fear.

She needed to speak to Richard, but first things first. After hanging up, she went into her brother's room where he was lying on his bed, listening to his iPod. They were due to leave for Richard's shortly. He saw the look on her face and immediately removed his earphones. After she'd told him what was up, he jumped up from the bed and started pacing the room. 'Idiot! Fucking idiot!' he exclaimed. 'I can't go back to that clinic now, can I?'

'No, of course you can't,' Charlotte said evenly. 'Try to stay calm, we need to think clearly.'

'How can I stay fucking calm? I've been identified, twice! I saw the hooker, but I didn't think she'd go to the police. I thought she'd be too scared. It won't be long before they find me.'

Charlotte went up to her brother and placed a hand on his shoulder. 'You need to leave the country, Isaac.'

He looked at her as if she was mad. 'You're banishing me? After all I've done to help you pull this off?'

'Do you see any other way? It's not forever, just while I take care of things, and all this blows over.'

'What do you mean, take care of things?' A sick sensation ran through Isaac.

'Don't worry about that. For now, you're going to take a little vacation. Start packing, while I go and book your ticket to Florida.'

'Florida? Dad's condo?'

'Yep. I know for a fact it's empty right now. I'll make sure Dad knows. I'll tell him the stress of last week got to you and you needed a break, OK?'

'What about tonight?'

'We'll tell Marianne the same crap. That you're stressed, and you needed time away. Once I've booked your ticket, I'll call Richard and let him know Steve fucked up. Now pack!'

Back in the living room, Charlotte opened her laptop and searched for the first available Virgin Atlantic flight to Orlando International.

It had all been going so smoothly, but suddenly it felt like their plan was unravelling at the seams. She needed to repair the damage before the whole thing fell apart, but none of the others were going to like what she had in mind.

Chapter Twenty-Eight

Dinner at the Barkers' passed without a hitch. Everyone, even Stephen, managed to play their part, and the evening ended with neither Marianne nor Celeste any wiser about their secret. But underneath the smiles, the laughter, the carefree contentment at having escaped with their lives, was a sick feeling of dread. Dread of being found out, and a grim realisation that they'd slipped up. Big time. Although Richard didn't like the idea of what Charlotte had proposed on the phone, he didn't see any other way. And neither did Matthew. They agreed to keep it a secret from Stephen. He was freaked out enough already, and it might tip him over the edge.

Matthew would deal with it before the end of the week, and then their biggest problem would be eliminated.

'It was a woman?'

Wednesday, 8 a.m. Drake had just burst into Carver's office with some interesting news. A Bahamian police officer had been on the phone. Confirmed that a Czech woman, named Marie Brabec, had set up Pellingtons two months ago using local Nassau law firm, Jasper Payton & Co. No one at the firm had met Brabec in person, which apparently wasn't unusual when it came to foreigners establishing offshore bank accounts using locally incorporated companies, and all correspondence between them had been via email. Brabec had filled out the necessary one-page form, and provided photocopies of her driver's licence and passport, both of which had looked in order. Within forty-eight hours of the company's incorporation, she had instructed Jasper Payton to open a bank account at Ansbacher in Pellingtons' name. Shortly after this was done, twenty thousand pounds was wired to it.

But Brabec had turned up in person at Ansbacher Bank the morning after the six million had been wired from Sullivans' account to Pellingtons'. She withdrew two hundred thousand pounds, and transferred the rest to a Gibraltarian account, held in the name of Jericho Ltd, set up by Brabec using local lawyers, as originally suspected. She was described as being around five-seven, well-spoken, highly attractive, chicly dressed, in her mid-fifties, with cropped, probably dyed, Marilyn-blonde hair, a slim frame, and wearing black butterfly frame sunglasses. She had provided the usual identification and had spoken with a slight Eastern European accent.

'Did they have any idea where she was staying, where she went?'

'No, sir, she appears to have well and truly disappeared. She could be anywhere.'

'And the CCTV?'

'It's not clear at all. She kept her head down the whole time. Never removed the shades.'

'Clever woman.'

Just then, there was a knock on the door. It was the post boy. He handed Carver a medium-sized brown jiffy bag. Intrigued, Carver hurriedly opened it, and for a moment, looked confused. It was a diary for 2015–2016. He opened it, started reading, and soon realised who it belonged to.

'What is it, sir?' Drake asked.

'It's Mary Jacobs' diary.'

Drake's mouth fell open. 'But how? Who?'

'One of the kidnappers, has to be. We need to get forensics to check for prints although they've no doubt been wiped.'

Carver sat down and read more. Before long, he realised he was holding damning proof of Davenport's guilt. His resignation hadn't been enough. The kidnappers had wanted more. The question was, how the hell had they got hold of it?

'We need to bring Davenport in,' Carver said, holding up the diary. 'And talk to Frank Gerard. See if he knows anything about this.'

Later that day, Carver sat across from Davenport in an interview room. He went straight for the jugular and blindsided him with Mary's diary. The colour immediately drained from Davenport's face.

'But how do you know it's authentic?' he asked Carver. There was a desperate, rather than defiant, tone to his voice. A last-ditch attempt at avoiding the past which had finally caught up with him.

'Because I've just had a call from one of my officers, who's currently with Frank Gerard. He's confirmed it's Mary's handwriting.' The bad news was, as expected, no prints had been detected on the diary. Another dead end.

Davenport flew into a rage. He banged his fist down hard on the table and glared at Carver. 'You should be more concerned with finding out who sent it. It's clearly those crazy men who took four of my staff, but you're sitting here interviewing me for something that allegedly happened well over thirty years ago, when you should be out there, finding them!'

The man had schemed and plotted his way to the top of the corporate stratosphere for three decades, and now he was attempting to engineer his freedom. But it was wasted on Carver. He had enough to charge him, and the custody officer agreed with Carver. Davenport was charged and locked up in a cell, pending a bail hearing.

In the end, it was all immaterial. That same night, a guard found Davenport dead in his cell. He'd hanged himself with a torn bedsheet.

Chapter Twenty-Nine

Carver phoned Maddy on her mobile early the next morning before Davenport's suicide hit the headlines. She'd just made it to the office when he called. For a moment, she stood stationary, lost for words. 'You OK?' he asked.

'Yes, just a bit shocked. I'd never imagined him to be the kind of man to take his own life.'

'Don't feel too sorry for him. He was guilty, and he knew he was facing at least eight years behind bars. To go from being the top of his game to that, his reputation in tatters, I guess death was the preferable option.'

'Have you told the Gerards?'

'No, but I'm on my way there now. It'll break soon after.' He paused, then said, 'So we should get a drink or something?'

Maddy's lips curled up at the sides. 'I take it Drake's not with you?'

'You guessed right. He's tied up on something else, so I'm going solo this morning.'

'A drink would be good. And don't worry, you've been busy, you work crazy hours. I get that, I understand.'

Carver smiled as he sat in slow-going traffic on Kilburn High Road. 'Guess that's one thing our jobs have in common.'

Thirty minutes later, sitting at her desk, Maddy remembered something urgent she had to do. She picked up her phone and called IT. 'Hi, I need to get access to Charlotte Dempsey's PC. She was working on a couple of matters for me the week before last, and I need to make sure all of the correspondence has been printed out and filed.'

She'd meant to ask Charlotte the other evening how up to date her filing was, but their discussion had turned quite heavy and she'd decided not to mention it after all. Maddy was meticulous about files being kept up to date, every piece of correspondence printed and filed in chronological order. Who knew when they might need to refer to it in the future? There could be no breaks in the chain of communication, no chance of anyone disputing what had been said at the time.

She went over to Charlotte's desk, switched on her monitor and let Alex in IT do his thing. In less than a minute, he was in, and Maddy had access to every email, document and folder created by her trainee. Even her internet history, if she wanted to be particularly nosy. She didn't. At least, not at first. Not until something curious caught her eye. Something, she realised, the police wouldn't necessarily have picked up on.

Trawling through Charlotte's inbox, dragging and dropping the relevant correspondence to the relevant folder, Maddy came across an email from someone at Jenson Woods, a medium-sized firm in the West End. She suspected Becky Roberts was another trainee, possibly a friend from law school. The email was personal, not work-related, and Becky appeared to be in some distress. It was sent at 5 p.m., the Friday before the kidnappers showed up. Becky explained how she and her fiancé had broken up, that she was devastated, could barely focus at work. He'd been seeing someone else but had refused to move out. She'd just come off the phone with him, they'd had a blazing row, and she was beside herself. She was going home to her parents for the weekend but couldn't face another week with him. She'd asked Charlotte if she could crash at hers the next week, possibly for longer, until it was all resolved. But Charlotte, although sorry for what her friend was going through, had point blank refused with no credible explanation given. They were obviously close, and Maddy couldn't understand how her trainee could have been so heartless. She'd told Becky that things were crazy at her end right now, that the next few weeks weren't good for her, so she'd be better off finding somewhere else to stay. Becky had responded with a terse, 'Thanks for nothing, bestie,' and that was that.

It seemed so out of character, that Charlotte would be so dismissive of a friend in need. And Maddy knew for a fact that she hadn't been that snowed under at work. In fact, lately, they'd been fairly quiet. Maddy grabbed a pad and pen lying next to Charlotte's keyboard and scribbled down Becky's full name and contact details. Something didn't feel right, and she had a hunch that Becky might be the person to help her with that.

Frank Gerard looked shell-shocked by the news of Davenport's suicide. His son was solemn-faced for Carver's benefit, despite inwardly wanting to leap for joy. The plan had worked. Finally, he had justice. Finally, all was right in the world. He felt almost delirious with success, power, invincibility. If only the hooker hadn't opened her mouth, they'd be home and dry.

Although he'd never had his prints taken or given a sample of his DNA, he hadn't wanted to chance things. So, wearing a pair of latex gloves, he'd wiped his mother's diary of his fingerprints using a damp sponge with some fairy liquid, removing not just his prints but any trace of the tear he'd shed when he'd first read it. It was a technique he remembered his father mentioning criminals sometimes used back when he was a policeman. Now there was no possibility of it being traced back to him.

He and the others had nearly pulled it off, and tonight, with one final act, he'd ensure their secret was buried forever.

'It's not what Mary would have wanted.' Frank shook his head. 'She'd have wanted him in jail, I know that, but not for him to take his life. What of his wife?'

'She's been in France since Sunday, as we understand things,' Carver explained. 'Staying with friends. I gather she plans to travel back soon.'

'Dad, surely you're not feeling sorry for him?' Matthew couldn't hide his astonishment. 'After what he did to Mum?'

Frank said nothing, just stared into space. Then he gave his son a sad look. 'What I don't understand, is how they got hold of the diary?' Looking at Matthew, he was almost sure he knew the answer to his question. But he hoped to God the police never discovered the truth.

'You're certain you knew nothing about your wife's diary, Mr Gerard?'

Frank shook his head. 'No, and the strange thing is, it never turned up when we cleared out Mary's stuff, did it, Matthew?'

Matthew had a split second to respond in a way that would make Daniel Day-Lewis proud. 'No,' he said flatly, 'we cleared all that out together, not long after the police found Mum's scarf on Southsea beach.'

'Did anyone else have access to your wife's things? A friend, a cleaner, anyone at all?'

'Not that I know of.' Frank shook his head again. He smiled. 'We couldn't afford a cleaner. Mary did all that.'

'Well, someone must have sneaked in at some point and taken it, there's no other explanation,' Matthew said. Carver observed Matthew closely. He hadn't shaved since last Saturday. It made him look different. Older. Less wholesome.

'You're right,' Carver said. 'She may have kept it at work of course. Whoever these people are, they're as good as ghosts at covering their tracks.'

Chapter Thirty

She could tell he was a handsome guy. Smouldering dark eyes, nice bone structure, trim physique. Despite keeping his good looks hidden under a baseball cap, beard and Harry Potter glasses. And, rather oddly, he was wearing gloves. Perhaps he was one of those clean freaks. It didn't bother her. She'd seen it all. He hadn't stopped staring at her the whole time she'd been cavorting on stage. As she'd gyrated her ample hips in his direction, enjoying the power she held over men like him – no doubt an introvert held at bay by a domineering mother, needing to satisfy his throbbing loins somewhere mama would never find him – he'd shyly slipped a fifty-pound note in her G-string, laying his claim on her. Shy, maybe, but not without means. She'd make sure his money was well spent, and that he went home to mama with a grin on his face.

In the dimly lit room, she danced for him. He sat on a chair and gazed up at her. She was a beautiful girl. In a cheap kind of way. Those long, luscious blonde curls, exquisite large breasts, taut waist, pert bottom. But she wasn't Charlotte. She hadn't been through what they'd been through. And what they shared was more alluring, sexier, than any lap dance this hooker – who threatened to dislodge everything they'd worked for – could ever perform.

She came towards him, straddled his hips, brought his face between her breasts, surprised he wasn't hard yet. And that's when he did it. She hadn't noticed the knife buried in his lap underneath his left palm, and which he'd then slowly gripped in his right hand as she came towards him in the near dark. Shock took hold of her eyes, wild and starry, as he plunged it into her smooth, soft flesh, then once again, just for good measure. He was shaking as he lay her down on the floor – mindful of the blood on his gloves, his clothes – then slipped the knife into his rucksack, and snuck away and out of the club, not daring to look over his shoulder until he was well out of sight.

He was still shaking two hours later as he buried his head in Charlotte's lap and prayed his darling mother would understand.

Carver looked up at the ceiling and cursed. 'Shit, she was our best lead.'

Friday morning. Drake had just delivered the news that Cherry was dead. Eyewitnesses remembered her disappearing into a room with a tall, bearded man wearing a cap and glasses. But the lighting in the club had been dim, and the description was patchy, at best. As well as feeling frustrated that their best line of enquiry had been eliminated, Carver's heart felt heavy. Despite what she'd done for a living, he'd liked her. She'd been a nice girl. Brave enough to do the right thing and come forward.

But now she was dead, and Carver couldn't help feeling he'd played a part in that by persuading her to help him. Somehow, her killer knew she'd come forward, and possibly knew about Sophie Baines. He needed to warn Sophie to be careful, although he didn't expect the scarred man to show up at her work again.

'They found glove prints on the girl, sir, and on the chair, but no other means of identification.'

There was only one thing for it. 'We need to go public with Cherry's sketches. I'll check with New Scotland Yard about holding a press conference later today. Sophie said she thought the more recent one was reasonably accurate, so there's a chance someone out there will recognise him. Frankly, Drake, right now it's our best option.'

'You seeing this?'

Richard watched Carver hold up the sketches of fat and thin Isaac. A sea of hungry reporters chomping at the bit, a million flashes rebounding off his face.

Since shedding the weight, Isaac had kept a low profile, apart from his visit to Cressingtons. Aside from the scar, the sketch wasn't a perfect fit. There were lots of olive-skinned, dark-haired guys out there. Plus, she'd made him two inches shorter than in real life, and better looking in Richard's opinion. But it was still a concern. He was glad Charlotte had been quick to pack him off to the Sunshine State.

'I am. Matt's here with me.' Charlotte put Richard on speaker.

'How is he?' he asked.

Charlotte looked at her lover. Less edgy than last night, but still having a hard time coming to terms with the fact that he'd crossed the line. He'd become a killer. And there was no turning back.

'He's getting there.' She gave Matthew a loving smile. When he'd turned up on her doorstep the previous night, trembling, incoherent, she'd feared for his sanity. In bed, he'd tossed and turned, woken up in a sweat, panting for breath. She'd massaged his back, soothed him, stroked his hair, assured him he was safe, that it was just a dream. But it wasn't really. What he'd done was very real and it was haunting him. He'd been so sure he could handle it, even after she'd offered to do it herself. But now it seemed he wasn't as strong as he or she had believed.

'Do you think we need to deal with Sophie Baines?' Charlotte asked.

Matthew flinched, looked at her in alarm, his eyes manic, his stomach flipping. He knew Sophie. She was a nice girl, and despite their differences, Stephen would be horrified by the suggestion of any harm coming to her. He suddenly saw Charlotte in a different light. He wondered at her coldness, her calculated willingness to do whatever it took to survive. He'd killed someone last night, somehow justifying it by the fact that they were doing all this for his mother. But was he, in the end, no better than Davenport?

'No, I don't want any more bloodshed,' came Richard's firm response. Matthew breathed a sigh of relief. 'Murder was never part of the plan, and it's all spiralling out of control. Your brother's not going back to that clinic, and she doesn't have a credible name or address. The police have nothing to go on but these sketches which are far from perfect.' He paused, then said, 'You're quiet, Matthew?'

'Sorry, got a lot on my mind.'

'I suggest you go back to work soon. Take your mind off things. In time, this will all blow over. We just need to stay calm.'

'And how are you, Richard?' Charlotte asked.

'I'm just dandy. Loaded up on morphine. Marianne and I are going to the cottage next week. I expect it'll be our last trip there together.'

Charlotte and Matthew marvelled at his courage. They'd had plenty of time to come to terms with the fact that his illness was terminal, but having spent so much time with him, devoting their energies into pulling off the impossible, they'd almost forgotten the sad truth, or rather, had pretended to forget it. But now it was over, now they had time to stop and think about the imminent death of a man they'd come to admire and care about, it came as a crushing blow.

* * *

'So you want Chinese or Indian?'

When Carver had invited Maddy over for dinner on Saturday night, she'd assumed he was cooking. But the case was monopolising all his time, and he hadn't had a moment to restock his long-neglected fridge. Which consisted of sour milk, suspicious-smelling eggs, a quarter-full tub of butter, and yesterday's pizza.

'Do you ever eat a home-cooked meal?' Maddy asked as she ploughed her way through a dozen takeaway menus.

'Sure I do.' Carver grinned. 'I usually have dinner at Lionel's once, sometimes twice, a week. His wife, Lorraine, makes a mean shepherd's pie.'

Lionel was Carver's sparring partner at the gym. A larger-than-life beefcake, scary as hell to look at, but inside he had a heart of gold.

Maddy rapped Carver over the head with a menu. 'That's not what I meant, and you know it.'

Carver shrugged. 'I don't know, usually my hours are so erratic, it's not worth getting much in. Or I'm too knackered and want something quick. Plus, it's no fun cooking for one.' He stopped and stared at her. She leant forward, kissed him on the mouth.

'Well, there won't be as much of that going on now, will there?' Her pulse quickened as she said this, hoping she hadn't overstepped the mark and scared him off.

But Maddy had yet to realise that Carver was more worried about her being scared off. There'd long been a void in his life, and it had been her absence.

'I like the sound of that,' he said.

They settled on Chinese and opened a bottle of red as they waited for it to arrive. They talked about each other's week, Carver's, in particular. He told her he felt guilty about Cherry and was worried for Sophie. It felt good telling her all this. Before, he'd had to keep it bottled up inside, deal with stuff as best he could. Which usually involved launching himself at a punchbag.

Since yesterday afternoon's press conference, they'd had the usual nutters, dead-end callers, claiming to know Cherry's scarred man, but nothing that amounted to much.

'Do you have any idea who's behind it all?' Maddy asked.

'Other than the fact it's someone who knew Mary Jacobs and bore a massive grudge against Davenport, no.'

'But we know there's a man with a scar...'

'Not anymore,' Carver interrupted. 'Or, at least, not such a noticeable one.'

'OK, so he *did* have a prominent scar, plus we know a woman withdrew the money from Ansbacher Bank.'

'Correct.' Carver shook his head. 'If only we'd had the order sooner, we could have had officers waiting for her when she arrived.'

'You can't worry about that now.' Maddy paused, then said, 'You say she was about the same age as Mary Jacobs?'

'Yes.'

'So maybe she was in the same class at Cambridge?'

'We've questioned all her classmates. Well, the ones who aren't dead or gone to live abroad.'

'Hmm.' Maddy frowned. Then she thought of something: the email from Becky Roberts she'd accidentally read. She'd left a message on Becky's work phone for her to call her back, but so far, hadn't heard from her.

'What is it?' Carver asked. Maddy explained.

'And that's out of character?'

'Well, yes, I think so. Charlotte's not with anyone, she lives with her brother. Why would she turn away a friend in need? Especially when I know for a fact she's not been that busy. I get the feeling they're close. Or, rather, they were close. I mean, it's not like she knew she was going to be abducted the following…'

Maddy and Carver froze. They locked eyes, wondering if the other was thinking the same thing.

Maddy laughed. 'No, it's preposterous! They could never have pulled it off.'

Carver was suddenly pacing the room. He'd forgotten how hungry he was, adrenaline pumping through him like a juggernaut. He needed a pen, paper. He dashed to the kitchen, found both, started writing.

Someone who knew Mary – Matthew Gerard and Richard Barker.

Someone with a grudge against ND – RB witnessed rape/lost out on senior partnership; MG's mother raped by ND.

Someone who had access to ND's office to bug it – all four hostages.

Stephen Baines is MG's friend from primary school.

RB dying from cancer. What has he got to lose?

SB's responses unnatural, as if speaking from a script; didn't totally match with MG's.

Charlotte Dempsey – a straight A student/shone at interview, but like a different person at the firm.

CD whispers to her father that he is to blame.

He handed it to Maddy, his pulse racing as he wondered if the victims were, in fact, not victims at all. Whether they'd duped everyone, including him, all this time?

'Well, what do you think?'

Maddy's heart was racing too, but it was too fantastical to comprehend. 'But the injuries, how?'

'Could have been self-inflicted. Fooled us all, didn't they?'

'I... I just don't know.' Maddy shook her head. Charlotte had always seemed like such a nice, normal girl. They'd shared a friendly drink together only four days ago. What kind of a person would endure self-inflicted injuries?

Carver sat down, gripped her shoulders, his eyes luminous. 'Think about it. It seemed random, but they all share a connection in some way. Richard Barker knows the firm inside out, plus Matthew could have had access to his mother's diary, erasing his prints just to be sure. He's a policeman's son. I'm sure he's learnt a trick or two over the years.'

'But what about the woman?'

'I don't know who she is, but she's clearly in on it. Perhaps she acted as their mole on the ground while they were in hiding.' He took a short breath, didn't allow Maddy time to speak. 'And it explains the absence of bodies, doesn't it? They drove themselves there, then one of them – this woman perhaps, whoever she is – blew both vans up remotely.'

'Why bother? Why not just give you an address to pick them up from? Make out they'd been abandoned? Much simpler, less risky.'

Carver half-smiled. 'I think that was their plan. But I ruined it.' He explained.

'And all this to get revenge on Davenport?' Maddy wasn't entirely convinced. Or maybe she liked Charlotte and Richard too much and didn't want to believe them capable of such a thing.

Also, certain things didn't add up. Carver read her mind. 'I know what you're thinking,' he said. 'It sort of fits with Matthew and Richard. But why would the others agree?'

Maddy nodded.

293

'Charles Dempsey was there that night, when Davenport raped Mary. You know how Charlotte feels about her father. She hates his guts by all accounts. Her mother killed herself, and I wouldn't be surprised if she blames him for that.' Carver stood up and paced the room again. He was hyper. Maddy had never seen him like this.

'And what about Stephen?' she asked, still desperate for it not to be true. 'Surely he wouldn't have agreed to this just because he's best mates with Matthew? Something else must have driven him to take such a massive risk.'

'You're right, something else must have motivated him, and right now that eludes me.'

Carver sat down, took Maddy's hands in his. 'I need your help, Maddy. Right now, I've only got my gut feeling to go on. But I need something solid.'

'What are you saying? You want me to snoop around?'

'I trust you. You've got inside knowledge, access to things I don't. Plus, I already know you've got great detective skills. You'd be like my undercover spy.' He grinned, as if one gorgeous smile was enough to sway a strong, independent woman like her.

It was. But not just because he was cute, and she fancied him rotten. She was strangely exhilarated by the thought of getting to the bottom of the mystery, just like Carver. She saw that now. That aside from their physical chemistry, it was what they had in common.

'OK, I'm in,' she said.

'Great.' He kissed her, then pulled back, and said, 'If this Becky Roberts returns your call, try and get her to talk about Charlotte's relationship with her parents. If she's as close to Charlotte as you think she is, she's likely to know how her friend really feels about her father.'

Chapter Thirty-One

Stephen was feeling calmer. The press was saying the police had no new leads on the abduction, and that since the murder of their only credible witness, the investigation had come to a virtual standstill.

He wasn't a fool. He suspected his friends had played a part in that unpleasant business, even if the victim had been in a potentially risky line of work, liable to meet all sorts of weirdos. Point was, they hadn't admitted it to his face, and he wasn't about to ask. They'd got away with it, and soon, once Pamela had deposited the money, he'd be a very rich man. Then he could wipe the slate clean, and finally give Celeste the life she deserved.

'Drake, I need you to do a background check on Stephen Baines.'

Having been summoned to the station at an obscenely early hour on Sunday morning, Drake had barely stepped foot in the building, Danish in one hand, latte in the other, when Carver came whistling past and practically jostled him to his office. He'd fought the impulse to object, seeing the no-mood-for-arguing look on Carver's face, and had dutifully followed, stuffing the pastry into his mouth en route. Now, as he washed it down with milky coffee, hoping he didn't get indigestion, Carver's request sparked the obvious question. 'Can I ask why, sir?'

Carver checked the door was closed, even though there was hardly a soul in sight, then returned to his desk, and offered Drake a seat.

'I've got misgivings about the "victims".' He did the quotation mark thing, something he abhorred, but which Drake did constantly. He was being sardonic, but it didn't faze Drake. He was used to his sarcasm, and too enthralled by Carver's remark.

Drake cocked his head, thought for a while, then sat up straight as if an electric current had shot through him. 'Sir, surely you…'

'Humour me, Drake. You got any other bright ideas? Because if you have, I'm all ears.'

Drake felt his own ears go pink. 'No, sir.'

Carver relayed everything he and Maddy had discussed the night before. Leaving out the part that they'd been together at his place at the time.

'Wow,' Drake mumbled.

'Wow indeed. This goes no further than these four walls, got it?'

'Got it, sir.'

Monday morning. Exactly two weeks on from the kidnapping. Maddy closed the door to her office, flung her bag on the floor and sat down at Charlotte's desk. Matthew and Stephen were returning to work today, and there would be welcome-back drinks for them at 5.30.

She rang Alex in IT, and inwardly sighed with relief when he didn't question why she needed access to Charlotte's files again. She hadn't resigned yet, but she might soon, and Maddy needed to act quickly before her account was terminated.

Carver had asked her to trawl through every document and piece of correspondence on Charlotte's PC. 'As if I don't have work of my own to be getting on with,' Maddy mumbled to herself as she scrolled through email after email. He'd also asked her to check Charlotte's calendar. Look out for anything odd, like weekly time blanked out, meetings with the other hostages. He knew it was highly unlikely any of them had been that careless – Richard certainly didn't strike him as the slapdash sort, and they'd only managed to fool everyone this long by being meticulous in the run-up – but it was still worth pursuing.

An hour later, realising she'd have to stay late to finish the billable work she'd yet to start, Maddy had almost given up hope when something caught her eye.

It was amazing how far back calendar searches allowed you to go. July 2016 detailed a lunch with Richard. His secretary had sent the appointment to Charlotte. Maddy's heart raced as she clicked on the other invitees. There was only one. Matthew Gerard. It still didn't prove anything. They'd only been at the firm four months, and Richard was their mentor. No doubt he'd taken them out to lunch to see how they were getting on. It was standard practice, and nothing that would raise eyebrows.

But maybe that was exactly the point? A partner mentor taking his mentees out for lunch wouldn't raise eyebrows. It made Maddy wonder. If Richard was behind the abduction, had he engineered Charlotte and Matthew as his trainee mentees deliberately? So he had an excuse to meet with them, bring them in on his plan? As she considered this, she didn't hear the door open in time for her to close Charlotte's calendar without being caught red-handed.

'Hello, Maddy, why are you at my computer?'

It was Charlotte. Back. Unexpectedly. Maddy quickly closed the calendar and swivelled round.

'Charlotte, how are you?' She got up and embraced her trainee's stiff shoulders. 'I needed access to your account to see if all the filing was up to date.' She gave a forced smile. 'But now you're here. Does this mean you've decided to take my advice and finish your training?'

She noticed the way Charlotte's eyes kept flitting to her computer. She'd seen the calendar, and suspected Maddy had been snooping. It was written all over her face. A face that didn't seem innocent or timid anymore. A face that was hiding something.

'Yes,' she replied with an equally artificial smile.

'What made you change your mind?'

'Like you said, I've come this far. Might as well see it through.'

'Good. That's the spirit.' Their eyes remained locked on one another, the air suddenly thinner. Maddy could scarcely breathe.

Just then, her phone rang, breaking the painful silence. *Thank God,* she thought, racing to pick it up.

'Ms Kramer?'

A woman's voice. Alien to Maddy. She glanced up at Charlotte who'd yet to sit down. They exchanged another forced smile. Finally, she removed her jacket and sat at her desk.

'Yes?'

'This is Becky Roberts,' the caller said. 'I got your message.'

Maddy's heart pounded. *What a time to call. Typical!*

'Oh, hello, thanks for calling me back.' She tried her best to sound nonchalant, as if she was addressing Counsel or a client. 'I'm just going into a meeting,' she lied. 'Can I call you back in, say, an hour?'

'Oh, I see, OK.' Becky sounded unimpressed. Maddy didn't blame her. After all, she'd made the effort to call back, and was going through what sounded like a rancorous split. She had every right to sound pissed off.

'Thanks, look forward to speaking then.'

'You've got a meeting?' Charlotte asked. 'Should I come along and take notes?'

'No, no, you're fine. It's just a quick internal catch-up on a new matter. You get yourself settled in, and I'll be back shortly.'

Maddy dashed out of the room and made a beeline for the lifts. Luckily, one came immediately, and she took it all the way down to ground. There were ten individual phone cubicles on the ground floor, equipped with a table, seat, phone, pads and pens, where staff could make private calls. Maddy just prayed Becky was still at her desk when she called.

It rang twice, then Becky picked up.

'That was a short meeting,' she said drily.

'Yes, sorry about that. I was stuck in a rather awkward situation when you rang, and I needed to get out of it somehow. Are you still free to speak?'

'Yes. You mentioned in your voicemail that you wanted to talk to me about Charlotte Dempsey?'

'Yes, she's my trainee. I understand you and Charlotte are good friends.'

Becky grunted. 'Yes, well, that's what I thought. I thought we were best friends.'

'I take it you haven't been in contact with her since the hostage crisis?'

'No. Naturally, I was shocked to hear about it, and I'm glad she's OK. But I guess I'm still too pissed off with her.'

'Why?'

'Let's just say, when I really needed her, she let me down. Badly.

299

Christ, we were as thick as thieves at school, and at uni, but since she joined your firm, she's changed. Really changed.'

'How so?'

'It's like she never has time for me anymore. Guess she thinks she's too good for me now, working at a hotshot firm like yours, while I'm slumming it in the little league. I suppose she's your star pupil?'

'No, actually. Between us, Charlotte's performed poorly throughout her training contract. She makes silly mistakes, lacks initiative, generally appears overwhelmed. The partners are far from impressed.'

Becky was silent. 'Well, I never,' she finally said. 'That makes no sense at all. Lottie's always been a brilliant student, the teacher's pet. She was on the moot team at uni, would slaughter her opponents.' Another pause, then, 'Why are you asking me these questions? Telling me confidential information about your trainee? You could get into trouble.'

'Because I have reason to believe Charlotte is hiding something, and I think her acting out of character – giving you the cold shoulder, et cetera – might be part of that something. I think she may have been forced into acting the way she did.'

A brief pause, then, 'Does this have something to do with her being taken hostage?'

Maddy bit her lip. She was taking a risk letting Becky in. She was still Charlotte's friend, after all, and their conversation might get back to her. But Becky knew Charlotte better than anyone, and Maddy needed her help.

'Yes, I mean, it might. Please, this can't get back to Charlotte. Do I have your word?'

Another pause, then, 'It's unlikely I'll be speaking to her anytime soon. To be brutally honest, I don't have the slightest urge to call her. So yes, you have my word.'

'Thanks. Does Charlotte have a close relationship with her father?'

Becky sniggered. 'No, not at all. She hates him. Especially since her mother died. Charles was never at home when she and Zac were kids. Diana practically brought them up single-handedly. When they were little, they assumed it was because he was working late at the office, but as she got older, Lottie clued up.'

'About what?'

'Let's just say, he went out a lot. Particularly with his mate, none other than your deceased ex-senior partner.'

'Davenport?'

'Yep. They struck up a friendship at Cambridge. Later, Davenport brought him to Sullivans as a client, and from what Lottie told me, they were always out together. Splashing out on bottles of DP at strip clubs, sleeping around. Can't say I'm sorry Davenport topped himself, he was a disgusting man.'

'And Charlotte's mother put up with all that?'

'Diana was a sweet, loyal woman. But she wasn't a beauty, and I guess she thought she owed Charles her loyalty for marrying her, and for never having to worry financially. The way I understand things, her parents weren't well off. Plus, she loved her kids rotten. She didn't want to upset them.'

'Her death must have hit Charlotte and Isaac very hard?'

'Yes, they were devastated. Lottie and I were travelling in Thailand when Zac rang with the news. She got on the first plane home, but insisted I carry on. She's kind, thoughtful like that. Or rather, she used to be.'

'Did she complain a lot about Nigel Davenport?'

'Yes, all the time. She hated his guts. Not so much when she was younger, like I said. But more so after she found out how he'd led

Charles astray. I remember him standing by Diana's coffin at the funeral. With his fake grief, fake tears. Charlotte barely spoke to her dad after that.' Becky sighed, then said, 'To give Charles his due, I think he genuinely regretted the way he'd neglected Diana. But by then, it was too late to make things right with either of his kids.'

'And Isaac, what does he do?'

'Not much. He's always been a bit strange, a bit of a drifter. A real IT nerd. Think he worked in Starbucks in Hampstead for a while, also had a rock band going. But I don't think I've seen him more than two or three times since the funeral. Last time was around two months ago. Passed him on the street and I remember being surprised at how much weight he'd gained. He's always been skinny as long as I've known him.'

As she said this, a startling realisation hit Maddy. The family photo on Charlotte's desk. Isaac had a scar on his chin. How had she not remembered earlier? Was he a part of this too? Was he the anonymous scarred man? And then there was Cherry's sketch. A fat and thin version of the same suspect.

'He lives with Charlotte, right?'

'Yes.' There was a moment's pause, then Becky said with an edge to her voice, 'Look, as pissed off as I am with Lottie, we go back a long way and I'm starting to feel a little shady telling you all this.'

Maddy sensed Becky was about to hang up, but she needed to keep her on the line a little longer. 'Please, believe me, I'm asking you all these questions for Charlotte's benefit.'

A big fat lie, but a necessary one. At least, that's what Carver would have said.

She sensed Becky's hesitation. She was an intelligent, professional woman, after all. An aspiring lawyer, who had every right to be suspicious. Maddy added, 'The men who took Charlotte and the others are still out there.' Still nothing. She went for broke. 'Between us, the police are concerned for their safety, and I've offered to help in any way I can.'

'How kind of you.' Becky's tone was caustic.

'Look, Becky, I was in that room when Charlotte and Richard were taken. I keep thinking how it could have been me. How lucky I was to come away unharmed.'

Becky finally took the bait. 'OK, what else do you want to know?'

Phew. 'Just what you meant by Charlotte changing? I mean, when did that start?'

A brief silence, then, 'I don't know, maybe last summer. A few months into our training contracts. At first, I put it down to her being snowed under at work, but then she kept blowing me off, time after time, even at weekends. She said it was work, but I know she lied. It was *him*.'

'Him?'

'Matthew Gerard.'

'They're together?'

'Yes, I presumed you knew. Or is Sullivans funny about work relationships? My firm doesn't have a problem, but I know it's seriously frowned on at some places. Probably why they kept it a secret.'

'But they told you?'

'No, I found out by accident. Got fed up with her blowing me off, so I decided to go round to her place one Saturday morning. Think it was last December. Must have been around 9 a.m. as I wanted to catch her before she went out. I parked opposite her block of flats and was about to get out of my car when she came out the front door and got into hers. Then she drove off.'

'Did you follow her?'

Another pause. Maddy sensed Becky's guilt, embarrassment. 'Yes. Sad, I know, and whatever you might think, I'm not a stalker. But

I was curious. She used to tell me everything, but it felt like she'd become a stranger.'

'Where did she go?'

'To a hotel in Harrow.' *That's on the Bakerloo line*, thought Maddy. *Matthew's line.* 'He was waiting for her outside. I figured they were having a romantic getaway, although it was a strange location; I mean, they might as well have stayed at her place, why hide out there, in Harrow? I watched them kiss, then go in. And before you ask, no, I didn't wait for them to re-emerge, or see if they went elsewhere. I felt foolish enough for following Lottie in the first place and headed straight home.' Becky sighed. 'Look, my boss will be back any second, and I need to get off the phone. Is that everything?'

'Yes,' Maddy said. 'You've been a big help. Thank you.'

'We never spoke, OK?'

'Understood.'

When Maddy got back to her desk, Charlotte was busy filing. 'You were right,' she said. 'I was a bit behind, but I'm nearly up to date now.'

'Thanks.' Maddy tried to act normal, but it wasn't easy. Especially when Charlotte then asked, 'Good meeting?' Her tone was casual, but her eyes were searching.

Did she suspect the meeting was bullshit? *Probably.*

'Fine, it was fine.' Maddy sat down at her desk and pretended to check her emails. She stared at her computer screen but sensed Charlotte's gaze from the corner of her eye. With every passing second, Maddy was more convinced by Carver's theory. Plus, it just seemed too coincidental that Charlotte's brother had a scar on his chin.

Charlotte was no 'victim', that much was clear. But how to prove it?

Chapter Thirty-Two

At 11 a.m. that Monday morning, Marianne Barker stepped inside the cosy cottage and laid her cotton scarf on the hall table.

The Barkers' cottage was situated on the quiet edge of Lower Slaughter, one of the most famous villages in the Cotswolds, and boasted an opportune position straddling the shallow River Windrush. It was a stone-built property, originally commissioned by a well-to-do family for their estate workers in the late nineteenth century. With beautiful local mellow stone and rustic architecture, it was a serene, picturesque escape from London, set amongst open countryside and yet only a stone's throw away from the amenities of Stow-on-the-Wold and Bourton-on-the-Water.

She loved this cottage. Loved the fact that when you woke up, all there was to hear was the joyful tweeting of birds. No honking of horns, angry yells, screaming school kids, shrill police sirens. Here, she could find peace, a chance to step back, recharge her batteries and let time slow down. She knew she couldn't slow down Richard's disease, but at least here there would be no distractions. They could cook, eat, sleep, talk, read, play board games, take gentle walks, do all the simple things life had to offer, alone and in peace. Life was just simpler.

When Richard had first bought the cottage, it had been in sore need of repair. Damp, dark, gloomy, it had required a complete refurbishment to transform it into the fabulous holiday home they had today. Now it was not only damp-proof, but sound-proof, with a bright, airy open-plan kitchen-diner where the Barkers had entertained on many occasions. On the first floor, new stone mullion windows brought a flood of welcome light into the two bedrooms, while every other room in the property had been modernised to an equally luxurious standard.

There was also a traditional cottage garden, complete with pretty, intricate flower borders, pristine manicured lawns and a sweeping gravelled drive. But what really set the cottage apart was a new annexe which Richard had designed and completed in 2012. Fashioned from a few derelict outbuildings on the boundary of the cottage grounds, it housed a sitting room, bedroom, bathroom and kitchenette, also acting as a quiet space where Richard could work away from the main building if he needed to.

The place hadn't been lived in for some time, and so, despite the warm weather, it felt chilly. Marianne shivered, and went around the ground floor, pulling curtains.

No sooner had they parked up on the drive than Richard had quickly disabled the alarm, unloaded their bags into the house, then driven off again. Although the journey had clearly taken its toll, he'd insisted on driving into Salperton, less than half a mile away, to grab some essentials they'd forgotten to bring in their haste to escape the City. Bread, milk, and such like.

He was putting on such a brave face, far braver than hers, despite his swift deterioration in health. Each day a little gaunter, a little weaker, a little more breathless. Oh, how she wished he'd take it easy and let her do more, but it was as if he wanted to grasp every second of life being offered to him. He was a chivalrous man, who had always taken care of her, and it was like a knife to his side seeing their roles reversed.

When she'd first brought him home from the hospital, they'd hugged long and hard, thankful to be together once more, clinging to each other for fear of being torn apart again. And then she had broken away, grown angry with him, vented a tirade of abuse, needing to expel all the tension, hurt and grief she'd felt at discovering his illness, and the fact that he'd hidden it from her for so long. That had never been the deal. They had agreed to love each other in sickness and in health, and he hadn't kept his side of the bargain as far as she was concerned. How could he have done that, suffered for so long without her there at his side? It wasn't selfless, it was selfish, with a capital fucking S, and she had hated him for it. He'd allowed her to curse, scream, bang her fists against his scrawny chest because he'd expected it, and having let her rant run its course, she'd finally collapsed into his arms once more, the tears flowing thick and fast.

She filled the kettle and popped two teabags into a pot, then, waiting for it to boil, decided to carry their bags up the sturdy oak stairs to the master bedroom. It had been blessed with sun all morning and felt much warmer than downstairs. A little dusty, though, making her sneeze several times. She opened a window to let some fresh air in, and had just lugged their cases onto the bed, when she heard a boy yelling at the top of his voice. She darted to the window and recognised William Bradshaw, the son of their nearest neighbours, Martha and John, sprinting up the path.

He looked up, as if sensing her gaze, and when their eyes met – when she saw the fear in his, the heartfelt pity – she knew.

Richard would never make it back.

Richard had collapsed and suffered a fatal heart attack outside the grocery store. Minutes earlier, he'd been chatting to William in the bread aisle, asking him why he wasn't in school. It was the summer holidays, of course, and he was just running an errand for his mother, but later, they were off to Cheltenham to buy him brand new trainers.

William had told all this to the coroner later, between sobs. He was only thirteen: a well-mannered, conscientious boy, who'd never seen a dead person in the flesh before. When people had come flurrying to Richard's side, Jack Briggs, the store manager, had ordered William to run like the wind and get Mrs Barker while he called for an ambulance. But William was a smart boy. He'd seen the way Richard had lain in the road, stiff and lifeless, as a local nurse who happened to be passing tried to resuscitate him, performing mouth-to-mouth as other grown-ups looked on helplessly. They all saw how ill Richard was, and had instinctively put their hands together in silent prayer. Calling an ambulance was more a matter of routine than hope. And by the time Marianne arrived, their worst fears had been confirmed. The illness had weakened his heart, and his body could take no more.

A few hours later, William and his mother came by the cottage to see how Marianne was doing. Her son and daughter were on their way, but for now, Martha and William would have to do. This was no time for her to be alone.

As expected, she was a mess. When she opened the door, her face was deathly white, her movements laboured, her voice feeble and choked with grief.

'There, there,' Martha said, guiding Marianne through to the sitting room. Small, baby steps. She gently sat her down on the cream leather sofa. Her frame stiff, her face vacuous. The carpet was also cream, the walls off-white. It was a bright, cheerful room, decorated with pretty vases of artificial Lady's Mantle on both window sills, and a traditional wood-burning stove which added character and warmth. But right now, aesthetics had no bearing. There was no light or warmth in the room. It felt dark, cold and austere.

Martha told William to sit with Marianne while she made tea. They'd stay until her children arrived. She was in no fit state to do anything for herself, and Martha worried what she might do alone in a home filled with treasured memories. Not to mention a lethal block of kitchen knives she'd spotted before.

William sat on an armchair opposite Marianne, watching her nervously. Her gaze fell his way, but it was as if he didn't exist. As if she was looking right through him. William didn't much like uncomfortable silences, and he felt the urge to speak. In his mind, he wished his mother would get a move on. 'I'm really sorry about your husband, Mrs Barker. He was a really nice man.'

For a moment, she didn't appear to hear him, her guise still vacant. Then, finally, she made eye contact, gave a faint smile. 'Thank you, William, that's very kind of you. But you're right, of course. He was the nicest man I knew.'

Marianne had yet to cry properly. *She's still in shock*, Martha had whispered into William's ear before heading for the kitchen. But the tears would flow soon enough.

More silence. At last, after what seemed like an eternity, Martha came through with a tray holding two mugs of tea, a glass of squash for William, and some rich tea biscuits she'd found unopened in the cupboard. Having given up a high-powered job in PR when William came along, she kept herself busy with the gym, PTA and local Sunday school. She was a naturally chatty woman and knew everything there was to know in the village. At least, she thought she did.

'Here we are,' she said lightly, laying the tray down on the coffee table. She placed Marianne's tea on a side table next to her, but Marianne didn't appear to register.

Martha caught William's eye, a signal to offer up the biscuits. He did as he was told, but got a flat, 'No thank you, dear.'

The three sat in awkward silence, then, looking around, Martha said, 'I really hope you decide to keep this place. It's so lovely.'

'I'm not sure,' Marianne said softly. 'I'm not sure there's much point without Richard.' Her eyes were glassy – the tears were imminent.

'He loved it here, didn't he?' William blurted out, unable to withstand more painful silence. 'Did you go away somewhere nice and hot those weekends he came without you?'

Marianne turned her head sharply. As if she'd just been stabbed with an adrenaline shot. A defunct wind-up toy brought back to life. 'What do you mean those weekends he came without me?'

William's cheeks went bright red. He glanced at his mother, who looked equally embarrassed. Marianne continued to glare at him. 'I'm waiting,' she said, her tea still untouched.

William swallowed hard. 'I… I just used to see him arrive some Saturdays, not every weekend, maybe once a month, occasionally twice.'

Marianne thought she might be sick. She'd never questioned those Saturdays he'd said he had to work. Working weekends at a top firm like Sullivans was standard practice. Particularly when there was a big trial to prepare for. It was necessary, unavoidable. Why Richard had earned so much. Plus, on weekends, you often got more work done without the phones ringing constantly.

But had he lied to her about something else? Had he been having an affair? It's not like he was ever away for more than a day at a time. But there were Saturdays when he didn't return home until almost midnight. She clutched her waist. Thank goodness she was sitting down because her legs were suddenly like jelly. Unlike her son, Martha knew exactly what was running through Marianne's mind. 'William, stop upsetting Mrs Barker. You must be mistaken.'

William was a sweet, honest boy. The mere thought of being labelled a liar upset him greatly. 'No, I'm not, Mum. I saw him, and he wasn't alone, he had guests.'

'Guests?' Marianne repeated faintly.

'Yes, I think it may have had something to do with his job. He works long hours, doesn't he, Mrs Barker?' William blushed, having realised he'd got his tense wrong. 'Sorry, what I mean is, he *did* work long hours, didn't he?'

'What did these guests look like?' Marianne asked weakly.

'Well, I remember seeing a lady, not very old, maybe twentysomething. And at least two other men, not old either.'

Marianne felt panicked. She was relieved it wasn't just a woman William had seen. But who the hell were these people Richard had considered important enough to bring to their retreat in the countryside? And why had he kept it a secret from her?

'Did you get a good look at them?'

William nodded. 'I didn't know their names at the time, though. But I do now.'

'How's that?'

'It was the same three who got taken with your husband. I saw their pictures in the newspaper the other day.'

Marianne's stomach flipped again. 'Charlotte Dempsey, Matthew Gerard and Stephen Baines?'

Another nod. 'Sounds familiar, yes.'

'William, I think you've said quite enough,' Martha said with a pinched expression. She'd always encouraged her son to speak up, but sometimes it backfired. She had no idea what was running through Marianne's mind at that moment. She just thought William was making a bad situation worse and hoped Marianne's children would turn up soon and rescue her.

'When did you see them?' Marianne demanded, her eyes boring through William.

'I can't remember exactly.' William was starting to wish he'd kept his mouth shut. 'Maybe only a few times last year. More so this year.'

'Like William said,' Martha interrupted, 'it must have been work-related. They were Richard's trainees, weren't they? Maybe they were working on a case together, which somehow involved the kidnappers. Maybe that's why they were taken?'

Marianne's head was spinning. It was a nice idea, but she knew better. Richard had told her innumerable times what a hopeless trainee Charlotte was, that he never used her, that she wasn't being kept on. Plus, all three trainees hadn't sat in Litigation simultaneously. And they certainly wouldn't have sat there for more than six months. So, what was he doing inviting all three of them to their holiday cottage Lord knows how many times? She thought back to last week, and the dinner she'd hosted to celebrate their safe return. At the time, she'd been struck by the closeness between them. Yes, they'd been held together under dangerous circumstances for five days, but there had been an over-familiarity between them she'd found rather odd. As if she'd been the guest, almost a stranger in her own home. Not part of a club that had long been initiated.

'Thank you for the tea.' She managed a smile. 'But I think I'm going to have to lie down. I'm suddenly feeling very tired.' She stood up and extended her open palm in the direction of the hallway.

'Yes, yes, of course,' Martha murmured, grateful for the chance to leave. She'd take a punt on the kitchen knives staying put; she couldn't stand the unpleasant tension a second longer. William was up like a shot. It had been a taxing day for one so young and he was craving the comforts of home.

After a stilted hug and goodbye, Marianne was alone once more. She didn't need a nap. She needed some answers. And she knew the best place to look for them.

Richard had said that aside from wanting a last weekend alone with her in the cottage, he needed to sort some papers out, which he kept in a desk in the corner of the annexe sitting room. He'd claimed he didn't want her being put to the trouble of working out what should and shouldn't be kept after he died. That was a task he'd set himself for some point during the week.

Marianne raced outside, grabbing the keys to the annexe on her way out. She couldn't get in fast enough, disabling the alarm and marching into the sitting room. Next to Richard's desk in the far-right corner, there was a four-tiered bookshelf and a small filing cabinet. She decided to start with the desk drawers. The top ones were filled with odd bits of stationery. She shut them impatiently and moved on to the larger bottom drawers which held various papers separated by dividers in alphabetical order. There were numerous research memos, planning and other legal documentation regarding the cottage, utility bills and so forth. Feeling increasingly exasperated, she rifled through them, still harbouring the same uneasy sensation in the pit of her stomach. And then she saw it. A divider towards the middle of the left-hand drawer, labelled 'Project M'.

She pulled out the file and opened it. Lots of loose papers held together with a bulldog clip. The first document was a detailed floorplan of Sullivans' building. Davenport's room, the ground-floor conference suite and reception were highlighted in red, as were the basement toilets and back entrance. There were also two highly dubious-looking sublease agreements, both allowing for exorbitant one-off lump sum payments in cash. One was for a light indus-trial unit in Leyton Industrial Village, where the hostages had been released, the other for a similar unit at Riverside Industrial Estate in Barking. Both were made between Isaac Dempsey and a company called Stanislav Textiles, and both immediately sent Marianne's heart racing. Although she hadn't met him, she knew Isaac was Charlotte's brother, who'd bailed on dinner last week. Both subleases were due to expire at the end of the month. Just three weeks away. There were also maps of both sites. Unit 25, which backed onto a large playing field was circled in red.

Seeing all this, her heart sank, and she could no longer avoid the ugly truth. But the worst was still to come. She found printouts from the internet, giving information on SWAT guns, black-market companies, bugging devices, hacking, constructing remote-control explosives, setting up offshore companies and bank accounts, Bahamian and Gibraltarian law firms, forensic analysis, police procedure, number plate fraud and, curiously, how to obtain a fake passport and driver's licence.

Marianne could scarcely breathe. It was almost too incredible to grasp. But she had the evidence in her hands. They'd engineered the

314

whole thing. It was the only explanation. They'd met here, in secret, away from unsuspecting eyes and ears, to make and fortify their plan. They'd fooled everyone, including her. And she realised that Richard had planned on destroying the evidence this week. He'd thought he had enough time, but time had run out.

Why had he done it? Guilt for keeping quiet about Mary Jacobs? Did the 'M' in 'Project M' stand for Mary? Revenge against Nigel Davenport for conspiring his way to senior partnership at Sullivans? Both?

Whatever it was that had motivated him, she was now faced with a terrible choice. A choice between her conscience and her love for her husband. Between her head and her heart.

Chapter Thirty-Three

Monday, 1.45 p.m. 'She's onto us, I know she is.' Charlotte and Matthew were looking out over the water in Butler's Wharf. It was another scorcher, suits like them out in droves, blending into each other in a collage of black and grey against the cloudless blue sky and bright yellow sun. Charlotte had texted Matthew, asking him to meet her there urgently. She'd been standing alone for ten minutes when he'd finally shown up, having spotted her casually leaning against the wall as if waiting for no one in particular. She'd sensed his presence but didn't touch him or make eye contact. There was a restlessness to her voice.

'How do you know?' he asked, trying to keep his cool. Charlotte wasn't one to panic, so he knew she must have good reason to be concerned. Even so, he prayed she was wrong.

'She was looking at my calendar when I came in this morning. I could have sworn it was that first meeting we had with Richard. Fuck, why didn't I delete it?'

'There was no reason to delete it. Richard was taking his mentees out to lunch in their first seat. Like all partners do. It would have looked more suspicious if you had deleted it.' He paused, shrugged his shoulders. 'It doesn't prove anything. We were careful never to communicate by email or landline. She and the police have nothing to go on.'

'Let's hope so. If she was a complete bitch like most of them, I'd be tempted to deal with her.' Matthew cringed. Although work was a distraction, his hands still felt stained with the hooker's blood. It tormented his dreams, and when he saw his father, he found it hard to look him in the eye. His conscience couldn't take more bloodshed. Where would it end? They were running out of lives, and surely couldn't expect to keep getting away with their crimes scot-free?

Charlotte knew what he was thinking. 'Don't worry, she's safe,' she assured him. 'It's just that she looked at me like she didn't trust me. And she pretended to have a meeting. She didn't have a meeting, I checked with her PA. It was just an excuse for her to leave the room after she got a call from somebody she clearly didn't want to speak to in front of me.'

'You're being paranoid,' Matthew said, getting irritated.

'Maybe,' Charlotte said under her breath. She sighed. 'I wish we could get away from here. Somewhere far away.'

'That'll only attract suspicion. We just need to ride things out till qualification next March, then we can make plans.'

'How's Stephen?'

'OK. Seems pretty chilled actually.' Just then, Matthew's phone alerted him to a new email. He pulled it out, went to his inbox. 'Oh, Christ.'

Charlotte looked at Matthew for the first time since he'd arrived, saw the anguish on his face.

'What is it?' she whispered.

'Mark Simmons has just sent an email. Richard's dead.'

Monday, 2.45 p.m., French time

The women met in a cute bistro in La Défense. Two smartly attired working women in their mid-fifties, both in designer suits, armed with designer handbags, wearing designer shoes, enjoying a late business lunch in the financial district of Paris. One of them was very beautiful. She wore a blonde wig and dark glasses. The other was plain, and she had no need for a disguise. She wasn't the one presumed dead.

'I have the money here,' the blonde said under her breath, lowering her shades, her gaze directed towards the Louis Vuitton ladies' briefcase she'd carefully placed at her feet. Despite everyone around them minding their own business, it still felt like she was being watched.

Knowing you'd committed a crime did that to you. Being on the run all this time did that to you. Every day you became more suspicious, more paranoid, that today was the day when the game would be up. Her paranoia had intensified ever since learning that local police had questioned the manager of Ansbacher (Bahamas) Limited about their mysterious customer who'd emptied her company's account of six million pounds.

'Good. I'm taking the Eurostar at 5 p.m. It's too risky for me to go to his flat, so I've arranged for a locker at King's Cross.'

'Good plan.' The blonde hesitated, then asked, 'How has Matthew been? Does Richard tell you much?' Both women were still clueless as to Richard's death.

'Last time we spoke, Richard said he was doing fine. As I understand things, he and Charlotte are very much in love.'

The blonde smiled. 'I'm so pleased for him.'

'It's too soon to even consider coming back yet – you know that, don't you? When Richard approached you, he made that clear. You make contact now, and Matthew's a dead man walking. We all are.'

'I know,' came the woeful reply. 'I just wish there'd been some other way.'

When fifty-three-year-old Mary Jacobs first heard a voice she hadn't heard in thirty-four years, memories came flooding back to her. Good and bad, but mostly bad. The bad made worse by the fact that she'd just left the home of a sixteen-year-old girl who'd been repeatedly raped by her stepfather and, consequently, Mary was walking past the Royal Marsden Hospital on the Fulham Road in something of a daze.

It had been Mary's dream to go to Cambridge and eventually become a human rights lawyer. When she'd first arrived at Trinity College she'd felt like Dorothy in *The Wizard of Oz*. She wasn't in Kansas anymore, she was in a whole other world, full of promise and opportunity. Glittering and bright, like the Emerald City. A world away from her frugal, sheltered, yet loving upbringing. Her mother had been a cleaner, her father a librarian. But they'd encouraged their only daughter to study and reach for the stars. It didn't matter where she came from, she could go places if she believed in herself, like they believed in her.

And Mary had believed in herself. She'd studied day and night, passing the entrance exam with flying colours, and impressing the hell out of Stewart Larson, the master of Trinity, in her interview. Little did she know then that he was a conniving toad of a man, with an eye for beautiful young women, and little regard for their dignity. A year and a half into the course, Mary's confidence would be shot to pieces, her dreams of becoming a lawyer similarly shattered.

She remembered that night as if it were yesterday. It never left her. It was always there. The pain, the humiliation. The feeling of worthlessness. And later, the anger.

As usual, he'd been off his face, trying it on with her at a hall party, egged on by his pathetic, sycophantic hangers-on. Worst of all – Charles Dempsey. An overweight, weak, easily manipulated young man, predisposed to hero-worshipping those stronger, more popular, than him. She'd tried to brush him off politely, but he wouldn't take no for an answer, and became aggressive. So, she'd told him to get lost, before leaving the party to a chorus of jeering and foul taunts. She'd been upset with her supposed best pal, Katherine Reid. Too chicken to stand up for her friend, she'd kept her mouth shut, hadn't even offered to walk home with her.

Scurrying back to her halls in the dark, no more than a five-minute walk, she'd heard footsteps approaching from behind. Gaining pace on her. Fear had gripped her like a bracing wind. It had been a raw February night, and there had been no one about. Just the odd stray cat, and the drunken mob tailing her. She'd picked up her speed, desperately rummaging around in her handbag for her key as she reached the door to her digs. And that's when he'd seized her by the hair from behind. Unlocking the door with his free hand, he'd shoved her inside and up the stairs to his bedroom, his motley crew tagging behind. She hadn't been strong enough to fight back. She'd tried to scream but his hand had been pressed firmly against her mouth, and she could scarcely breathe.

He'd pushed her into his room so hard she'd fallen to her knees, sobbing hysterically, begging him to stop, begging him for mercy. But mercy had not been an option. He hadn't known the meaning of the word. As he'd lowered himself down on top of her, feral with rage and lust, she'd seen the pitiless look in his eyes. And then he had roughly turned her over, like meat on a spit, ripping her knickers off before pushing her up against the foot of the bed, her naked rear exposed, her dignity erased for good in that split second. And then he had penetrated her while the others had looked on, laughing, cheering, delighting in her pain and in her violator's triumph.

All except one. A young man who had burst into the room the second Mary's life changed forever. He had a kind face, but at that moment, it was creased with angst and pity because he had been in love with her from the first moment he'd set eyes on her. She'd heard him say, 'Stop it, Nigel, stop it at once! If you don't, I'll… I'll report you to the police.' But there was no stopping Nigel. He'd simply sneered back; told the young man he'd ensure his legal career was over before it had even begun, and that he'd see to it that Mary ended up dead in a ditch somewhere if he didn't keep his mouth shut.

And that was that. A kind face, but also someone who had been too scared to stand up to the cruellest man Mary knew. Scared for his own survival at the college, scared for his future as a lawyer. Scared of turning Nigel Davenport – a ruthless young man from a highbrow family with contacts in all the right places – into an enemy for life. She remembered turning her head and locking eyes with her admirer, willing him to do something, but he never did. The deed was done, and then they had tossed her out of the room like rubbish, yelling expletives in her wake.

She'd been in horrendous physical pain, but her mental state had been a hundred times worse. Having made it back to her room, doubled up in agony, she'd stripped herself naked, and taken a bath. Submerged all but her face for forty-five minutes, until the water turned cold, her skin was mottled, her body numb. And then she'd slowly got out, wrapped a towel around herself, before sinking to her knees, hugging them to her chin like a baby in its mother's womb.

321

The next day, after she'd plucked up the courage to go to the master's office and tell him what had happened, he'd laughed in her face, telling her not to have such a wild imagination, that girls often got themselves into serious trouble making up stories to get attention.

Stinging with hurt, shame and anger, she'd threatened to go to the police if he didn't take action, pointing out that his name, as well as Davenport's, would be dragged through the mud. And that's when he'd pushed her up against the wall, his right hand around her neck, nearly choking the life out of her. Looking back, she remembered his eyes, wild and demonic, could still smell his whisky-laced breath on her face. 'I will ruin you if you so much as breathe one word,' he'd snarled. 'I gather your parents are good, honest people. Do you want them to be publicly humiliated when it turns out their whore of a daughter made false accusations against one of our top scholars? A young man whose father makes handsome donations to the college. A young man with a promising legal career ahead of him. A young man who'd politely turned down a poor working-class girl. A desperate girl with a vivid imagination, and no doubt as high as a kite. Who'd seen banging him as her golden ticket to a better life?'

'But… but none of that's true,' she'd stammered. 'He attacked me. I wanted nothing to do with him.'

He'd given her a psychotic smile, pressed his lips against her cheek, dragged them leisurely down her neck, making her want to vomit. 'But that's not what the police will hear from me. I am a powerful man, with powerful friends. You have no chance against the establishment. You are nothing.'

He'd let his last three words, spoken slowly and deliberately, sink in. Then he had cut away, still eyeing her with disdain as she'd stood rigid against the wall, trying to catch her breath.

322

'Now get out,' he had ordered, pointing to the door. 'And never forget what I said. You can't win, and you'll only end up hurting others as well as yourself.'

Mary had left Stewart Larson's office a broken young woman. She'd realised she was no match for Davenport. He and his family were part of a network that lay entrenched in the bowels of the college. They were part of a fraternity that stuck together. A vicious clique that would rather roll over and die than see 'trash' like her try to topple them. She'd known then that it was useless to try to right the wrong that had been done to her. She'd lost the battle before it had even begun, and Mary had quit her degree at the end of the following week, slipping out unnoticed.

It had been Richard Barker's biggest regret in life, not intervening that fateful night. And so, when he had, quite by chance, bumped into Mary as he was coming out of the Royal Marsden, he'd seen it as fate, having just received the devastating news that he had cancer. This was no chance meeting. It was a signal from God. His chance to right the wrong that had consumed him for over three decades. He'd had nothing to lose, and everything to gain.

Lynsey, the young rape victim Mary had been counselling, had got to her more than usual that day. Although, over the years, she'd become used to dealing with horrific cases like this, she'd never become fully immune. She could never stand back and be completely neutral. She was a victim herself, and so, for her, it had always felt personal. Making her both the best and the worst at her job. She'd never told her parents why she'd quit her Cambridge degree, she'd felt too disgusted with herself. But she'd always suspected they knew, deep down in their hearts. Her father had been a gentle soul. Not one to beat down Larson's door and demand answers. Both he and his wife had naturally been shocked and saddened by their daughter's decision.

But being the kindest of people, who'd loved and supported Mary no matter what, they'd respected her decision to begin a local social studies course, and were delighted for her when she found a job with Hammersmith and Fulham County Council as a social worker. They were even more delighted when, shortly after, she met Frank Gerard, a decent, honest man, who they knew would take care of their fragile daughter, haunted by demons she never revealed to the outside world.

But unlike her parents, Mary had confided in Frank, on the night he had asked her to marry him. A warm, still night in late June – the night he had presented her with an engagement ring as they'd sailed along the River Thames in a private boat he'd hired, and which had cost him an entire month's salary. She hadn't wanted to enter the marriage with secrets between them, and she had needed to know that her past humiliation wouldn't affect the way he felt about her. She'd realised that if she didn't tell him, it would always hang over them, like a dead weight – an everlasting void between them that would only grow bigger and eventually tear them apart for good.

She'd told him later that night, at his place, and to her relief it hadn't changed the way Frank felt about her. If anything, it had made him love her more. But it had also enraged him. He'd punched the wall, made his knuckles bleed, talked about wanting to kill Davenport, make him pay. She'd let him vent his anger; she'd expected that. But she didn't want him to revisit something she'd consciously buried. Six years had passed, she was dealing with it, she was happy with Frank, and she didn't want her name, or his, being plastered all over the papers. She also knew that Davenport had a wife, and the last thing she wanted was for her name to be blemished for something her husband had done. Mary wasn't a vindictive person. She always considered others' feelings, even if they were strangers to her.

Reluctantly, Frank had promised never to speak of it again, never to her or to anyone, and they'd gone on to spend twenty-eight blissful years together. A life made more joyful by the arrival of Matthew.

But bumping into Richard had touched a nerve inside Mary. She'd already been feeling unsettled by a conversation she'd had with Matthew the night before. Learning that he was going to work for Davenport. Of all the firms to train at, why did it have to be that bastard's? She'd wanted to be happy for him, but instead she'd felt sick to the stomach. Matthew was exceptionally bright, and all she could think was what if Davenport took him under his wing, like he'd done with Charles Dempsey? Introduced him to all sorts of unsavoury characters? It had brought back memories of that fateful night, as had seeing Lynsey.

The poor girl had been attacked as her stepfather's drunken friends looked on, revelling in her pain and indignity like a pack of wolves. Lynsey had been brave enough to press charges, and it looked like she had a good chance of getting the bastards. It had made Mary think. What if she'd stood up to Larson? Ignored what he'd said. Maybe it had all just been hot air, designed to call her bluff, scare her into submission. Had she been too weak? So weak, in fact, she'd not only granted Davenport his freedom, but also ensured he'd gone on to have a flourishing legal career, making fortunes, while she'd been forced to shelve her dreams because of what he'd done.

At first, she'd been frosty with Richard after he'd called out her name and she'd swivelled round and caught his eye. She'd recognised him immediately, despite thirty-five years having passed. And he himself could never forget those large, luminous chocolate-brown eyes despite the lines that had developed around the edges. He'd walked up to her, said, 'Hello, how are you?' and they'd exchanged a brief account of their lives since the night they'd both wanted to forget but never could. He'd suggested grabbing coffee nearby. She'd refused at first, but then he'd told her about the cancer, and her heart had melted. They'd ordered two coffees at Caffè Nero, a five-minute walk away, and sat in a quiet corner, the sordid memory of all those years ago still hanging over them like a black cloud.

'Why didn't you intervene, do more to stop him?' she had asked. 'I saw the look in your eyes – you knew it was wrong. Was it your way of getting back at me? Because I didn't want to go out with you?' She'd looked at him with pleading eyes, desperate to make sense of his decision to stand there and watch her suffer.

'No, of course not,' he'd answered, and she'd seen the honesty in his face. 'I was simply too weak, too aware of the hold Davenport's family had over the college, too caught up in my own ambitions for the future, too young and self-obsessed to know that, as time went on, all the trappings of success and money would seem immaterial. I know that now, more than ever. Now that I am dying.'

'What you mean is, once again you're scared for yourself. Only this time it's your soul you're concerned about, not your status.' She hadn't raised her voice, but there'd been no compassion in her tone. Just bitterness.

Richard had lowered his eyes, talked down into his coffee. 'Maybe.'

'How could you have worked with him all this time?'

Richard had explained how they'd happened to land articles at the same firm and, both being brilliant lawyers, soon found themselves on the fast-track to partnership. He'd met and married Marianne, had a son. It had all been too cosy, too good a deal to walk away from and take a chance elsewhere. So, he'd sucked it up, carried on. And yes, once again he'd been too weak to stand up to Davenport after he'd cheated his way to senior partnership.

'Do you know that my son, Matthew, has a training contract with your firm? He starts next March.'

This had been news to Richard, and it had distracted him from his illness. 'Does he know?'

'About what happened? No, of course not. There's no way he'd have taken a job with you if he knew. Good God, I don't know what he'd do. The very thought frightens me.'

'But your husband knows?'

'Yes, I told him the night he proposed. Made him promise never to mention it again if he wanted to marry me.' Richard had smiled at her feistiness, felt a pang of sadness when he thought of what she might have been, had he intervened that night.

'How can you let him train at Davenport's firm?' he'd asked.

'It's your firm too.'

'No, it isn't really. Davenport's at the helm, the whole firm reeks of him and his decisions.'

Mary had sighed heavily. 'It kills me, if you must know, but what am I to do? I can't tell him why I'm against it.'

'He has a right to know, Mary.'

'I'm afraid of what he'll do.' Although her son was kind by nature, Mary also knew that he frequently let his emotions get the better of him. When he felt wronged, he found it hard to put a check on his anger, and being a staunchly loyal person, he would defend his family and friends to the death.

'Don't you want Davenport to pay?'

Mary had shaken her head slowly. 'It's too late for that.'

'It's never too late.' His eyes were steely.

'What are you saying, Richard?'

'I'm saying I don't want to leave this world knowing Davenport got away unpunished.' He had paused, a disgusted look on his face. 'Nothing's changed. He and Charles Dempsey still act like they did thirty years ago. Visiting strip clubs and whorehouses behind their wives' backs. Treating women like dirt. Is that the kind of man you want your son to work for? I know how desperately unhappy his poor wife is. She's suffered at his hands for far too long. She's a lovely woman and she deserves so much better.'

Somehow, after she'd got over the initial shock of Matthew joining Sullivans, Mary had forced herself into believing that Davenport was perhaps not the same man he'd been back then. Told herself, over and over, that perhaps he'd mellowed, settled down, turned over a new leaf.

She'd therefore been especially devastated to hear that this had been wishful thinking, and the thought of Matthew associating with the bastard had horrified her once again. She'd thought of poor Lynsey lying bruised and broken in her bed; how men like Davenport continued to get away with their crimes, often because women like herself were too weak to stand up to them.

But she also hadn't been able to see a way out. 'You go to the police now, it's his word against yours, Richard. It'll come to nothing. You have no proof.'

'You could go to the police,' Richard had said.

'They won't believe me after all these years. Larson will deny it, Davenport will deny it. And in any case, I can't drag Matthew's and Frank's names through the papers.'

Richard had paused. A faraway look in his eyes, as if he was seriously contemplating something.

'What is it?'

'What if you had a diary?'

'A diary?'

'A diary Matthew happened to find. Diaries always tell the truth. That's the point of them.'

She had realised what he meant. 'I see where you're going with this, Richard, but I can't face Matthew confronting me about it. I can't face telling him what happened. I can't bear to see the pain in his eyes. And like I said, I'm scared of what he'll do.'

It had been tempting, though. Like Richard had said, diaries were journals of the soul. People only wrote the truth in them. Who would doubt a diary's authenticity?

And then it had come to her. A thought as exhilarating as it was terrifying. She couldn't bear the thought of leaving her husband, her son. But she also couldn't bear the thought of her precious boy working for Davenport. Possibly moulded over time into a carbon copy of him, the way he had moulded Dempsey. Marrying some poor, devoted girl, ultimately forced to suffer the way Davenport's wife had suffered. All this had made her shudder, and she'd realised she had to save him, save his inherent good nature, before it was lost for good.

Mary had known exactly what she had to do. Who wouldn't believe the diary of a dead woman? Devoted mother, devoted wife, devoted social worker, loved and respected by friends, families, clients alike. A woman so tormented by her demons, she'd felt compelled to take her own life.

She could disappear for a while, maybe a year or two, then come back. It happened all the time. People had funny moments, breakdowns. They went away to 'find' themselves, and then they came back, families reunited, everyone happy. She had hated the thought of causing Matthew pain, terrified of what he'd do under the stress and strain of her 'death', and that's when things had become clear; she had no choice but to let Frank in on the plan. Father and son shared a strong bond, and so she could count on him to help Matthew through his grief. She'd been certain Frank would agree to the plan if she made it crystal clear it was what she wanted, more than anything. She knew he'd go to the ends of the earth for her, and he would be the one to steer Matthew towards the diary. Although, of course, Matthew would believe he'd stumbled upon it by chance.

Mary's eyes had grown animated, and Richard had realised then that she wanted in. They'd continued to talk, make plans – plans that soon became much bigger than they'd ever imagined, and which had led Mary to this Parisian café in early August 2017, two hundred thousand pounds in cash sitting between her ankles.

She smiled at Pamela Davenport, who looked so different to when Richard had first taken a chance and recruited her into their scheme. Confident, sexy, a new woman, now that she was free of her repugnant husband.

'OK, so I'll give it another year, let all this blow over. But you'll keep me posted on Matthew? I need to know he's OK.'

'Don't worry, you have my word.'

'Sometimes I wish we'd just left it at the diary. That's what I'd imagined at first. That Matthew would find it and take it to the police. But Richard somehow convinced me that wasn't enough, and when I look back now, I can't help thinking that for him, it was as much about pulling off the unthinkable, as getting his revenge. Don't get me wrong, I know he deeply regrets doing nothing that night, but I also know that working towards the plan excited him, kept him going. He somehow roped me, Frank and Matthew into his elaborate scheme, but I still can't help worrying, because if we get caught, it'll ruin Matthew's life. I don't care about mine, but I can't bear to see him waste his behind bars.'

'Don't stress, that's not going to happen. It's all gone smoothly so far, hasn't it? The police have nothing.'

'They had the hooker.'

'But she's been dealt with.'

'Tell me Matthew had nothing to do with that.'

'I told you before, Matthew played no part in that,' Pamela lied. She knew from Richard that he had; but telling Mary might break her. A second's pause, then, 'And besides, Richard's right. The diary alone might not have been enough, and Nigel would have escaped a second time. Instead, we got six million out of his firm, and a substantial donation to a worthy cause and...'

'And Nigel's death. Is that what you wanted, Pamela?'

Pamela hesitated, then, 'No, I didn't want that. But I'm not going to spend my new-found freedom crying over it. That man shamed and humiliated me for years, while I devoted my entire life to him and raising our children. He ended up paying the price for a terrible thing he did to you, and he deserved to suffer in the most public, humiliating way possible. Richard's plan has helped right the wrongs done to three women Nigel hurt, directly, and indirectly – you, me and Diana Dempsey.'

'Yes.' Mary smiled faintly. 'I suppose you're right. I just pray Richard's left no stone unturned.' She paused for a second, then said, 'So you'll meet Frank once you've got Nigel's funeral out of the way?'

'Yes. I'm dreading the funeral, to be honest. I'm so grateful to my children for taking care of the arrangements. Of course, I told them it was because it was too painful for me. They didn't know I had more pressing matters to deal with.' She paused, then said, 'Let's just hope I can resist the urge to spit on my husband's grave.'

Chapter Thirty-Four

After hearing Maddy's account of her conversation with Becky Roberts, as well as her observation that Charlotte's reclusive brother, Isaac, had a scar on his chin, Carver was more convinced than ever that the abduction had been faked. But the fact that Charlotte and Matthew had been lovers for some time didn't prove they'd conspired with Richard to forge their own abduction. The reality was, they still didn't have absolute proof, and now one of the suspects was dead.

In Carver's mind, Richard Barker had to have been the brains behind the operation. He knew the firm inside out, had an axe to grind and a conscience to appease. But now he was gone, leaving his three trainees, and almost certainly Isaac Dempsey, as Carver's chief suspects.

It was Tuesday night. Maddy was curled up against Carver on his sofa, watching but not really watching some inane quiz show on TV. It was another sultry evening. All the windows were open, but this, and the portable fan Carver had blowing in their direction, did little to cool the oppressive air. Richard's funeral was on Thursday. Marianne had wanted it done quickly, and out of the way. Maddy understood completely. Why drag out something so painful? She, along with many from the firm, would be attending the church service at St Saviour's in Pimlico, while Carver planned on putting in a low-key appearance at the back. Right now, all he and Maddy could do was watch Matthew, Charlotte and Stephen closely. Hope that one of them made a wrong move. Either that, or Richard slipped up from the grave.

'What's wrong?' Maddy asked, looking up at Carver. She was still finding it hard to come to terms with the fact that Richard had been the likely ringleader. The fact that he'd put her and her colleagues through forty-five minutes of hell, made them wonder if they'd ever see the light of day again, all so he could get revenge on Davenport. He'd always been nice to her. Always supportive, fair-minded. Making it that much harder to be cross with him. Especially now that he was dead. Even so, he hadn't had the right to toy with people's lives like that. All because his life had been coming to an end. She thought about Marianne, the lies he must have told her, on top of keeping his illness a secret. What would she say – how would she cope? – if she knew he'd planned his own abduction? It might very well destroy her.

Carver looked down at Maddy with raised eyebrows, a grille of lines running across his forehead, a slight smirk forming around his mouth. 'What, you mean aside from the fact that four of your colleagues appear to have got away with faking their own abduction, facilitating money laundering, fraud, theft, blackmail, bribery, and possibly murder along the way?'

Maddy sat up. 'Don't forget the brother and the anonymous woman. That makes six suspects in total.'

'Ah, yes, of course, they'd slipped my mind.' He grinned at her. Maddy knew they hadn't slipped his mind. Nothing did. He was just being cute. Jesting with her.

'Who do you think the woman is?'

'Judging by Davenport's history, it could be any number of women bearing a grudge.'

Maddy chewed this over for a second, then finally said what had been weighing on her mind since she'd spoken to James Canton about Davenport's funeral earlier that day. 'Here's a thought. What about his wife?'

Carver's interest was piqued. 'Go on.'

'I mean, has anyone seen her much since all this happened? She buggered off to France after kicking Nigel out of the house, made a brief appearance for his funeral this afternoon, but disappeared straight after. Didn't even hold a wake, or small gathering. Canton said she was as calm as calm can be. Didn't shed a tear.'

'Can you blame her? She's furious. Furious after discovering her husband was a liar, a rapist and a philanderer. How can you cry for someone like that? Plus, she was probably embarrassed to hold a social event after the funeral. I mean, what would she talk about? What a wonderful, kind, loving husband she'd had?'

'Yes, but wouldn't you expect her to be a bit less calm about the whole thing? Personally, I think I'd be beside myself, hysterical even. In the space of a fortnight, she found out her husband was a rapist and a serial cheat, he was blackmailed, resigned, arrested, then killed himself. Wouldn't you expect her to be a little less in control?'

'There is something in that,' Carver agreed.

'But just humour me for a second. What if she'd been mad for some time? Knew about his affairs, et cetera. What if she'd had all the time in the world to prepare for what, to the rest of us, was an unexpected bolt from the blue. What if she was their mole on the inside? I mean, she had access to her husband's office, she could have planted the bug. She knew his movements, she could have told them when he was out with Charles Dempsey, where they went. Christ, she could have blown up the vans remotely for all we know.' Maddy got up, her eyes dancing. Carver could have kissed her right then.

'You could be onto something there,' he said. 'But Richard or any of the other three could just as easily have planted the bug. And besides, Nassau police said the woman who handled the account was Czech, blonde, slim and very attractive. I hate to say it, but Pamela Davenport is none of those.'

'She may have been wearing a wig, dolled herself up a bit. And I've heard people get away with fake passports all the time.'

'Hmm, perhaps. But we know the transactions were made in person the morning after the hostages were released. Pamela kicked Davenport out on Friday night. She would have had to have boarded a plane to Barbados the same night, to make it to Nassau the following morning.'

Maddy frowned. 'Hmm, good point.'

'It's not impossible, though. Barbados is a ten-hour flight away, but five hours behind the UK. We can check the passenger manifest.' He paused, then said, 'If she is the one who emptied the account, surely she'll make contact with the others soon?'

'Who's to say she hasn't already?'

Wednesday, 11 a.m.

'You've spoken to Stephen?'

'Yesterday evening, after he picked up the 200k from King's Cross. Mary will transfer the rest of the two million he's owed to each of the various accounts he's opened in stages.' A brief pause, then, 'He could barely contain himself over the phone. Can't say I'm surprised. Have you seen the dive he lives in?'

'I have. Poor boy's been unlucky, but hopefully this'll set him on the straight and narrow. He's got a lovely girl, and she deserves the best.'

'The rest of the cash, the four million, has gone to Cancer Research, as per Richard's instructions. Strictly anonymous, with clear instructions not to leak it to the press.'

'Good.' A pause, then Frank asked, 'How was the funeral?'

'Dry-eyed.'

'That's good to hear.'

'That coward Dempsey looked the most bothered. My children didn't even shed a tear between them.'

'Can you blame them, after what he did?'

'No,' Pamela sighed, 'I can't. I just wish I'd had the courage to leave him years ago. Then I might have had some sort of a life. Instead, I've wasted most of it.'

Frank felt genuinely sorry for Pamela. She was a good woman. Everything she said was true, and it was a sad situation. Still, she wasn't even fifty-five yet, still young by today's standards and it wasn't too late to start again. And at least she didn't have to hide. Not like his beloved Mary. 'At least you're free now. You can go where you want, do what you want, see who you want. Think of my poor Mary. She's been in hiding for the last year and a half, and I've only seen her twice in all that time.'

Frank sipped his cappuccino in the corner of the café. A small family-run affair on Salusbury Road, just a five-minute walk from Queen's Park Tube station. They were seated at one of three tables, the other two occupied by a young couple engrossed in each other, and an elderly man engrossed in *The Times*. Pamela hadn't wanted to meet like this, but Frank had been certain there was no risk. Neither were suspects. As far as the police were concerned, they were victims. Innocent by-products of Nigel Davenport's crimes.

336

Pamela watched his eyes water. She thought how lucky Mary was to have found him. She'd have traded places with Mary in a heartbeat. She saw how he ached for her, and she wondered how that must feel. Incredible, no doubt. Like no other feeling in the world.

When Mary had first told Frank about Richard's plan, he'd hit the roof, said they were both nuts. It was insanity to even think about pulling off such a ploy. Having been a policeman for thirty years, he'd struggled with the idea of breaking the law. And what about her job, her life with them? How could she even consider leaving them?

But when she'd reasoned with him, told him how much she regretted not pressing charges, how that wretched night still haunted her as much as she'd tried to push it to the back of her mind, he'd relented. All he had to do was place the diary where Matthew would find it. They both knew Matthew loved his mother more than life itself. Like Frank, he idolised her, and learning the truth would be torture for him. Although he was a loving boy, he was also a passionate soul, and when something riled him, he found it hard to let go.

Of course, Frank had been scared for his boy. Scared he might get caught – scared it could all go horribly wrong and he'd end up facing a life behind bars. And it had been hard taking a step back, pretending he was ignorant of the elaborate scheme Matthew was a part of. But it was a chance he had taken. Having met with Richard, he'd felt he could trust him, and he'd given him tips on police procedure, forensic analysis, obtaining weapons, black-market activities, number plate cloning, CCTV and so on. Information Richard had fed to his younger partners-in-crime as if it had all stemmed from his own research. Of course, Frank had warned Richard that, should they be forced to implement plan B, the police would ultimately conclude the kidnappers hadn't been in the van when it blew, but Richard had insisted it had to be this way, that Isaac needed a distraction to make his escape, and Frank had once again relented. Told himself that so long as everyone kept their cool, there was no reason why it shouldn't work.

And now, to his relief, it seemed he'd been right.

'Does she look well?' Frank asked Pamela.

'Yes, she looks good. Just think, another year, tops, and you'll be together again.'

'I just worry she'll get caught with that passport. Despite changing her hair and wearing lenses. A fake is a fake after all.'

'Immigrants use fake passports all the time. Sure, if she tries to board a plane in Europe she'll be in trouble, but provided she keeps to the water, she'll be fine. No one even gave her a second look getting on at Portsmouth, or in Bilbao.' She paused, then added, 'Besides, the police stopped looking for her over a year ago after finding the note and scarf. As far as everyone's concerned, she's dead.'

'But they never found a body.'

'So what? She might be lying at the bottom of the English Channel for all they know, having filled her pockets with bricks. Please stop stressing yourself out.' She paused, then said, 'Will you ever tell Matthew the truth? That she planned her disappearance all along?'

Frank shook his head, sighed. 'I don't know. I can't decide how he'll react. He might hate us for not including him in the plan from the beginning. But we couldn't. He had to find out for himself, his reaction had to be natural, and Mary didn't want him trying to contact her, or asking questions about what happened.'

'Are you going to Richard's funeral?'

'No, it wouldn't make much sense for me to be there, despite being Matthew's father. I'm not supposed to have known Richard. It saddens me, though. I'd have liked to have been there.'

Pamela reached across the table and squeezed Frank's hand. 'He knows that, Frank. Wherever he is, Richard knows that. Just as he knows I would have been there if it wasn't for the fact that I'm stained with my husband's filth. The last person Marianne Barker will want to see is me. Now that she knows what kind of a man Nigel really was. That he cheated her husband out of senior partnership.'

'If only she knew that you and her husband were allies.'

'That's one thing she must never know, Frank. Never.'

Rivers watched from her car, parked on Salusbury Road. Watched Frank Gerard leave, Pamela Davenport slipping out ten minutes later. She then got out, popped across the road to the café, confirmed her suspicions with the manager, before returning to the driver's seat. She picked up her phone and dialled Carver's direct line at the station. 'Sir, it's me.'

'Yes? What you got?' He'd asked Rivers to keep tabs on Pamela's comings and goings, prompted by his conversation with Maddy the night before.

'Pamela Davenport has just met with Frank Gerard at a Queen's Park café.'

'Frank Gerard? That's odd, isn't it?'

'Yes, sir.'

'Do you have any idea what they were discussing?'

'Sorry, sir, Gerard knows me. I had to stay well away, and it wasn't the sort of café I could hide in. It was tiny. They were in there about forty minutes, though. He left first, then her, ten minutes later.'

'And you're certain they were together?'

'It was a three-seater café, sir. Plus, after they left, I went inside, and asked the manager who confirmed that the two of them had coffee together.'

'There's no reason for Frank Gerard to have coffee with Pamela Davenport, unless…'

'Unless he's in on it, too, sir.'

'Precisely.'

Chapter Thirty-Five

Wednesday afternoon, 1 p.m., and Drake had more interesting news.

'The background check on Stephen Baines came back, sir.'

'And?' Carver had just wolfed down a sandwich and was taking a ten-minute break. He looked up keenly from his newspaper. Break over.

'He's up to his ears in debt. Appears he has a bit of a gambling problem, or at least had one. Owes roughly two hundred grand to various creditors.'

'Shit, two hundred?' Carver repeated, folding his paper. 'So, he's in it for the money, pure and simple – has to be. Good work, Drake. Keep an eye on his comings and goings. I wouldn't be surprised if he moves out of that flat soon.'

'Will do, sir.'

Carver told Drake about Frank Gerard's meeting with Pamela Davenport.

'You think he's part of it too?'

'Why else would he be having coffee with the wife of the man who raped his wife?'

'Perhaps she was apologising, sir? After all, they've both been hurt by Davenport, albeit in different ways.'

'It's possible, I suppose.' Carver nodded with a slight smile, marvelling at how Drake always tried to see the best in people, despite his job. 'Still, their choice of café seems telling – as if they were trying their hardest not to be seen.'

Thursday, 10.30 a.m. The day of Richard's funeral. Carver and Drake had just had a quick catch-up meeting. Catch-up over, Carver stood up. 'I'm off to Barker's funeral.'

Just then, Rivers came crashing through the door.

'Ever heard of knocking, Rivers?' Carver said irritably.

'Sorry, sir, but something big's come up.'

Carver's heart jerked. Things were suddenly moving quickly. 'What?'

'I got a call from a bloke in Newcastle. He saw Cherry's sketch in the paper. Said he's certain he sold his blue Ford Transit van to the same man three months ago.'

A breakthrough. Finally. 'Why the hell didn't he come forward earlier?'

'Same reason a lot of folks don't, I guess. They're either scared, apathetic, or they've done something wrong themselves.'

'Did he give a name? He must have required several forms of ID from the buyer before selling it?'

'He sure did, sir. Isaac Dempsey.'

Carver gave a triumphant clench of his fist. His suspicions had been confirmed. Even so, he asked, 'As in son of Charles Dempsey?'

Rivers beamed. 'And sister of Charlotte, sir.'

'So now we know for certain. He's our anonymous man. The blue van driver, the one who bribed Cherry.' Carver muttered this more to himself than to the others. And he wondered, did Isaac also kill the poor girl?

'He lives with his sister as you know, sir. Want me to go pick him up?'

'Change of plan.' Carver grabbed his coat. 'I'm going with you, Rivers. Drake, you go to the funeral.'

'What about Charlotte Dempsey, sir? Surely this confirms they're in it together?'

'I'd bet my last pound coin on it. But we still have nothing solid on her, just hunches. Hopefully we can make the brother talk.'

Ten forty-five a.m. Maddy sat in the back of a black cab with Charlotte. She'd hoped to escape the office unseen, but Charlotte had caught her at the lifts, almost as if she'd been tailing her. She'd asked if Maddy wanted to share a cab to Richard's funeral, and finding it increasingly hard to act normal around her trainee, Maddy had had no choice but to say, 'Sure, why not?'

The heatwave had broken once more, and a light drizzle hung in the air. The roads were busy and hectic, City workers on their way to meetings choosing to hail a cab, rather than risk arriving at their destinations frazzled and wet. Maddy had deliberately put her handbag on the seat next to her. Thankfully, Charlotte had got the message and sat opposite, enabling Maddy to keep Carver's text to herself.

Got a tip about C's brother, Isaac. On my way to pick him up. J

Maddy's heart galloped, but she tried hard to suppress her excitement.

'Something up?' Charlotte asked. (Evidently not hard enough.) She stared at Maddy intently.

'No, I mean, not exactly,' Maddy replied nonchalantly. 'Just thinking how this is going to be tough.' She smiled at Charlotte. 'It's nice to have company, though.'

What a lie!

Charlotte gazed out of the window at the gloomy grey sky, and almost whispered, 'Yes, it is. Poor man didn't have enough time with his wife. He deserved at least another couple of months.'

'Was that his plan, do you think? To have more time?' Maddy searched Charlotte's face for the truth.

'Plan? What an odd turn of phrase,' Charlotte scoffed, frowning. 'Of course he wanted more time. His doctor was pretty confident he had another three to six months.'

'You seem to have got incredibly close to him in such a short time. I'm surprised you don't resent him. He was your mentor, after all, but he didn't fight to keep you on. You must know that?'

That was harsh. Had she gone too far by saying the one thing she'd previously vowed to keep to herself? Probably. But the game had changed, and Charlotte needed to be pushed.

'That's what being held hostage does to you, Maddy,' came the bitter response. 'Shared trauma, shared tragedies, shared misery, brings people together. Makes material issues seem, well, immaterial.'

Maddy suspected she wasn't just talking about being held hostage. Rather, she was referring to her mother's death, and the fact that she and her accomplices had all, in some way, suffered at Nigel Davenport's hands. 'Are Matthew and Stephen coming?'

'Of course, we all suffered together. We'll share a common bond forever.'

A common bond of deceit, fraud and murder, thought Maddy. It was maddening. She felt like shaking her, screaming at her, 'You were all in this together, admit it!'

But she knew that wouldn't do, and Carver wouldn't thank her for it. They needed quantifiable proof. Hopefully, Isaac would provide that.

The cab pulled up outside St Saviour's. Mourners were already pouring in. Sombre expressions all round. A sea of black, some shaking out umbrellas at the door, all of them pausing to offer their condolences to Marianne Barker, who was ready to greet them with her two grown-up children either side of her. Dressed in an elegant black crepe shift dress and jacket, with matching black patent leather shoes, she was the epitome of elegance. But no amount of make-up could disguise the sorrow in her eyes, the hollowness of her cheeks. Again, Maddy couldn't bear to imagine her reaction if she knew what her husband had done.

They embraced tenderly as Maddy tried, at least for a moment, to blot this thought out. 'I am so sorry,' she said.

Marianne managed a weak smile, then spotted Charlotte. All at once, there was panic in her eyes. As if Charlotte's presence had seriously unnerved her.

Does she suspect something after all?

'Mrs Barker,' Charlotte began, leaning forward to embrace Marianne, 'I'm so sorry, he shouldn't have gone so soon.'

Maddy watched the touching scene. Noticed the way Marianne seemed to freeze, her shoulders stiff, her manner still anxious. She caught Maddy's eye, a look that said it all. She knew something. She knew all was far from right with this seemingly innocent young woman.

Charlotte broke away, and Marianne managed a soft, 'Thank you,' before moving on to the next mourner. As she sauntered up the aisle, Maddy realised she somehow had to get Marianne alone after the service and find out what she knew.

'Goddammit!'

Exasperated, Carver thumped his fist hard against the door. Isaac wasn't home. In fact, neighbours hadn't seen him for some time now, not since his sister had been released, they thought. Apparently, he used to work at Starbucks on Hampstead High Street, but he hadn't been seen in there for over a month. Carver suspected he'd done a runner. No doubt Sophie Baines had told her brother she'd spoken to a couple of detectives about Isaac, and Stephen had told him to get the hell away. Even so, Carver had just sent Rivers to check out the coffee chain.

'Can I help you?' a male voice said from behind.

Carver swivelled round. Charles Dempsey. This was a surprise. He'd expected him to be at Richard's funeral.

'Mr Dempsey. You know that Richard Barker's funeral is today?'

Dempsey gave a half-smile. 'I'm afraid Richard and I were never friends. We never saw eye to eye. In fact, on several occasions, we nearly came to blows. I'm sorry for his wife and family, of course, but it would have been hypocritical of me to attend.'

'Unlike your daughter?' Carver said.

There was a flash of alarm in Dempsey's eyes. 'My daughter worked for Richard, but more importantly, she was held captive with him. I should imagine such a situation brings people closer together.'

'I should imagine it does.' Carver's eyes lingered on Dempsey for a few seconds.

'Why are you here?' Dempsey broke the awkwardness.

'I wanted to have a word with your son.'

'My son?' A look of surprise. 'Isaac is in Florida, staying at the family condo.'

That figures, thought Carver. 'In need of a break, was he?'

'I just think the stress and strain of the last few weeks got to him. He's an introspective sort, doesn't handle pressure well.'

'He's had a lot to deal with. First his mother's death, then his sister's abduction.'

'He was very close to his mother, and he's just as close to Charlotte. Is there something wrong with that?' Dempsey's tone had turned hostile, clearly irritated by Carver's fishing.

'When did you last see your son, Mr Dempsey?'

Dempsey thought for a second. 'Hmm, it must have been here, the Friday Charlotte was released. I drove her home from the hospital.'

'I don't think I've seen him once since all this happened. Not at the press conferences, or when Charlotte was freed.'

Again, Dempsey thought. 'Yes, I believe that's right.'

Carver took a step closer. 'Don't you think that's a little odd? That a devoted brother wouldn't choose to plead for his sister's return, or be there at the scene, the moment she was released?'

Dempsey scratched his head. 'Like I said, Isaac's a nervous, reclusive sort. He doesn't like crowds or drawing attention to himself.'

'I see. But you must have seen him at some point during the week Charlotte was taken?'

'No, we only spoke on the phone.'

'You only spoke on the phone? Again, isn't that a little peculiar? Surely it's a time when family members reach out to each other for support?'

'We're not a normal family,' Dempsey snapped. 'My children hate my guts, OK? Is that what this is all about? What you wanted to hear?'

'Why is that?'

'Because they blame me for their mother's death. Ever since Diana died, they've wanted nothing to do with me.'

Carver studied his face. Bloated and blotchy. A face full of excess. Drugs, booze, women. 'So why are you here?'

'Because I have nowhere else to go, I suppose. Because I wanted to

347

make things right with Charlotte.' He pulled out an envelope from his pocket. Held it up.

'What's that?'

'A letter to my daughter. Telling her I'm sorry, and that I'd like to make it up to her, be closer.'

'Sorry for what?'

'Not being there.' A pause, then, 'I'm fifty-five years old, retired, with so much money I don't know what to do with it. But I have no wife, no real friends to speak of now that Nigel is dead, and my only flesh and blood won't talk to me. Plus, I keep thinking about what Charlotte said to me after she was released.'

'What was that?'

'That I was to blame for what happened.'

'Is she right?' Carver stared at him long and hard.

'Perhaps. Maybe partly.' Dempsey lowered his eyes with shame.

'Did she say anything else?'

Dempsey looked up again. 'Yes.' He nodded. 'That Nigel's sins were mine, and that I deserved to rot in hell.' He appeared to hesitate.

'There's something else, isn't there?'

'Yes. Something I still can't get my head around.'

'What?'

'She said that Nigel was very much mistaken if he believed he'd got away with it.'

Carver and Rivers drove back to the station in silence. Like Drake, Rivers was a fast learner. She knew better than to speak when her boss was thinking. She'd noticed his tendency to drift off into a world of his own when something was grating on him.

Charlotte had sent a clear message to her father that she wasn't done with Davenport. It had been risky of her to do so. But perhaps she hadn't imagined he'd ever dare to repeat it. He was her father, after all, and maybe she'd been relying on his guilt at having been such a poor one, to keep his mouth shut.

As they'd parted company, Carver had seen the look in Dempsey's eyes. The suspicion, and yet, at the same time, desperation not to believe his daughter had helped engineer his old friend's demise. The horror of knowing he was responsible for driving his own flesh and blood to such lengths clearly consumed him. His daughter considered him a monster. And yet, because of the way he'd behaved, he'd helped fashion her into a monster of sorts. All the money in the world couldn't atone for what a terrible father he'd been.

Chapter Thirty-Six

It was a beautiful service. Not a dry eye in the church. A poignant blend of warmth, respect, love and grief filled the air. A stark contrast to Nigel Davenport's funeral, where emotions ran cold. Richard's son, Justin, gave a moving speech about his wonderful, loving, brave father, while Mark Simmons praised his partner's sharp intellect, brilliance as a lawyer and unflinching loyalty to the firm. Throughout, Maddy kept a close eye on the three suspects. And Marianne.

She looked distraught, of course. But there was more to it than that. She didn't look quite there, as if something else was preying on her mind, making her appear vacant, rather than fully present in her grief. She fidgeted in her seat, every now and then looking over her shoulder as if she expected some rude interruption.

But Charlotte, Matthew and Stephen were Emmy Award winners. Each giving a performance that would make Meryl Streep proud. But maybe that wasn't entirely fair. Perhaps at that moment they weren't acting. United in grief for a man who had become a firm part of their lives. Not just a partner, or an employer to them. But a brother-in-arms, who'd had their backs at every turn.

Back outside, the skies had cleared, and Maddy was suddenly warm in her jacket. As she lingered amongst the crowds, she heard a voice call out her name from behind. She turned around sharply. It was Drake. He came up close, whispered in her ear, 'Nice service. Isaac wasn't there. Took a sudden trip to the family pad in Florida. Which makes it even more likely he's involved.'

'Shit.'

'Quite. Carver's fuming.' *I can just imagine*, thought Maddy. Drake quickly recounted Carver's conversation with Charles Dempsey.

'So that's what she said,' Maddy murmured. 'That makes sense.' She'd always suspected Charlotte had said something more to Charles that day, other than the fact that he was to blame, but both father and daughter had lied to her in the hospital.

'Maddy.' Charlotte was suddenly there. Sneaking up on them like the grim reaper. 'Want to share a taxi to Marianne's?'

Maddy had originally intended to skip the wake and go straight back to the office. But in light of Marianne's odd behaviour, she now saw it as a golden opportunity to get her alone. Most of the partners and several of the litigation associates were going, so her absence at work wouldn't be frowned on. 'Sure.' She feigned a smile.

'Great.' Charlotte turned to Drake, said pleasantly, 'Hello, DS Drake. Any more leads?'

Drake put on his best poker face. 'No, not yet. But we're not giving up. My boss isn't one to rest when it comes to catching criminals. Even if it takes him forever.' He fixed his eyes on Charlotte, but she didn't bat an eyelid. As if ice ran through her veins, rather than blood.

In contrast to Stephen, who, together with Matthew, had just appeared, catching Drake's comment. His ruddy complexion was suddenly peaky. 'Well, I'll see most of you back at the office,' he said. 'I've got a mound of work to get through, and I need to leave promptly this evening.'

'Oh, why's that?' Maddy asked.

'Celeste and I are looking at flats in the Angel area.'

'Nice part of town. Buy or let?' Drake asked.

'Buy actually. It's about time, really, we've been together three years now.'

'They must be paying you well at Sullivans?' Drake let his gaze linger on Stephen, whose previous unease had been replaced by a look of outright fear. The subtle, yet highly effective, questioning continued. 'From what I read in the papers, it seems students are so riddled with debt these days, the only way they can afford a property is by relying on their parents.' He paused. Grinned. 'Either that, or by robbing a bank.'

Stephen had started to perspire. A faint bead of sweat coated his top lip. But he managed a light chuckle. 'Fortunately, Celeste and I have been saving for years, and we finally have enough for a deposit.'

'Well, good for you, mate.' Matthew patted his friend on the back. 'Now, you'd better get going. Celeste'll kill you if you don't make it out on time later.'

Stephen gave Matthew a grateful smile, excused himself, then was off like the wind in the direction of the Tube.

Drake and Maddy exchanged a brief look. He was their weakest link. Their next target with Isaac out of the country.

Trying to pin down Marianne at the wake was no easy task. Richard had been a popular man, and his home was brimming with friends, colleagues, clients alike, wanting to celebrate his life, and pay their respects to his widow. Marianne had hired a catering firm whose employees circled her house with trays of artistic canapés and seemingly endless bottles of champagne. Maddy watched her work the ground-floor living room, acting like the perfect hostess when inside she must have been dying.

Finally, she excused herself from a couple she'd been talking to and left the room. Maddy waited a couple of seconds, checking Charlotte and Matthew were still deep in conversation with another guest, then followed. She found Marianne in the kitchen, standing against the sink, her back to Maddy.

'Marianne, are you OK?'

Marianne spun round, startled by the sudden intrusion. Tears streamed down her cheeks. She clearly wasn't OK. Maddy went and put her hand on Marianne's shoulder. 'It's been a difficult day. I'm not surprised you're crying. I'm in awe of how you're managing to keep it together in there.' She motioned in the direction of the living room.

Marianne grabbed a piece of kitchen towel and blew her nose. Then looked up at Maddy, a tortured look in her eyes. 'Have you ever been forced to make a difficult choice, Madeline?'

Maddy thought back to January 2015.

'Yes. You know I helped put my best friend away. In my heart, as much as it killed me, it was the right choice.'

Marianne sniffed, grabbed another piece of kitchen towel and wiped her eyes.

'I'm sensing you're in a similar situation,' Maddy continued gently. 'I want to help in any way I can, but you need to open up to me. Tell me what it is.'

Marianne looked up at the ceiling, as if seeking help from some higher entity, then let her gaze fall back on Maddy, the same pained look in her eyes. 'I think the abduction may have been faked.'

Maddy's heart skipped. She tried to act surprised. 'What do you mean?'

Marianne glanced around, spoke in hushed tones. 'As you know, Richard and I drove to our cottage in the Cotswolds last Monday, where he died.'

'Yes.'

'Well, I hadn't been there for some time. But one of our neighbour's sons, William, said he'd seen Richard several times over the last year. With three, possibly four others. Always on weekends, and when I thought he was in the office.'

'Do you know who the others were?' Maddy had an idea, and her heart was thumping at the prospect of Marianne's response.

'William said he recognised three of them, from the papers. Charlotte, Matthew and Stephen. He said he'd seen them arrive at the cottage a few times.'

'What are you saying exactly?' Maddy needed to hear it from Marianne's own lips.

'I'm saying I think they may have planned the whole thing. I also found a file in Richard's desk drawer.'

'In the cottage?'

'In the annexe we had built several years ago. Where Richard kept a desk, a filing cabinet and a bookshelf. The file contained a detailed floor-plan of Sullivans. Certain areas were highlighted in red – the basement toilets, the ground-floor conference suite, reception, and Nigel's office.'

Maddy's pulse was racing. Carver needed to hear this. 'Anything else?'

'Yes. There were two sublease agreements between Isaac Dempsey and Stanislav Textiles, for the subletting of industrial units at Leyton Industrial Village and Riverside Industrial Estate. They looked pretty dodgy.'

'Christ,' Maddy said. The same money-laundering outfit masquerading as a legitimate company the NCA was hunting, and whose directors appeared to have vanished into thin air. This was the proof they needed. The evidence couldn't be more damning.

'I think that's why he was so keen for us to have one last stay at the cottage. It wasn't about us. It was about destroying the bloody evidence.' The tears were there again. 'How could he, Maddy? How could he have done something like this? Lie to me, plot and scheme behind my back, let me go through hell? I feel like I never knew the man.'

She buried her head in Maddy's chest, sobbing like a child. 'Hush,' Maddy soothed, stroking her hair. 'I'm sure it wasn't just about that. I'm sure he genuinely wanted to spend time there with you.'

Marianne broke away. Gave Maddy a forlorn look. 'I never realised just how much he hated Nigel. He could never get over that night.' She paused, then said, her eyes narrowing, 'You don't really seem that shocked. Do the police already suspect something?'

Maddy nodded slowly. 'Yes.' Then she told her what they already knew about Isaac, the meeting in Charlotte's calendar, and what she'd said to her father after being released. 'Marianne, will you tell the police all this? Will you hand over what you found in Richard's desk?' She looked at her searchingly. She knew what she was asking of her. She was asking her to betray her husband. When all this came out, his reputation would be blackened forever. He'd be labelled a fraud rather than a hero, and Marianne would have to suffer the brunt of that. The bitching, the stares, the wagging tongues, she could picture it now.

But Marianne didn't hesitate. 'Yes, I'll do it. But I didn't bring the papers home with me. They're still in the annexe, locked away. I panicked. Nearly destroyed it all. But then I thought maybe if I came away, allowed myself time to think, I'd know what to do.'

'Can you fetch them?'

'I'll go first thing tomorrow.'

'Thank you, Marianne. You're doing the right thing.'

'What the fuck are we going to do?'

Charlotte had heard every word of Maddy's conversation with Marianne. She'd noticed Maddy leave the room not long after Marianne, and had concealed herself in a tiny alcove outside the kitchen, with a view to listening in. She'd tried not to retch as she realised Richard hadn't been as careful as she'd imagined.

Now she and Matthew were in a cab headed for the office. She turned off the intercom, but still whispered.

'We'll have to destroy the evidence before she gets to it.'

'How?'

'Richard gave me a key, remember? And the code for the alarm. Maybe he'd anticipated something like this happening.'

This wasn't what Matthew had signed up for. The plan had always been about getting justice for their mothers. About destroying Davenport. Because of that, he'd never considered himself, or any of them, to be criminals. More like caped crusaders. But that's exactly what they had become. Caped crusaders only lived in storybooks. This was real life, and there was never a happy ending for criminals.

He looked at Charlotte, and hardly recognised the woman he'd fallen in love with. She'd changed almost beyond recognition. She'd become so hard, so conniving, so ruthless. But he realised someone had to be. It was either that or wait for the police to turn up on their doorsteps.

'Don't worry, you've done enough, I'll do it.' Charlotte squeezed his hand. 'In the meantime, don't tell Stephen. It'll only scare the shit out of him, and we can't have him folding.'

Chapter Thirty-Seven

Stephen was feeling much happier, his conversation with Drake a fading memory. He'd simply been paranoid. The guilt talking, nothing more. Last night, he and Celeste had seen several flats, and fallen in love with one of them. They'd made an offer, and fingers crossed, would soon be able to quit their shack for a smart two-bed apartment in a much nicer part of town. He hadn't seen Celeste this happy in ages. Nothing gave him greater contentment than seeing the delight in her eyes. They'd had the best sex in a long time, and later today, he planned on buying her the biggest diamond engagement ring he could find in Hatton Garden. He had to admit, it had been a little unnerving knowing he had two hundred grand in cash hidden behind the cylinder in the airing cupboard – the one place he knew Celeste would never go. She hated small, enclosed spaces, especially ones susceptible to spiders, her biggest phobia. Even so, now he could rest easy. First thing that morning, he'd deposited it into his current account. No more hiding.

What's more, he'd recently opened several savings accounts, and soon, the one point eight million being held in a Gibraltarian account would be distributed amongst them, his debts wiped clean.

Celeste had asked how it was that they were suddenly able to afford a nice apartment in Angel, and he'd simply said he'd been saving in secret. After all, they didn't have a joint account and he'd never told her the extent of his debts. Just that he'd racked up the typical student debts. No big deal, just a sign of the times.

He intended to pay the deposit in cash. And then, over time, he'd keep making small deposits from his savings accounts into his main current account, so as not to raise suspicion.

Stephen contemplated this on his way to an internal meeting with the head of corporate, George Bussard. He had no clue what the meeting was about and could only assume he'd been summoned for a ticking off about something or other. His unpopularity amongst the partners still puzzled him. They never seemed especially displeased with him, and they must have thought highly of him to overlook his debts. He was a hard worker, always proactive, good with clients, and so Richard's revelation that he had no chance of being kept on had hurt him to the core. Still, he no longer gave a crap. He was loaded, and his new-found fame in the City made him eminently more hireable.

He reached the room and knocked on the door.

'Come in,' came Bussard's booming voice. He was already seated. A broad, brute of a man, with thick, club-like hands, and a Friar Tuck double chin.

He asked Stephen to take a seat, enquired after his well-being, with reference to the abduction, then got down to the nitty gritty.

'You must be wondering what this is all about?'

Stephen was suddenly nervous. Surely, they weren't onto them? 'I'd be lying if I didn't say it's all a bit mysterious, George. Should I be concerned?'

Bussard laughed heartily. 'Concerned? No, not at all. I've called you here to try and convince you to apply to my team when the time comes for you to list your choices next month. I know Property's your last seat, and I don't want them nabbing you at the last hurdle.'

Stephen nearly fell off his chair. 'Come again, sir?'

'You're coming to the end of your time with us, and I would think that, by now, you'll have some idea of where you want to qualify. We've all enjoyed having you here. In fact, you're one of the best trainees we've had in a long time. The consensus is that we'd like you to join us when you qualify next March.'

'So, the partners like me?' Although his mid-seat appraisal had been OK, it had been with Sam Trent, a quiet, lacklustre associate who never got excited about anyone or anything.

'That's what I said, didn't I?' Bussard sounded mildly irritated. *What was wrong with the boy?*

Stephen thought back to when Matthew had first approached him, in January. It now seemed like a lifetime ago – so much had happened since. When his friend had looked him in the eye and told him he had no hope of being kept on. A fact echoed time and time again by Richard as they'd honed and rehearsed their plan. Had they lied to him, just to get him on board? Had his best friend played on his biggest weakness – his debts – to seduce him into their personal vendettas? Risking his neck, his freedom, when all along he could have kept his head down and secured a stable job at the end of his training. A job that would see a fifty-grand salary rise to at least seventy. What's more, a *legal* way to pay off his debts.

He felt sick, when he should have been doing cartwheels. He'd been so naïve.

'Well, aren't you going to say something? You look flabbergasted.'

Stephen did his best to hold it together. 'No, I, er – it's an honour, George. I'm truly flattered, and I can't tell you how grateful I am. Corporate's always been my first choice, and you can guarantee that I'll be putting it top of my list.'

Bussard's face broke into a smile. 'Pleased to hear it,' he said. 'And I'm glad we had this little chat. I always think it pays to be upfront about these things. I'm not a man for harbouring secrets.'

Stephen tried his hardest not to vomit on the spot, shook hands with Bussard, then left and bolted for the nearest gents'.

It was Friday morning, and Carver was expecting a visitor in the next few hours. Marianne Barker. He was closing in on the suspects, and it was only a matter of time before he'd have them. He'd bring them in and hit them separately with Richard's papers. Grill them on their sightings at his cottage, as well as Isaac's sudden disappearance following his visit to Cressingtons, and his purchase of a blue Ford Transit van, suspiciously similar to the one in which the kidnappers had made their getaway. One of them would crumble, and he was putting his money on Stephen. Earlier, he'd learnt from Stephen's bank – obliged by law to disclose such information to him – that Stephen had deposited two hundred thousand pounds into his current account. It wasn't millions, but it was still a lot of cash for a young trainee lawyer who was immersed in debt, even if he had told Drake that he and Celeste had been saving for some time. And unless he'd got lucky on the lottery, or received some unexpected inheritance, it could only mean one thing.

He checked his watch. 11.30 a.m. Maddy had told him last night that Marianne was aiming to take the 8.30 a.m. train to Stow. She'd quickly gather the papers but didn't plan on hanging around. Assuming she stuck to the plan, he could expect her by 2 p.m. at the latest.

Carver had to admire Richard Barker and his band of brothers. It had been a hugely ambitious plan. One they had probably viewed as noble and just, and certainly not one that would result in murder. They'd been thorough and clever. But not clever enough. It had been a mistake choosing Isaac as their anonymous point man. It may not have been huge, but scars, like moles and birthmarks, were identifiable features – marks that might seem immaterial to a family member over time, but which stuck in the minds of strangers. Poor Cherry had been a victim of that.

Just then, the phone rang. Carver jumped to attention. He recognised Maddy's number and picked it up immediately. 'Yes?'

'Bad news.' Her voice was flat.

'What?'

'Marianne just called. Someone broke into the annexe last night. Richard's papers were gone when she got there this morning.'

Maddy was livid. She'd called Carver from a private phone booth at the firm. It was becoming a bit of a habit, but it couldn't be helped because Charlotte had been with her when Marianne's call had come through, her gaze hanging on her like a suffocating fog. The poor woman had been beside herself. She'd felt violated, shaken, scared for her life. All Maddy could do was give bland yes and no answers, pretending she was on the phone to a client. Marianne had understood, told her to call her back when she could.

Maddy suspected Charlotte had overheard her and Marianne talking the previous day and had somehow broken into the cottage that same night, removing any trace of evidence.

But that was the weird thing. Marianne had said there was no obvious sign of a break-in. The door to the annexe had been intact, not an item out of place, save for the missing papers. Plus, the alarm hadn't gone off. The only explanation was that Richard had given Charlotte a key and the alarm code. Perhaps foreseeing the possibility that something might happen to him sooner rather than later and giving Charlotte the chance to save her skin.

Carver had immediately called Marianne and told her to stay put while he jumped on a train to the Cotswolds. He also ordered a local forensic team to get there quick sharp. Although Charlotte was smart, she wasn't a professional, and there was always a chance she'd tripped up somewhere. He took a cab from the station and arrived to find a van parked up in front of the pretty cottage, which was now crawling with a team of identically clad individuals in yellow protective clothing. Their team leader, aptly named Gary Comb, came up to Carver, and filled him in on their findings so far. Which roughly amounted to a big fat zero.

The girl was no amateur, it seemed. She'd been scrupulous. Although they could often make out imprints of gloves – giving them a rough idea as to whether they were after a male or a female – it seemed whoever it was, had wiped away any impressions, making even this distinction impossible. And of course, it wasn't London, it was the Cotswolds. CCTV wasn't nearly so widely used or considered necessary.

Assuming it was Charlotte, she'd done her homework. Marianne had already asked her neighbours if they'd seen anyone suspicious lurking about the place, but no one had. Not even young William, although Marianne did wonder if he'd been told by his mother not to say anything. She'd clearly been upset by his interference the other day, perhaps wondering whether he'd let his imagination run riot, as opposed to seeing what he claimed to have seen.

'I'd like to speak to the young man,' Carver said to Marianne. She hadn't left the sofa since he'd arrived. A terror-stricken nervous wreck. Poor woman.

'I'm not sure that's going to be possible,' she said weakly. 'His mother was very upset with him.'

'He's an eyewitness. The only one who appears to have seen Dempsey, Gerard and Baines meet with your husband here.'

'Yes, but what does it prove? Without Richard's papers, it doesn't prove they were planning to fake their own abduction to get revenge against Nigel. As far as I can tell, unless one of them confesses, you have nothing concrete. Just guesswork.'

'We have the brother.'

'He's in Florida as I understand things.'

'He can't stay there forever. We can get an extradition order.'

'Maybe, but who's to say he won't go somewhere else, keep moving? I've heard of people disappearing forever you know.'

'Someone will yield.'

Marianne shuddered. 'I've seen the look in that girl's eyes. She's as hard as nails. She'll never admit it.'

'Yes, but I know which of them might, and when I get back to London, I'm going to pay him a visit. He doesn't know that I've found his weak spot.'

On his train journey back to London, Carver found an almost empty carriage and called Drake. Thankfully, he had some good news, sure to give them leverage over Stephen. Stephen had put down a deposit on a flat in Angel. One hundred thousand in cash. Few had that kind of money lying around in hard cash, especially someone with two hundred grand's worth of debt, and Carver hoped he'd crack when asked about it. After all, he'd stumbled the first time Carver had questioned him, and despite the rehearsed feel to his answers, his story hadn't quite matched Matthew's. His behaviour in general had also been odd, jittery, as if he was harbouring a guilty conscience.

A man who'd been held hostage had every right to portray a whole range of emotions. Joy, relief, hysteria, melancholy. But Stephen had exhibited none of these. There had been a wariness in his eyes during that first interview, causing Carver to suspect he was hiding something.

And now that Carver knew what that something was, he was going to prise it out of him.

Chapter Thirty-Eight

'What's up, Stephen? Why have you asked us here?'

'Come in.'

Saturday, 2 p.m. Charlotte handed Stephen her jacket, then followed him into the compact living room. Matthew was already there, standing by the window, and she immediately went up and kissed him before sitting down on the springy sofa. He came and sat next to her. There was no background music or TV, just the sound of distant traffic and children's chatty voices through the open window, and it looked like Stephen had tidied up. The atmosphere was sterile, uninviting. He didn't bother offering them a drink.

'You know what this is about?' Charlotte asked Matthew.

Matthew shrugged. 'Beats me. Stevo?' He looked up curiously at his friend, still standing, and this only served to stoke the fire in Stephen. 'Celeste's out with friends, so we can talk freely.' His voice was calm, yet terse.

'Freely about what?' Charlotte asked. 'And why the grim face? Thought you'd be over the moon now that you're debt-free, and able to move out of this place.'

Stephen narrowed his eyes at Charlotte, amazed. She seemed to have lost any trace of softness. Consumed by her desire for revenge, she'd lost sight of reality, of right and wrong.

'George Bussard called me to a meeting room yesterday morning.'

'What about?'

'About my performance.'

Matthew's heart fluttered. He'd always known there was every chance this day would come, but foresight didn't make it any easier. Charlotte didn't flinch, but, like Matthew, she was pretty sure where Stephen was headed.

'Apparently, I'm one of the best trainees they've ever had, and he practically begged me to list Corporate as my first choice.'

Matthew smiled uneasily. 'That's great, mate,' he said. 'What you always wanted. They must have come to their senses.'

Stephen's face grew red and twisted. He looked down at them with a hatred that chilled Matthew to the bone, and caused him to shrink back in his seat, fearing that his old friend might hit him.

'Don't you fucking pretend this is news to you! You fucking lied to me! You said the partners didn't consider me a good fit, and that I had no chance of being kept on. And like the stupid trusting fool I am, I believed you.'

Matthew and Charlotte exchanged a brief look of alarm. 'Steve, please, mate…' Matthew began, but he was cut short.

'Don't you *mate* me. I thought you were my best friend, but you deceived me, made up some bullshit story to get me on board with your sick plan. I had no beef with Davenport.' He looked at them both with wounded eyes. 'You used me because you knew I was shit-deep in debt, a secret I confided in you, Matt. You knew I couldn't afford to be jobless.'

Matthew got up, tried to put a hand on Stephen's shoulder, but it was roughly brushed off. 'Please listen to me, Steve,' he pleaded. 'Richard said it was the only way. I knew I could trust you to keep a secret, but Richard said you needed to feel like you had no choice. You needed to be desperate to see the plan through.'

'Of course I had to be desperate to do something like that – we committed a fucking crime, for God's sake. Several in fact! And don't talk to me about having a choice. I *did* have a choice.' Stephen raised his fist. 'I still have a choice, and I choose my freedom.' He paused, then said, 'Did you know the police are ninety-nine per cent sure your brother was involved in the abduction?' He glared at Charlotte. 'He can't run forever. They'll get an extradition order, and once he's caught, we're done for.'

'Calm down,' Charlotte said. 'I'll tell him to disappear for longer, go to Mexico or something.'

'And you actually want that kind of life for him? Living like a fugitive, constantly looking over his shoulder. What kind of life is that?'

Charlotte was getting rattled. Stephen saw it in her eyes, her demeanour. The unflappable ice queen was starting to melt under the heat of the moment. He kept going. 'I should have just carried on, kept my head down, looked forward to a future with Celeste. But I can't now, can I? It's going to hang over us until the day we die. You're both so selfish. As was Richard. You all set me up to suit your own ends. None of which had anything to do with me.'

Charlotte stood up and faced Stephen square on, her face suddenly angry. 'Our mothers killed themselves because of that bastard. He raped Mary, cheated Richard out of senior partnership, and treated his own wife little better than a dog. You should be proud of what you did. Would you really have wanted to work for a man like that?'

Stephen didn't respond. He looked at Matthew. 'You've changed, mate. You're not the same guy I grew up with.' He felt tears gather in his eyes.

'Don't say that.' Matthew tried to hug his friend again, but Stephen immediately backed away. 'It's true. You killed that hooker, didn't you?' He gave Charlotte a vicious look. 'It can't have been you; CCTV footage confirmed a man was seen going into that room with her, and Richard was too ill.' He turned back to Matthew. 'So, it had to have been you.' His face was draped with horror, disbelief. And perhaps a shade of pity, despite the wrong done to him. 'How can you sleep at night, Matt, knowing that you took a life?'

Matthew said nothing. He'd been trying to blot out what he'd done with work, and he had allowed Charlotte to persuade him that they'd had no choice – the hooker's murder for their freedom. But he wasn't free. He was anything but. In truth, he was locked in a torture chamber of guilt. It gnawed at his soul every minute of every day, and he knew he would never be the same again. He thought of his mother. She'd confessed in her diary that she'd never been the same after Davenport raped her. But unlike her son, she had been the victim of a crime. Her conscience had been clear. His could never be. He was no victim.

Matthew fell to his knees and started to cry. A little boy again, who badly needed his mother. Charlotte sank down beside him, rubbed his back, then looked up at Stephen with vicious eyes. 'Get a fucking grip, will you, and leave him be! No one forced you to come in on the plan. You made your choice, and now you need to look forward. They've got nothing on us, I made sure of that on Thursday night.'

'That's where you're wrong, I'm afraid, Ms Dempsey.'

Charlotte froze. Matthew slowly raised his head, locking eyes with Stephen. A look of mutual recognition. Resignation.

Carver came closer, Drake and Rivers just behind. Then all three faced Charlotte and Matthew, both still on their knees.

'You set us up?' Charlotte said to Stephen, almost inaudibly. Matthew looked horrified.

'Mr Baines agreed to wear a wire in return for leniency.' Carver came closer still. Noticed Charlotte glance over her shoulder towards the open door. An automatic reaction, even though there was no chance of escape.

'I had no choice, they knew,' Stephen said blandly.

'There's always a choice,' she said. 'You're doing this because you're pissed at us.'

Stephen narrowed his eyes at Matthew. 'Now you know what it feels like to be betrayed by your best friend.'

Word of their arrests spread like wildfire the following day, Sunday, telephone lines sizzling with gossip, email accounts clogged with juicy intrigue. And it was all anyone could talk about at the firm on Monday morning. Everyone was stunned. Including Gavin Turner. Unable to grasp the fact that they'd been fooled by their colleagues right under their noses, and that Charlotte Dempsey, their 'mealy-mouthed, incompetent trainee' had been playing them all along.

But there was also talk of a mole. A mole who'd helped them on the ground, a mole who'd been their eyes and ears as they'd waited for Davenport to accede to their demands. A mole who clearly hated Davenport as much as they did. Who was this mole, and were the police on the verge of finding him or her?

Chapter Thirty-Nine

It hadn't taken long for Stephen to crack. After he'd got back from the Cotswolds, Carver had headed straight for the station, biding his time in his office until he felt it reasonable to enquire whether Stephen had left work for the night. On learning that he had, he'd turned up on Stephen's doorstep a little after 8 p.m. Luckily for Stephen, Celeste had been at the gym, so he'd at least been able to confess his guilt without having to face her reaction at the same time.

There had been no magic to Carver's approach. The plan had been simple. Hit him with the debts, the sudden injection of money into his current account, the deposit in cash, his sightings at the cottage, his conversation with his sister about Isaac, and Isaac's subsequent, all too swift, disappearance. And finally, Richard's papers, which had mysteriously disappeared.

Stephen wasn't a dishonest person by nature, and when Carver had fired the evidence at him like a volley of bullets, the guilt had been written all over his face. And, fortunately for Carver, although he hadn't known this at the time, Stephen was already feeling seriously pissed off with Charlotte and Matthew after his meeting with George Bussard. They'd lured him into their plan on false pretences, and he no longer felt any loyalty to them. The only thing that troubled him was the thought of how he was going to explain it all to Celeste. He couldn't help but curse himself for jumping the gun with the flat; he'd just been so excited, so desperate to get Celeste out of that shithole, but his desperation had been his undoing.

Carver had sat and listened as Stephen had explained how, in late January, Matthew had approached him with Richard's plan. How Richard had first recruited Matthew and Charlotte over a year ago, somehow knowing that his two charges wanted Nigel Davenport's blood. How they had blamed him for their mothers' deaths, and how Richard had still felt guilty for failing to protect Mary and had resented Nigel for stealing senior partnership from him. Stephen had also explained how he'd been desperate. Seriously in debt, facing financial ruin without the promise of a steady income, Richard's revelation that he had no future with Sullivans had sent him into panic mode. The only future he'd seen ahead of him was one marked by bankruptcy and the end of his relationship with Celeste. She was the best thing that had ever happened to him and losing her was not an option. Plus, he'd loved Matthew like a brother and Mary had treated him like a second son. Knowing what Davenport had done to her had therefore forced his hand. Richard had also been convincing. He'd had a way with words, he knew the firm inside out, and he'd managed to make his plan sound foolproof. No one would get hurt, justice would be served, and Stephen would have a solution to his debts.

'And the injuries suffered by Charlotte and Matthew?' Carver had asked. 'How did they come about?'

'The plan was only going to work if Davenport succumbed, and Richard knew that roughing up at least two of the hostages was the only way to make him cave. Along with the video, of course. Make-up

371

wouldn't cut it if we were to reappear after four days. The injuries had to be convincing; they had to be real.'

'You still haven't answered my question.'

Stephen had shaken his head, smiled wryly, almost as if he didn't quite believe it himself. 'Charlotte was passionate about her cause, I'll give her that.' At that moment, he had briefly lowered his eyes, before looking back up at Carver. 'The burn mark was her own doing. As for her face, Isaac wouldn't do it, so she asked Matthew.'

'They're lovers, right?'

'Yeah, like Romeo and fucking Juliet.'

'And what about Matthew? Who beat him up?'

Stephen had sighed. 'That was Isaac.'

'Tell me again how Matthew found out about the rape?'

'I already told you, he and his Dad were clearing out his mother's belongings, and he stumbled across her diary.' A slight pause, then, 'You don't need me to tell you what's in it because you got it in the post.'

'Matthew?'

'Yes. In the end, Davenport's resignation wasn't enough for him. He wanted him to suffer, be disgraced, account for what he did by serving time. And I think Richard felt the same way.'

'The way Matthew's mother had suffered – been disgraced?'

'Yes.'

'And was it Isaac who drove you to the drop and set off the explosions?'

'Yes. After you scotched our original plan. He also disabled the CCTV at the firm.'

'And the bug in Davenport's office? Who planted that?'

'That was Richard.'

'I need to know how you got the money, Stephen. We know someone else has been helping you on the ground. The account at Ansbacher Bank in Nassau – where you instructed the six million to be wired – was handled by a woman with a bogus Czech passport. Using a local law firm, we know she set up a shell company in whose name the account was held. She withdrew the 200k and transferred the rest to an account in Gibraltar set up by her in the same way. Who is she?'

Stephen had hesitated. He had no issue with Pamela Davenport, who he genuinely believed had handled the money. She'd suffered a loveless marriage and, as far as he was concerned, deserved to have her revenge on her husband. But he had seen no way around it.

Looking up at Carver with guilty eyes, he'd replied, 'Pamela Davenport. Richard recruited her too. She'd long suspected Nigel had been up to no good behind her back, but in late 2016 Richard contacted her and told her about the affairs, the brothels, the rape. She refused to believe him at first, apparently told him to get lost. But once she'd calmed down, and Richard showed her photographs, she wanted in. After all, what did she have to lose? Her children were grown up and gone, she had no life really. And she wanted vengeance.'

'Hello, son.'

Frank Gerard was close to tears. His heart had stopped when he'd heard the news of his son's arrest. His worst nightmare had materialised. They'd been too ambitious, too greedy in their thirst for revenge. They should have left it at the diary. But Richard had wanted to humiliate Nigel on a grand scale, and Mary had allowed herself to be sucked into his grand plan. He'd had nothing to lose, and everything to gain. A dying man wanting to go out with a bang; do something so bad, so outrageous, so against the grain and everything he'd stood for all his life. But Matthew was young and healthy. He had his whole life ahead of him, and now he was facing a substantial portion of it behind bars.

Frank was almost certain Matthew had murdered that girl. He'd been acting strange ever since she died, his eyes sad and haunted – a hint of madness, even – and Frank knew it would torment him for the rest of his life.

He wondered if Mary was aware yet. He hadn't had the courage to get word to her himself. He knew she'd be devastated. Locked in her self-loathing, she'd convinced herself that Matthew would be OK. That with Davenport punished, they'd all be free, her son no longer in his clutches. But now he was far from free, and that would be hell for Mary.

'Hi, Dad.' Matthew looked up at his father, his eyes full of shame. Alone in his cell, with time to think things over, he'd realised he'd let his emotions get the better of him. He'd deluded himself into believing the plan would work. Richard had played on his anger, his hurt, to satisfy his own guilty conscience. He'd been at the end of his life and had gone to his grave relieved of the guilt that had eaten away at him for so many years. Matthew's physical life was far from over, but now he wouldn't be free to live it.

'Matt…'

'I'm sorry, Dad.' Matthew cut his father off. 'I let you down, I let Mum down, and I'm sorry.'

Witnessing his son's guilt was too much to bear. 'Son…'

'When I found Mum's diary, I guess it tipped me over the edge. I was already angry with her for leaving us, but reading the diary made me understand why, and I was relieved not to be angry with her anymore. I was angry with *him*, and I needed to make him pay. I didn't know how at the time – I didn't want to make the diary public – but then Richard came along with his plan, and I couldn't help myself. I saw him as my best chance. It was like I didn't care about law, my career, anymore. I was just so goddamn angry.' He paused, looked directly into Frank's eyes. 'Please say you understand, Dad. Please say you forgive me.'

It was no use. He couldn't hold it in any longer. His son deserved to know the truth, to know about his part in all this, and that Mary was still very much alive. But just as Frank was about to confess, the guard appeared. 'Time's up.'

Chapter Forty

Carver sat on a bench watching his son throw chunks of bread to a battalion of militant ducks and geese. Today was Rachel and Carl's wedding anniversary, and he'd agreed to have Daniel for the night.

This time last year, he'd never have agreed. On principle. But he was no longer a sad, lonely, bitter singleton. He had someone, a plus one, and it had softened him.

It was 6 p.m. on Monday. A warm, tropical evening. People were out in droves, a feeling of optimism, vigour and frivolity permeating the air. Loved-up couples strolling hand in hand, elderly folk ambling along at their own steady pace, lucky suits who'd miraculously managed to escape the office early and looked like they might combust with relief, carefree toddlers up later than usual owing to the hot weather, yummy mummies dressed in fancy gym gear exposing their impossibly toned tummies while pushing their buggies at breakneck speed, others just picnicking on the grass, gossiping over nibbles and prosecco. All of them enjoying the early evening sunshine in Regent's Park, adorned with colourful flora and fauna, healthy green trees, the smell of life, ice cream and barbecued food.

Daniel looked back at Carver, his face woeful. 'It's nearly all gone, Dad.'

'They've had a good feast, don't worry. Make the chunks smaller, you don't want to choke the poor things. And I'd watch your back when you're finished, you might find yourself being chased.' A temporary look of alarm swept across Daniel's face, before he plucked up the courage to finish the feeding frenzy.

As Carver sat there, he pondered his day. Spent interviewing Charlotte and Matthew. Their reactions had been very different. Cherry's death clearly tormented the boy, and he'd admitted to letting himself get swept away by his hatred for Davenport. Losing all sense of reason, perspective. But Charlotte had shown no such remorse. She regretted nothing, was positively proud of what they'd tried to pull off. Then again, it was perhaps easier for her. She hadn't taken another human life.

There'd been other developments that morning. Pamela Davenport had been spotted and picked up at King's Cross station, no doubt attempting to board the Eurostar to her freedom. Rivers and Coombs had been tactful with her arrest, asking her to come quietly if she didn't want the embarrassment of a scene. She'd realised all was lost, and had confessed to reporting Davenport's movements to Richard, and depositing two hundred thousand pounds in cash in a locker at the same station, which Stephen Baines had collected twenty-four hours later. In addition, Isaac Dempsey is currently on a plane back to the UK, an order for his surrender having been granted under the Extradition Act 2003.

But Carver wasn't confident he'd fitted all the pieces of the puzzle. He'd quizzed Pamela on her rendezvous with Frank Gerard, and she'd been adamant that she had simply wanted to say sorry in person. Apologise for what her husband did to Mary at Cambridge, nothing more than that.

Carver wasn't sold, but without solid proof otherwise, he had no reason to bring the elder Gerard in for questioning. Suspicion that something didn't quite add up wasn't enough, even if, nine times out of ten, his suspicions were proved correct.

And then there was the issue of how Richard had managed to recruit Charlotte and Matthew. When questioned, they had both confirmed he'd first approached them in July 2016. A lunch meeting dressed up as a casual appraisal of how his new trainee mentees were getting on. Richard must have felt he had a good chance of hooking them. But how had he been so sure? He hadn't known them from Adam before they joined the firm. How would he have known that they both harboured a deep hatred of Nigel Davenport? How would he have known that Matthew had discovered his mother's diary, and that she'd been raped? And how would he have known that Charlotte also despised Davenport for leading her father astray and indirectly causing her mother's suicide?

And then there was the six million. Someone had handled the account with Ansbacher Bank, and it couldn't have been Pamela Davenport, no matter what Stephen said. The physical description – both by the bank manager and the image of the woman caught on CCTV in reception – didn't match, but, more importantly, eyewit-nesses had seen Pamela enter her home off the King's Road the same day the two hundred thousand had been withdrawn, with one point eight million transferred to Gibraltar, the remaining four million given to Cancer Research. There was also no record of her having boarded a plane to Barbados. That being so, they were still none the wiser as to who had handled the money.

Pamela was refusing to say, while it appeared that Stephen, Matthew and Charlotte genuinely didn't know.

So who was Pamela protecting, and why?

Tuesday morning. Maddy sat at her desk and read the headlines on BBC News online. The hostages' arrest had made the second top story, usurped only by Brexit.

She'd spoken to Carver on the phone last night, after he'd put Daniel to bed. She'd heard the frustration in his voice, the feeling that they still didn't have the whole story. There was another guilty party out there, hiding in the shadows, but he didn't have a clue who it was.

Maddy noticed that the story was cross-referenced to a special features report on each of the accused. She clicked on the article and started to read. Much of it went over stuff she already knew, but then something caught her eye. She scrolled down to a section dealing with Mary Jacobs and her disappearance. Apparently, she'd left the family home to get groceries on New Year's Day 2016, but never returned, having left a note. Two weeks later, they found her scarf on Southsea beach, and she was presumed dead. Soon after, Matthew found his mother's diary, in which she'd specifically referred to being raped by Davenport. Speculation abounded that she'd never been able to get over this and had ended up killing herself.

But her body had never been found. It was assumed that it was lying somewhere at the bottom of the ocean, and that, more than likely, Mary had filled her clothes with heavy items and drowned herself that way. But if that was the case, why had her scarf ended up on the shoreline? Surely it would have been fastened around her neck, and therefore lying at the bottom of the ocean with her? Why had that item, and that item alone, not perished? Could it be because…

Maddy picked up her phone and dialled Carver's direct line. 'Hey, it's me.'

'Hi.'

'They never found Mary Jacobs' body, did they?'

Carver sat back in his chair, his attention caught. Her breathless tone told him she was cooking something up in that smart brain of hers. He was all ears. 'No, why?'

Maddy explained her theory about the scarf.

'It's a good thought, but at the time they said it was a parting gesture from Mary. A signal to her family that she was gone.'

'But she left a note. Surely that was enough of a sign? Why bother with the scarf as well? It seems too much. What if *she* planted it there as a signal to someone in on the plan that she was OK?'

'You think she's still alive and a part of this?'

'It's possible, isn't it? The bank said the account was handled by an attractive woman in her mid-fifties.'

'That doesn't exactly narrow it down a lot.'

'But what if it was Mary, wearing a blonde wig and shades?'

'Hair colour can really change a person, I suppose.'

'Yes, exactly. And the eyes are a real giveaway, hence the shades. This woman was clever. She knew she might be caught on camera. She kept her head down, wore dark glasses, so we couldn't see her face.' A brief pause, then, 'You need to show the image to Frank Gerard. He, more than anyone, should know his wife when he sees her.'

Silence. Maddy grew frustrated. 'Jake, talk to me, you still there – what is it?' she probed.

'I've just had a thought myself,' Carver said.

'What?'

'Well, you know how it still bothers me how Richard felt so confident Matthew and Charlotte would sign up to his plan?'

'Yes.'

'Well…'

'I know what you're about to say!' Maddy interrupted. 'That my theory may go some way to explaining that. At least, in the case of Matthew. That Richard got all his information on Matthew from Mary. I still can't figure out his insight into Charlotte's mindset, though.'

'No, me neither. But in the case of Matthew, if Richard and Mary hatched the plan, she might have planted the diary before faking her own death. Capitalising on Matthew's grief. They were extremely close, as you know. Matthew admitted as much when I questioned him. He said that when he saw the diary, it was as if a fuse blew in him. From then on, reason didn't come into play; it was all about getting justice for Mary.'

'But how would Mary have known he'd react so strongly?'

'No one knows a son like his mother.'

A pause, then Maddy said dramatically, 'Or his father.'

'What are you saying? That Frank's a part of this, too?' Carver thought about Frank's rendezvous with Pamela at the Queen's Park café.

'Makes sense. I mean, you didn't buy Pamela's explanation as to why she met up with him, did you?'

'No, I didn't. I think I need to pay Frank Gerard a visit.'

'DCI Carver, please, come in.'

Carver followed Frank Gerard into the living room. He was offered coffee but declined. They sat down, Carver on the sofa, Frank on an armchair opposite. Carver took a moment to study his face. It looked drawn. No doubt the stress of his only child being locked up, certain to face a lengthy jail sentence, taking its toll. *But is it just that?*

'So, what can I do for you?' Frank's voice was listless.

Carver leant in, asked simply, 'Is your wife still alive?'

It took him by surprise. Carver saw the tensing of shoulders, a faint, yet sharp, intake of breath. Then an incredulous look, almost a snigger and quick swipe of the hand. Quick, defensive movements. 'What a ridiculous question, Chief Inspector, why on earth would you ask that? I only wish it were true.'

Carver reached into his inside pocket and produced a photograph. A slightly blurred image of a slim, stylishly dressed woman, ash blonde and wearing dark sunglasses, head down, striding through the reception of Ansbacher (Bahamas) Limited in Nassau. He handed it to Frank, who took it, studied it for a few seconds, then looked up with a quizzical expression. 'Who is this?'

Carver smiled. 'You tell me, Mr Gerard?'

'I really don't understand.'

'I think you do.' Carver leant in closer still, and spoke with a quiet, yet unnerving, authority. 'I think you know that this woman is your wife.'

Frank looked panicked. There was no way of disguising it. His breathing became shallow, his right hand, still holding the photograph, trembling.

'Richard Barker was an intelligent man, but he wasn't a mind reader. He didn't know your son before he joined Sullivans, so he had to have spoken to someone who did. Someone who knew exactly how much Matthew hated Nigel Davenport. That person gave Richard the confidence to approach your son.'

Frank avoided eye contact with Carver. Continued to stare down at the photograph, although he seemed to be looking right through it. His heart rate was up, and his chest hurt.

'In fact, I think he spoke to the two people who knew Matthew better than anyone.' Carver's eyes tore through Frank, who finally looked up. 'You, and your wife, Mary Jacobs.'

He saw the resignation in Frank's eyes, a look as if to say, *There's no use pretending otherwise.*

'It's true, isn't it, Frank? You and your wife were in on this as well. But you never told your son. Your son still thinks his mother is dead.'

Frank remained silent, a single tear rolling down his unshaven cheek. 'Tell me!' Carver demanded, laying on the pressure. 'Isn't that the truth, Frank?'

'Yes, it's the truth.' Both men's heads jerked towards the door. Where the woman's voice had come from. Initial bewilderment turning to recognition.

'Mary!' Frank darted up. Leapt to his wife's side. He took her face in his hands, tears streaming down his own as he showered her with kisses. Her forehead, her lips, her cheeks. Covering every inch of her lovely face with love. Finally, they broke away. Carver saw the tears flowing from her eyes now. She was still wearing the blonde wig, but no shades. He looked at the family photograph on the mantelpiece, then back at her. The eyes were the same. Big, dark pools. Beautiful, but sad. He was in no doubt. It was Mary.

'Hello, Mary,' Carver said, standing up.

'Hello, DCI Carver.' She turned to Frank. 'I'm sorry, love, I couldn't stay away, not with Matthew in custody.' She looked at Carver. 'Please, Frank and I are the guilty ones. It's us who should stand trial, not

Matthew. He'd never have got caught up in this if it wasn't for us. We planted the diary where we knew he'd find it.'

'That may be true. But your son is a grown man, old enough to make his own choices. He willingly chose to commit various crimes, including murder. He must pay the price for that.'

Mary clutched her middle, then looked at Frank, aghast. 'He killed that girl? Pamela assured me he didn't.' Carver saw that she was desperate for it not to be true.

'She was trying to protect you, my love,' Frank said gently, putting his arm around Mary's shoulder.

Mary broke away sharply, shaking her head. 'I should never have let Richard persuade me. Christ, I lived with it for over thirty years, why couldn't I have just said no for another thirty?'

'It's my fault. I should have convinced you it was too risky. But I guess the part of me that had long wanted Davenport to suffer got the upper hand. It skewed my judgement.'

Carver fixed his gaze on Mary. 'Mrs Gerard, it was you who handled the money, wasn't it?'

'Yes.'

'Tell me, how did Richard know Charlotte bore a grudge against Davenport?'

'Richard already knew what her father and Nigel got up to. But it was only through my relationship with Diana Dempsey that he learnt how desperately unhappy Diana was, and that Charlotte hated Nigel's guts.'

'You knew Diana?'

'Yes. I used to hold a weekly help group for women suffering from depression. Diana started coming to it in the summer of 2015. She didn't miss a session until she took her own life the next year.'

'And she opened up to you? About her husband's activities?'

Mary nodded. 'Yes. She knew exactly what her husband got up to. And she put much of the blame on Nigel. Said Charles followed his lead like a puppy. Had done since Cambridge.'

'Did you tell Diana what Davenport did to you?' Carver tried to phrase his question sensitively. Even after all his years on the force, rape was never an easy term to use.

Mary shook her head. 'No, I didn't. She was my patient, and I didn't want to inflict my problems on her. My sessions were all about her confiding in me. Overcoming, or at least coping with, her depression.' Mary paused, her eyes sad. 'But I failed. And now Charlotte and Isaac don't have a mother. All they're left with is a vain, selfish father. The same as he was back then, all those years ago.'

Frank squeezed his wife's shoulder. 'You can't blame yourself, love, you tried your best.'

Carver kept going. 'So you knew how unhappy Diana was, and that she blamed Davenport. But how could you have known how much Charlotte hated him? That she'd be prepared to risk everything to make him pay?'

'The last time I saw Diana was mid-December 2015, the day after her wedding anniversary. Charles had forgotten about it and gone out with Nigel instead. Diana broke down in front of Charlotte. Told her what Charles got up to with Nigel. She said Charlotte was beside herself with anger and hated her father for treating Diana so badly. She said although Charlotte was a good daughter, she had a ruthless streak and she'd seen pure and utter hatred in her eyes when she talked about Nigel leading Charles astray.' Mary paused, then continued. 'Two months later, shortly after I disappeared, Diana killed herself. Charlotte was abroad at the time, as I understand. I was so sad to hear the news and I became more convinced that Richard was doing the right thing.' She paused, looked directly at Frank. 'That we were all doing the right thing.'

'And you told all this to Richard?' Carver asked. Mary nodded. 'And he took a chance that Charlotte would come on board with his plan?'

Another nod. 'It was riskier with Charlotte than with Matthew, but we figured she'd blame her father and Nigel for Diana's death.'

'What do you think your son will say, when he finds out you faked your own death, and were in cahoots with Richard from the beginning?' Carver was sorry for what had happened to Mary at Cambridge, but a crime was a crime, and he had to separate the past from the present. She and her husband had committed a serious crime, a crime they'd let their son become a part of.

'I'm not sure,' Mary replied.

'I think he's going to be pissed as hell.'

Frank became angry. 'Don't say that, you don't know that.'

Carver glared at him. 'I don't have to know it. You made him endure the worst kind of grief. Grief for the mother he loved more than life itself and thought he had lost. You stood by and watched him suffer, all the time knowing she was still alive.' A pause as he let this settle, then, 'I don't know how you had the stomach for it.'

He got no response. There was nothing more to be said. He cuffed husband and wife, and they drove in silence to the station.

Chapter Forty-One

Maddy was nervous. Today was a big day. A very big day. Her heart was beating double time as she strode towards Pizza Express on the Southbank, a light wind whispering through the air, taking the edge off the heat. She felt more nervous than she had done before any of her job interviews. Because the person she was meeting today held more power in the palm of his hand than any of her potential employers. This person would say it like it was. There would be no mincing of words, no tactful questions, no hiding behind a facade of outward civility. No cutting corners, no second chances, no time to ponder her strengths and weaknesses in the spirit of meritocracy. This was all or nothing. He'd either like her and give her a chance or hate her and tell her to back off.

She reached the entrance, took a deep breath, then walked in, making her way to the main seating area.

'Over here, Maddy.' She turned her head in the direction of Carver's voice, spotted him and gave a little wave hello. Her stomach was doing cartwheels as she did so, but to her relief, she received a toothy grin from Carver's dining companion: Daniel. That was a good sign, surely? They were sitting at the far end of the sprawling restaurant, big by Pizza Express standards, and mostly filled with families enjoying a lazy Saturday lunch south of the River Thames.

Daniel was already tucking into dough balls. 'Sorry, he couldn't wait,' Carver apologised with smiling eyes. He and Maddy shared a polite kiss on the cheek, then Carver looked at his son. 'Daniel, this is my friend, Maddy.' He switched his gaze to Maddy and stated the obvious. 'Maddy, this is Daniel.'

Clearly, Carver was as nervous as her.

'Nice to meet you,' Daniel said with another broad grin. 'My dad talks a lot about you.'

He was adorable. A mini Carver. Same hair colour, same distinctive grey eyes, cheeky grin. She felt instantly relieved and sat down beside him. 'Want to see the menu?' Daniel offered her his.

She took it, glancing at Carver, who gave her a sly wink. 'Thanks,' she said. 'What can you recommend?'

The rest of lunch went by without a hitch. She'd passed the test. She had the job. Daniel considered her a suitable girlfriend for his father, and she was formally initiated into the fold.

She asked him about school, football, his favourite superhero, and listened intently as he poured out answers one after the other. As Carver sat watching them, he too felt a sense of relief. He'd feared his son would be able to tell how much younger than him Maddy was, making for an awkward lunch. But he never alluded to her age, just that she was very pretty, and his dad was very lucky. This had drawn laughter all round. Whether or not Daniel was aware of the age difference, he certainly didn't show it, and Carver felt immensely proud of him. Knowing that he had his son's approval would make things much easier for him and Maddy. A great weight off his mind. And hers.

Later, as Daniel tucked into dessert, the grown-ups discussed the case. Work had been so frenetic for both, they'd barely spoken since

Tuesday evening. 'So, tell me more about Matthew's reaction to his mother still being alive?'

Carver sighed, leisurely sipped his espresso. 'Naturally, he was in shock at first. Kept saying I must be mistaken. But then, when he realised I wasn't, when I relayed every detail of my conversation with Mary and Frank, he started to cry. Sobbed like a little boy. It was horrendous, Drake will tell you. There's no excusing what he's done, but I couldn't help feeling sorry for the boy. Set up by his own parents.'

'Of course, I do, too. He feels betrayed. His parents were the two people in this world he felt he could trust. But realising they'd planned the whole thing, conspired with Richard behind his back, must have been devastating.'

Carver leant in. 'But here's the thing. He said even if his parents had been upfront from the start, he still would have wanted to make Davenport pay. It wasn't her death as such that drove him to it; it was the events of thirty-five years ago. The thought of his mother being violated, humiliated. Robbed of her dream, her dignity.'

'So he's not going to plead coercion, or temporary insanity?'

'No, and I admire him for that. He's taking responsibility for his own actions, and he seemed buoyed by the fact that we've arrested Larson.' He paused, then said, 'Ms Dempsey hasn't tried to pass the buck either.'

'What did she say?'

'She knew Mary was alive.'

Maddy's eyes popped open. 'She did?'

Carver nodded. 'Yes, it surprised me too. I was convinced she didn't know who handled the money. She's a very good liar. Very believable.'

'You're telling me.'

'Apparently, Richard told her in secret, about six months ago, after they recruited Stephen.' He paused, sighed heavily. 'She and Matthew weren't going to have much of a relationship locked up in a cell for the foreseeable future, but her confession has definitely put paid to that. I think he's madder at her than he is at his parents.'

Maddy shook her head in disbelief. 'Just goes to show you, never judge a book by its cover. I should know that, more than anyone.' She paused, then asked, 'What of Stephen?'

'He'll do some time, but most likely get out early. After all, he cooperated, plus he was tricked into the whole thing. And he surrendered the money.'

'What about his girlfriend?'

'Gone back to Venezuela. Can't say I blame her.'

'If only…'

'If only what?'

'If only Mary had had the courage to go to the police at the time. Then none of this would have happened.'

'That's life. Full of ifs and buts.' He paused, then grinned.

'What?'

'Well, I may not have met you if your flatmate hadn't been a raving lunatic.'

She smiled back. 'There is that, I suppose.'

'Every cloud has a silver lining.'

Carver turned his head, looked out of the window at the sky which had suddenly gone very grey. 'Speaking of clouds, we'd better get the bill and make a run for it. How does *Avengers Assemble* at my place sound?'

Daniel's eyes lit up. He looked at Maddy keenly. There was only one possible response.

'How could I refuse an offer like that?' She grinned.

THE END

Acknowledgements

There are a whole host of wonderful people I'd like to thank for helping me bring this book to the shelves, both when it was first published back in December 2019 and more recently with this updated version published six years on. Also, more generally, for being an immense source of friendship and support through the ups and downs of my writing journey.

Firstly, my agent, Annette Crossland. Your boundless enthusiasm for the book since I sent you the first draft back in 2015 has been so uplifting, while your unflinching support, encouragement and belief in me over the years, through all the highs and lows, has been such a blessing. I can't thank you enough for always spurring me on and urging me to believe in myself. I'm incredibly grateful and lucky to have you in my corner.

Thank you to James Faktor, Publishing Director at what was then Endeavour Media back in 2018, for picking this book up alongside *The Lawyer* (previously *The Scribe*), and for seeing huge potential in the Carver and Kramer partnership! Huge thanks also to Marie-Louise Haig and Kate Ballard at Lume/Joffe Books for being so passionate about getting the book into the best shape possible, and for all your hard work on the creative side. You've both been so great to work with, no query ever too much trouble, and I feel lucky to be published by such talented, genuinely nice people.

Jon Appleton, for being such a brilliant copyeditor and saying such lovely things about the book! Your eagle eye and intuitive observations were invaluable, and have helped make it a more compelling read! Also, to the proofreader, Sharon Rutland, for helping to make it as error-free as possible.

A massive thanks to ex-DI turned Amazon bestselling crime writer, Roger A. Price, for his invaluable advice on police procedure back in 2019, and for letting me bug him with my ceaseless questions! Also, to Dr Kath Mashiter, MBE, for her forensic advice. With forty years of forensic experience as a case working scientist and Force Scientific Support Manager, I feel extremely lucky to have been advised by Kath.

All the lovely, kind and talented authors who read an early copy of *The Partner.* I'm immensely grateful to you for taking time out from your busy schedules to do so. It's always such an honour to have such incredible writers read and endorse my books.

The amazing book blogger and reading community on all forms of social media who've supported the Carver & Kramer books over the years. I wish I had the space to list out all your names (!) but I hope you know who you are and how grateful I am to you for constantly championing the series. With a special mention to Danielle Price, who's been a massive fan of Carver and Kramer from the beginning, your support really means the world.

To all my wonderful friends and family, especially those who have taken the time to read early drafts of my Carver & Kramer novels, as well as my standalones, (my dad, Janet Sage, Chika Ripley and Jessica West especially) – it really means a lot. A special mention also to Awais Khan, not just a supremely talented author and fantastic launch partner, but a wonderful friend who always gives me great advice and makes me laugh out loud with his sharp wit.

Last, but by no means least, a very special thanks to my parents, Diane and Mukul, my husband, Chris, and my gorgeous boys, Adam and Henry, for their constant love, support and patience with my writing.

The Lume & Joffe Books Story

Lume Books was founded by Matthew Lynn, one of the true pioneers of independent publishing. In 2023 Lume Books was acquired by Joffe Books and now its story continues as part of the Joffe Books family of companies.

Joffe Books began in 2014 when Jasper agreed to publish his mum's much-rejected romance novel and it became a bestseller.

Since then we've grown into the largest independent publisher in the UK. We're extremely proud to publish some of the very best writers in the world, including Joy Ellis, Faith Martin, Caro Ramsay, Helen Forrester, Simon Brett and Robert Goddard. Everyone at Joffe Books loves reading and we never forget that it all begins with the magic of an author telling a story.

We are proud to publish talented first-time authors, as well as established writers whose books we love introducing to a new generation of readers.

We won Trade Publisher of the Year at the Independent Publishing Awards in 2023. We have been shortlisted for Independent Publisher of the Year at the British Book Awards for the last four years, and were shortlisted for the Diversity and Inclusivity Award at the 2022 Independent Publishing Awards. In 2023 we were shortlisted for Publisher of the Year at the RNA Industry Awards.

We built this company with your help, and we love to hear from you, so please email us about absolutely anything bookish at feedback@joffebooks.com

If you want to receive free books every Friday and hear about all our new releases, join our mailing list here.

And when you tell your friends about us, just remember: it's pronounced Joffe as in coffee or toffee!